PRAISE FOR CHILDREN OF THE KNIGHT
(BOOK 1 OF THE LANCE CHRONICLES):

"I have worked with youth for over 30 years. I've seen the effects of Zero Tolerance, juveniles moved to adult courts, incarceration, "intervention projects". So Children of the Knight struck home. King Arthur returns when his country (in this case, the US since it was a British colony at one point, apparently) needs him most. He gathers around him new knights - the young people who have been discarded, ignored, abused, and he sets out on a quest to show the value of the youth that he has gathered around him. They set out to prove their worth, and the story is an awesome telling of how a charismatic adult can honestly change the direction and fate of so many young people. It's hard to read this if you have any empathy for today's youth and our society as a whole. I cried through almost all of the 344 pages. And I didn't sleep after the climactic scenes near the end. Get this, read this. Be prepared.

–J.g. Murphy

"The children we meet in the story are broken, but beautiful inside. They are your children and mine. What they all have in common is this: they are forgotten. I fell in love with these children: Lance, Mark, Jack, Chris and so many more. We witness what these children can do when a glimmer of hope is shown, when genuine love is given, when they feel their worth.

Reading this book was an emotional journey for me as a parent and a former high school teacher. One of the themes of this book is having second chances. These children are given second chances, the two main cops, Jenny, the teacher, and even Arthur gets a second chance. I even get a second chance, to examine my role as a parent, as an educator, and as a member of our society. Children Of The Knight is thought-provoking, gut wrenching, hopeful, and a fantastic story. It will stay with you even after The End. It is highly recommended and I am anxious to read the rest of the series. Well done, Michael, and thank you!"

–Kari

"WOW, what a roller coaster ride Michael sent me on with this second installment of his Children of the Knight series. I was crying with sadness, then spell-cast, then crying with happiness."

– Dallas Vinson

"I am not sure I can remember reading a book that tugged my heart strings in this way. Up, down, backwards, forwards, in, out, over here, over there...simultaneously... and TIGHTLY! I started Running Through a Dark Place and could not put it down. My emotions ran rampant, crying regularly, lying awake angry at one character or another, mostly just trying to internalize a story that consumes you from word one. I was mesmerized with Michael J. Bowler's second novel of children who are trying to take over the world. The book draws you in from the foreword (penned by Mia Kerick) and beyond that, you are on your own."

– Jay

MICHAEL J. BOWLER

THERE IS NO FEAR

THE LANCE CHRONICLES 3

Published by Michael J. Bowler, USA stuntshark2.0@gmail.com

There Is No Fear
(The Lance Chronicles 3)
Second Edition Copyright © 2018 by Michael J. Bowler

Cover Art and Interior Formatting by Streetlight Graphics

Edited by Karen Scutts and Cindi Lynn ewriteediting@gmail.com

Print: ISBN: 978-0-9903063-3-7
Mobi: ISBN: 978-0-9903063-4-4
epub: ISBN: 978-0-9903063-5-1

Printed in the United States of America Second Edition
July 2018

As with the first two books in this series, *There Is No Fear* is dedicated to all of the astonishing children and teens I've worked with over the years, especially those who all too often had no word for their fear, and no one to understand it even if they'd heard. I always tried my best to hear and understand. Just being that friendly ear, that empathy, that small gift of understanding enriched both the kids and me beyond measure. I also want to give a shout out to the outstanding probation staff I've worked side-by-side with over the years, those who understood that their job was more than just custodian. The best of them were more often than not the friendly and sympathetic ear these kids needed to get them through another day of incarceration, another day away from their loved ones, another day confounded by a system that seemed designed to reject outright their basic humanity. To those staff, I say, thank you for caring. Oh, and I can't leave out the real Ricky, a boy I met when he was twelve years old in juvenile hall. If there was ever a boy with a bigger heart, I never met him. Ricky managed to convince everyone in his unit, including the staff, that I was his father because his passionate need for one was so genuine. I happily accepted the job as best I could, but that boy gave me so much more than I could ever have given him in return, just by being himself. As Lance so often says of the fictional Ricky, he was truly amazing. For those of you who don't believe there is anyone to understand your fear even if they hear, trust me, there is. Don't ever give up trying to find them. All kids deserve a second chance, and a third. Hope endures…

WHAT HAS GONE BEFORE...

THE LEGENDARY KING ARTHUR APPEARED in Los Angeles with a mission – to save and empower youth. He started a new Round Table of knights made up exclusively of children and teens. A vision from Merlin led him to Lance, a homeless fourteen-year-old who was destined to lead his Children's Crusade. Arthur trained Lance in swordsmanship and archery, taught the boy discipline and self- control. He came to love Lance beyond measure, and Lance finally found the father he'd longed for growing up as an orphan in "the system."

In turn, Lance taught Arthur the complexities of 21st Century American life. They recruited hundreds of "disposable" youth - gang members looking for something better, homeless kids, gay kids, kids of every race and color – the ones most marginalized by society. And they built New Camelot, a safe haven for every child in need. They mobilized youth through social media and forged a ballot initiative that would give fourteen-year-olds in California adult rights, including the right to vote. Their initiative, to be voted on in the upcoming November election, divided the people of California, but united the youth behind its bold premise that kids need more rights to protect them from out-of-control adults and over-reaching government.

But Lance's journey has not been an easy one. His abusive past and resultant fears of what he might become pushed him into dangerous behaviors that put his life at risk and embarrassed New Camelot. As The Boy Who Came Back, Lance was catapulted into worldwide prominence, and the sudden fame threatened to topple him and all that he and Arthur had accomplished. Only Ricky, the newest member of the Round Table—and Lance's closest friend—could steady him, especially when Lance was inexplicably drawn to an unstable teen named Michael. Michael introduced the boys to a partying lifestyle that neither of them liked, but because of personal doubts and fears, they allowed themselves to be drawn into it.

After several failed attempts on Lance's life, an abuser from his dark past rose up one night to confront him, and that fateful encounter led to his arrest on a charge of attempted murder.

The Lance Chronicles Continue…

AND JUSTICE FOR FEW

CHAPTER ONE

HE WOULDN'T HURT ANYONE

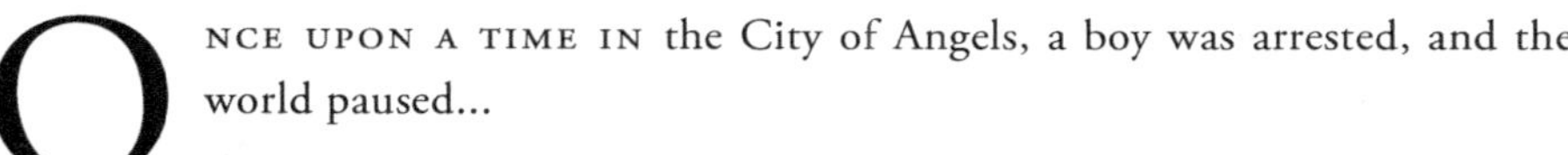

ONCE UPON A TIME IN the City of Angels, a boy was arrested, and the world paused...

The media trailed the black and white all the way to the Hollywood station, and many reporters arrived there first. Cameras rolled when Lance was pulled from the back of the cruiser by the aggressive cop so hard his shoulders shrieked with pain, and then shoved up the steps into the station. He had to keep shaking his unrestrained hair out of his face just to see where he was going because of the pushing and dragging by the officer.

Reporters had already massed within the lobby. They snapped pictures and threw out questions right and left, but Lance still felt slightly dazed by the crack to his head, and the enormity of his circumstances. All he could do was look uncertainly from beneath his hair as the faces and cameras flew past.

The cop dragged him to a room with one door and no windows and slammed him hard into a stiff-backed wooden chair. Pain shot up his back, but he forced himself not to make a sound, not to even grimace. The aggressive cop and his partner stepped from the room and closed the door. Lance heard the lock click, sealing him within.

His mind whirled as he sat painfully in the chair. His hands had long since gone numb, and his shoulders felt like they were being wrenched from their sockets. Attempted murder? What the hell? Who was he supposed to have almost killed? Or was this another attempt to derail their election objective, a trumped up scandal to destroy his credibility in the eyes of the voters, credibility he'd worked so hard to regain after those early drunken escapades? He shook his head, trying to clear his thoughts. He hadn't done anything wrong. They'd have to see that soon and let him go, right?

His mind then fixed upon the desperately lost and terrified look he'd seen in Ricky's wide brown eyes. His bro. His best friend. The most remarkable boy he'd ever known. In many ways, more remarkable than Jack, Lance realized, as he sat quietly in that tiny room, waiting for who knew what. His heart felt hollow as he thought of his family, of his mom and dad and brothers and sisters. But Ricky filled the largest place in that hollow heart. This was the first time they'd been apart since Ricky joined the family, and Lance felt lost and alone without him, as though the better half of him had been ripped away.

"Oh, Ricky..." he murmured to the empty room.

It didn't take long before a fortyish-looking guy wearing a nicely tailored coat and tie stepped into the room and closed the door. He was Caucasian, tall and well groomed, flashing a badge before Lance's disinterested face.

"Good morning, Lance," the man said amiably, slipping his badge back into his pocket. "I'm Sergeant Cooper. I believe you've already met my partner, Sergeant Wallace?"

Lance said nothing. He merely looked up at the man's face impassively. His thoughts remained on Ricky.

Cooper indicated the camera in the upper corner of the room. "This camera is recording everything, Lance, so there'll be no doubt that I've read you your rights as the law requires."

Lance remained mute.

Cooper sighed and slipped a well-worn, laminated three-by-five card from his pocket and proceeded to read from it.

"You have the right to remain silent. If you give up your right to remain silent, anything you say can and will be used against you in a court of law. You have the right to speak to an attorney and to have an attorney present during any questioning. If you cannot afford an attorney, one will be provided for you at government expense. Do you understand these rights as I've read them to you?"

Lance nodded.

Cooper frowned. "I need an audible response for the camera, Lance."

"Yes, I understand."

Cooper smiled and slipped the card back into his jacket pocket. "Good. Knowing and understanding your rights as I've explained them to you, are you willing to answer my questions without an attorney present?"

"No, sir."

Cooper put on the good-cop face and seated himself across from Lance.

"You know, Lance, though we have an arrest warrant, you're not yet formally charged with a crime. My questions are merely for the purpose of determining your whereabouts last night. All I'm trying to do is establish where you were in relation to where the crime occurred and lay out an approximate timeline. You don't need an attorney for that, do you?" He flashed perfect white teeth, making Lance feel like the guy should be on one of those toothpaste commercials.

"I grew up in the system, Sergeant, and I know all your guy's tricks, all that good-cop crap." Lance chuckled sadly. "Known a grip 'a kids who went to jail 'cause you guys just wanted to, what did you say, 'establish a timeline'? No thanks, man. I'll wait for my dad and my lawyer."

Cooper frowned. "You know it could go much worse for you if you don't cooperate, especially you being the 'The Boy Who Came Back' and all. A lot of D.A.'s like to make examples out of famous people like you."

"Like I don't already know that? Like I don't know how you cops treat us kids like crap 'cause we got no rights in this country? Well, things'll be different when our prop passes. For now, feel free to leave and take your BS with you. Sir."

Lance gazed up at the man without expression. No smugness, no haughtiness. Just a steady look that masked the fear churning through him.

Cooper smiled admiringly and stood. "Cool as a cucumber, eh? Well, we'll see how cool you are when you're booked for attempted murder and sent to the hall." He left the room.

Lance exhaled the breath he'd been holding and turned his eyes upward toward the camera in the corner. He knew they were watching, but he also knew giving them attitude would not help his case. So he refrained from sticking out his tongue. Just the thought of doing that almost made him smile because he saw in his mind's eye Ricky twisted up with laughter at the sight. The ache in his heart grew stronger just thinking of the other boy.

Lance waited, the cuffs no longer painful because his forearms and shoulders were numb. He wondered briefly if this was what frostbite felt like.

He knew his dad and Sergeant Ryan would be along any minute, so he tried not to dwell on just how much trouble he might be in. He'd never committed any crimes, so had never gotten caught up in the so-called justice system. But he'd known enough kids who hadn't been so lucky, and once in the system, they never seemed to get out. He had often thought getting arrested was like sinking in quicksand, except it was more like slow-sand because everything took forever, and yet you still never got out. At least, he never saw most of those kids on the streets again.

After some time passed—Lance had no idea how long, but he was thirsty and hungry—the door opened and Cooper returned. Lance scowled, until Arthur stepped in behind him.

"Dad!" Lance exclaimed happily as he leaped to his feet, his heart beating wildly with love and relief.

Arthur was followed by Ryan and Sam, and Lance instantly felt better. This would all be resolved now and he could go home. Home to… he'd meant to think of everyone, but it was only Ricky's face that came to mind.

Sam eyed Lance's hands cuffed behind him and looked at Cooper. "Uncuff my client, Sergeant."

Cooper hesitated.

"Has he been booked?" Sam asked curtly.

"Not yet," Cooper admitted, and Sam glowered at him.

Reluctantly, Cooper went around behind Lance and released his painful wrists from their imprisonment. When Lance slowly and stiffly lifted his arms to lay his hands on the table, Arthur gasped at the deep red welts around his wrists, sharply contrasting against the light brown of his skin. Sam shook his head with disgust.

"Was this necessary, Sergeant?" Sam asked, lifting one of Lance's arms to indicate the red and already swelling wrist. Lance winced just from the touch, but at least blood was returning to his arms and hands.

Cooper shrugged matter-of-factly. "Just routine, Counselor, especially when a suspect is considered dangerous."

Lance eyed the man with astonishment. Him? Dangerous?

Cooper waved in a few more chairs, delivered by the cop who'd slammed Lance's head into the car.

The men sat around the table, Arthur and Sam near to Lance, and Ryan on Cooper's side.

Arthur put a hand on Lance's shoulder and it took all Lance's willpower not to hug his father.

"Shall we begin?" Cooper asked cheerily, eliciting a scowl from Sam, who turned to Lance.

"You don't have to answer any questions, Lance, and if I think a question is inflammatory or out of line, I'll advise you not to answer."

Lance nodded.

"Now then, Lance, let's start with your whereabouts last night. Where were you between the hours of eleven p.m. and one a.m.?"

"Asleep at home," Arthur put in immediately.

Sam held up a cautionary hand. "Let the boy answer, Arthur."

Lance bowed his head shamefully before looking at Arthur. "I snuck out, Dad."

Arthur's mouth dropped open in shock, and Lance felt—more than saw—the disappointment in his father.

"And where did you sneak out to, Lance?" Cooper asked, as though he already knew the answer.

Lance swallowed and gazed uncertainly at Sam, who nodded. "A park in Hollywood."

"What park?"

"De Longpre."

"What time was this?"

"I left the house around eleven, I guess."

"Why were you going to De Longpre Park so late at night, and why did you feel the need to sneak around to do it?"

Lance glanced again to Sam.

"Just tell us what you're comfortable with, Lance," the attorney advised.

"I went to meet someone."

"Knowing, as we all do by now," Cooper went on, "that you like 'variety', was this person male or female?"

Lance blushed, realizing the man's implication.

Sam shook his head in disgust. "Caution, Sergeant. He is a minor."

Cooper nodded.

"Male," Lance whispered, head bowed. He didn't know why he felt so embarrassed. After all, he didn't meet Michael for anything inappropriate. But just the way the man looked at him made Lance feel dirty.

"And why did you meet this *male*?" Cooper asked, emphasizing the word.

Lance looked up at him. "I needed to talk to him, that's all."

"And that couldn't have been done over the phone?"

Lance shook his head. "Sometimes you gotta look a guy in the eye, you know?"

"I probably wouldn't know about that."

Again that tone caused Lance to burn with shame.

Cooper gazed across at him. "Care to share the name of this unidentified male you met?"

"No," Lance said quickly. "He's got nothing to do with this. Whatever it is."

"Very well." Cooper reached into his pocket and slipped out a photo, keeping the white back facing Lance. "Do you recognize this man?"

He turned the photo around and Lance gasped.

"I see you do."

Lance gulped, his heart rate increasing, his breathing ragged. Even the man's picture had that effect on him, and he hated himself for being so weak.

"It's Richard," he whispered. Richard just as he'd looked when he…

Arthur studied the picture, and Sam leaned forward to get a better look.

"And who is Richard?" Cooper asked, though it was obvious that he already knew the answer.

Lance shivered and fought to control his breathing. "He was an old foster parent of mine."

"At what age?"

Lance blew out a breath and struggled to keep his voice from quavering. Somewhere deep inside, he knew Cooper was enjoying this, enjoying how rattled he was making him. "From six to nine."

Arthur placed a hand on Lance's shoulder to help calm him, and Lance shot him a weak smile of gratitude.

Cooper sat back confidently, still holding the picture in front so Lance couldn't help but see it. "At one of your press conferences, you alleged that a foster parent raped you. Is that correct?"

Weakly, unable to look up at that photo any longer, Lance looked down and nodded.

Cooper leaned forward and shoved the picture under Lance's downturned eyes. "Is this the man who raped you, Lance?"

"I object," Sam exclaimed loudly. "What has this boy's traumatic past to do with our being here now?"

Cooper eyed the attorney coolly. "Merely trying to establish motive."

"Motive?" Sam repeated angrily, and then turned to Lance. "You don't need to answer these questions, Lance."

Lance raised his gaze from the photo and pinned it to Cooper's face. "Yeah, he's the one."

"Again, Sergeant," Sam boomed with irritation, "what is the relevance of these questions?"

Cooper kept his eyes pinned to Lance. "Because someone attacked, mutilated, and left this man for dead last night."

Lance gasped in shock, and so did Arthur.

Sam was incredulous. "And you think my client… that's preposterous."

Cooper's eyes never left Lance's face, even as he spoke to Sam. "Is it? The timeline fits. There was supposedly some secret liaison with another 'male,' who as far as we know, never existed. And there's motive."

Lance was so rattled he blurted out, "He was fine when I left him. I swear it!"

Arthur gasped again, as did Ryan.

Sam leaped from his chair. "Lance, not another word!"

But Cooper had gotten what he wanted. He lay the photo face down on the table and sat back calmly. "Anything else you'd like to share, *Sir* Lance?"

Lance nervously eyed Sam, who shook his head. "My client is finished, Sergeant."

Cooper stood. "Very well." He opened the door and ushered the two cops back in, handing them the cuffs. "Stand up, Lance."

His legs shaking, Lance stood. The same angry cop slapped the cuffs back onto his wrists, hard, and Lance couldn't believe that they were even tighter than before.

"Lance Pendragon," Cooper intoned very authoritatively. "You are hereby charged with attempted murder, great bodily injury, mayhem, and assault with a deadly weapon." He turned to Sam and Arthur. "Given the gravity of the crime, and the evidence we already have, I'm confident your client will be sent to adult court, Counselor. If convicted, he'll likely never see the streets again."

"What evidence do you have to justify this arrest, Sergeant?" Sam asked indignantly.

"A video of your client threatening to mutilate Mr. Thornton with a knife. No confession needed."

Lance's mouth dropped open in shock. How could this be happening? A video? What video? Richard had been fine when he'd taken off the night before. Lance's knees felt weak, and his head spun.

Cooper nodded to the uniforms and they shoved Lance toward the door.

"Dad!"

Before Arthur could even reach for him, Lance had been pushed out into the hall.

Cooper turned to both men. "I believe we're done here, gentlemen."

Staggered by all that had happened, Arthur dolefully followed Sam and Ryan from the interrogation room just in time to see Lance dragged through the phalanx of reporters, who hurled question after question at him. Lance tried to look back to catch his father's eye, but the cops shoved him forward.

Then he was gone.

The reporters swarmed around the distraught Arthur, and Sam kept repeating, "No comment, no comment" until they were out of the station and back in Ryan's sedan.

By the time Arthur, Sam and Ryan returned to New Camelot, the hotel was in an uproar. The cops had left, but all the kids, and even the hotel staff employed by the Kabbalogy Center, were gathered with Jenny in the Throne Room, eyes riveted to the television. All heads turned when the three men stepped into the room.

Ricky's despairing look turned to horror when he saw Lance was not with them. "Dad, where's Lance?"

Jenny hurried over, as did Chris.

Arthur's expression told the tale. "He has been placed under arrest."

Chris gasped, and Ricky's face collapsed into despair.

"For what?" he blurted. "He didn't do that." He pointed back at the TV.

Sam cleared his throat. "We were only told the charges, not any details about the actual crime in question."

Jenny nodded sadly toward the television. "It's all over the news."

They all turned to watch CNN recapping the top story against images of Lance, in handcuffs, led away to the police car. There was a picture of Lance on screen right beside a picture of Richard – the same photo Cooper had shown Lance at the station.

The on-camera female anchor said, "To update you on our top story. Lance Pendragon, son of King Arthur, also known as Sir Lance and The Boy Who Came Back, has been arrested in the brutal assault and mutilation of this man."

Richard's photo filled the screen momentarily, along with his name: 'Richard Thornton, age forty'.

The anchor came back on screen. "While the police have not revealed any details as to the arrest or what evidence they may have against Sir Lance, here's what we know of the crime. At approximately twelve-thirty this morning, Mr. Thornton was struck from behind and rendered semi-conscious. His hands were tied behind his back by cloth apparently torn from a shirt, and his eyes were similarly covered. The attacker then – and if you have young children watching this broadcast, we strongly advise you to remove them from the room." She glanced over at someone in the studio before turning back to camera and looking grave. "Once the victim was tied up, his genital area was mutilated by a sharp knife of some kind."

Sam gasped loudly, and Arthur's mouth dropped open in shock.

"My God," Ryan muttered.

"The victim would've bled to death," the anchor continued, "were it not for a 911 call alerting authorities to his location. The caller did not leave a name and the call was made from a pay phone. Mr. Thornton is in stable condition at this time and apparently, though this has not been confirmed by police, named Sir Lance as his attacker."

"It is not possible," Arthur murmured, and Jenny took his hand lovingly.

Ricky glared up at the TV in anger.

"All police have said is that charges have been filed against Sir Lance and that, due to the gravity of the crime, the District Attorney's office will petition the juvenile court judge to send the case to adult court. As to a motive for the crime, speculation runs rampant that Mr. Thornton, a former foster parent, may be the man Sir Lance alleged raped him at the age of six. All of these reports are unconfirmed at this time, but our sources indicate the likelihood that what we are reporting is accurate."

Ricky quivered with increasing rage.

Arthur turned to him. "What do you know of Lance's whereabouts last night, Ricky?"

"Uh, Arthur," Sam piped up. "Perhaps you and I and Sergeant Ryan should talk with Ricky in private? We shouldn't discuss the case in front of everyone."

Arthur and Ryan agreed.

Chris ran up and hugged his father. "Lance is gonna be okay, isn't he, Dad?"

"Of course, Chris. We know he is innocent."

"He could never hurt anybody."

"No, Chris, he could not," Arthur agreed. "Stay here with your mother while we talk with Ricky."

Chris sadly returned to Jenny's side.

Arthur put his arm around Ricky and led him out of the Throne Room. Ryan and Sam followed. They went to the library and sat around a small table set aside for reading and writing.

Arthur squeezed Ricky's shoulder gently. "Tell us, son, what you know."

Ricky took a deep breath, and began. "We went to bed like ten, maybe. I knocked out quick 'cause I was tired. Next thing I know, Lance is shaking me awake."

"What time was that, Ricky?" Ryan asked, his notebook and pen ready to jot down the information.

"Not really sure. Once he got settled down I saw the clock and it was like around two o'clock, I think."

"What did Lance say to you, Ricky" Sam asked. "Try to remember as much as you can of exactly what he said and how he was acting."

So Ricky recounted in as much detail as he could Lance's words and terrified state of mind, how he'd gone to confront Michael and Richard had found him, how he'd been petrified and pulled a knife on the man who'd raped him.

Ryan took copious notes the entire time. "How was Lance dressed when he woke you?"

"Just workout shorts, no shirt. Why?"

"Did the police go through his clothes, his hamper, the laundry room? Did they take any of his clothes that you know of?"

Ricky thought a moment. "They went through everything, yeah, but I don't think they took anything. Why?"

"Is that relevant, Sergeant?" Arthur asked.

"It should be, Arthur," Ryan answered. "The crime, as described on the news, would've meant a lot of blood that the perp would've gotten on his clothes. No way around that. I'll find out what I can, but it's likely all of Lance's clothes would've been checked for blood stains."

"And when none are found?" Arthur asked, his tone hopeful.

"It doesn't really matter, Arthur," Sam put in. "Lance could've disposed of the clothes before re-entering the house."

"He didn't," Ricky said with authority. "All of his stuff is still here. I checked."

Ryan jotted that down.

Ricky gazed desperately at Arthur. "Dad, how could they think Lance did something like that?"

Arthur turned to Sam.

"Apparently, Ricky," Sam said with a sigh, "the police have a video of Lance threatening Mr. Thornton."

"No way! He wouldn't hurt anyone. Dad, you know that! Besides, Richard scared the crap out of him, just thinking about the guy!"

"I know, son," Arthur replied sadly.

"Arthur," Sam said after a pause, "I'm not a criminal attorney and Lance needs one. A good one. I suspect since the D.A. is up for re-election, he'll try to make an example of Lance, really act tough on crime and, to boot, prove that trying children in adult court is good for society."

"I agree," Ryan added.

"I know some top criminal defense lawyers, Arthur," Sam went on. "I'll get you someone today."

"Dad," Ricky said, his wide eyes looking desperately at his father. "What's gonna happen to Lance? Where is he?"

Uncertain, Arthur turned to Ryan.

The sergeant gazed at Ricky with compassion. "He'll be housed at juvenile hall,

Ricky, until his arraignment. It sounds like this will bypass the juvenile courts, so he'll most likely be held where the kids being tried as adults are kept."

"What about bail, sergeant?" Sam asked.

Ryan shook his head. "Even though these kids are being tried as adults, most are not given the option of bail like real adults are. And if bail is set, it will be upwards of a million, my best guess."

Ricky's eyes grew even wider, and his heart felt even more devoid of hope. "*Dad...*"

Arthur reached out and took his hand. "I know, son," he said softly. "I feel as you do."

Sam stood. "I'm going to get in touch with some attorneys, Arthur. I'll let you know who's willing to take the case." He looked over at Ricky. "Hang in there, Ricky. We'll get him back." Then he strode quickly from the room.

Ryan stood, too. "I've got Gib down at the station trying to find out whatever he can, Arthur, but those homicide guys think they own the world and us gang cops are lowlifes." He paused. "Plus, they know Gib and me are partial to you and Lance, so they're not likely to share info. Still, we have connections. I'm gonna go make some calls." He patted Ricky gently on the shoulder and left the room.

Ricky felt like crying and screaming and breaking things, all at the same time. But he knew he couldn't do that. "Dad," he said helplessly. "What am I gonna do without him?"

"Hope and pray, Ricky. Keep watch over Chris. He will need you now more than ever."

Ricky knew that. He also knew he should tell Arthur that Richard was the man who'd called himself 'Dick' out on the streets and had hurt him so badly. He'd recognized the creep instantly from the photo shown on the news, even though the hair was different. But would anyone believe his story, other than Arthur and Jenny? Ryan would, but could it help Lance in any way? He didn't see how at this point, since it was Lance who'd been accused of the crime, and Lance was all he cared about now. Arthur had so much on his mind Ricky didn't want to add to his father's pain. So he decided to keep silent and share his own degradation later, if the need arose.

Exercise. That's what he needed. That might at least burn off some of the frustrated energy coursing through him.

"Can I take Chris to the training room?" he asked. "I need to do something or I'll go crazy."

"That sounds like a good plan, son."

Ricky hurried from the library, leaving Arthur staring off into space. He clasped his hands together and bowed his head.

"Dear Lord, I do not pretend to know your plans for myself or my children, but I cannot believe you would return my Lance to me only to take him again in such a cruel fashion. I defer to your wisdom, Lord, and ask that you watch over my son in his hour of need. Protect him, and give us the wisdom to bring him home safely."

Then, almost as an afterthought, Arthur slipped his phone from his pocket and sorted through his text messages until he found it again – the message Lance had sent months ago just before he'd been kidnapped. The one Arthur hadn't seen until much later, after he'd nearly lost his son forever. The message read: "Hey Dad, I'm coming home. I'm sorry for being weak. I love you."

With a heavy sigh, Arthur rose, shoulders slumped in dejection, slipped the phone back into his pocket, and quietly left the library.

CHAPTER TWO
YOU A GOOD ENOUGH LAWYER TO GET LANCE BACK?

LANCE ENDURED THE RIDE TO juvenile hall by tuning out the angry cop who kept talking trash to him the entire journey, saying things like, "Finally getting what you deserve" and "What a sicko you are" and how "All the boys at juvy will love a pretty boy like you, especially in the showers."

His partner told him, weakly, Lance noted, to "Leave the kid alone," but the older man kept up the trash talk. Lance's temper rose, but he fought it down, focusing instead on Arthur and Jenny and Chris and what was going on at home and what they might be thinking about all of this. But mostly, his thoughts went to Ricky.

They wouldn't be together tonight, or any other night for the foreseeable future. They were soul brothers, two pieces of the same toy, and Lance already felt that part of him was missing. He didn't know how he would get through this night, or any other, without that boy.

And how long would all of this take before he was set free? He was innocent. What video could the cops have? It was just him and Richard talking. Even Michael hadn't gotten there until...

Michael.

Lance considered the possibilities. Could Michael have been hiding and recording them? He had the video equipment, Lance knew, and he loved to record stuff. But why? And why give it to the cops? Revenge, because Lance rejected him? Would Michael be that cruel? Ricky believed him so, but Lance knew better. Or thought he did. Could he have been wrong about Michael all this time? Would Michael let him go to prison for the rest of his life out of spite?

Finally, after what seemed like forever, the police cruiser stopped at a small booth, behind which were the towering red brick walls twisted with razor wire all along the top, and a monstrous sliding metal door leading into Barney J. Nelson

Juvenile Hall. The gate guard pressed a switch in his little booth, opening the sliding door, and waved the cruiser through. Reporters were already hovering around the entrance, snapping pictures of the car, and fighting to get shots of Lance through the barred windows. The cruiser eased through and the door slid casually shut behind them, signaling the end to his freedom.

The older cop yanked Lance from the car as soon as they parked and dragged him forward to a locked gate fronting redbrick buildings. A man wearing a dark blue polo shirt emblazoned with his last name on the right front breast, and a gold shield that said "Los Angeles County Probation" on the other, opened the gate from the inside, staring in wide-eyed amazement as Lance was hauled through. He locked the gate and led the officers into the building through another locked door, escorting them to the intake section.

A second probation officer turned as they entered, saw Lance, and gaped. "Holy crap! It's The Boy Who Came Back!" He had a kind, round face and the name Brown emblazoned on his shirt. Recovering from his initial shock, he said, "You can uncuff him now."

The other probation officer who'd let them in stood to the side as the younger cop slipped a key from his pocket and gently unclasped the handcuffs. Lance's arms fell free to his sides, numb and almost useless.

The older cop chuckled and exited the room.

The younger officer looked sheepishly at Lance. "I'm sorry about that, Sir Lance, but see, I'm just a rookie and..." He trailed off helplessly.

"It's okay. I understand."

The officer left Lance alone with the two probation officers, both of whom stared at him with something resembling awe.

"We watched you die..." said the one who'd opened the gate.

Brown nodded silently.

"Yeah. Might have been better if I stayed that way, huh?"

Brown shook his head. "Hell, no. My kids love you, Sir Lance. You're a hero to 'em."

Lance's eyes went wide, and he gulped down his uncertainty. "Do, uh, do you guys even know what I'm supposed to have done?"

The two men exchanged a glance, and then the first one shut the door to the hall. Lance noted that his name was Wilson. They hurried him over to a small TV monitor with the sound turned down. It was a news broadcast, repeating essentially the same information CNN had broadcast earlier. Brown turned up the volume enough to hear. Lance gasped loudly when the reporter described what had been done to Richard.

"My God," he whispered, in shock. "I didn't do that! I couldn't do something like that. Even to him."

He looked imploringly at the two men, who exchanged a glance, but didn't respond. Wilson turned down the TV volume and indicated a chair for Lance sit. Brown took his personal information and typed it into the computer while Wilson excused himself and returned to his gate duties.

After all of the data had been put into the system, Brown escorted Lance across a hallway lined with grey lockers set against stark, bluish-green walls and into another room. Lance waited while the man pulled out some clothes – pocket-less dark-gray pants, gray t-shirt, plain sneakers, underwear and socks. He handed the clothes to Lance.

"Uh, where do I change?" Lance asked, fearing he already knew the answer.

"Right here." The man actually looked a little embarrassed.

Against his will, Lance blushed. "In front of you?"

The man nodded.

"Everything?"

"The underwear can stay."

Feeling more humiliated than at any time since he'd been nine, Lance slipped the shirt over his head and dropped it. Then he slipped off his skate shoes and socks, all the while trying to keep from shaking. The last time he'd been naked with a grown man had been with... Richard.

Trembling, but fighting the panic, he slid his pants down and stepped out of them. Now he wore only his boxers, his wide eyes gazing imploringly at the obviously uncomfortable probation officer.

"Turn around please."

"Huh?" Lance said in a shaky voice, his body trembling with mortification.

"You, uh, have to squat and cough."

"What?" Lance didn't think he could feel even more degraded than before. His whole body trembled.

"Policy, Lance," the man said. "Gotta check for drugs."

Lance blanched with embarrassment and reluctantly turned his back to the man. To Richard.

No, it *wasn't* Richard.

Stop going there!

"Now squat," he heard from behind him.

Lance nearly fainted. He shook with trepidation, the memories of his violation flooding back in.

Bend over for me, my little fag boy, and play with little Lance while I make you feel so good.

Not sure if he would faint or not, Lance squatted, exposing his buttocks to a grown man, hearing Richard's voice, feeling Richard's probing fingers, feeling Richard's...

He coughed.

"That's enough," he heard from behind, and stood up faster than he thought was possible.

"You can get dressed now." The man indicated the clothes and then turned his back to give Lance some semblance of privacy.

Lance pulled on those clothes faster than he'd ever gotten dressed before, the sweat beading on his face and back, causing the t-shirt to cling to his skin.

The door opened and Lance whirled around.

Wilson stuck his head in. "Word came in on Lance. Juvenile judge signed off on adult court. Unit W." Then he was gone.

Brown turned to Lance, who eyed the man cautiously. "What does that mean?"

"It means the compound." He opened a locker and pulled out heavy metal restraints, causing Lance to step back in fear.

"You're gonna put those on me?" he asked, forcing his voice to be steady.

Brown looked genuinely sorry. "It's policy, Lance. Compound kids are never moved without restraints."

"Why?"

"You're considered more dangerous than the others."

Lance took a deep breath and let it out slowly.

You can do this, he told himself. *You got to. Can't show fear in here, just like on the streets.*

He gritted his teeth and held out his hands. "Go ahead."

The handcuffs wrapped tightly around his wrists and another restraining chain wrapped around his waist so his hands were kept snugly together against his body. Presumably, he figured, this was done so he couldn't lift his arms and attack the staff. Brown took a set of thick plastic cuffs and chained his ankles together so tightly he could barely shuffle.

Lance stood taut and tense, memories of his childhood restraints flooding his mind and heart. He could hear Richard's giggling sort-of chuckle as he tied him to the bed with black leather straps.

"You ready?" Brown asked, pulling Lance out of his haunted past. He nodded and Brown opened the door, holding it open so Lance could shuffle through, awash in mortification.

Brown led him down the hallway, past the rows of gray lockers. In the offices to his right, everyone ceased their work to stare silently through glass windows as he passed by.

He kept his head lowered, his eyes to the ground, his hair covering his shame.

Brown unlocked a door at the end of the hallway and weak sunlight struck Lance as he stepped through. There was an enormous, mostly glass booth in front of him filled with computers and TV monitors and staffed by six or seven probation officers.

Lance looked up at them as Brown locked the door behind him, and they all stopped what they were doing to stare.

Brown guided him to the left past the long booth to an open metal gate that could obviously slide shut when needed. He shuffled through the gate and saw buildings to his left, each with letters above their entryways. A and B were at the top of the hill, followed by C and D, E and F, G and H and J and K near the bottom. To his right he spotted buildings R/S and T/V. Lance now thought he understood what Wilson had meant by 'W'. That would be his unit number. Serene-looking mountains rose up behind the facility with rolling hills of green that seemed to placidly watch his disgrace, and their simple beauty somehow deepened it.

Brown led him along a concrete path abutted on either side by grassy playing fields, toward an enormous red brickwork structure right in the center, surrounded by high fencing topped with more razor wire. This must be The Compound, he figured, and suddenly it hit him – he was now a criminal.

Him.

The Boy Who Came Back.

The boy behind the proposition that would change things for the better.

Or would it? Might it just mean more kids like him would end up in this forbidding-looking place? More kids tried as adults because now they would already *be* adults?

Feeling like a baby learning how to walk, Lance zombie-shuffled his way toward the massive fence and its double-door gates. Brown used his key to open the gate and swung it open, ushering Lance through. Within were two-story buildings to his left and right, with a concrete path leading straight between them up at an angle to better access the upper units. He saw Y and Z to his right, but Brown turned him to the left where he saw W on the bottom and X above it. Lance waddled his way toward that giant 'W,' realizing this was to be his new home. But for how long? How long would it take his Dad and Sam to get him out?

Brown stopped in front of a heavy glass door and slipped out his key once more. Opening the door, he ushered Lance forward. Lance hesitated, looking into a large concrete dayroom with metal tables populated by a number of juveniles eating their lunch.

Brown eyed him with compassion. "No fear, Lance. They'll be all over you if you do."

Lance got his breathing under control. "It's okay, Mr. Brown. I got this."

Lance stepped inside and Brown closed the door behind him. He heard from one of the tables, "You know who that is?" but he refused to seek out the speaker.

Every set of eyes, juvenile and adult, was pinned to him as Brown led him past the tables. Lance made it a point to gaze straight ahead and not make eye contact with anyone. He felt like a zoo animal, and suddenly experienced great empathy for those poor creatures being gawked at day and night.

He kept his eyes pinned to the mirrored-glass enclosure they were approaching. As he neared the mirrored door, it swung open from within, and Brown followed him inside past the young female staff holding it open.

Lance looked around and saw what looked like a big control center, almost like the bridge of the Millennium Falcon. There was a huge semi-circular control panel behind which sat several more probation staff.

Behind them, separated by windows, were what looked like observation rooms, or maybe solitary confinement? Lance couldn't tell which, but he was sure he'd find out soon enough. As in the dayroom, all gazes settled on him like he was the most expensive art exhibit they'd ever seen. Maybe he was.

After another moment, the tableau broke and a large, broad- shouldered man, well over six feet and attired in the standard khaki pants and navy polo of probation, rose from the center console and strode forward. He nodded to Brown, who began the almost complex task of un-restraining Lance. This process took a minute or two, but seemed to go on forever as the bigger man and other staff watched.

Finally, hands and feet once again allowed their freedom, Lance smiled his thanks to Brown and looked up at the larger, bearded man before him.

"Never expected to see you here," he said, and Lance could detect a note of sadness, or maybe disappointment, in his voice. "I'm Mr. Mansfield, the senior." He stopped and eyed him a moment, before shaking his head in amazement. "I watched you die, Lance..." he said quietly, almost with reverence. "And come back." He looked like what he was seeing now was even more impossible than that.

Though he'd never met this man, Lance felt awash in remorse for somehow letting him down. "I didn't do it, Mr. Mansfield," he said, expecting the man and the other staff to smirk knowingly, because he was sure every kid probably said the same thing.

But Mansfield didn't smirk. "The other minors will be going back to school after lunch," he said, his voice sounding heavy. "Because you're new, you'll be kept in your room until tomorrow, except to eat and shower. We gotta monitor every new minor before they mix with the others. You hungry?"

Lance wanted to say no, but he'd missed breakfast and now it was lunch, and he was starving. "Yes, sir."

Mansfield nodded to one of the staff, who exited the office back into the dayroom. "We'll feed you in back, by yourself."

Brown cleared his throat. "Well, good luck, uh, Lance." He nodded to Mansfield and exited the office as well.

Lance was directed by a short, young female staff with the name Hawkins on her polo to the door at the rear of the control room. She unlocked the door and ushered him through. There was a small table and a couple of plastic chairs.

"Have a seat and we'll bring your food," she said crisply, all business.

"Thank you." He'd barely sat down before the door was closed and the mirrored glass cut off his view of the control room.

Lance looked around his stark surroundings. He'd been at Central Juvenile Hall for a short time after he'd finally run away from Richard and gotten picked up by the cops, but they'd kept him in the infirmary because he was only nine and hadn't committed any crimes. He'd refused, of course, to return to Richard's house, but had never told anyone why.

He'd only been housed there a few days before DCFS found him another foster home. Those people weren't evil like Richard, but they spent almost none of the money they were given on him, and he had to wear the same clothes until they either got too small and he couldn't fit into them anymore or until they fell apart. They also locked him in his closet as a punishment. After Richard, however, that place was the Garden of Eden.

Hawkins returned within a few minutes with a Styrofoam plate shrink-wrapped with plastic that covered what appeared to be dog food mixed in with some vegetables and a slice of bread. She also brought him a small milk and a plastic spork, depositing the items on the table and returning to the control room without a word.

Lance didn't care if it was dog food or not – he ravenously devoured every bit and drank all the milk. The small portion put a dent in his hunger, but in no way assuaged it. Then he sat and waited to be assigned a room, wondering what was going on back at New Camelot and what everyone over there was doing at this moment. What would Ricky be doing now? Lance sighed heavily, despondency enveloping him like a cocoon.

New Camelot was a scene of turmoil. News outlets rang the phone off the hook wanting a statement from Arthur or Ricky or Jenny about Lance's arrest. The Throne Room TV remained tuned to the news for updates. Despite it being a school day, both Bridget and Ariel had texted Ricky to find out what was going on, and both said they'd be over as soon as school let out. Bridget was stunned by what had happened, but Ricky didn't have any inclination to text back and forth with either of them. He said he'd see them later.

Instead, he'd taken Chris to the Training Center as he'd promised Arthur. The cops had taken the short handled knives and dirks, but there were still plenty of weapons to practice with. The boys sparred with swords until their shirts were soaked in sweat. They also practiced on the archery range, and Ricky even taught Chris some wrestling moves. But none of it was enough to release the pent up energy and rage burning within him.

He knew Chris was hurting, as well, and tried to distract the younger boy with exercise.

Reyna and Esteban had been with Arthur and Jenny trying to come up with something to say to the press, and what they would do now about the proposition commercials that were supposed to feature Lance.

When the criminal defense attorney—a tall, rail-thin man wearing wire-rimmed glasses named Arnold Ryerson—finally arrived later that afternoon, he asked to confer with Arthur and Jenny alone, so Reyna and Esteban went looking for Ricky and Chris.

They found the two boys sitting on a mat in the Training Centre, swords beside them, panting and sweating and trying very hard not to cry with despair.

Reyna hurried over and knelt down to grab Ricky in a tight hug. "Oh, baby," she said as soothingly as she could. "We'll get him back."

Esteban stood looking down at Chris. "Hey, little man." He smiled as best he could. Chris jumped up and threw his arms around the older boy. "It's okay, Chris, it'll be okay."

Like an exhibit in a wax museum, the four remained locked together for several moments, no one moving, no one speaking.

Reyna pulled back from Ricky and looked him in the face with genuine love and compassion. "He'll be all right, Ricky. He's not only younger, prettier and can shoot better than me, he's also more badass."

Despite his pain, that drew a smile to Ricky's face.

"With Lance gone, baby," she went on, now serious, "we need you to step up and do what he would normally do."

Ricky looked confused. "Like what?"

"Like talking to the media."

Ricky's face crumpled. "Hell, no, I can't."

Esteban stepped forward and placed a hand on his shoulder. "Ricky, it's gotta be you. Everyone knows you're, like, Lance's other half, and they need to hear from you, man. They need you to tell 'em straight up that Lance is innocent."

"I can do that, 'cause he is."

Esteban squeezed his shoulder supportively. "Now that's my other badass *carnal*."

"When?" Ricky asked nervously.

Reyna said, "Soon as Arthur's finished with Lance's new attorney. They'll go outside to make a statement and you need to say something, too."

Chris grabbed Ricky in a hug. "I'll help you, Ricky."

Ricky hugged him back. "Thanks, little man."

By the time Lance was led to a room, the other kids had already gone back to school, which Lance was told were several caged-in classrooms behind The Compound. His room was tiny, smaller than he'd ever been in, like being locked in a cereal box, he guessed. There was a scratched and tagged up window with glass so thick he figured it could withstand a nuclear blast. The bed was a slab of concrete extending from the wall with a two-inch thick plastic mattress on top. Other than that, the room was bare. When the door closed and locked behind him, the totality of his predicament finally slapped him in the face.

He was a prisoner.

He was a criminal.

He might never taste freedom again.

Weighed down, as he'd never been even under all of his Round Table responsibilities, Lance sat on the rock-solid bed and leaned back against the cold, concrete wall. His eyes fell on the locked door with its tiny window looking out into the dayroom, and silently broke the promise he'd made to John. For the first time since that amazing boy had died, Lance once again wished he could've died too, back when he was supposed to, because now his return was meaningless.

Once again within the privacy of the library, Arthur and Ryerson concluded their initial consultation, and Arthur sent for Ricky, who'd taken a fast shower and dried his hair. Ryerson curtly instructed Ricky to repeat everything he'd told Ryan and Sam, and took copious notes. When finished, Ryerson told them it was time to make a statement to the media and answer some questions.

"No losing your temper, son," he admonished sternly, eyeing Ricky above his glasses, "and if I say do not answer, you do not answer. Clear?"

Ricky bristled. "You a good enough lawyer to get Lance back?"

The man smiled, apparently impressed by Ricky's chutzpa in standing up to him. "Yes, Ricky, I am."

Ricky looked at his dad. "Let's do this."

Reyna, Esteban, Jenny, Chris, and Ryan joined them in the lobby. Then everyone stepped out the front door and down the walk to the gate. Arthur signaled to the guard and he opened the gates. Ryan waved forward several of Chief Murphy's men to stand at attention near Arthur as he eyed the crowd warily. The media swarmed in like a horde of voracious locusts, led, as usual, by the always-tenacious Helen and Charlie.

Questions were shouted, one over the other, and a general scene of chaos ensued. Arthur raised Excalibur above his head until everyone settled down. He lowered the sword and introduced Ryerson as Lance's attorney. The tall, dapper man stepped forward.

"Ladies and gentlemen of the press, I'll make a very brief statement and then I'll allow for some questions. However, bear this in mind – I have, as of now, only conferred with Arthur and Ricky on this matter. I have not yet conferred with my client, nor have I seen the official charges leveled against him. By tomorrow I will have the police report and will have met with Lance at juvenile hall to hear his story. So any questions relevant to those areas I cannot answer at this time."

Helen threw her hand into the air and he pointed to her.

"Mr. Ryerson, have you heard that there is purportedly a video of Lance threatening the victim, and what's your comment on that?"

Ryerson frowned. "I've heard a great number of rumors being bandied about by you people in the media. If such a video exists, I will see it at some point when the D.A. shows me his evidence. Thus, I have no comment at this time."

Another hand went up. "This is for King Arthur," the reporter announced.

Arthur stepped forward.

"What effect do you think this arrest will have on your proposition, King Arthur? As you know, the District Attorney favors a yes vote for the very purpose of prosecuting more kids like your son in adult court."

"I am well aware of the district attorney's opinion, but I also know many of his colleagues prefer a no vote so they will not have boys like my Ricky sitting on juries to try other boys like my Lance. Thus far, we do not know how the public will react to this misunderstanding."

"Misunderstanding?" the reporter asked.

"Of course," Arthur continued. "My son is no more guilty of such a heinous crime than you are, sir. Most of you standing here today have had ample opportunity to gauge his character and good qualities, so you should already know this is a clear case of false arrest."

The yellow-haired reporter, who always seemed to be present, threw up his hand. Arthur reluctantly pointed him out.

"As you say, King Arthur, we have seen your son in action. In fact, we all saw him hung over, scream at us, and imply that I wanted to molest him. Such behavior would indicate an unstable personality, wouldn't you say?"

Arthur opened his mouth to respond, but Ryerson stepped forward. "We have no comment on that at this time."

Helen raised her hand again and Arthur pointed.

"I have a question for Sir Ricky," she said formally, but gently.

Arthur turned and ushered Ricky forward.

"Sir Ricky," Helen began, "you probably spend more time with Sir Lance than anyone else, by all appearances. Do you think it's possible he committed this crime?"

Ryerson threw a stern look Ricky's way, but did not forbid him to answer.

Ricky looked at Helen soberly. "Lady Helen, you knew Lance even before I did. Do *you* think he did this?"

Helen was taken aback a moment. "As a journalist, Sir Ricky, it's not my place to offer an opinion."

Ricky accepted that answer, not wanting to put her in a bad position. "Lance is the best, most amazing, most caring guy I'll ever know. He finds the good in people

I think are monsters. Says he can see the good in them, see it in their eyes, like soul-whispering." He shook his head in incredulity. "Would he do something so nasty and evil as this, even if the guy deserved it? Hell, no."

Helen nodded. More questions were fired at Ryerson and Arthur, but most went unanswered due to lack of information or the fact that it was "Too early in the case to comment."

After about fifteen minutes, Ryerson announced that he and Arthur had work to do and that he'd answer more questions after the arraignment on Friday. The uniforms, under Ryan's watchful eye, ushered the media out the front gate, making certain none tried to sneak back inside. Helen tossed a small smile of encouragement Ricky's way before she left with the others and Ricky followed the adults back into the house.

Frustrated, Ricky asked Esteban if they could spar together. He had already worked out with Chris, but he needed an opponent he could go all out with to release his pent up energy. Also distressed, Esteban readily agreed. Reyna took Chris to the kitchen to make sure the despondent boy ate something.

Ricky and Esteban sparred for an hour, and both were breathing heavily when the door to the Training Center opened and Reyna ushered in Bridget and Ariel.

Ricky knew he should've felt happy at seeing Ariel, but he just felt empty.

The normally shy girl threw her arms around him, not even caring about his sweat-soaked tunic. "Oh, baby, I'm so sorry about Lance," she whispered, and held him.

Bridget joined them and took Ricky's hand, squeezing it gently. She looked devastated. Her eyes were puffy and red and her usual colorful eye shadow had smeared. She eyed Ricky sadly. "You okay?"

"No, I'm not."

Ariel released him and Bridget engulfed him in a hug of her own. When they separated, she turned her wide, fearful eyes to his. "Have you heard from him?"

He shook his head, unable to speak, afraid of his feelings gushing forth and embarrassing him.

"I been in juvy before, Bridget," Esteban said, and the girls turned to him, looking surprised. "I used to be a bad kid, if you hadn't heard," he went on with a knowing look toward Reyna. "Anyway, there's only certain times staff'll let the kids use the phones, and then it's mostly collect calls."

Bridget's face fell. "You mean he can't call me?"

Esteban shrugged. "Not 'less he uses the brown phone."

Both girls scrunched up their faces in confusion.

"That means the staff phone, in the office, and the senior staff has to let him."

"Oh, God..." Bridget whispered, and Ariel wrapped an arm around her.

"You can set up a pre-paid account on your cell phone, if you want," Esteban went on. "Then Lance could call you from the pay phone."

She brightened at that.

"I don't know how it's done, 'cause my mom couldn't afford it," Esteban added solemnly. "But I'm sure you can find out."

She nodded, and held Ariel close.

Ricky stood by helplessly, knowing he should be the one with his arms around Ariel, maybe even be comforting Bridget, and yet he remained immobile, uncertain of what to do and distrustful of his feelings.

Ariel took his hand. "Any time you wanna talk, Ricky, I'm here for you."

Her smile and the tone of her voice were so sincere, so filled with love that Ricky felt even worse. He knew he should want to talk with her, should want her comfort, but he didn't. He just felt the loss of Lance. Nothing else.

"Thanks, Ariel," he muttered weakly, "but right now I can't... I just need to, like, work out my anger and everything. I can't talk right now." He lowered his eyes in shame at the hurt look drifting across her face.

"Oh, okay. Call me?"

"I will."

Ricky felt Bridget's eyes on him and turned his head. Her look was intense, but unreadable, but it made him squirm with discomfort.

"If you talk to Lance, Ricky, tell him I miss him," Bridget said with such earnestness that Ricky's heart lurched. He suddenly realized just how much she really cared for Lance.

He gulped awkwardly. "I will."

"And tell him to call me," she added with urgency. "I'll figure out that phone thing."

He nodded.

She hugged Ricky one more time, and then Ariel hugged him. He knew she expected him to kiss her, but he felt self-conscious and awkward. So he let her pull away and the hurt in her eyes only intensified his own. Feeling guilty, he watched as they slowly shuffled from the Training Center with Reyna.

Ricky's eyes remained downcast until the girls were gone. A cleared throat caused him to raise them.

Esteban eyed him questioningly. "Anything you wanna tell me, Ricky?" His deep voice sounded softer than usual, more laced with understanding. "You know, man to man?"

Ricky couldn't meet Esteban's eyes. "Naw. Thanks, though."

Esteban raised his sword. "Wanna keep going?"

Ricky raised his own sword. For the next hour, his mind remained fixed on not getting his ass handed to him by Esteban, not on the girls or Lance or... himself.

CHAPTER THREE
I'D LIKE TO BE A WARRIOR OF LIGHT

LATER THAT AFTERNOON, LANCE WAS taken from his room and once again escorted into the enclosed area behind the control booth. But this time he wasn't alone. A man sat at the table where he'd eaten his lunch, and stood when Lance entered. The staff stepped back into the dayroom and locked the door, sealing Lance in with this stranger.

The man was a priest or minister of some kind. Lance could tell by the black clothes and little white square in the collar. An older guy, he was tall, thin, and bald on top. He had short, gray hair on the sides, and a trimmed gray beard and mustache. He had an impish-sort of face, with eyes that seemed to twinkle. His demeanor instantly put Lance at ease. He stepped forward and stopped before this stranger.

"Hi," he said, extending his hand. "I'm Lance."

The man's lips curled into a small, knowing smile. He shook Lance's hand. "I know. I'm Father Mike, the Catholic Chaplain here. I like to meet the new kids, in case they want to talk." He waved a hand toward the chair beside him. "Please, Lance, sit."

Lance did so, and the priest sat across the table from him, eying him with an expression of wonder. "So, how are you feeling?"

It was a stupid question, Lance knew, a typical adult question that required a non-committal response. But somehow, coming from this man, with that hint of an Irish accent causing the words to roll pleasantly off the tongue, Lance sensed the man really *did* want to know. So he told him the truth.

"Like crap," he answered. "Like my life is worthless. Like *I'm* worthless."

Father Mike sat back and appraised him silently, as though digesting his words. "*Are* you worthless, Sir Lance? After all you've accomplished out there?"

Lance considered a moment. "What does any of it matter if I go to prison for something I didn't do?"

The older man nodded, an understanding look on his face. "Everything we do matters, Lance," he finally said, waving his hand around him. "Do you think that these other boys here, because they're accused of a crime, because they may have *committed* a crime, have no value, and everything good they may have done is for nothing?"

"No," Lance assured him. "I didn't mean it like that. It's just ... why would God bring me back just to put me here?"

"What makes you think God put you here?"

Lance shrugged. "Isn't that what people say, you know, this is God's will and stuff?"

"Some do."

"You don't believe that?"

"That God put you here? No. But I do believe God never puts obstacles in our path that He knows won't make us stronger."

Lance considered those words. "How can this make me stronger?"

"That I cannot tell you, Lance," the priest said wisely, reminding Lance of Merlin. "We see the hand of God after the fact."

Lance considered that. It sort of made sense to him.

"All of us are better than the worst thing we ever did, Lance. Remember that," Father Mike went on, and Lance absorbed those words while the priest eyed him appraisingly. "I have a group I work with in this unit, and I'd like you to join. We meet tonight, and every Wednesday, right here."

Lance frowned. "What kind of group?"

The priest leaned forward and placed his arms on the table. "We call it a meditation group where we discuss different issues each week. They're all good kids like yourself. You'll like them."

There was something about this man, a positive energy that was infectious.

"Won't they like, you know, stare at me the whole time?"

"Of course they will, Lance. You're The Boy Who Came Back. A living miracle."

Lance instantly felt embarrassed, and shocked by the man's straightforward honesty. "I don't know."

"Lance," Father Mike went on earnestly, his soft eyes twinkling with truth, "you've no idea what you've already given these youngsters here, just from what you've done out there. Most of them will spend decades in prison, and they need all the hope they can get. You *are* hope, Lance, hope for a better life for kids like them, and hope for life after death."

Lance sat back in his chair, stunned, and disconcerted, that he could mean so much to these incarcerated kids he'd never even met. "How can I be hope, Father, when I've been running in this dark place for so long? I thought maybe I finally found my way out, but here I am, right back in the dark."

The man nodded, and Lance knew Father Mike understood exactly what he was saying. "We have all been there, and these other boys well know how to be a warrior of darkness. That's how most of them have lived their lives. In here, we seek to make everyone a warrior of light."

Lance considered that, and smiled. He was already a Warrior of Right within the Round Table. Being a Warrior of Light sounded cool, too. "I'd like to be a warrior of light, Father Mike."

The priest stood. "You already are, Lance."

Lance felt his face redden. "I'd like to join your group."

"Good," the man said. "I'll clear it with staff." He looked at Lance with deep compassion. "Any time you need to talk, Lance, just let the staff know and they'll call me. You're important."

"Thanks, Father Mike." He stood and they shook hands. "Do you think, Father, that everyone will stop staring at me after a while? I really hate it."

He shrugged. "Hard to say, Lance. You are the most high-profile kid we've ever had here. Actually, you're the most high-profile kid in the world. I suppose once the others figure out you can't walk on water, things'll settle down."

He smiled, exaggerating little dimples in his cheeks. Lance grinned. Then the priest used his key to open the door into the control booth, and a staff member escorted Lance back to his room.

Dinner that night at New Camelot was a somber affair as everyone sat around the table and Arthur said a prayer for Lance's deliverance, before food was listlessly passed back and forth. All life, it seemed, all the usual exuberance, was drained from the room, from the entire family, from the Round Table itself.

Finally, Chris mumbled to no one in particular, "Wonder what Lance is doing right now."

Esteban and Reyna exchanged a look, but Ricky kept his head down. Esteban glanced up at the clock. It was six o'clock. He cleared his throat. "Uh, he'll be in his room right now."

Everyone lifted his or her eyes to him.

"Dinner's around five, and then they stay in their rooms till seven. That's dayroom time, but since it's Lance's first day, they probably won't let him come out till tomorrow."

Everyone stared at him, and Esteban shrugged sheepishly. "Been in a few times, remember?"

Arthur and Jenny nodded, but Ricky looked over at Esteban. "Will he be safe in there?" There was an edge to his voice, but he kept it steady.

"I never been to the compound before, but since he's so famous, I'm sure they'll watch him real close."

"When can he call us?"

Esteban shrugged again, and Ricky fell silent.

"Are you gonna visit him, Arthur?" Reyna asked hopefully.

Arthur nodded. "I have been told visiting is Saturday and Sunday afternoons. I shall go both days, if it pleases you, Jenny."

She smiled lovingly. "Of course. I'll watch things here."

"Can I go, Dad?" Ricky asked, his heart beating wildly at the thought.

"Alas, Ricky, only adults of twenty-one years or higher are permitted. Mr. Ryerson told me."

Dejected, Ricky slumped back down into his seat and stared listlessly at his food. He wasn't hungry anyway, and now he lost his appetite completely. "May I be excused?"

Arthur nodded. Ricky silently rose from the table, took his plate into the kitchen, and then passed back through the dining room in the direction of the stairs. A pall settled once again on the diners, and nothing else was said the entire meal.

Esteban had been correct. Lance was given dinner in his room—another plastic-covered Styrofoam plate of dog food—but he was so hungry he ate every scrap and was thankful for what he had.

After the night staff took away his plate, Lance waited for Father Mike to call him out for that group. He'd never had any experience with Catholic priests before, or any organized religion, for that matter, but he found himself liking the older man. There was something gentle and comforting, just being in his presence, and he suspected all the kids here probably felt the same way.

His thoughts drifted to Bridget. How had she reacted, he wondered? He didn't think she'd believe him guilty and knew she'd miss him, but why didn't he miss her more? Shouldn't he? Of course, it had only been one day and he was still somewhat in shock. And yet, try as he might to focus on Bridget, his thoughts continually drifted to Ricky.

Lance sighed just thinking of him.

His shadow. His protector. His sparring partner. His keeper of secrets. His better half. His... everything.

How would he live without Ricky?

Finally, Lance heard a key in the door and it swung open to reveal one of the night staff, Ms. Harrison, a short, pretty lady with a serious look on her face. She ushered him from his room and when he stepped out into the dayroom, all activity ceased. Every head turned to find him, as though by magic. He acknowledged them all with a little nod and followed Harrison back into the closed-off area behind the office.

This time, he found Father Mike sitting with a circle of eight boys, six Latino and two African-American, all gazing at him in silent wonder. Father Mike stood and offered the impish smile Lance found so comforting.

"Come in, Lance, and join us," he said with that Irish lilt, indicating a chair directly across from him in the circle.

No one said a word as Lance stepped forward and seated himself on the plastic chair. Father Mike acted like this was business as usual, even though the other boys were gawking.

"Everyone, I think you all know Lance," the priest said by way of breaking the ice. "He needs no introduction."

"Hi," Lance offered, pushing hair away from his face and trying his best to not reveal the fear and embarrassment coursing through him. "Thanks for letting me join."

Father Mike looked around the circle, obviously amused by the spellbound faces of his charges. "Why don't we go around the circle and introduce ourselves, eh? I'll start. I'm Father Mike, Catholic Chaplain here at Sylmar."

He nodded toward the boy beside him. When the boy said nothing, Father Mike nudged him with an elbow.

"Oh, yeah, I'm Joey."

Lance nodded, noting the scruffy black hair and little rat-tail dangling from one side. The litany of names continued, and Lance knew he'd never remember them right now, so he didn't try. After a minute or so, the names ceased and everyone continued to stare in wonder.

Joey blurted, "Did you really die, man?"

That caught Lance by surprise, and he took a moment before answering. "Yeah. Yeah, I did."

Joey's mouth hung open comically, and the others gaped, as well.

Lance sighed. "I'm just not sure why God would bring me back only for me to end up here."

A tall, lanky boy near Father Mike piped up with, "We all been seein' how youse out there trying to help kids like us, with yo prop and all, you know, us kids bein' tried as adults? So maybe God wanted you in here so's you could know some 'a us first hand. That way you'd know better what to tell them people out there."

"Well said, Anthony," Father Mike said with a knowing look toward the boy.

Lance's jaw dropped open. He'd never thought of it that way. Damn, these kids were pretty smart. "*If* I ever get back out there, you mean."

"You will," Anthony said with assurance. "You're too important to stay here for long."

"If you feel comfortable, Lance," Father Mike said, breaking the awkward silence, "would you tell us about your experience with death?"

Lance looked around the circle, saw their faces, and almost gasped. In every pair of eyes there was the same desperate need to know what he alone, of anyone on earth, could share with them. So he did. He described his experience in much the same way he had to John, adding a few more details as he remembered them, especially about Mark and Jack and how at peace they both looked as they turned to cross that field toward that endless light.

When he finished, the gawking had gotten even more extreme – every mouth hung open like a bunch of Venus Fly Traps Lance had once seen in a plant store.

Then one of the boys blurted out, "I never knew fags could go to Heaven."

"Angel," Father Mike admonished quietly, but firmly.

Angel turned to the priest. "Oh, my bad, Father Mike, but I just always been told fa—gay people go to Hell."

He turned back to Lance, but the gaze was not harsh or threatening in any way. Just curious. Had these guys seen that video of him and Michael, he wondered for the first time? If so, he could be in a world of hurt.

Lance cleared his throat. "You guys probably know a lot more about the Bible and God than me," he said, gazing around at each of them, "but I always thought only the bad people go to Hell. Jack and Mark were good. The best."

No one said anything, and Lance turned to Father Mike.

"You're right on the money, Lance," he said with a smile. "My colleague, Father

Greg, who all these guys know, has a saying – you're exactly what God had in mind when He made you."

Lance had never heard that, and he liked it. Arthur said things like that too, but he liked the way this was phrased. "So Jack and Mark and other gay people aren't, like, you know, mistakes or something?" he asked the priest, hoping the edge in his voice wasn't too obvious.

Father Mike just chuckled. "God doesn't make mistakes, Lance. We are all here for a reason, and God wants us all back with him one day. No exceptions."

Another boy to Lance's left blurted out, "What about the guy who raped Lance?"

Lance blanched and lowered his eyes, and the speaker suddenly looked mortified.

"Oh, my bad, Lance, it's just, well, if you did do what they said, I'm on your side, man. That guy had it coming."

Lance looked at him incredulously, trying to pull up his name.

Father Mike did not look angry, as Lance thought he might. He just cast his interested eyes toward Andy. "Is that what we're about here, Andy, revenge?"

Andy looked sheepish, but stood his ground. "No, Father Mike, but that guy raped a little boy, man, and got away with it."

Lance felt increasingly uncomfortable as they talked about him like he wasn't there.

Father Mike obviously felt his discomfort because he said, "Joey, explain to Lance what being a warrior of light means, and what is restorative justice."

Joey turned to Lance. "A warrior of light fights battles with the word of God, not with weapons or fists. And restorative justice is about healing, not just the victim, but the offender and the community."

Father Mike nodded. "Well said, Joey. Healing only comes when we forgive and are forgiven. That doesn't mean men like that shouldn't be punished by the law, but as human beings we must repair the damage done." He turned those blue eyes onto Lance and held him with his gaze. "Do you ever see yourself confronting this man, telling him how much he hurt you, perhaps even forgiving him?"

Lance's mouth dropped open in shock. His first impulse was to blurt out, "Hell, no," but he bit back the words. Could Father Mike be right? Would Richard somehow cease haunting his dreams, tearing his insides apart with terror, if Lance were able to somehow forgive him? He didn't think such a thing was possible. He broke eye contact. "I don't know, Father Mike."

The old priest nodded, satisfied with that answer. "So, that brings us to our meditation for tonight, which just happens to be on forgiveness."

Lance looked up quickly and met Father Mike's eyes. The man offered a small smile, and Lance felt like this was someone to whom he could tell anything. He settled into his seat as the priest admonished everyone to relax and get into a calm, contemplative state.

Lance listened to the meditation, which detailed a story Lance had never heard before, about a man with two sons. One did everything his father asked, while the other took his share of the inheritance and then left home to party. Except Father Mike set the story in a modern day barrio and updated the characters to kids like him.

Lance was amazed when the father in the story forgave his younger son for wasting all the money, and disobeying him. It made him think about Arthur, and how Arthur forgave everything he'd done, even those embarrassing episodes. Now he suddenly understood the power of forgiveness, especially since the older son in the story was jealous and wanted his father to take revenge against his brother. But that wouldn't have done any good, Lance realized. It just would've made everything worse.

After the mediation and discussion, which Lance eagerly joined, Father Mike passed out little snacks and the guys talked and joked around. Joey moved to sit beside Lance and started telling him about the history of punk music, and Lance was grateful that the subject was finally about something other than him.

When it was time for Father Mike to leave, he invited Lance to join them on Sunday morning for mass, and the kids all encouraged him to attend. So he agreed, feeling more a part of this incarcerated group than he ever would've thought possible.

Unfortunately, after Father Mike's departure, Lance experienced the next humiliation, one he'd have to endure daily. He had to shower with other guys, right in front of the staff! And if he needed to do a "number two," what the guys there called a "sit down," it would be on toilets that were in plain view of the dayroom. The bathroom was mostly a giant window through which everyone could see everything, for "security reasons."

In his room, Lance slowly stripped off his county-issued clothes, including the underwear, and slipped a small white towel around his waist as quickly as possible. He shook with anxiety because he'd never been naked in front of anyone before, not even Ricky.

Only Richard.

He shivered at the thought, reflecting back to Father Mike's story and wondering if he could ever bring himself to forgive Richard. He knew he was innocent, and most likely it had been one of Richard's other victims who had attacked him. But didn't the man deserve it? Now he wasn't so sure.

Suddenly his door swung open and he must've looked like a deer in the headlights. A male staff named Whitaker stared at him in surprise. "You okay, Lance?"

Whitaker was the one who'd earlier explained shower and bathroom procedures. Lance nodded, though not convincingly. "I just never been naked with anybody since, well, since what happened to me."

Whitaker looked empathetic, but spread his hands helplessly. "It's policy, Lance. Sorry."

Lance forced down his fear, and stepped from the room. He glanced over at the shower room – three other boys were already heading in that direction, similar white towels wrapped around their waists. He noted their physiques, and at least felt a tiny bit better that he was in better shape than them.

Heart pounding, Lance made his way into the showers. He averted his eyes from the naked boys, slipped off his own towel and stepped beneath the warm water. It was the fastest shower he'd ever taken. Supposedly they had three minutes, but Lance managed to finish in less than two. He threw some county shampoo into his mass of hair, rubbed it in and rinsed it out. Then, keeping his privates turned inward, washed all over with nasty feeling soap and snatched his towel from where he'd hung it. A quick shake of his long hair and a few rubs with the towel and then it was wrapped around his waist again. After the door had been unlocked, Whitaker gave him a second towel as darted from the shower room.

"For your hair," Whitaker said as he handed over the second towel. Lance thanked him with a nod, his blood still pounding, his heart and breathing at hyperactive levels.

As he finished drying himself in his room, Lance realized this was what Richard had reduced him to all those years ago, and nothing had really changed. Could Father Mike be right? Could forgiving that man, even for something so evil, actually bring him peace of mind? He didn't know. Soon, he was dressed for bed in a plain white t-shirt and underwear and his first night as a prisoner came to a quiet conclusion.

School at New Camelot was off for the month of August, but knights drifted in and out all morning because of the situation with Lance. They were all stunned, but continued their duties in the Computer Lab, or sparred in the Training Centre, in stoic silence.

Ricky stayed in Lance's room and slept on Lance's side of the bed. Or tried to. He'd hoped doing this would minimize the ache in his heart, but it only made it worse. He'd ended up pacing the house most of the night, meeting up with Arthur several times because he, too, couldn't sleep. Once again, due to the police raid and current crisis, the hotel had been closed to paying guests, so the silence of the night was nearly oppressive in its totality.

By morning, both Ricky and Arthur were exhausted, but neither would allow the tiredness to show. Ricky made it a point to play with Chris and distract him, while Jenny did her best to keep Arthur's mind on matters other than Lance.

Since Lance had been scheduled to record some TV ads for their prop campaign, that task now fell to Ricky. The filming was scheduled for the following week, and Jenny gave Ricky the scripts so he could prepare. Given what had happened to Lance, Ricky asked if he could change some of the words, and Jenny agreed. She would check it later for clarity and focus.

For Lance, the day began at six o'clock when he was awakened by staff to get dressed and do "head and water calls" -- translation: use the bathroom, and/or drinking fountain, and wash up for breakfast.

This time, Lance was brought out to eat with the other minors. The guys from last night's group acknowledged him with a nod, but the others just stared at him like he'd grown an extra head. The food consisted of milk, wheat bread, powdered eggs and a baked potato. Lance ate every bite – he was *really* hungry.

Breakfast, as all meals, he'd been told, was to be eaten in silence. Talking was a punishable offense. So he kept his head over his food, long hair draping the sides of his face and hiding him from the others. After breakfast, the boys were returned to their rooms.

At eight, everyone was released from their rooms and lined up double file for the short trek outside the unit and into the caged classrooms. Since the classrooms were effectively part of the Compound, and thus sealed off from the rest of the institution, no shackles were required.

As he stood outside his door, Lance glanced around the triangle-shaped day room and took in some of the decorations. There were bulletin boards with positive slogans on them, as well as 'integrity', 'honesty' and 'teamwork' painted onto the pillars protruding from the wall every four rooms or so. Just outside his door was a large poster proclaiming: 'Everyone is different. Respect the differences'. Lance momentarily considered how that sentiment echoed the mantra of New Camelot, and wondered if anyone in this place took it seriously.

Instructed by staff, "Hands behind your back," Lance fell in at the end of the line because the exit door to the school was across the dayroom from him. The staff intoned crisply, "No talking and start walking." Lance did as he was told, doing his best not to appear scared or nervous. He knew guys in places like this postured a lot, always wanting to punk new kids just to show how tough they were. He didn't believe his celebrity status would exempt him and might, in fact, encourage more of these guys to challenge him. But he had a plan. He was ready.

They filed out of the building and up a slight ramp to a walkway. To their left were caged-in basketball courts that looked more like extra-large dog runs, and to their right more brick buildings with open doors, obviously the classrooms. Each one sat within its own separate cage, so if anyone ran out of one he couldn't get into the room next door due to locked gates.

Lance followed the others into a classroom that looked sort-of like those he'd had at Mark Twain High—posters, charts and pictures of famous people adorning the walls, stacks of books on countertops lining the back wall—but instead of desks, there were square tables for the kids to sit around. The teacher was an old man who looked positively ancient to Lance, like maybe he'd taught the real Abraham Lincoln or something.

Staff ushered them into the room and made certain everyone took a seat. Lance sat with Joey next to him and a burly Latino guy from the other half of his building, called W-1, directly across. Once everyone was seated, Mr. Lincoln's personal tutor passed out worksheets with stuff Lance had done in the sixth grade.

Man, he thought, *this is lame.*

But he kept his mouth shut. Once everyone had work to do and pencils to use, the ancient teacher hobbled back to his desk and sat. The probation staff eyed everyone a moment before stepping outside and closing the door. Lance could see his head through the little glass view window – the man was obviously standing guard. Joey glanced over at Lance and rolled his eyes at the paperwork, mouthing the words "long term sub" and flicking his eyes back toward the old man up front.

Lance gave a tiny grin and set to work. Everything was calm for a while, but he kept noticing the burly guy mad dogging him. He could literally feel the kid's eyes boring into him. At first he ignored it – after all, the W-1 guys hadn't gotten a look yet at the world-famous boy who came back. But after about fifteen minutes the staring got really annoying, so Lance flicked his hair from the side of his face and glared at the unknown kid.

"Can I help you?" he whispered.

Burly boy eyed him with a look of pure disgust. "You're a faggot, aren't you?"

Lance heard a gasp from Joey, but also from other kids around him, as though calling The Boy Who Came Back such a name was a huge no-no.

"The hell did you call me?" Lance whispered, his voice as cold and dangerous as he could make it.

Burly boy glanced over at Mr. Ancient and saw him snoozing at his desk, and turned back to Lance. "I saw that video of you making out with that dude," he practically spat, as though that was the worst thing he could ever see. "Man, that's nasty. I don't like queers."

Lance didn't think it likely these incarcerated guys had seen the video in here, so this kid probably saw it before he got locked up. Fighting down his embarrassment, Lance said, "I don't like idiots, either, but I'm sitting across from one." Burly's face pulled into anger, but Lance wasn't finished. "Know what I'm here for, scumbag?"

The kid nodded, anger still there, but Lance was pleased to see a slight flicker of fear dancing across those cold brown eyes. "Good. Cause here's the deal," he went on, keeping his voice low and steely. "You wanna come over here and call me a faggot up close and personal, bring it on. I don't need a knife to mutilate your junk – I'll use my teeth and then I'll laugh while you bleed out."

Burly boy blanched white with shock.

"So, come at me," Lance went on quietly, continuing the best impression of Michael he could muster. "I already died once. How many lives have you got to spare, huh?"

Burly's face dissolved into a look of horror, and fear. "You're psycho."

"And don't let your dumb ass forget it."

Burly quickly broke eye contact, and Lance returned to his work, calm as could be on the outside, but shaking like crazy inside. He hated having to act that way, but he knew guys like this too well, and going all Michael on 'em was usually the best way to shut 'em down.

He flicked a glance over toward Joey, whose mouth hung open in shock. He winked and saw the boy's face dissolve into a grin of admiration. Joey shook his head in wonder and turned back to his work.

Mr. Ancient never even knew anything had happened.

Lance finished all of his work very quickly, as did Joey. It was obvious the other boy was also way too smart for the likes of this baby work.

The other teachers that morning were far more interactive and Lance felt he might actually learn something from them. Finally, it was lunchtime. The staff re-entered and escorted the kids back into unit W, with burly boy keeping his distance from Lance as that line peeled off to enter the W-1 side.

The guys who'd witnessed Lance's encounter with Burly all patted him on the back or high-fived him during head and water calls, and then took their places at the metal tables.

Lunch was eaten in silence, with hotdogs being the fare of the day. Before school resumed, a day staff named Mr. Watkins, short and thin with a shock of black hair, approached Lance's table and stopped before the boy. "Your attorney's here to see you, Lance," he said calmly.

"Okay. So what do I do?"

Watkins looked a little uncomfortable. "He's in the visitor's center. That means I gotta shackle you. Sorry, Lance, it's policy."

Lance nodded, and Joey tossed a grin toward Watkins. "Hey, how come you never apologize for shackling me, Watkins?"

"That's 'cause your ass needs it, Reynoso," the man threw back, obviously joking.

Angel piped up with, "And how come he's Lance and the rest of us goes by our last names?" Again, the tone was playful, not angry.

Watkins thought it was a serious question, however, and said, "Well, he *is* Lance, isn't he? What else would I call him?"

Angel and Joey laughed and high-fived.

Watkins smiled, realizing they were messing with him. He directed Lance to follow him to the office.

"Good luck, man," Joey said, offering a fist bump.

Angel did the same.

Lance was once more shackled with metal restraints around the hands, and plastic ones around the ankles, and led out across the dayroom, past the tables with all those gazes pinned to him. He followed Watkins through the thick glass exit door and back outside.

CHAPTER FOUR
YOU REALLY HIM?

I T WAS A HOT AUGUST day and the blinding sun made Lance squint. He hobbled along the pathway to toward the huge booth he'd seen yesterday, which Watkins told him was called Movement Control.

"The Visitor's Center is on our left. There's little rooms in there for minors to meet with lawyers or psyches or social workers. Catholic Chaplain's office is in there, too."

"Is Father Mike here today?"

Watkins shrugged. "Don't know. I'll check while you're in with your lawyer."

They didn't talk any more as Watkins led Lance toward a large single-story building made up mostly of huge windows overlooking the playing fields and The Compound. They entered through a glass door, unlocked at the moment, but Lance noted the large key slot as they passed through. He guessed every single place in the juvenile hall could be locked for security purposes. There was a control booth of sorts just to Lance's left as they entered. Watkins stopped him there, but Lance's eyes scanned the large visiting area and settled on the glass door at the other side bearing the words 'Catholic Chaplain'.

Watkins informed the staff person in the control room whom he'd brought, and the heavy-set woman rolled her eyes at him. "Like I don't know who *that* is?"

He shrugged.

"Room two," she said, eying Lance with the same mix of wonder and sadness he seemed to get from all the staff in here.

Watkins removed the shackles from Lance's hands and pointed to the middle of three glass rooms. A tall, skinny guy with sunken cheeks sat at a table, checking his iPad and phone, an open briefcase on the table and a tape recorder and notepad beside it.

Watkins used his key to open the door and the man looked up. He had a severe-looking face, Lance thought, as though he seldom smiled. *This* was his attorney? He hobbled into the room and heard the lock click behind him.

"Sit," the man said brusquely, and Lance complied. "I am Mr. Ryerson, your attorney, and the best criminal defense lawyer in California." He looked at Lance with a gaunt face and piercing blue-gray eyes that seemed to go right through him. "Now, I understand from your father that you snuck out of the house to meet someone, and the victim found you. Correct?"

Lance nodded. Boy, this guy didn't waste any time!

"He also said you refuse to give up the name of the person you went to meet."

"He's got nothing to do with this," Lance insisted. "Richard was already gone before he got there."

"He?" the man repeated sharply. "Was this a boyfriend? Is that why you don't want to give his name?"

Lance blushed. "No." He already didn't like this man and couldn't believe his dad had hired him. "I was meeting a friend. To talk."

"Then tell me his name."

"This isn't about him, it's about me. About making an example outta me, isn't it?"

The man sat back a moment and steepled his fingers before his face.

"You want it straight – here it is. The D.A. is running for re-election in three months. You have a prop on the same ballot, a prop this D.A. is in favor of. Why? Because even though it will allow kids like you to sit on juries, it will also allow him to send that many more of you to prison, something he's intent on doing. Does he care if you committed this crime? No. Do I? No. The point of going to court in this country, Lance, is to win, however you can. So yes, he wants to make you, The Boy Who Came Back, the most famous person in the entire world, into a teenaged Jack the Ripper. In so doing, he can gain re-election and bolster his contention that all kids should be treated as adults for every offense they commit. Now, I'm going to allow you to withhold your 'friend's' name, for the present. But, if down the line I need it to establish that this crime was not premeditated, you'd better cough it up. Clear?" The man's eyes blazed, making him look like a demonic scarecrow or something.

Lance scowled. "Crystal. Sir."

"Good." Ryerson turned on his tape recorder and shoved it in front of Lance. "Now tell me everything that happened that night between you and the victim, every word he said and you said, with as much exactness as possible."

Lance told his story as best as he could recall. He concluded with the arrival of Michael, without giving up his name, of course, and Ryerson eyed him keenly.

"Those were your exact words to him, Lance, as you pointed your knife?"

"Yeah, as far as I know. I was, like, shaking and afraid. He made me feel six-years old again and helpless." He looked down at the table and fell silent.

Ryerson turned off the recorder. "Any questions for me?"

"The cops said something about a video."

"I haven't seen it yet, but apparently the victim had it in his front shirt pocket, recording you through a small hole he'd made."

Lance was stunned. "He set me up?"

"Perhaps. Sick prick like him maybe just wanted more jack-off material."

Lance turned red with embarrassment.

"Thornton has been living under the alias Dick Trimble," Ryerson went on, "which likely explains why the police weren't able to locate his whereabouts prior to him finding you."

"What's gonna happen on Friday?"

"Arraignment." Ryerson looked long and hard at Lance. "No matter what that D.A. says about you, Lance, you may only utter two words. When the judge asks how you plead, you say 'not guilty'. Period. Nothing more. Got that?"

Lance nodded.

"Good." The man stood and started slipping everything back into his briefcase. "I'm off to Parker Center. I need your official arrest report and the victim's statement." He slipped a small cardholder from his jacket pocket and popped out a business card. "Call me if you think of anything important. But do not waste my time with stupid questions. I am a busy man."

Lance took the card. Ryerson snapped his briefcase closed and stepped around the table to rap on the glass door. As soon as Watkins opened it, the lawyer stepped out and was gone without a backward glance.

Lance's mouth hung open in shock. This guy was a jerk! How could his dad have...?

"You okay, Lance?" he heard Watkins ask, and realized how he must have looked at that moment.

"Yeah. I'm good."

Watkins held up the restraints.

"No Father Mike?" Lance asked hopefully.

Watkins shook his head. "Maybe later. I left a message on the door for him."

Lance smiled gratefully. "Thanks, man."

Within minutes, Lance was once more shackled like Hannibal Lector and shuffling back to The Compound.

Reyna and Esteban stayed that night at New Camelot, having been assigned by Jenny separate rooms on different floors because she didn't want any trouble from Reyna's parents. They all had to be up extra early the next day to head to the criminal courts building in downtown Los Angeles for Lance's arraignment. Everyone was tense and on edge, especially Arthur and Ricky. Thus far, Lance had not called, and the ache in Arthur's heart at not hearing his son's voice kept him awake most of the night. Again, like sentries passing one another on patrol, he met up with Ricky in the various halls and corridors of the massive hotel. The two would stop, hug one another for however much time they needed, and then silently continue their aimless rounds.

Lance was awakened at four-thirty Friday morning for court. Once he'd done his head and water calls, he and Angel, who also had court that day, were given a quick, very inadequate snack for breakfast. They wore bright orange prisoner jumpsuits, and shackled with metal cuffs around the ankles and wrists. A chain connected the ankles even more tightly than usual to the wrists, forcing Lance to walk hunched over like an old man. This made his humiliating descent from hero to criminal complete.

Angel shrugged and grinned – this was clearly business as usual for him. Lance nodded in acknowledgement as they were led out of The Compound. It was dark outside, but already warm – today would be another scorcher. The night staff led the boys past Movement Control and down another corridor Lance had not seen before. It was caged in, like everything else in this facility. They stopped before yet another gate and the staff opened it with his key. As they shuffled through, Lance saw up ahead a huge Los Angeles County Sheriff's bus with two deputies lounging beside it.

The Night Staff stopped just outside the gate and said, "Good luck, guys," and indicated the bus. Then he stepped back inside, closed and locked the gate, and headed back the way he'd come.

The deputies smirked when they saw Angel, and something in their faces set off alarm bells in Lance. Angel led the way, long curly hair tumbling around his neck, head held high, refusing to be submissive before the intimidating deputies, who wore their full khaki uniforms.

"Well, well," said the taller of the two. "If it isn't our favorite angel boy. Shot at any more deputies lately, punk?"

Angel didn't answer, but merely stepped forward to board the bus. The shorter deputy unobtrusively stuck out a foot and tripped him. Angel went sprawling on the hard driveway. With hands and feet bound in chains, the boy crashed hard to the ground, turning slightly to avoid smashing his face into the concrete. He landed on his shoulder, a painful cry coming from his mouth, but nothing else.

Lance was stunned. "The hell!" He tried to stumble forward toward Angel before stopping, realizing he could not even help his friend get up.

The taller deputy eyed Lance mockingly. "Oooh, Celebrity Boy wants to butt into something that's not his business."

Shorter said, "You got somethin' to say, Celebrity Boy?" His tone was cold, and threatening.

Though Lance recognized the danger, he stumbled closer to the deputies. "Yeah. What's wrong with you? He could of smashed his face in."

The deputies exchanged a chuckle. "Oh, gee, we didn't know that."

Lance fought for control. "What the hell's wrong with you guys? You're supposed to protect people."

Taller deputy glared at him. "Yeah, people. Not garbage like this one who take shots at our colleagues." With that he gave Angel a slight, but hard, kick to the stomach, eliciting another groan and causing him to pull in his legs protectively.

"Hey!" Lance shouted and stepped around Angel to get between him and the deputies. He figured there must be cameras recording this area and that's why the deputies stood between them and the building, hiding their actions.

The two men eyed Lance like he was a cockroach. Then the shorter one leaned in so close Lance could smell his breath. Lance was easily a couple of inches taller than the deputy, but the guy looked thick and muscular.

"You're real lucky, Celebrity Boy, that you got so many high level people looking out for you," he whispered, his breath nearly causing Lance to gag. "Otherwise, we'd mess up that pretty face of yours. You need to learn to shut up and mind your own."

Lance wasn't cowed, though he knew he was treading dangerous waters here. "My friends are my own," he stated defiantly, never breaking eye contact with the man.

The man smiled, and ever so slightly, slugged Lance hard to the stomach. Pain ripped through him, the air poured from his lungs and he crumpled into a heap beside Angel, struggling for breath, gagging and coughing and fighting to keep from passing out.

The taller deputy gave the rolling, gagging boy a discreet kick to the midsection, and Lance nearly lost consciousness for lack of air.

"The pretty face may be on camera later, but the body won't be," the short one said with a chuckle.

At that moment, Probation Officer Wilson hurried over, and Lance saw genuine concern on his face. Wilson confronted the deputies. "We saw these kids fall. Is everything okay here?"

The taller deputy casually answered, "Yeah. They tripped over their shackles."

The shorter one hauled the boys to their feet, and Lance met Wilson's worried look, but said nothing.

"They're okay, aren't you, boys?" the short deputy said as he pretended to check them for injuries.

Lance didn't even look at him. Neither did Angel. They knew what would happen if they snitched.

"We're good, Mr. Wilson," Lance said, his voice a little breathy as he fought to get more air into his lungs. "Just clumsy."

Wilson looked dubious, but nodded, and then watched as the boys were assisted up the steps into the bus.

There were individual cages toward the front, and each deputy pushed his boy into a separate one. Lance struggled to breathe, the pain in his gut and side excruciating. Still, he refused to even let on that he was hurting. He caught a glimpse of Angel's grateful expression before Short Deputy slammed him down onto a wooden bench and wrapped a restraining bar around him, locking his manacled hands to its front, and securing the band so tightly Lance could barely catch his breath.

He glared at the man, and the deputy grinned wordlessly before slamming the cage door and locking it. He was facing forward and couldn't see Angel, similarly battened down behind him, but he heard a quiet, "Thanks, Lance," from behind and smiled to himself, despite the pain he was enduring.

As the bus pulled away, Lance saw Wilson returning through the gate into the facility.

The ride downtown was slow and torturous, with every bump in the road digging the restraining bar and manacles deeper into his already enflamed flesh. The dull ache in his stomach and ribs throbbed, but became manageable after a while, and Lance considered what he now realized – these deputies, and others like them, might beat up kids all the time, and there was nothing the kids could do about it.

Lance suddenly began to see his proposition to make fourteen- year-olds adults in a new light. Sure, they could vote and sit on juries and hear cases involving their peers. But wouldn't its passage also mean even more kids at the mercy of sadistic sheriff's guys like these? It would be another – what had Michael called it – unintended consequence.

The bus stopped at Men's Central Jail, a forbidding-looking structure in downtown Los Angeles, to pick up adult inmates for travel to CCB, the abbreviation, Lance had been told, for Criminal Courts Building. Every one of these men grew wide-eyed upon seeing Lance shackled in the cage up front, and it was obvious that they all knew who he was, even if they hadn't yet heard of his arrest. By now, the pain in his entire body had turned to numbness, and he felt as though everything from his midsection down had gone to sleep.

The ride from MCJ to CCB was, mercifully, the shortest leg of the journey. The adult inmates were escorted off the bus first and led away by the taller deputy. A new deputy, one Lance had not seen before, boarded the bus and eyed him curiously, as though wondering if he could actually be guilty of the crime with which he was charged. Then he unlocked the cage, and proceeded to release Lance from the restraining harness. Blood immediately began flowing to his lower extremities, but it still took a shaky moment for him to gain enough balance to exit the bus. The same deputy then released Angel.

CCB was a huge, twenty-one story concrete and glass building on Temple Street, not far from City Hall where, only a few months before, Lance had been holding court with the mayor and chief of police.

He shook his head at the irony of it all.

The boys were taken to a holding tank with other prisoners awaiting their moment in court. There were benches within the holding tank with restraining bars similar to the ones on the bus. Lance and Angel were told to sit side by side on one such bench, and then clamped onto it by the curved metal restraint. Once again, their hands were manacled to the device so their arms rested uncomfortably at almost a ninety-degree angle to the floor. The shackles on their feet remained untouched.

Lance glanced over at Angel, who eyed him with amazement. "You got balls, Lance, standing up for me back there. Thanks, man."

Lance nodded, the numbness rapidly returning to his arms and hands.

"How long we gotta wait here?" Lance asked, almost afraid to hear the answer.

Angel shrugged. "Depends on when they call each case. Could be all day."

"What if we gotta piss?" he asked.

Angel laughed hollowly. "In your pants, or hold it."

Lance knew he shouldn't have been shocked, but he was. And to think Angel and those other kids at Sylmar went through this humiliation every time they had court!

The boys fell silent then, as adult prisoners were brought in and similarly shackled to the benches around them. Every gaze fell upon Lance, and he squirmed with even more discomfort than he had from the restraints. One man, big with tattoos all over his face and wearing the standard orange jumpsuit, leaned slightly forward to scrutinize Lance.

"You really him?"

Lance shrugged. "Depends on who *him* is?"

The man looked at Lance like he was crazy. "Him! The Boy Who Come Back."

Lance looked at him self-consciously. "Yeah, I'm him."

"Hell, no...," the man mumbled, drawing out the words in shock.

"I'm innocent," Lance felt compelled to say, somehow feeling as though he was letting this man down just by being there.

The man just gave him that 'You crazy?' look. "Course you is," he said, as much for his benefit as Lance's. "If youse a criminal, Sir Lance, then we's all doomed, cuz there be no hope fer no one."

Lance almost blushed, he was so stunned by the man's affirmation, and all the heads nodding around him.

"Thanks, man," he said quietly, looking down in embarrassment. He still couldn't get over the effect he seemed to have on people. Probably never would.

"Um," the man continued, suddenly shy and hesitant, almost comical for a man so large and intimidating. "My case ain't lookin' so good, Sir Lance. Might you find it in yer heart to pray over me?"

Lance sucked in a sharp breath, but he saw the expectant eyes of the man gazing at him in wonder. Everyone else watched the exchange with anticipation.

Angel shrugged. "I could use a prayer, too, Lance. Who better from than the boy who saw God and come back to tell us about him, huh?"

Lance felt stunned, and inadequate to the pedestal upon which everyone seemed to put him. But he looked around at those faces, all so filled with the hope he represented in their minds, and couldn't say no.

He nodded to Angel and then looked back at the man. "What's your name, sir?"

The big man gave a little smile. "Ain't no one called me sir my whole life, Sir Lance. It's Daquan."

Lance smiled back and then lifted his eyes toward heaven. "Father God, you called me once to be with you, but then you sent me back. I know you had your reasons, and maybe I'll understand 'em someday. I know I'm in trouble down here, but so are my brothers in this room. Angel and Daquan and all the rest, Lord, well, they really need your help. So if you, you know, don't have enough magic to go around, help them first, before you help me. Maybe you can talk to their judges or lawyers, or something, but please help them, Lord. They're your children same as me. Amen."

He lowered his head and gazed across at Daquan, who smiled his thanks. "That was a right proper prayer, Sir Lance, and I thank you fer it."

Lance smiled and looked at Angel, who smiled back, and then the room fell silent.

Reyna drove everyone in her parent's Escalade, including Ryan, who, as always, provided armed security for Arthur and the others. Knights converged on the courthouse from around the city to lend their presence and support to Lance. By the time Reyna got the car parked and they made it up to the twentieth floor, the courtroom was quickly filling up with Arthur's young knights. Arthur, Jenny, Ricky, Chris, Reyna, Esteban, and Ryan sat in the second row behind the defendant's table. Ryerson was already there and he acknowledged Arthur with a curt nod.

Ryan leaned over to Arthur and pointed out the man standing at the state table. "That's the head D.A., Arthur. He never prosecutes a case unless it's high profile, or an election year."

Arthur nodded. He well understood the mentality of men like that. He eyed the man, sizing him up. Tall, distinguished, with gray at the temples and stylish short hair, the district attorney was decked out in an expensive-looking navy blue suit with a light red tie. His name, Arthur had been told, was Dooley.

The media had been barred from the room so all cameras and reporters were stationed in the hall outside the court. They had inundated Arthur with questions as the group made their way through the gauntlet into the courtroom, but Ryerson told Arthur to say nothing without him present.

Arthur permitted Helen to enter with him, but not her cameraman. She was allowed to observe and take notes, but not record, the bailiff told her upon entering, and she sat apart from Arthur's group.

Ricky and Chris sat between Arthur and Jenny, both boys silent and apprehensive, gazing in fear at the judge's bench, the Great California Seal behind it, the words 'Superior Court' emblazoned on the wall. Both well understood they weren't in Children's Court anymore.

The D.A. and his assistant, a young, attractive woman, appeared confident. Ryerson shuffled some papers and looked bored, as though he had something else more important to do. Ricky didn't like the man's attitude, but Sam had assured him Ryerson was the best, and that's all that mattered.

The judge entered from his chambers behind the bench, and the bailiff announced, "All rise."

Everyone stood until the judge, whose name was Jackson, adjusted his black robes and took his seat behind the bench. Once he did, the bailiff made a downward motion with his hand and everyone sat.

The judge looked around at both tables, and at his full courtroom. "Are both sides ready?" he asked.

"State is ready," the D.A. said confidently.

"Defense is ready, your honor," Ryerson said.

The judge nodded. "Bring in the defendant."

The bailiff exited the courtroom through a door behind the court clerk's desk.

Ricky tensed up, taking Chris's hand and squeezing it. The little boy looked up at his brother and Ricky offered his most confident nod. Arthur and Jenny exchanged a glance over the heads of their boys. The door re-opened and the bailiff stepped through, leading a shackled, chained, hunched over, manacled and jump-suited Lance, who shuffled his way slowly toward Ryerson's table.

Arthur's breath caught in his throat, and Jenny gasped loudly. Reyna threw a hand to her mouth in shock, and buried her face in Esteban's shoulder.

Ricky's mouth fell open in stunned horror, and he gripped Chris's hand hard. "Oh, Dad…" he whispered, almost without any air in his lungs. He sat frozen.

Lance had his head tilted slightly up, shyly peered through his loosely dangling hair at his family, and met Ricky's stunned gaze. He tried for that little smile, but Ricky was too shocked to even attempt an acknowledgment.

Lance was seated at the table, his back to Ricky and the spectators, and Ricky finally breathed again.

"Dad," he began, but Arthur just looked at him in despair and Ricky hugged him, pulling Chris in on the other side. How could they do this? They were treating Lance like some kind of wild animal!

His thoughts were interrupted by the court clerk announcing, "State of California versus Lance Pendragon."

The judge looked over his bench. "This is your arraignment, Lance, do you understand that?"

Lance nodded.

"You need to answer out loud, Lance, for the court reporter," the judge said, without any trace of irritation.

"Yes, Your Honor," Lance said, his voice quiet and more scared than he wanted it to sound.

Ricky's heart leapt into his throat upon hearing Lance's voice.

It seemed like forever since he had.

The judge turned to the district attorney. "The state will present its charges."

The D.A. stood and picked up a piece of paper. "The State charges the defendant, Lance Pendragon, with one count of attempted murder, one count of assault with a deadly weapon, one count of aggravated mayhem, and one count of assault to commit great bodily injury."

Lance listened to the charges leveled against him and knew if he were found guilty, he'd likely spend the rest of his life in prison. Joey had explained about a new law called SB 260 that would guarantee minors convicted of adult crimes a chance at parole after twenty-five years, but twenty-five years without Ricky was intolerable.

But I'm not guilty, he wanted to scream. Instead, he stole a quick glance behind him at Arthur, his arms still around Ricky and Chris.

The judge turned to Ryerson and Lance. "Lance Pendragon, you have heard the charges leveled against you. How do you plead?"

Ryerson glared over his glasses at Lance, who whipped his head back around to face the judge. He gulped. "Not guilty, Your Honor."

Ryerson stood. "As to the matter of bail, Your Honor, my client has no criminal record and his contributions to our city have been well documented these past two years. He does not pose a threat to the community." Ryerson sat.

The judge looked over at Dooley. "Mr. Dooley?"

The D.A. stood smartly, holding a manila envelope in one hand. "The state recommends no bail, your honor."

"On what grounds?" the judge asked. "I know it's unusual to give a minor bail, but this is no ordinary minor."

"I agree, Your Honor," the D.A. went on, his voice calm and very self-assured. "He is a monster that needs to be caged for the rest of his life."

Reyna's voice could be heard saying, "What the hell?" and then someone shushed her. The spectators rumbled with anger at the D.A.'s words.

The judge pounded his gavel. "Order in the court." Everyone settled down and he squinted at the D.A. "Mr. Dooley, your rhetoric is overly harsh."

"If it pleases the court, Your Honor, I'd like to enter these crime scene photos into evidence as proof that this minor, whatever he may have done in the past, is now far too dangerous to allow on the streets. We also believe him to be a flight risk if released."

"Present your evidence, Mr. Dooley."

The D.A. strode to the bench and handed the judge the manila folder.

The judge opened it, recoiling slightly at whatever he was seeing. He took a moment to leaf through all the photos, before handing it to the clerk. "Mark that People's A."

"Yes, Your Honor," the clerk said.

"May the defense see this evidence, Your Honor?" Ryerson asked with an annoyed look over at the D.A. The judge waved the clerk over to the defense table and the man handed Ryerson the folder.

The attorney opened it and Lance leaned over to look. His gorge rose and he choked back a stifled gasp of horror. He heard a shocked intake of breath behind him and flicked his wide eyes over his shoulder. Ricky had a hand to his mouth, his own eyes saucer- wide and filled with revulsion as he leaned forward and craned his head to see the images.

Lance turned back as his attorney scanned the photos. Each one showed different views of mutilated flesh with blood pooling everywhere. Ryerson emotionlessly flipped through the pictures, but each successive image caused more blood to drain from Lance's face and he felt faint, as well as nauseous. They actually thought he could do something this horrific, even to Richard?

Silently, without emotion, Ryerson handed the photos back to the clerk and he took them to the evidence table for filing.

"May I address the court, Your Honor?" Ryerson asked the judge.

"Of course, Mr. Ryerson."

Ryerson stood. "Those are certainly graphic images and difficult to stomach. However, my client is innocent until proven guilty and there is no evidence in those pictures that establishes guilt or culpability."

Dooley stood. "If it please the court."

"Yes, Mr. Dooley?" the judge said soberly.

"The State has in its possession a cell phone video of the defendant brandishing a knife at Mr. Thornton and threatening to, and I quote, 'cut your balls off'," Dooley announced in a disgusted tone.

The judge looked over at Lance, who lowered his eyes in shame. The judge sighed. "In light of the gravity of the offense and the evidence presented, bail is denied at this time."

Ryerson clucked his tongue in annoyance and resumed his seat. Lance didn't even react to the news about bail. His mind was still fixed on those horrifying images and the fact that anyone could think him responsible.

"We need to set a date for preliminary," the judge went on. "Does the state have any time constraints?"

Dooley stood once more. "Your Honor, the state wishes to proceed as soon as possible."

The judge appeared surprised, but glanced over at the clerk. "Very well, Mr. Dooley. Clerk, prelim one month from today? Check the calendar."

The clerk checked his calendar and looked up at the judge. "That date will work, Your Honor."

The judge looked down at Ryerson. "Does the defense have any objections?"

Ryerson was looking at his phone. "No, Your Honor. One month from today looks clear."

The judge gazed out at the lawyers and the assembled. He then turned his eyes on Lance, but Lance could not discern the feeling behind the man's look. "Court will reconvene on September second at ten a.m." Then he pounded his gavel once.

Lance finally snapped out of his shock and grabbed Ryerson's arm as the man stood to leave. "A month? I gotta stay in that place a month?"

Ryerson shrugged. "As I suspected, Lance, the D.A. is ramming this case through to make an example out of you before the election. He intends to crucify you, and he wants to do it quickly."

"But I'm innocent," Lance protested. "I could never do... *that*!" He shivered at the thought.

"The district attorney doesn't care if you're guilty or not, Lance. I thought I explained this to you. It's about winning, and this trial will be political theater at its most histrionic."

Lance was stunned. "What did flight risk mean?"

Ryerson looked at him as though he was an idiot. "Flight, Lance? As in fleeing to another country?"

"What country?"

Again, that look. "Mexico? Ever hear of the place?"

Lance became more muddled. "I was born here. I don't even know nobody in Mexico."

Ryerson sighed, angering Lance even more. "It's 'I don't know *anybody* in Mexico', Lance, and it doesn't matter. You have brown skin. To the system, that means you'll flee to Mexico. Now, any other useless questions?"

Lance gaped at him in astonishment, and shook his head.

"Good," Ryerson asserted with a tone of dismissal. "I need to get to work on your defense. I'll be in touch."

He snapped shut his briefcase and turned to exit the courtroom, signaling to Arthur that they would talk outside. Lance turned his head and met Ricky's wide-eyed look of fear and misery. He opened his mouth to say something, but a hand to his shoulder stopped him. He turned and saw the bailiff standing before him.

"Time to go."

"Can't I talk to my family a minute?" Lance asked, trying not to plead, but feeling desperate all the same.

The bailiff shook his head. "Sorry."

Lance cast one quick look back at his family and tried to freeze their faces in his mind and heart. He was uncertain when, or if, he'd see them again. The bailiff took his arm and guided him from the courtroom.

Ricky remained seated, Chris's face buried in his shoulder, his eyes fixed upon the door through which Lance had disappeared. A month. A whole month, and who knew how much more? And that D.A.! Lance, a monster? His heart thumped so wildly in his chest that Ricky feared it would burst. He couldn't lose Lance. He couldn't. Not now, not ever!

Arthur's gentle hand on his shoulder told Ricky it was time to go, and silently he followed the other lost and dispirited knights as they filed from the courtroom.

Out in the corridor, reporters and cameras swarmed the group, especially Arthur and Ryerson, and threw questions at them right and left.

Ryerson held up a hand for quiet, and the questions ceased. "Prelim will be one month from today, September second at ten a.m., in this courtroom. That is all."

"Mr. Ryerson," a reporter called out, "how did Lance plead?"

Ryerson looked at the man as though the guy was from Mars. "Not guilty, of course."

Another reporter shoved his head forward and Ricky saw the yellow hair of the guy who always heckled Lance. "Do you think he's guilty?"

Ryerson glowered at the man, but Ricky's anger over Lance's denial of bail boiled to the surface. He pushed his way to the front.

"You people think that Lance, after all the things he's done for this city, hell, for all the kids in this state, could do that to someone? What the hell is wrong with you people, huh?"

Arthur stepped forward and threw an arm around Ricky. "That's enough, Ricky," he whispered, and then addressed the crowd. "I apologize for my son. He is, as are we all, upset that Lance will not return home with us. I thank those of you who have come to know and care about Lance over these past two years, and who know in your hearts that he is incapable of such a monstrous act. Thank you for your time." He leaned down to the fuming Ricky and whispered, "It's time to go, son."

Gritting his teeth as he caught Yellow Hair smirking, Ricky allowed Arthur to lead him to the elevators. Ryerson and the others followed.

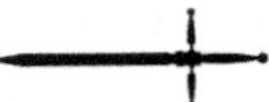

Lance sat shackled to his bench in the holding tank until after lunch. One hand was partially freed so he could stuff the tiny peanut butter sandwich between his lips and wash it down with milk. Even with that he had to bend over to actually get the food into his mouth and his dangling hair kept interfering. Angel came back from court before lunch, and the boys laughed at the idiocy of how they had to eat.

Angel told Lance his prelim was put off again for two more months, and Lance suddenly didn't feel so bad for himself, having to wait only one. Angel had been waiting almost two years just for his prelim, and quietly told Lance that what the deputies did to him that morning at the bus happened every time he was transported.

Lance digested that news soberly, his mind going back to the sickening images he'd seen of Richard's mutilation. What kind of monster did something like that? Sure, Richard was a monster too, and, Lance supposed, on some level even deserved what he got, but who could bring themselves to actually do something like that? He also considered Father Mike's admonition that forgiveness was the path to healing. Lance knew he needed to be healed, but could he ever bring himself to forgive that man for defiling him?

CHAPTER FIVE

THE DRIVE BACK TO NEW Camelot was somber, no one saying anything, each in his or her own world of pain over losing Lance's bid for bail. Arthur didn't say a word to Ricky about his outburst, and Ricky was grateful. He hadn't intended to blow up, but this whole thing was so crazy, and that one reporter was such a prick anyway.

When they got home, Ricky went to Lance's room and sat on the bed, looking at everything with an even deeper sadness than he'd felt the past couple of days. Lance was gone, and who knew when he'd be back? Ricky felt the urge to cry, to just grab Lance's pillow and sob into it like a little kid, but he didn't want to. He was a boy, and he could deal, right? That's what boys did. Only girls cried – that's what his father had always told him since he was tiny, and smacked him upside the head if he ever saw tears in Ricky's eyes.

A sudden fatigue overwhelmed him, so he lay down on Lance's side of the bed, grabbed the pillow, and curled himself into an almost fetal position. In his mind's eye, he saw Lance chained and manacled and hunched over like a wild animal, that sweet, gentle smile on his lips, those amazing green eyes reaching out to him across the space of the courtroom.

Despite his previous promises to himself, the tears came anyway, burning from the backs of his eyes to the front, spilling in waves and soaking Lance's pillow like rain. Mercifully, he cried himself to sleep and slept away the day without dreams or nightmares to haunt him.

That evening, there was a phone call from juvenile hall on the hotel landline. It was a collect call from Lance, but a recording informed Arthur that he needed to put money on an account in order to accept it. Frantically, he put Jenny on the line to interpret the message and she said, "I need your debit card."

Arthur fished out his wallet and handed her the card. She followed the instructions, which seemed to take forever, and put fifty dollars on the account, eight of which was subtracted immediately as a 'service fee'. She scowled and punched in the correct buttons, but by the time the process was complete, Lance had apparently hung up.

Dejectedly, Jenny replaced the phone in its cradle and turned to Arthur.

"It took too long, Arthur. Either Lance hung up or they cut him off. I'm sorry."

She put a hand on his arm, pain stabbing her heart at the look of abject loss on his face. How she loved him, and so wished she could make this time better for him. But she knew that wasn't possible.

"He'll call again, and next time we'll be ready."

She offered a faint smile, and he returned it, pulling her into a loving hug and just holding her a moment. Then he released her and ambled dejectedly from the lobby toward the Throne Room, and she knew he needed to be alone.

Inside Unit W-2, Lance sagged as he hung up the phone. It was attached to a wall inside the dayroom, one of two available for the minors' use. He couldn't understand what happened. He'd heard nothing for a long time, and then the recording ended the call because no one on the other end said "yes" to accept it. It was seven-fifteen and dayroom was in progress, which was the usual time for phone calls.

There was a list, and Lance's name had finally come up. For nothing. Dejectedly, he sat down where Joey and Angel were engaged in a chess match.

"What's goin' on at New Cam, Sir Prince?" Joey asked with a grin.

Lance shrugged. "Don't know. They didn't take the call."

"That's the worthless phone company this place uses," Angel said as he made a move that took Joey's knight. "Yer family's gotta set up an account to take calls, and it's a big ole rip-off."

Lance's face fell. "Oh."

"Your dad coming to visit tomorrow?" Joey asked.

Lance shrugged. "Don' know. That's what I wanted to find out."

Joey punched him on the arm and tried for a cheerful demeanor. "Tomorrow's comin' pretty fast. For now, watch me whip this fool's ass."

He made a move, which Angel instantly countered.

"Checkmate," Angel announced, and Joey's smirk dropped.

Despite his disappointment at not talking to his dad, Lance smiled at the look of stunned surprise on Joey's face.

"Damn, I didn't even see that," Joey offered by way of explanation.

"So, whose ass were yew gonna whip again?" Angel said playfully, and all three of them laughed.

Saturdays in the hall were lazy days. Breakfast was still at seven o'clock, but with there being no school, the kids went back to their rooms to sleep or read until morning dayroom. Family visiting didn't begin until one in the afternoon, and ran till three on Saturday and four on Sunday.

Lance ate his breakfast, his stomach twisting and turning with anticipation. He knew only adults could visit him and he desperately wanted to see Arthur, to hug him, to just be with him. Since Arthur had recruited him to be First Knight, Lance had never spent so much time away from him without being able to at least talk on the phone, as they had so often when his dad was campaigning in Northern California. He said a silent prayer before eating that Arthur would show up.

By now, most of the other guys had gotten used to Lance and ceased their looks of wonderment every time he left his room. He decided they'd finally must have realized that he was human after all. Lance still rushed his showers, and dreaded doing sit-downs, but he was acclimating to this new kind of life, mainly because he'd made some friends and they helped him adjust. Some of them had been here so long, they didn't feel any embarrassment talking with volunteers or anger management instructors, wearing nothing but a towel, while on their way to or from the shower. Lance still felt naked and exposed even wearing the towel, and always hurried to his room to put on his underwear, at least.

During morning dayroom, he aimlessly played some card games with Angel, Joey and Hector, another boy from Father Mike's meditation group, but always had to be reminded of the rules because his brain was focused on visiting. Lunch was bread and some kind of beef stew with rice. The portions were small, but Lance's stomach was learning to do more with less.

After lunch, all the minors were returned to their rooms. Only those whose parents showed would be out in the dayroom until dinner. Lance sat on his concrete bed, knees pulled up, arms wrapped around them, looking out the slatted window as parents began to trickle into the facility, breaking off in different directions, depending upon where their kids were housed.

Ryan drove a very anxious Arthur out to Nelson Juvenile Hall for his visit with Lance. Ryan had been there numerous times, dropping off this kid or that one, and knew well how to get there. He'd told Arthur he would stay in line until the king entered the facility and then return at three to pick him up. Arthur dressed in casual, modern clothes – khaki pants and a long-sleeve tunic and a pair of skate shoes Lance had asked Jenny to order for him as a Christmas gift.

He smiled at the memory as he glanced down at the semi-high-top DC skateboard shoes on his feet. Lance had replaced the yellow laces with purple, the color of royalty.

Ryan turned down a small side street and the juvenile hall came into view. Arthur saw the high brick walls, razor wire rolled along the top, and his heart pulled tight in his chest.

Oh, my Lance ...

Ryan flashed his badge to the man in a little booth, then pulled into a wide parking lot. Arthur saw just ahead another large brick building with the words 'Superior Court – Juvenile Division' above a glass entryway, now closed for the weekend.

Ryan parked and they got out. Arthur had a leather strip tied around his head, rather than anything metallic, because Ryan had told him about the metal detector he must clear to enter the facility.

When they exited the car and walked toward the line of waiting parents, Arthur noted that there were already at least twenty people in front of him. Heads turned when the two men joined the line, and several parents gasped and pointed. Despite attempting to appear inconspicuous, Arthur was too well known to go anywhere unnoticed.

Ryan excused himself and went to the front of the line where a probation staff stood ready to usher each parent forward in turn. Arthur smiled at the people in line and they eyed him with uncertain glances, as though unsure whether or not to speak to him.

Arthur noted, with dismay, that most of the parents in line were mothers. Besides himself, there were only two other fathers waiting. Alas, he knew, such was the cause of hurt for most of his knights, and no doubt most of the children incarcerated within these walls, as well.

Ryan returned a moment later with the probation staff.

"King Arthur," the staff said with a nod, "you don't have to wait in line. We can get you in first so you won't have to deal with all these people, or the press if they show up."

"It's a good idea, Arthur," Ryan agreed. "Keeps you out of the spotlight."

Arthur glanced over at the people in line ahead of him, noted their anxious faces as they observed the scene, and recognized their fears for their own children. He turned back to the probation staff.

"I thank you, sir, for your kind offer, but these others ahead of me are as anxious to see their children as I am, and it would not be fair-minded of me to enter before them. I am content to wait my turn."

The staff looked at Ryan, who nodded, and the man returned to the front of the line. Ryan eyed Arthur silently, but said nothing.

Arthur turned to face forward and found every person gazing at him with astonishment. Someone began to clap, and others joined in until everyone in line was applauding him. That seemed to break the ice, and Arthur was suddenly greeted by one mother after another. Each wanted to shake his hand, to thank him for not cutting in front of them, for helping their kids all over the city. Many spoke Spanish, but Arthur was proficient enough to converse with them.

The mothers greeted him warmly, some asking if they could hug him. The men shook his hand. All of them expressed the hope that Lance would be out soon. Arthur discovered through these interactions just how much these parents loved their children and wanted the best for them. Sadly, as some of the ladies told him, their sons were going to go to prison, and there was nothing they could do to stop that.

One by one, the line grew shorter until it was Arthur's turn to be called forward. There was a table with several probation staff, each holding lists of names. Arthur presented his California I.D. and the female staff eyed him with a sense of wonder before glancing down at the paper and handing him back his I.D.

"Straight ahead, through the metal detector, King Arthur," she said, almost shyly.

Arthur smiled warmly. "Thank you."

Ryan watched as Arthur cleared the metal detector and entered the interior of the facility before he turned and strode back to his car.

Accustomed by now to people staring at him, Arthur smiled and greeted each staff member he encountered as he passed into the facility. His charm and easy manner were infectious, and he seemed to put them at ease. The Compound was pointed out to him, "Just ahead," by another female staff, and Arthur's heart tightened yet again.

It is a cage, he thought, *a cage to house wild animals. And my son is within.*

Sighing heavily, he strode up the walkway with the slip of paper that he'd been given in one trembling hand. A staff person standing by the open gate didn't even check the paper Arthur held. He merely shook the king's hand and pointed at unit W to his right.

Lance had stopped sitting by the window after seeing mother after mother enter the facility, but only two men, and neither was his dad. He sat curled up on his bed, leaning back against the wall, feeling an oppressive loneliness such as he hadn't felt since Jack's death.

A key in his lock startled him out of his reverie, and one of the day staff, Perkins, grinned. "Dad's here."

Lance's heart leapt and he jumped off the bed. Stepping out the door, he hurriedly slipped into his sneakers and turned to look around. Arthur sat at the far table, nearest the office, grinning with pure joy.

Lance's breath stopped and he moved slowly forward. He wanted to run and throw himself into his father's arms, but he knew everyone was watching. All conversation had ceased and every gaze followed his progress. Arthur stood as Lance neared and held out his arms, and suddenly Lance was within them, encircling him in that comforting way only Arthur could do. Lance hugged him harder, and with more emotion, than he had even that night so long ago when he'd confessed his inner torment to this man and the king had accepted him nonetheless.

Lance held on, not wanting to release his dad, not wanting the moment to end. But he knew it had to, and slowly pulled back to look into his father's eyes. Lance saw the beginning of tears, and his own eyes began to burn. He knew he shouldn't cry here, in front of the other guys, but he couldn't help himself.

"Oh, Dad..." he whispered, and hugged him again.

"I love you, son," Arthur whispered back, his voice clogged with emotion. They separated and sat across from one another at the metal table. Every other family drifted back into their own conversations, so Lance was able to stare longingly at Arthur.

"I miss you so much," he said, swiping at his eyes as discreetly as possible.

"Not as much as I miss you, Lance," Arthur said in return, dabbing his own eyes with a handkerchief.

"I tried calling last night," Lance said after they'd pulled themselves together.

"I know. Your mother attempted to set up some kind of account to take your call, but by the time she had done so, you were gone."

Lance lowered his gaze. "I was afraid you wouldn't take my calls."

Arthur reached out and lifted his chin gently with one hand so their eyes met. "Never would that happen, Lance."

Lance smiled. "How's everybody?"

"Lost, without you."

"I'm lost without them too." He hesitated, and looked up shyly at his dad. "How's Ricky?" Against his will he felt his face grow hot, and lowered his eyes again.

"He is adrift, Lance, missing half of his soul and fighting to maintain himself as best he can," Arthur answered. He smiled slightly. "He paces the house nightly, as do I. We pass one another like sentries, except there is nothing to guard because you are not there."

Emotion welled up within Lance, and for a moment he couldn't say anything. Ricky missed him that much? Just the thought filled him with warmth, but left him all the more desolate, knowing that it could be a long time, maybe years, before he'd be face-to-face with his other half.

"Tell him I..." Lance trailed off uncertainly.

Arthur smiled. "It is acceptable, Lance, to say you love him."

Lance looked down again. "I know. Will you tell him for me?"

Arthur nodded.

"And Chris too," Lance hastily added, so Arthur wouldn't think his thoughts were only on Ricky.

Arthur and Lance went on to discuss the previous day's arraignment, and Lance pulled a face at the mention of Ryerson. "He's rude, Dad."

"He is abrupt, but Sam assured me he is the best at what he does. We must have faith."

Lance hesitated, and then, in a near whisper, asked, "Dad, does anybody out there, you know, actually think I did... what they said I did?"

"No one who knows you, Lance," Arthur answered. "But Sir Techie has informed me that many on the Internet have turned against you, feeling that you had to be too good to be true, and that now the real you has come to the fore."

Lance blanched with dismay. "How could anyone think I'd do something like that, Dad? Did you see those pictures?"

"I caught a glimpse, yes. But it seems to be within our human nature to believe the worst of someone else, perhaps to, in some way, excuse our own failings. Do not let your heart be troubled, Lance. You are loved."

Lance nodded, but it did trouble him that anyone could think such a thing.

They spoke of the commercials that Ricky, Chris and Reyna would be recording in lieu of him, and he was happy the others would be involved. He'd always hated the whole crusade being so focused on him, especially after he came back.

All too soon, it was three o'clock and Arthur had to leave.

"You coming tomorrow?" Lance asked hopefully, as they stood to say their goodbyes.

Arthur smiled lovingly. "Nothing could keep me away."

Lance feared he would tear up again, so he threw his arms around his father in a tight hug. "I love you, Dad."

Arthur hugged him back. "I love you more."

They separated, and Lance had to watch the man he loved more than any adult he'd ever known walk out the door without him. Once again, he was just another prisoner, and that's all he'd be for at least another month. Sighing with deep emotion, Lance returned to his room, slipped off his shoes, and entered the tiny cubicle to await his meager dinner.

The moment Arthur and Ryan entered the lobby of New Camelot, Ricky, who'd been pacing nervously back and forth, almost accosted them.

"How's Lance, Dad? Is he okay?"

Arthur nodded, and Ricky breathed a sigh of relief. "He said to tell you he loves you."

Ricky's eyes burned with loss and hope and dread all at the same time. "He did?"

Arthur smiled, and Ricky felt himself immersed in a soothing warmth that almost relaxed him.

"When can I talk to him?" Ricky asked, his brown eyes alive with expectation.

"The next time he is allowed a phone call, I suppose."

"Did they have him in those... chains?" he asked, his voice barely a whisper.

"No, son, not when he is within the unit," Arthur explained. "Those... chains... are used for transport only."

"Dad, he's not an animal!" Ricky exclaimed, images of the shackled Lance weaving their way through his mind.

"I know, Ricky." Arthur sighed. "In some ways, this era is more barbaric than mine own." He patted him on one shoulder. "Where is your mother?"

"In her room, I think," Ricky answered with a shrug.

"Find Chris, if you would, Ricky, and bring him to me so I may assure him that Lance is well and unharmed."

"Okay, Dad," and he went off in search of his little brother.

Arthur exchanged a look with Ryan.

The sergeant looked more weather-beaten these past few days than he ever had. The older man sighed. "I got my own people investigating this, Arthur. That D.A.

may want to railroad Lance, but he's got nothing except that so-called video. If there's any evidence to clear Lance, my people will find it."

"Thank you, Sergeant." Then he ascended the stairs.

The following morning was Sunday, and Lance looked forward to seeing Father Mike and attending his service. Initially, Protestant volunteers entered the unit to do some sort of Bible study, and Lance was told by staff that the Catholic service followed at around nine-thirty.

After breakfast, with head and water calls complete, Lance remained in his room until he was let out for the service. When the staff unlocked his door, there was Father Mike smiling at him.

"Good morning, Lance," he said cheerfully. "You look well."

Lance couldn't help but smile back. "I'm good, thanks, Father."

The priest ushered Lance forward and used a key to open the mirrored door into the office. There was a hallway with closed, blue-green doors on either side extending out from the office and running between the two sides of the building. There were chairs and a small table already set up and several volunteers there to greet him. They seemed happy to meet him, and introduced themselves.

Father Mike explained that he wanted Lance up front because he was going to take part in the homily.

Lance didn't know what a "homily" was, but he already trusted Father Mike enough that he didn't ask.

On the table there was a crucifix, a candle, some white wafers in a bowl, and a large plastic bowl of water.

"What's the water for?" Lance asked Father Mike.

He turned from what he was doing and smiled. "We have a baptism today," and resumed fishing through a messy-looking carry bag filled with papers and other stuff.

Lance sat where the volunteer indicated and eyed the bowl of water. A baptism? He'd never seen one before, and he was pretty sure he'd never been baptized.

There were about twenty plastic chairs set up, and the kids began filing in from both sides of the building. The burly kid from school who'd called him a faggot ambled in, saw Lance, and paused. Lance hadn't seen the kid since Thursday because Friday was taken up with court. Burly stared a second, then gave a little chin nod and sat in a chair way in the back. Lance smiled to himself and turned back around.

The kid getting baptized was Eric, another of Father Mike's meditation group.

A new volunteer entered with two ladies, who were introduced as Eric's mother and aunt. The aunt would be his godmother for the baptism.

When Father Mike asked for volunteers to read something, Lance raised his hand and the priest asked him to read the gospel when it was time. The priest opened the service by explaining about Eric's baptism and how it represented the death of sin and rebirth to a new life with Christ. Lance was fascinated, especially since he'd already been reborn once.

When it was his turn, Lance stood and read the gospel in a clear, strong voice, as he had always been an excellent reader, thanks to his many hours hanging out in public libraries growing up. The story was about Jesus' followers not washing their hands before eating, and all the bigwigs in town criticized him for that. Jesus gave a simple explanation: nothing that comes from outside can defile a person, only the things that come from within. Lance had never thought about it, but knew in his heart that those words were true. Richard had always been impeccably clean and well groomed, and look what evil came from within him. He shuddered as he finished the reading and resumed his seat.

After the gospel, Father Mike stood and talked about rebirth, and he introduced Lance, bringing him forward, and draping one arm around his shoulders. All eyes were pinned to him and Lance once again felt the weight of who he was bearing down on him.

"This is Lance," began Father Mike, "the boy we all saw die and come back to life. He was reborn, just as Eric will be reborn when I pour the water over him." He asked Lance to briefly describe his experience with death, as many of the attendees were not part of the meditation group.

Lance repeated to a rapt audience what he'd told the Wednesday group. The two women blessed themselves several times during his story, and when he fell silent, Father Mike smiled at the group.

"Hope. There is always hope, and this boy represents it. He is a warrior of light, just as Eric has become. So now, I ask the reborn Lance to assist with the baptism."

Lance was startled, but nodded when Father Mike moved him to stand behind the table with the water. Then he called Eric and his family forward and they stood beside Lance. The priest blessed the water and had Eric repeat a credo of some kind, rejecting sin and accepting God. Lance had never heard it before, but it reminded him of the oath he'd sworn to the Round Table when he'd been knighted.

Father Mike told Eric to bend down and place his head over the bowl. He then took a small seashell and filled it with water. He asked Lance to place a hand on Eric's right shoulder, while Eric's mom and aunt were told to place theirs on his left.

"Eric, I baptize you in the name of the Father," intoned Father Mike, as he poured a little of the water over Eric's head, "and the Son," the priest said, along with more water, "and the Holy Spirit." He poured the remainder of the water onto Eric's head, while Lance watched, mesmerized.

The lady volunteer handed Eric a towel and he wiped some of the water from his hair. Eric stood straight, water dribbling down his face and chin, and Lance saw that his eyes seemed to have a kind of glow that hadn't previously been there. He looked happy.

Father Mike hugged him, and then Eric hugged Lance, before turning to his mother and aunt and hugging them.

Father Mike said to the other kids, "*Fuerte aplauso, por favor*" and everyone burst into applause.

Lance returned to his seat, feeling oddly special in a way he never had before, as though what he'd done had opened a door in his heart that had been previously closed.

After the baptism, there was something called the Eucharist, which Lance understood was like the Last Supper of Jesus before he died. That's when the wafers were given out, and Eric received one of these for the first time. Lance crossed his arms over his heart for a blessing, as instructed, and didn't take the wafer because he wasn't sure he was allowed to.

After the Eucharist, Eric received something called Confirmation. Father Mike explained that it was asking the Holy Spirit to come down into Eric and to help him be a strong Warrior of Light.

Lance really enjoyed the service, and loved how Father Mike made everything so real to the lives of the kids, so relevant. But he also had a bad feeling in the pit of his stomach, and after the service, when Father Mike had finished taking pictures with Eric and his family, Lance approached the priest shyly.

Father Mike placed a hand on Lance's shoulder and tossed him an impish grin, his eyes almost twinkling. "Thank you, Lance, for your help."

"Oh, yeah, you're welcome."

He hesitated and the priest eyed him expectantly. "Something wrong?"

"Father Mike, I've never been baptized and, well, what would've happened to me if I'd like, you know, stayed dead?"

The priest smiled wisely. "God would have taken care of you, Lance. Trust me."

Lance nodded, but it still troubled him. "Father Mike, can I get baptized while I'm here?"

"Of course, but you need to get your father's permission."

Lance pulled a confused face. "Why? I thought I was an adult in here."

Father Mike placed a gentle hand on his shoulder and offered a wry smile. "Only for the purposes of committing a crime, Lance. Otherwise, you have no rights."

Lance shook his head in amazement. "My dad'll be okay with it. I'll ask him today."

The priest smiled. "I'll be visiting the units this afternoon. I'd very much like to meet your father, and we can discuss it then."

Lance beamed. "Thanks, Father Mike."

The staff then told him it was time to return to the dayroom.

After lunch, Lance returned to his room to await Arthur's arrival. This time his dad must've gotten to the hall earlier because as Lance sat at his window looking out at the incoming parents, Arthur was the fourth one to enter. Excited, he watched his dad walk up the concrete path, and banged on the window to get his attention. Arthur looked up and squinted, but Lance realized the window slats from the outside must be too small for someone to see in, especially through the fence.

He jumped off the concrete bed and ran to his door, bouncing on the balls of his feet and awaiting that glorious sound of a key turning in the lock. It took a few minutes, but then a staff appeared at his little window and the key turned. The door opened and Lance practically leapt into his shoes. If anything, he felt even more excited than he had yesterday. They'd been given the same table by the office and Lance hurried to embrace Arthur, holding on as though afraid to let go. When they separated and took their seats, Arthur gazed at the smiling Lance curiously.

Lance knew he must look foolish with his grin and bright eyes, but he was happy, both from the service this morning, and now seeing his Dad.

"You look better today, son," Arthur said. "Refreshed, somehow."

"I went to church today, Dad, and I helped baptize a kid named Eric."

Arthur's eyebrows shot up in surprise. "Indeed?"

Lance nodded excitedly. "It was so cool. And Dad, I wanna get baptized, too. There's this awesome priest, Father Mike, and he said I could be baptized if I got your permission and I really don' wanna die again without being baptized. Can I, Dad?" He finally ran out of breath and gazed hopefully at Arthur.

Arthur rubbed absently at his beard. "I had never given baptism much thought for you, Lance," he said with obvious self-recrimination. "Or for any of my children. But I should have." He paused, shaking his head at his own neglect. "If you wish to be baptized, son, of course you have my blessing."

Lance broke into a huge grin. "Thanks, Dad, I really do want to. Father Mike said if I'd stayed dead before, God would've taken care of me anyway, but I really wanna be baptized because then I'll be both a warrior of right *and* a warrior of light."

Arthur leaned forward on the table, clearly amazed to see Lance so excited about something positive, given all the problems he currently faced. "Might I meet this Father Mike?"

At that moment, the office door opened and out stepped Father Mike himself, wearing his basic black with the white collar.

"He's right there," Lance said excitedly, pointing.

Arthur turned and stood as Father Mike approached and extended a hand. They shook, and Father Mike sat at the table with him.

"You have an extraordinary son here, King Arthur," the priest said, tossing a smile Lance's way.

Lance fought back an embarrassed blush.

"I agree, Father Mike," Arthur said. "I thank you for being there for him in my absence."

"We do what we can. I must say, it's an honor to meet you, Arthur. You and I are working for the same cause, justice for these kids. Both I, and all the kids here, greatly appreciate everything you, Lance, and the others have done to help them."

"I am honored to have your support. Lance tells me he wishes to be baptized."

"That's what he told me."

Arthur glanced at the eagerly watching Lance, and winked. "He has my blessing, of course."

"See, Father Mike," Lance gushed. "I told you he'd say yes."

The old priest flashed the impish grin and turned to Arthur. "We'll begin instructing him this week."

Lance frowned. "How long will that take? I might be gone after my prelim on the second."

"Perhaps, but with the courts, slowness is a given. You may be here longer, Lance."

Lance felt a punch to the gut, and Arthur reached across the table to take his hand.

"We'll try to schedule you at around the time of your prelim, Lance," Father Mike told the anxious boy. "Don't worry over it." His easy smile loosened Lance's fears.

"Might I be able to attend his baptism?" Arthur asked hopefully.

"Of course," Father Mike replied, and turned to Lance. "You'll need a godparent, too, Lance."

"Godparent?"

"Someone other than Mom or Dad who will be in your life to help you as needed. Let me know who you choose so we can get them approved to come in."

Lance agreed, and Father Mike rose to his feet, extending his hand once more. Arthur shook it. "It's been a pleasure, Arthur. Enjoy your visit with your son." The priest smiled at Lance and moved off to another table.

"I'm pleased such a fine man is here to watch over you, Lance."

But Lance was thinking, his face scrunched up, his mind turning.

"Something wrong, son?"

"No, just thinking." He paused. "Dad, I wanna ask Sergeant Ryan to be my godfather. Is that okay?"

Arthur broke into a surprised grin. "It's very much okay."

Lance smiled to himself, thinking about his pending baptism, but also thinking how much he wished Ricky could be there and get baptized with him.

"Dad, you think Ricky's ever been baptized?"

That caught Arthur by surprise. "I don't know, Lance. I can ask him, if you'd like."

Lance bit his lower lip anxiously. "Did you, uh, give him my message?"

"That you loved him?"

Lance nodded.

"Yes, Lance, I did."

"What did he say?" Lance was actually nervous about the answer.

"He was quite speechless, and looked rather relieved, I'd say," Arthur replied honestly. "He cannot function without you."

Lance swallowed a lump in his throat, his breath almost stopping. He didn't trust himself to answer, so he changed the subject.

Soon the three hours were over, and Arthur had to leave.

"Will you come next week?" Lance asked, hope bright in his eyes and strong in his voice.

"I shall come every week, Lance," Arthur replied and they hugged goodbye.

This time, as Lance watched his father exit the building, his heart tugged almost into his throat because he knew it would be a whole week before they would see each other again. A lot could happen in a week.

CHAPTER SIX

IS RICKY ALL RIGHT?

THE FOLLOWING WEEK SETTLED INTO a daily routine for Lance. Life in juvy was the same, day after day, and he gradually adapted to the daily indignities of being naked in front of strangers, and having to use the bathroom in front of them, too. School was okay, except for Mr. Ancient, the long-term sub, but there wasn't anything Lance could do about him. The burly Latino kid from W-1 no longer said anything to him. In fact, after hearing Lance's story on Sunday, the kid seemed almost in awe of him, and Lance didn't press the advantage by messing with the guy. He always preferred to get along with people than not – it made life easier.

He didn't talk to his lawyer, and his weekly phone call wouldn't be until Friday night. A Catholic volunteer met with him during the week to teach him about baptism, the symbolism behind the ritual, the water and the oils used. Lance found it all fascinating.

He'd taken to reading the Bible in his room, starting with the Book of Matthew, so he would be better prepared, both for his baptism and for Father Mike's meditation group, of which he was now a regular member. Lance slipped with ease into the daily rote lifestyle of the incarcerated.

At New Camelot, life continued, though still subdued and listless as the weight of Lance's troubles hung over everyone like a heavy fog.

Ricky was played with Chris and trained with Esteban to burn off his pent up frustration, but there was no life in his soul, no joy in his heart, and no one was able to help him. He counted the days until Friday when he would hear Lance's voice again, and the minutes seemed to drag on endlessly.

He worked with Chris and Reyna on their TV campaign spots, and showed Jenny the one he'd written that specifically referenced Lance's situation, which Jenny approved. She corrected some of his grammar, but otherwise proclaimed it strong and heartfelt.

Arthur had told them all about Lance's decision to be baptized, and they seemed happy about it. Most, including Ricky, had been baptized as young children or babies. Ricky, of course, wished he could be there when Lance got baptized, but Arthur sadly informed him that minors were not allowed.

Lance's arrest, and the charges against him, were international news, and the phone continued to ring twenty-four-seven with interview requests for Arthur, Reyna, Ricky or anyone who wished to make a statement. On the Internet, Sir Techie kept track of how many images of Lance in handcuffs were downloaded or tagged, and the comments ranged from strong support to a fair number bashing him and claiming sentiments like 'I always knew he was too perfect to be real'. Some were downright nasty, connecting the images of Lance kissing Michael to mutilating Richard, comments like 'Sir Lance likes his junk any way he can get it' and 'This is why fags should all be killed'.

It sickened Ricky to read those comments, but he still went daily to the Computer Lab to check percentages - those who supported Lance versus those who'd turned against him. It seemed to be hovering around seventy percent for, twenty-five percent against, with five percent undecided. It amazed Ricky how many people believed that if a person was arrested, they were automatically guilty of the crime.

Friday finally rolled around and Ricky felt hyped and restless the entire day. He trained with Esteban for two hours until the much bigger boy called it quits, laughingly telling Ricky, "You tryin' to kill me, or what?"

The sweaty, panting Ricky cracked a grin at that, but the ache in his heart remained. After showering—he'd taken to using Lance's shower and even Lance's shampoo—Ricky began pacing the lobby at six-thirty, gazing with longing at the silent phone. At six forty-five, Arthur, Jenny, Chris, Reyna, Esteban, Justin, Ryan, and Gibson all appeared from different parts of the hotel to stand guard over the phone.

It had been agreed that since Arthur would visit Lance the following day, he would accept the call, place Lance on speaker mode, and allow the others to talk. The calls were only fifteen minutes, and everyone wanted a chance to speak. Ricky saw the same eagerness on all their faces that he held in his heart.

Losing Lance had created a massive hole at New Camelot, a void that no one could fill, especially him, though now it seemed everyone deferred to his will, when they previously would've sought out Lance. But Ricky didn't want to be in charge. He wanted Lance back, more than he'd ever wanted anything in his life. Except he couldn't have him. And that hurt, even more than his parents' abandonment.

He continued his anxious pacing, and Chris took to pacing r behind him like a shadow. Finally, at seven-fifteen, the phone rang, and Arthur snatched it off its cradle.

He heard, "This is Global Tellink with a collect call from" and then Arthur heard his son's voice sounding like it was inside a fishbowl, "Lance," and then the recording took over, "an inmate at Barney J. Nelson Juvenile Hall in Sylmar, California. To accept charges for this call, press 5. To hear the–" Arthur pressed 5. "Thank you. Your call is being accepted. You may begin speaking after the tone." There was a beep.

"Lance?"

"Hi, Dad."

"Hello, son," he said, taking a deep breath. "I'll be with you tomorrow, Lance, and since the whole family is here to talk I'm going to put you on speaker." He pressed a button on the phone and set down the receiver in its cradle. "You're on speaker, Lance."

"Oh, uh, hi everybody," came Lance's voice over the phone, tinny and unnatural, but unmistakably that of Lance.

Ricky's heart pounded as they all gathered round and stared at the phone like it was a miracle.

"I miss you so much, Lance," Chris blurted out, and began to tear up.

Ricky pulled him in.

They heard a slight sniffle and Lance said, "Miss you too, little man."

"Hey, Lance," Jenny said, her hand to her mouth, forcing herself not to cry.

"Hey, Mom," Lance replied, and they could hear him expelling a deep breath. "I'm okay, Mom, don't worry about me."

"I can't help but worry about you," Jenny said breathlessly. "I love you, Lance."

There was a pause, as though Lance was trying to maintain control. "Love you, too, Mom."

Reyna and Esteban chimed in with a simultaneous "Hi, Lance."

Reyna added, "You better still be prettier than me when you get out or there'll be hell to pay."

Lance chuckled. "I'll always be prettier than you, Reyna, so get used to it."

Reyna smiled, though tears were beginning to blur her eyes.

"You hangin' in there, *carnal?*" Esteban said, his deep voice etched with concern. "Nobody tryin' to mess with you?"

"No worries, buff guy," Lance answered. "I kicked *your* ass, remember?"

"How can I forget? You won't let me."

Lance chuckled again through the speaker. "It's okay, Este, I'm good. Take care of the others for me, 'kay?"

"You got it, Lance."

Justin offered his encouragement, as did Gibson, who assured Lance that he had people investigating every possible lead, and so far there was no hard evidence linking him to the crime. "We'll get you out of there. Trust me."

"Thanks, Sergeant," Lance replied. "Is Sergeant Ryan there?"

Ryan stepped closer. "Right here, Lance."

There was a pause. "Did my dad tell you I was gonna be baptized in here?"

"Yes, he did. Congratulations."

"I have a favor to ask you, Sergeant," Lance went on, his voice suddenly sounding hesitant and uncertain.

"Name it," the sergeant replied.

"Will you be my godfather?" came Lance's voice, quiet, yet tinged with emotion.

Ryan gasped slightly. It was obvious Arthur hadn't told him that part. He clearly didn't know what to say. "I don't know, Lance, I mean, I haven't been to church in, well, a long time."

"Father Mike told me I needed someone who would be there for me, Sergeant, someone I trust to always look after me and, well, I'd really like you to be that person."

The tone in his voice, the boyishness mixed with the deeper tones of impending manhood, the heartfelt simplicity of the request, clearly touched Ryan. He smiled. "Of course, I accept, Lance. I'll be proud to be your godfather."

Lance expelled a sigh of relief. "Cool. Father Mike will call you about when to come and stuff."

The clock was ticking down, and thus far Ricky had stood apart and silent, listening to the exchanges, his heart tight in his throat, his body stiff with uncertainty.

Arthur eyed him, but Ricky's face remained downcast, as though the floor tiles held all the secrets of the universe.

Almost as if sensing something wrong, Lance's voice came over the speaker, hesitant and hopeful. "Is Ricky there?"

All eyes turned to the boy everyone knew was closer to Lance than anyone. Ricky looked up when he heard his name, but didn't say anything. He didn't trust his tongue to work properly.

"Dad?" came Lance's voice again, now tinged with fear. "Is Ricky all right?" The words sounded breathless, as though Lance was struggling to breathe.

"He's fine, Lance, and we're all going to leave now and allow him to speak with you in private. I love you, son, and I'll see you tomorrow."

"We all love you, Lance," Jenny said, her sentiment echoed by the others.

"I love you all, too," came Lance's choked reply. "I hope to be home soon."

"We hope so, too," Reyna said, and they all wandered out of the lobby, leaving Ricky alone to stare helplessly at the phone.

"Hello?"

Ricky heard that most precious of voices, and couldn't respond.

"Anybody there?"

"Hi," Ricky said, barely a whisper.

There was a sharp intake of breath from the speaker. "Ricky."

"You really all right in there?"

"Yeah, I'm good. Really."

Ricky fought to control his emotions. "Those chains, man..."

"Just part of the deal," Lance answered, obviously trying to sound nonchalant about it all. "I got it covered."

"Yeah," Ricky said, wanting to say so much, but not knowing where to begin.

Then the operator came on, "You have 120 seconds left on this call."

Crap, Ricky thought. *Two minutes to say everything?*

"You okay, Ricky?" he heard Lance ask breathlessly.

"No. Not without you."

"I know the feeling," Lance said in reply. Then he asked, "Have you heard from Michael?"

Ricky's face screwed up into instant anger. "Why would I hear from him, Lance?"

There was a slight pause. "I don' know. Thought he might be worried about me."

Ricky fought his anger. "I thought you were done with him."

"I am," Lance's voice said quickly. Too quickly. "I just wondered, that's all."

Ricky struggled to control himself. "This is all his fault anyway, Lance," he said with a hiss. "If you hadn't gone out to meet him, none of this would've happened, so don't talk to me about Michael, okay?"

"You have sixty seconds left on this call," came the recording.

There was silence from the other side and then, "Sorry, Ricky. I don't wanna argue with you."

Ricky calmed. "Me, either. Oh, and Bridget wants you to call."

"Okay," Lance replied, his tone neutral.

"You have thirty seconds left on this call," the recording announced.

"Ricky..." The voice was breathy and tremulous, not a question, not even a statement. The name itself was an emotion.

"Lance..." he breathed quietly back.

There was a pause.

As the seconds ticked away, Ricky heard a soft, emotional, "Miss you, man. *So much.*"

Ricky's breath choked off his reply, and he fought back the burning tears. Finally, expelling a breath, he said, "Miss you too. *So* much."

Then there was silence. The call had been terminated.

Trembling, Ricky reached out a finger and pressed the end button, gazing down at the silent phone in abject despair, his heart empty and filled with longing. With heavy sadness, Ricky tromped up the stairs and into Lance's room. Lying on Lance's side of the bed, he hugged the pillow and wept.

In Unit W-2, Lance hung up the phone, and gazed at it in silence, his chest heaving with emotion, his eyes burning. He needed to be alone. He signaled to a staff, who came over. "Can I go back to my room, please?"

He must've looked spooked because the staff cocked his head. "You okay, Lance? Need to see the nurse?"

Lance shook his head. "No," he whispered. "Just need to be alone."

The staff nodded and walked him down to his room. Lance slipped out of his shoes and stepped inside, hearing the door close and lock behind him. He crossed to his bed and sat, pulling up his legs and wrapping his arms around them. For the first time since being there, he cried.

Life for the fractured family continued. Debate about Lance raged daily on the Internet with headings like 'The Boy Who Came Back – Angel or Devil?' and 'Is Sir Lance a Psychopath?' On Talking Heads shows, supporters and opponents debated the possible latent violent tendencies of sexual abuse victims and how that instability can manifest itself in the teen years, almost like schizophrenia.

Arthur visited Lance on weekends, and Lance got his home phone call on Fridays. He continued to attend Father Mike's Wednesday group and Sunday services, and continued to read the Bible. He worked with the volunteer, a nice old guy named

Deacon Bob, in preparation for his looming baptism. And the campaign for their prop heated up.

The District Attorney wasted no time in issuing statements to the press about how it was exactly this kind of crime, committed by "Latent sociopaths like Lance Pendragon that make passage of Prop 51 a necessity for California. Let's stop coddling these kids. They need to be put away for the protection of society."

Fortunately, since live TV was not permitted to the minors, Lance only heard of these remarks through Arthur during their visits, and was thus spared the indignity of hearing himself impugned for all the world to see and hear.

Ricky, Chris, and Reyna recorded pro-51 commercials, but for very different reasons than those of the D.A. The film crew arrived the third week in August to record all the spots. The standard message Chris and Reyna delivered was along these lines:

"A yes vote won't take rights away from parents or adults, but will give more basic human rights to kids fourteen and older. At least then, if we are charged with a crime, we can have a real jury of our peers. A yes vote will also strengthen our schools because the system will be accountable to both parents *and* students, and everyone will have to step up their game to make education relevant for the twenty-first century."

That was the gist of most of them. Only Ricky had a different one, the one he had written himself. But even as he recorded it, he kept seeing Lance in chains, Lance hunched and shuffling across the courtroom, kept hearing Lance's voice over the phone, kept seeing in his mind's eye the D.A. posturing to the press. And he began to question which vote might be best. Was a 'yes' vote the right one, or might 'no' be more appropriate? After all, a 'no' vote would return childhood to the kids of California, and never again would kids be treated like animals, at least, not by the legal system.

Ricky was torn, but he also knew he couldn't change the message at this point. Now it would be up to the voters to decide.

As he sat in the Throne Room of New Camelot, in the chair normally reserved for Lance, Ricky looked straight into the camera and recorded these words:

"My name is Sir Ricky Pendragon. Most of you know me already, but you know Lance even better. The Boy Who Came Back. The most amazing boy I'll ever know has been falsely accused of a horrible crime he could no more commit than he could kill me. Yet he's in shackles and chains. He's treated like a dangerous monster and caged for the so-called protection of society. If he goes to trial, he'll have a jury of adults, people who have no clue what it's like for kids today. That isn't fair. If he, and other kids are adults when charged with a crime, then we can also be adult enough to vote for laws like this one. Lance needs your protection. He needs your vote. We all do. Look into your hearts and ask yourselves this question – after all you've seen Lance do for the people of Los Angeles and California, do you really believe he deserves to be treated this way? Please, vote yes on Prop 51. Thanks."

They did multiple 'takes' because Ricky would become too emotional to continue. The young director assured him they would edit together the best parts to play beneath images of Lance in his triumphant moments, alongside the ones of him in handcuffs.

Ricky kept repeating the lines until he was told they had enough. The director thanked him, and Ricky took Chris by the hand to get some lunch. The commercials would begin airing by the end of the month, right around the time of Lance's preliminary hearing, he was told. An anonymous donor had kicked in a lot of money to run these spots in prime time, so they would get plenty of exposure.

At first, Bridget and Ariel called or texted Ricky every day, or dropped by after school to see how he was. Ricky sat with them on the living room couch while Bridget prattled away about all the gossip around school, especially as it related to Lance and his case. Ricky was slightly buoyed by the fact that most teenagers seemed to be on Lance's side. Of course, many of them had experienced negative run-ins with the police or authority figures and didn't necessarily support Lance, just hated "the system." Still, it made Ricky feel a smidgen better.

Bridget also reminded Ricky to have Lance call her. He explained about Lance's limited phone time, and she was clearly disappointed. He knew he could invite her over on Friday night for Lance's weekly phone call, but he considered that family time. He also realized he just didn't want her there when he talked with Lance.

Another realization was his discomfort at being physically close to Ariel. He still kissed her when she arrived and left because he knew she wanted it, and he let her hold his hand as they sat and chatted with Bridget. The absence of Lance had clarified his feelings for Ariel, and Ricky knew why. But he had to keep trying, for Lance. It was what Lance wanted, wasn't it?

He felt badly for his indifference to her, but didn't seem able to overcome it. So their relationship devolved into a rote obligation he felt compelled to keep up with, but his heart wasn't in it. Had it ever really been, or had he just been flattered that a girl liked him because it had never happened before?

Ariel clearly sensed his diffidence, and the visits became less regular as time went by, replaced by phone calls or Skype sessions. Ricky had noted Bridget scrutinizing him on more than one occasion, as though she sensed what was in his heart, but he put on the best face he could and kept going. For Lance.

Lance's baptism had been scheduled for the weekend after his preliminary hearing, and he anxiously awaited the moment. Especially now, with so little to look forward to in life, he latched onto that impending moment as something akin to graduating high school. Even bigger, really. He would officially become what Arthur always called him from the start – a child of God. That thought warmed his heart, slightly overcoming the dread of his prelim tomorrow.

Ryerson had finally come back to see him earlier in the week, so Lance once more had to make that shuffling, shackled and manacled trek down to the Visitor's Center.

"I'll never make fun of zombies again," he wryly told the staff who was accompanying him. The man chuckled, but said nothing in reply.

Ryerson was his usual curt self, abrupt and to the point. "The state has nothing on you, Lance," he announced when Lance had been deposited in the glass booth and the door closed. "I saw that video, and yes you're clearly pointing a knife and threatening to cut off the man's balls." He glowered at Lance as though Lance should've known what would happen, and thus should've controlled his temper.

"They have no weapon," the lawyer continued, "none of your clothes had even traces of blood, nor your shoes, and even the victim's own statement doesn't really help him. If the judge is smart, he'll throw this out of court tomorrow."

Lance gulped. "And if he isn't smart?"

"Too many of these judges don't want to actually make a decision, Lance, a decision that could come back later and bite them on the ass. He might very well bind you over to trial in hopes that another judge will have to deal with you. Happens all the time."

Lance nodded.

"Remember, no matter what D.A. Dooley says about you tomorrow, you say nothing, you do nothing. Clear?"

Lance nodded again, suddenly fearful. Ryerson had already told him his case was political theater. He knew he was probably the most high profile defendant Los Angeles had ever had, and this city had had its share. He feared the judge would, in fact, send him on to trial.

"What if, like, the judge does want to send me to trial?" he asked. "How much longer will I gotta wait in here?"

"It's how much longer will I *have* to wait," the man said, annoyed, "and the answer is, I don't know. I suspect the D.A. will rush this to trial before the election. Proceedings will likely begin in October to maximize the publicity factor."

Lance gazed at the man. "Why are you so mean to me?"

That caught Ryerson off-guard. "How am I *mean* to you?"

"You're rude and cold," Lance replied quietly, trying to keep the desperation from his voice. "This is my whole life we're talking about." He lowered his eyes so the man wouldn't see just how scared he really was.

Ryerson sighed heavily, but said nothing for a moment. He cleared his throat. "If I allowed myself to become emotionally involved with my clients, I'd be a basket case, young man. Trust me, my job is simply to get you off and that I will do."

He stood and snapped shut his briefcase. Lance raised his eyes and saw Ryerson looking down at him. His face was impassive, as usual, but Lance thought he caught a glimpse of sympathy in those blue-gray eyes. Then the man stepped around the table and rapped on the glass door. Lance heard the key in the lock, but kept his eyes downcast. He felt a hand gently rest on his shoulder—just for a second—but when he turned his head Ryerson was already exiting the room.

The following morning, Lance was roused at four-thirty for the long, painful trek downtown to the Criminal Courts Building. This time, Angel didn't accompany him, but Hector did. Once both boys were fitted with their orange jumpsuits, shackled and manacled, they were led by the same staff as before out of The Compound and across the facility to the waiting sheriff's bus.

Lance groaned when he saw the same two deputies standing by the enormous bus.

The staff wished them luck before locking the gate behind him and returning to his duties.

Lance and Hector exchanged a resigned look as they shuffled toward the bus. The tall deputy smirked, and the short one glowered as they stepped in front of both boys, keeping them hidden from camera view. Lance knew that wasn't good.

"Well, if it isn't our favorite Celebrity Boy," he said coldly. "We missed you, Celebrity Boy, didn't we?"

His partner nodded. "How's those ribs today, Celebrity Boy?"

Lance glared at them, but said nothing.

"My partner asked you a question, punk," the short one grunted, and subtly punched Lance in the stomach.

Lance crumpled to the ground, and Hector bent to try and break his fall. Lance hit his shoulder hard, but thanks to Hector's body pressed against him managed to miss cracking his skull on the cement. Searing pain ripped through his shoulder and into his brain.

"You punks need to respect your elders," the tall deputy said.

"Got that, Celebrity Boy?" the short one echoed, kicking out slightly with his foot at Lance's midsection. Hector threw himself in between Lance and the foot, and took the brunt of the kick to his side, knocking the air from his lungs and causing him to gasp with pain.

Each deputy grabbed one of the boys and yanked him painfully to his feet, shoving both toward the entrance to the bus. Hector stumbled hard into the first step, smacking his knees and sending him crumpling to the ground. Lance pushed him from behind so the boy didn't fall all the way, and Hector managed to press his manacled hands against the bottom step to partially break the fall.

Suddenly, Wilson was beside the deputies, but Lance could only get a glimpse of him through the hair covering his face. He heard Wilson say, "You okay, Lance?"

Lance shook the hair off his face as Hector staggeringly rose to his feet. Lance stayed right at his back for stability, and Lance eyed Wilson's suspicious face. Lance knew Wilson understood what the deputies had done, but unless either boy accused them, there was no proof.

Again, as before, Lance knew who held all the cards here, and if he told the truth, there would be retaliation by other deputies, maybe not against him, but against Hector and Angel and all the other Compound kids. He knew the police mentality – they would stick up for their own, even when their own were in the wrong.

He sucked in a breath, fought down the pain, and said, "Just can't get used to walking like a zombie." He tried for a reassuring smile, but didn't think he succeeded. Wilson looked very unconvinced as he stepped back.

The boys were battened down in their little cages and secured so tightly Lance was certain he'd pass out. Still, he wouldn't give these guys a moment's satisfaction by complaining or even grimacing. The pain in his arms and wrists was excruciating, but he endured it. So, he knew, would Hector. It was the only way to survive.

CHAPTER SEVEN
YOU BELONG TO EVERYONE

THE COURTROOM WAS EVEN MORE packed than before. Due to intense public interest in the case, and at the D.A.'s urging, the media were allowed inside this time. As Arthur and the others entered the courtroom, Ricky looked around in disgust at the media frenzy, and understood why Lance's lawyer had called this "theater."

Arthur and his family sat in the same second row behind the defense table. The first row was required to remain empty. The courtroom filled up rapidly, with New Camelot knights and media personnel and as much of the public as could fit, which wasn't many. Most were turned away and told to wait in the hall if they wished to know the outcome, or go home and watch it on the news. Most chose to go home.

District Attorney Dooley was dressed in a slick, shimmering gray designer suit and preened for the cameras. He was in full campaign mode, Ricky noted with revulsion. Mr. Ryerson, by contrast, was dressed austerely in a beige suit and navy blue tie. His pinched face viewed the circus around him with disdain.

"All rise for the Honorable Judge William Jackson," the bailiff intoned, as the judge appeared from behind the raised bench.

Everyone stood until the judge seated himself behind it. The spectators reseated themselves. The attorneys remained standing.

"Are both sides ready to proceed?" the judge asked.

"The State stands ready, Your Honor," Dooley announced.

The judge turned his gaze on Ryerson.

"The defense stands ready, Your Honor."

The judge turned to the bailiff. "Bring in the defendant."

The bailiff exited the court through the same side door as before, and Ricky held his breath, dreading the expected sight of Lance in bondage, but his heart thumped like a jackhammer just at the prospect of seeing him at all.

The door opened, and Lance appeared, bound hand and foot, clad in prison orange, hunched over like an old man. The cameras flashed in strobe-like succession as he shuffled awkwardly forward. Ricky caught his eye, and Lance offered a slight smile. But then Lance's eye must've caught sight of something behind Ricky, because his gaze shifted.

Ricky turned and froze. Seated in the very back row, in the chair closest to the aisle, was Michael. The boy gazed stoically past Ricky, eyes obviously locked on Lance, his expression unreadable.

Ricky turned back to Lance, who stopped his forward motion upon seeing Michael. He noted with a deep sense of dread that Lance's gaze remained fixed on the boy in the back row.

The bailiff nudged Lance forward. "Take your seat, Lance," he said, and Lance snapped out of his momentary trance to shuffle to his table and sit beside his lawyer.

Ryerson frowned at him. "What was that all about?"

"Nothing," Lance whispered. "Saw somebody I knew, that's all."

"State of California versus Lance Pendragon, Preliminary Hearing, is now in session," the judge announced with a pound of his gavel. "Is the state ready with its first witness?"

Dooley stood. "We are, Your Honor. The victim, Mr. Thornton, is still recuperating from the attack and cannot be here to testify, so the state calls Sergeant Mitchell Wallace to the stand."

The bailiff at the rear opened one of the doors and ushered in the big, burly detective, who Ricky recognized as the one that had arrested Lance. Wallace strode up the center aisle, entered through the small swinging gates, and approached the witness stand. He stepped up into the witness box and turned to face the court clerk.

"Do you swear to tell the truth, the whole truth and nothing but the truth, so help you God?" the clerk intoned.

"I do," Wallace announced formally and took his seat in the box.

Dooley strode forward, brandishing another manila folder.

"State your name for the court," Dooley told the man.

"Mitchell Wallace," he replied. He proceeded to spell his name for the court reporter.

"And what is your profession, Mr. Wallace?"

"Chief Homicide Investigator, LAPD, Hollywood Division."

"Sergeant Wallace," Dooley continued, "please tell the court your role in the Richard Thornton case."

"Certainly," Wallace announced. "When the report came in about the attack on Mr. Thornton, I was assigned to investigate."

"Did you, in fact, review the crime scene?"

"I did."

"Describe what you found, Sergeant."

"Blood, everywhere. The attack happened on a dark street in Hollywood at approximately twelve-thirty a.m. on the night of July thirtieth. The amount of blood pooling on the ground where the attack occurred was substantial. It's a miracle the victim survived."

"Objection, Your Honor," Ryerson said as he stood. "Witness is making a medical judgment."

"Sustained," said the judge. "Witness will focus on the police investigation only."

"Yes, Your Honor," Wallace said, as Ryerson reseated himself.

Dooley opened the folder and showed Wallace some photos. "Are these photos of the crime scene as you found it?"

Wallace flipped through them. "Yes," he said, handing it back.

"I'd like to enter these photos as People's B," Dooley said, striding to Lance's table and tossing the folder in front of Ryerson with a flourish.

Ryerson flipped open the folder and Lance gasped. These were just color pictures of the sidewalk, but there was so much blood everywhere that he nearly gagged.

Ryerson closed the folder and handed it to the clerk.

Dooley asked Wallace, "Were you able to interview the victim that same night, Sergeant?"

"That morning. He'd been rushed into emergency surgery and came out of recovery at approximately seven a.m. That's when he gave his statement."

"Describe what he said, Sergeant."

Wallace reached into his jacket pocket and slipped out a small spiral notebook, which he opened and flipped back a few pages. "He said he'd been walking home from a party when someone struck him from behind and he fell to the pavement, semi- conscious. He said he heard a ripping sound, like somebody tearing a shirt, and then a piece of cloth was tied around his eyes, and his wrists were bound behind his back. The attacker said nothing, but Mr. Thornton could hear him breathing and he said it sounded like angry breathing."

He paused, and Dooley urged him to continue. "Go on."

Wallace resumed checking his notes. "He then felt an excruciating pain plunging into his genital area."

There were audible exhalations of breath from the spectators.

"He was too dazed to fight back and nearly passed out from the pain. He recalled shrieking loudly and crying out for help before fainting. When he came to, the blindfold and wrists restraints were gone and he was being tended to by paramedics."

"You said he was struck from behind, Sergeant, but did Mr. Thornton have any suspicion who the attacker might have been?"

"Yes."

"Whom did he name?"

"The defendant, Lance Pendragon."

There were gasps from the crowd, and Ricky wanted to leap to his feet in protest. Lance leaned in to Ryerson, but the man put a hand out to silence him.

Dooley nodded. "And did Mr. Thornton give you any reason why Mr. Pendragon might commit such a horrific act of mayhem?"

"Yes, sir," Wallace answered, very professional and very serious. "He said the defendant had threatened him with a knife earlier in the evening. He'd recorded the threat on his cell phone."

Dooley strolled back to his table where he picked up a cell phone. He strode to the witness box and showed the phone to Wallace.

"This phone?"

Wallace took the phone and examined it. "Yes, sir. I remember because it had a chip out of one corner."

Dooley held the phone out. "I enter this as People's C. If I may play the video for the court, Your Honor?"

"By all means, Mr. Dooley."

Dooley nodded to his assistant, who walked to an area behind the clerk and grabbed a large-screen TV on a rolling cart, pushing it out in front of the judge. The TV sat at an angle so the judge could see, but so could Lance and the spectators on his side of the courtroom.

Dooley was obviously well prepared, for he strode purposefully to the TV and connected the phone via USB cable. Then he scrolled quickly through the phone for what he wanted, powered up the television, and turned to face the judge.

"The phone was in the victim's pocket, Your Honor, and the image was shot through a hole in that pocket, but I think you'll clearly recognize the defendant."

He pressed play on the phone, and Lance's terrified face appeared on camera.

The image was dark and grainy and the cloth of the shirt pocket slipped in and out, causing Lance's face to lose focus now and then.

Ricky almost gagged when he saw Lance's face, and the look of sheer terror pasted all over it.

Richard's voice could be heard. "How are you, son?"

Lance swung the blade threateningly toward the camera. "Stay back, Richard, or I'll cut your balls off!"

"Is that any way to talk to the man who loved you?" Richard's voice cooed.

Lance cowered, but still waved the knife. "You raped me, Richard, that's what you did, and I hate your guts! I swear I'll kill you if you touch me again!"

Dooley froze the image on Lance's terrified, almost animalistic expression.

Members of the audience made audible sounds of shock, and Lance bowed his head in shame.

Ricky gripped Chris's hand and pulled the smaller boy into an embrace.

Dooley detached the phone and turned off the TV, handing the phone to the clerk to catalogue.

"Thank you, Sergeant," Dooley said, "I have no further questions."

He resumed his seat.

"Do you wish to cross-examine, Mr. Ryerson?" the judge asked.

Ryerson, who'd been scribbling notes as he watched the video, stood. "Yes, Your Honor."

He stepped toward the witness box, all business, but without the theatricality of Dooley. "Sergeant Wallace, did Mr. Thornton actually, at any point during the attack, see the face, or hear the voice, of his attacker?"

"No, he didn't."

"So the attacker could have been anyone, correct?"

"Theoretically, yes."

"Obviously, Mr. Thornton is aware of what's on his phone, since he admitted to recording it, correct?"

"Yes."

"Did he say why he'd cut a hole in his front shirt pocket so he could record my client through it?"

"No, he didn't."

"Did you ask him that question, Sergeant?"

Wallace looked sheepish, no longer quite so confident. "No, sir, I didn't."

"On that tape, my client accuses Mr. Thornton of raping him. Did you ask Mr. Thornton about the veracity of my client's accusation?"

"No, I didn't."

"Why not, Sergeant?"

"Since Mr. Thornton was the victim, Mr. Pendragon's accusation seemed like a motive to me."

"As I watched that video, Sergeant, I saw fear in my client's face and heard it in his voice," Ryerson said calmly. "Did you consider the trauma of a child having been raped in evaluating my client's response to Mr. Thornton on that video?"

"No, I did not."

Ryerson shook his head in disgust. "From the victim's wounds, could your lab determine what kind of weapon was used?"

"A short handled knife or possibly a switch blade," Wallace answered. "Very sharp."

"Did you find the weapon among the possessions of my client or his father, King Arthur?"

"No, we did not."

Ryerson eyed the detective a moment before continuing. "Based on the photos we have been shown, both People's A and B, the attack was violent and very bloody. Would you agree?"

"Yes, sir."

"So the attacker, whomever it might have been, would likely have been covered in blood. Would you agree, Sergeant?"

"Yes, that's most likely."

"Did you or your lab experts examine all of my client's clothes and shoes?"

"Yes."

"And?"

Wallace glanced over at Dooley before fixing his gaze back on Ryerson. "We found no blood."

Ryerson dismissed him with a wave of the hand. "No further questions." He returned to sit beside Lance.

"Witness may step down," the judge said, and Wallace stood to exit the witness box, striding back through the swinging gate and down the center aisle to leave the courtroom.

"Call your next witness, Mr. Dooley," the judge said.

Dooley stood and glanced Lance's way a moment.

Lance didn't like that look. Something was up.

"State calls Lawrence Diosdado to the stand."

Ryerson leapt to his feet. "Objection, Your Honor. This witness was not made known to me."

The judge looked at Dooley with raised eyebrows. "Mr. Dooley?"

"With all due respect to my esteemed colleague, and the court, Your Honor, this witness only approached me yesterday with the desire to testify."

The judge frowned. "And have you verified the veracity of his proposed testimony, Mr. Dooley?"

"Not as yet, Your Honor, but since this is a prelim, I thought it best to allow him to share his story, since it appears to bear heavily on this case."

The judge considered a moment, then turned to Ryerson, who clearly looked miffed at protocol being ignored. "Mr. Ryerson, though Mr. Dooley's request is irregular, I'm going to overrule your objection at this time. As this is merely a prelim, I'd like as much pertinent information as possible."

Ryerson stiffened. "Very well, Your Honor, but I'd like my objection to remain on the record." He resumed his seat.

"So noted," the judge replied, and then called out to the bailiff in back. "Bring in the witness."

The bailiff opened the door and a tall man strode in wearing a crisp-looking, very stylish suit.

Lance turned to look as the man marched down the center aisle, and the blood froze in his veins. His heart accelerated, and his hands trembled.

The man glaring balefully in his direction was none other than Mr. D., the guy from Santa Monica Boulevard who'd wanted to rape him for two thousand dollars! He sported a beard and mustache, and the hair was colored and styled differently, but Lance would never forget the hungry look in those eyes or the nasty twist of his lip when he smirked.

"My God," he whispered as the man strode through the gate and up to the witness stand.

Ryerson frowned down at Lance. "Who is that man?"

Lance couldn't answer. His voice stuck in his throat along with his breath.

Mr. D. took the stand and raised his right hand.

The clerk asked, "Do you swear to tell the truth, the whole truth and nothing but the truth, so help you God?"

"I do," Mr. D. replied easily and sat in the chair provided, smoothing out the creases in his pants as he did so.

Dooley strode forward. "State your name for the court."

"Lawrence Diosdado."

"Spell that, please, for the court reporter," the judge said.

Mr. D. smiled. "Certainly, Your Honor. D-i-o-s-d-a-d-o."

"Thank you," the judge said. "You may proceed, Mr. Dooley."

"What is your occupation, Mr. Diosdado?"

"I'm a corporate lawyer with the firm of Hanley, Haskell and Keen."

Lance sat rooted to his chair, his eyes riveted to the man, his entire body trembling at the timber of that voice, at the memory of that night last fall.

Dooley paced back and forth. "Have you at any time made the acquaintance of the defendant, Mr. Pendragon?"

"Yes, sir, I have."

"Tell us about that, if you would."

"Certainly," Mr. D. said, sounding very calm. "It happened last year, sometime in October. I was driving home rather late one night when I spotted the defendant and another boy standing on a street corner with their shirts off."

"Did that strike you as odd?" Dooley asked.

"Objection!" Ryerson announced. "Leading."

"Sustained," the judge said.

"What did you do, Mr. Diosdado?" Dooley asked instead.

"As I got closer, I recognized Mr. Pendragon and the other boy as King Arthur's knights, so I pulled over and asked if there was a problem, if perhaps they needed a ride somewhere."

"Did you at any point step out of your car?"

Mr. D. looked sheepish. "Actually, yes. I confess, it was such a surprise to see the famous Sir Lance that I wanted to shake his hand, you know, to thank him for everything he'd been doing for our city."

Lance fumed. "That's not—"

Ryerson cut him off with a hand to his arm, and gave a slight headshake.

"Tell us what happened when you tried to shake Mr. Pendragon's hand," Dooley continued.

Mr. D. just shook his head in dismay, as though still unable to believe it had happened. "Kid went psycho. Pulled a knife and stuck it to my throat. Said I'd better get outta there or, and I quote, 'I'll cut your balls off and throw 'em down the sewer'."

There were more gasps from the spectators, and Reyna could be heard making an audible exclamation, but its exact nature was lost on Lance.

"You didn't provoke the boy in any way?"

"No way. He just went postal on me."

Dooley nodded in a very understanding fashion. "So what did you do?"

"What do you think I did?" Mr. D. said, his voice seeming to quake with remembered fear. "I got in my car and got the hell out of there."

Lance glared at the man and wanted to pull another knife on him. "He's lying!" he hissed to Ryerson, who shushed him again.

Ryerson stood. "Your Honor, I object to this testimony on the grounds that it is irrelevant to this case."

"With all due respect, Your Honor," Dooley said, approaching the bench. "I'm trying to establish a pattern here, that Mr. Thornton may not have been the first man Mr. Pendragon threatened."

"Objection overruled," the judge said. "The witness's testimony will remain on the record."

Dooley nodded for the cameras. "No further questions, Your Honor." He strode back to his table.

"Your witness, Mr. Ryerson," the judge announced.

Lance was livid as he grabbed Ryerson by the arm. "He's lying, I tell you!"

Ryerson turned to the judge. "If I may have a moment to confer with my client, Your Honor?"

"Go ahead," the judge agreed.

Ryerson shoved his face right down in front of Lance. "Now make this quick. How do you know this man and how did he lie?"

Lance took a deep breath, and whispered, "Last year, Jack and me were looking for our friend Mark on Santa Monica Boulevard. This guy would cruise the street picking up boys for sex. He'd already raped Jack a few times for money and he tried to buy me for two grand. He wanted to rape me. I swear that's the truth! So when he touched me, I pulled a knife on him." Ryerson's eyes narrowed. "I was scared, okay?"

"Were there any witnesses to this?" Ryerson whispered.

"Just Jack," Lance answered sadly, "but he's dead now."

Ryerson blew out a short, frustrated breath. "Then it's your word against his, Lance."

"But he—"

Ryerson held up a hand to cut him off. "I'll have my investigator dig up what they can on him, but for now, we have nothing."

Lance wanted to scream and jump up and down, denouncing Mr. D as a child rapist and liar.

Ryerson turned to the judge. "We have no questions at this time."

Lance cursed under his breath and glared so hatefully at Mr. D. that the man smiled as he left the witness box. Lance clenched his fists to regain control of himself as Mr. D. left the courtroom.

"Does the State wish to call any more witnesses?" the judge asked.

"No, Your Honor," Dooley answered, returning to his table.

"Does the defense wish to bring in any witnesses at this time?"

"No, Your Honor."

"Very well," the judge went on. "Does either side wish to make any closing remarks before I make my ruling?"

"Yes, Your Honor," Dooley stated, rising again to his feet with a flourish.

"You may proceed, Mr. Dooley."

Dooley paced back and forth as he spoke. "Your Honor, we have here a case of a seemingly innocent, very likeable boy who admittedly has charmed the entire world with his good looks and his miraculous return from the dead, clearly orchestrated for maximum media attention. However, as we know with most serial killers, the outward demeanor often harbors a dangerous, cold-blooded psychopath just waiting for the right moment to emerge."

He turned and cast a glare in Lance's direction. "You have seen evidence that on one, and perhaps two occasions that we know of, the defendant, Lance Pendragon, threatened to mutilate a man. And while he may possibly have had a motive in the case of Mr. Thornton, Mr. Diosdado was simply an innocent bystander offering to help the boy. Now, regardless of what Mr. Thornton may or may not have done to Mr. Pendragon in the past—and we only have his word on that—the attack on Mr. Thornton was violent and unprovoked, clearly showing a depraved mind at work. And further, while Mr. Thornton didn't see who attacked him, his wounds are similar to the threat issued earlier that evening by Mr. Pendragon. In light of this information, your Honor, I believe we have sufficient evidence to go forward with trial. Thank you."

He made his way back to his table.

The judge said, "Mr. Ryerson?"

Ryerson stood and stepped around the table. "With all due respect to my esteemed colleague, Your Honor, he has nothing that directly links my client to this horrific crime. No eyewitness account, no blood evidence, no weapon. All we have is a video showing my client, who appears very clearly to be in fear of his life, brandishing a knife and threatening Mr. Thornton, a man who may have raped the boy at the age of six. Then the district attorney presents some stranger who claims to have had a run-in with my client, but again, no eye witnesses, simply uncorroborated hearsay testimony."

He paused and indicated Lance, looking wide-eyed and scared. "Your Honor, my client is indisputably the most famous person in the entire world. There are literally hundreds of hours of video footage showing him doing nothing but good for this city and its people. That's real evidence of his character, Your Honor, something every one of us can all quantify. We have watched this boy grow and blossom before our eyes for nearly two years. He's like a son to everyone. Yes, he did stumble into stupid teenaged behaviors on a few occasions, but quickly righted himself. Could he truly be 'depraved,' as Mr. Dooley called him? A serial killer? And those tendencies to extreme, sadistic violence suddenly leapt to the surface like puberty? No, Your Honor. We know this boy seated behind me better than we know anyone else in this courtroom. And he could no more commit this crime than he could fly. I ask the court to dismiss all charges based upon lack of evidence. Thank you."

Lance's mouth had dropped open at Ryerson's positive, complimentary description of him, and it remained open as the man resumed his seat.

"Close your mouth, Lance," he whispered. "You look like a codfish."

Shocked out of his amazement, Lance complied, his anger of the moment before having dissipated in light of Ryerson's remarks.

"Court will take a fifteen minute recess to consider my decision." He slammed down the gavel and stood.

"All rise," the bailiff called out again.

Everyone remained standing until the judge disappeared into his chambers. Then the chattering and yammering began.

Lance leaned over to Ryerson. "Did you mean all that stuff you said about me?"

Ryerson looked at him noncommittally. "It's my job to get you off, Lance, remember that."

But something in the way he looked down at his notes rather quickly convinced Lance that maybe this arrogant, hard-edged, somewhat nasty man might have meant what he'd said after all.

Lance turned his head and craned his neck to see what Michael was doing. He sucked in a breath when his eye fell upon Michael's seat. It was empty.

Feeling eyes on him, Lance turned and looked behind him. Ricky was giving him a look that made Lance almost redden with embarrassment. Ricky had obviously caught him searching for Michael. He thought he spotted hurt in Ricky's eyes, but then Ricky smiled encouragingly and flexed his right arm and pointed to it. Lance grinned and then made eye contact with Arthur. His dad looked so much older than he had a year ago, and Lance felt a stab of guilt.

And I made him look like that.

He tried for a smile to ease his dad's pain, and Arthur gratefully returned it. So did Jenny, who sat clutching the king's hand tightly.

Reyna was clearly agitated by what she'd heard, and Esteban was trying to calm her. She caught Lance watching her and shifted gears quickly, blowing him a kiss and mouthing the words, "Love you, baby boy." That made him feel better.

It was only then that he spotted Bridget and Ariel in the very back, gazing intently his way and trying to get his attention. Instinctively, he tried to raise a hand to wave, but the chain around his waist yanked his hands back down. Instead, he smiled, and they waved back nervously.

His stomach churning with dread, Lance turned back around and eyed his attorney, now checking his smartphone for messages. "Do you think I'm gonna have to go to trial?"

Ryerson looked at him, obviously annoyed at having been interrupted. "It's 'going to have to go', Lance. Please work on your grammar."

Lance nodded, his face filled with trepidation.

Ryerson sighed. "This judge is very fair, Lance, but there is an election coming up and the head District Attorney wishes to make an example out of you. Do your own math."

Then he turned back to his phone, and Lance's heart sank even more deeply into his stomach. He was innocent! Why couldn't anyone believe that?

The minutes ticked by until the door to the judge's chambers opened and the judge stepped out.

"All rise," the clerk called out, and everyone stood. The judge resumed his seat and looked around the court.

Everyone sat.

"We're back on record in the matter of State of California versus Lance Pendragon," the judge began. He turned his head and looked directly at Lance. "Will the defendant please rise?"

Lance glanced nervously at Ryerson, who nodded. Trembling, he stood and faced the judge.

"Mr. Pendragon," the judge began, then halted, and sighed. "Lance. The charges brought against you today are serious. As your attorney may have explained, this is not a trial. In a trial the district attorney must prove to a jury beyond a reasonable doubt that you committed the crime. For our purposes today, only a preponderance of the evidence is required to bind you over for trial. Something your attorney said struck me as I pondered this case. We *do* all know you. You're Lance. You're the boy who charmed the city last year. You're the boy who broke our hearts when you died, and filled us with hope when you came back. You're also the boy who disappointed so many with your subsequent drunken escapades."

Lance lowered his eyes sheepishly at that. The judge paused and Lance looked back up to find the man gazing at him with compassion.

"In some sense, Lance, you are my son, and the son, brother, nephew, friend to everyone in this courtroom. You belong to everyone. And yet, as with all human beings, we don't know what is buried deep within you. I sympathize with what might have happened to you as a child, Lance, but in a court of law I must deal with facts and the current crime. I found your threats and violent behavior on that video very troubling, even as I understand the possible origin. Given the heinous nature of this crime, despite the lack of physical evidence connecting you to it, I feel there is sufficient cause to bind you over for trial on the charge of attempted murder. I'm sorry, son."

Lance gasped, felt his knees grow weak, and would've crumpled to the floor had Ryerson not leapt up to grab him and ease him back into his chair. Tears sprang to his eyes and he bowed his head in sorrow.

There were murmurs in the audience and Lance heard Ricky's voice call out, "He didn't do it!"

The judge banged his gavel. "Order in this court." Gradually, the ripples of conversation ceased. The judge looked over at Dooley. "Mr. Dooley, do you have a preference as to trial date?"

"As soon as possible, Your Honor," Dooley replied.

The judge eyed him a moment before turning to Ryerson. "Mr. Ryerson, would six weeks be sufficient for you to prepare your case?"

Ryerson stood. "Yes, Your Honor, that will be sufficient."

Lance had his head bowed, hair obscuring his face, not wanting anyone to see his tears, not wanting them to see his weakness.

The judge checked his calendar. "How is October the sixteenth at nine a.m. for jury selection?"

Dooley agreed without even checking his calendar. "Fine, Your Honor."

Ryerson did check his, and looked up at the judge. "That day will work."

"Very well," the judge concluded. "Trial will commence on October sixteenth at nine a.m. Defendant will remain in custody at Barney J. Nelson Juvenile Hall. Until then, this matter stands adjourned."

He slammed down the gavel and concluded the session. Casting a sympathetic gaze toward Lance, the judge rose and exited into his chambers.

Ricky turned to Arthur. "Dad, do something!"

Arthur threw his arms around him. The spectators went crazy with animated conversation, and the media strained to snap pictures of Lance, head bowed in sorrow, and the television cameras zoomed in for close-ups.

Ryerson awkwardly placed a hand on Lance's shoulder. "It is not over yet, Lance. In the end, I *will* win."

The bailiff approached and cleared his throat.

Lance didn't respond, just kept his head bowed.

"Lance," the bailiff said quietly.

Lance looked up at the deputy, and saw kindness in the man's eyes. After what the others had done to him on the bus, Lance found himself surprised.

The bailiff indicated the door behind him. "It's time to go."

Lance glanced at Ryerson, and then stood. He turned and locked eyes with Ricky, still cradled in Arthur's arms. Ricky looked so devastated, so hopelessly lost, that Lance nearly gagged with anguish. He felt, rather than consciously noticed, the camera flashes going off, not even caring if they saw his tear-streaked face. His gaze held that of Ricky for as long as possible. Then a gentle hand to the shoulder caused him to turn. The bailiff stood there, not hard and threatening, just there. Lance nodded and stumblingly followed the man from the courtroom without a backward glance.

The district attorney blithely waded into the spectator's gallery and out into the hall to answer media questions. Ricky mad dogged him the whole way, at one point causing the man to glance over as he left the court. Ricky was happy to see him lose that self-important, smug expression for a second before passing out of his line of sight in the dispersing crowd.

Ariel and Bridget hurried forward to express their anger and sorrow. Ariel, normally shy, but perhaps seeing the look of hopelessness on Ricky's face, pulled him into a hug. He turned red and pulled back, caught off guard with embarrassment to be hugging in a courtroom where Lance just got sent to trial for attempted murder.

A flash of anger roared through him at Ariel's callousness, and it must have shown in his eyes because she recoiled slightly, looking hurt.

The girls bade Ricky and Arthur goodbye and left the courtroom before their pictures were taken.

On the way out, Ryerson cautioned Ricky against any outbursts, no matter what the press may ask. He did not want a repeat of the boy's previous "performance."

Ricky nodded, but said nothing.

Out in the hall, the media surrounded Dooley, who looked large and in charge. The moment Arthur and his group exited the courtroom, however, Dooley was forgotten as everyone swept toward the king and his kids. The D.A. watched with a sour expression as the questions flew fast and furious, and Arthur did his best to answer them. Ricky spotted Yellow Hair in the crowd, but said nothing.

Arthur and Jenny assured the reporters that they fully believed in Lance's innocence, despite the video and impending trial, and that they stood by their son.

Ricky found Helen gazing at him, and when she caught his eye and raised her brows, he nodded.

She waded in with her question. "Sir Ricky, what was your impression of Lance's behavior on that video?"

Ryerson glared at Ricky. But there was no way Ricky would disrespect Helen, and he understood at once the purpose of her question. He gazed soberly at the crowd and the cameras.

"I know Lance bettern' anyone 'cept my dad. Every time he would even think of Richard and what he'd done to him, how he'd raped him and used him and..." Ricky paused, getting himself under control. "Lance, so badass, so strong and amazing, would melt like wax just at the memory. He'd shiver and shake and I'd have to hold him until he calmed down. That's what happened that night when he came home. Just seeing that guy, having him touch him, terrified Lance. I know the feeling." He paused and looked over at Arthur sadly. "I'm sorry, Dad, I never told you, but I met Richard when I was homeless, before I ever knew Lance or you. He said he'd take care of me, but all he did was rape me bad and then dump me back out on the streets."

Arthur's face collapsed with shock, and Jenny joined in the stunned gasp of the crowd.

Ricky continued to look at his parents. "I didn't know for sure till I seen his picture on TV. I didn't wanna worry you guys with everything already happening. I'm sorry I never told you."

Arthur placed a hand on Ricky's trembling shoulder, then pulled him into a hug. Ricky felt the love and security of his dad's body pressed against him, and knew without words that Arthur understood.

The stunned crowd watched as Ricky swiped a tear from one eye and turned back to Helen. "You wanna understand his reaction on that video, Lady Helen? It was fear, and that's all. It was Lance's deepest fear, and I would've reacted just the same to that guy if I'd been the one he came after."

He looked down at the floor and sucked in a deep breath.

Helen looked appalled. "Sir Ricky," she quickly threw out, "did you ever report the incident involving Mr. Thornton to the police?"

Ricky shook his head sadly. "I's homeless. He covered my eyes so I didn't know where he lived and I never even knew his real name for sure till, well, all this happened. 'Sides, it would've been his word against mine, anyway. Nobody believes kids."

As more hands flew fast and furious, Ryerson quickly stepped in front of Ricky. "Thank you all for your time and your support." He nodded to Arthur that now was the time to retreat.

Arthur wrapped his arm Ricky's shoulders. Ricky looked up at him and Arthur offered a sad smile.

"I'm proud of you, son."

Ricky smiled back, despite his shattered heart, and the family made its way to the elevators to make the long, painful ride home, once again without the boy they loved.

CHAPTER EIGHT

DO YOU MISS ME?

A DEJECTED LANCE SAT BELTED AND manacled to the bench in the holding tank awaiting his return to captivity. Another six weeks! And after that, what? Prison? Never to be with his family again? Despite Ryerson's arrogant assurances of ultimate victory, Lance saw the determined look in Dooley's eyes, and knew the man wanted him to be guilty so badly that he didn't really care if Lance committed the crime or not. What was it Ryerson had told him before? The purpose of the system wasn't justice, but to win? And Dooley looked to Lance like a guy who was accustomed to winning.

Then there was Mr. D. The vindictive smile he'd flashed in court confirmed Lance's initial thoughts regarding the man. This was payback, pure and simple. Payback because Lance had one-upped him. His only hope was that Ryerson's detectives would uncover some evidence to discredit the man, and hopefully put him in jail for having sex with underage boys. Jack, at least, deserved that much justice.

Lance's only positive moment came when Hector returned from court and announced that his attempted murder case had been dropped.

Lance's jaw nearly dropped open. "So how come you didn't just go home?"

"I still got a juvenile case pending," Hector told him from his chained position. "But no more compound for me."

Despite his own situation, Lance smiled with relief. "I'm happy for you, man."

Hector saw the look on Lance's face. "You going to trial?"

Lance nodded, the smile fading.

"Sorry, man. And I'm sorry to miss your baptism on Sunday."

Lance looked up, startled. He'd been so devastated by the court ruling that he'd all but forgotten. At least it was something to look forward to.

"You just wanted to see my hair plastered all over my face when Father Mike poured the water on me."

Hector grinned back. "Hell, man, I seen that lots of times in the shower."

Lance laughed. "Thanks, man, for, you know, helping me out this past month."

"No sweat. Good luck, Boy Who Came Back."

Lance nodded, and they fell silent until taken back to the bus.

It was late afternoon by the time Lance and Hector got back to The Compound, then Hector had to gather up his meager belongings to move out to one of the hill units. He said goodbye to everyone.

"Thanks, again, man, for being a friend," Lance said, realizing he would miss the other boy.

"Good luck in trial, dawg," Hector said.

Lance was shocked to see Hector led out without shackles.

Joey laughed bitterly. "That's cuz in here he's a dangerous animal, Lance, but out there in the hill units, he's just another kid."

"But he's the same kid," Lance said in astonished bewilderment.

Joey just shook his head. "Stupid as hell, huh?"

Lance nodded. Beyond stupid.

It being Friday night, Lance got his usual phone call home and, as happened every week, all the family gathered around the speakerphone to hear his voice. Arthur assured him he'd be there tomorrow and that he greatly anticipated Lance's baptism on Sunday.

"Me, too, Dad," Lance replied. At least it was one bright spot in this dismal life of his.

Reyna and Esteban were furious at the "creep," as Reyna called Mr. D., showing up to make Lance look bad. Briefly, so they'd understand what really happened, Lance told everyone about his previous encounter with Mr. D., and that made Reyna even angrier.

"Don't worry, Reyna," Lance assured her, "Ryerson said he'd put his investigators on the guy. A child molester like him's gotta leave some tracks to find."

Lance heard Reyna and the others assure him of their love, and the hope that this would all be over soon.

Chris told Lance that the commercials for their prop had begun to air. "And mine is the most popular 'cause everybody says I'm cute."

Lance laughed at that. "And so you are, little man. I love you, Chris."

"Love you too, Lance." The little boy's voice sounded so small and sad.

It had become customary to vacate the lobby and allow Lance and Ricky the last five minutes in private. As always, there was an awkward silence between them.

Lance whispered, "I miss you."

"Miss you too." Then Ricky added, "And, before you ask, no I didn't talk to Michael today and I didn't want to. 'Sides, he left during the break." There was a slight pause. "That's your great friend for you, Lance – didn't even wait to find out what happened!"

Lance heard bitterness, and something else he couldn't quite define in Ricky's voice. "I don't wanna talk about Michael." He fought to get hold of the emotions twisting him into knots.

Another moment passed in silence.

"You there, Lance?" Ricky's voice sounded panicked.

"Yeah," he answered, exhaling a deep breath. "Are we ever gonna be together again, Ricky, you and me? Cause I don't think I could live if... I don't think I'm strong enough to—"

"You are the toughest, baddest, realest boy I ever knew," came Ricky's voice, strong and filled with passion. "And damn straight we'll be together again! You just hang on, man. I got you."

Lance fought the burning behind his eyes, the one that always made him feel so weak. "For now and always?" he asked, almost breathlessly.

There was a pause, an exhalation of breath, maybe a sniffle. Lance couldn't be sure. Then he heard, quietly, but firmly, "For now and always."

The operator had already announced the one-minute deadline, so Lance knew they only had seconds left. And then Ricky would be lost to him for another week. He tugged back the tears and inhaled deeply to calm himself before whispering with just the slightest of breaths, "I *really* miss you."

There was another sniffle, and a deep sigh from the other end. "I really miss you too."

And then nothing.

Ricky was gone.

Slowly hanging up the phone, Lance motioned to the staff, who already knew he wanted to go back to his room. Lance became too emotional when he talked with the family, especially Ricky, and just couldn't handle dayroom afterwards. He couldn't seem too sensitive in front of these guys. It made him look weak, and Ricky had assured him he wasn't weak. God, how he loved that boy! He could say it to Chris and to Reyna, so why couldn't he actually say those words to Ricky? Why did he have to relay them through his father?

Jack's revelation from so long ago drifted back into his consciousness, as though from another plane of existence, "It's the things we don't say to each other that make the biggest difference."

Oh, Jacky, he thought to himself, tears springing to his eyes as he sat forlornly on his bed. *I still miss you, and I'm breaking my promise. I'm not supposed to let things go unsaid anymore, not to people I love, but I'm doing it anyway. What am I gonna do, Jacky? You promised to watch over me. Are you?*

Of course, there was no answer. Lance lay down on his bed, sorrowful and lonely, terrified by the possibility that he'd never again be with the people he loved.

As he had every weekend of Lance's incarceration, Arthur visited on Saturday. Rather than bring each other down by discussing the prelim, they talked about the family, the campaign, and Lance's impending baptism the following day. Lance was excited, but a little nervous too. Father Mike dropped by to remind Arthur to arrive at seven-thirty in the morning, because he wanted to introduce him to the other kids in the chapel at the eight-fifteen service. Arthur said he'd be honored. Then Father Mike showed him a book, one Lance had seen numerous times. It had a plain cover, but sported a cross made of individual little battery-powered lights that could be twisted to turn on.

Father Mike called this the Book of Life, and any kid who wanted to become a Warrior of Light was invited to sign the book, and his or her parents, as well. It was a commitment, a symbol of their desire to change.

The old priest's eyes twinkled as he looked at Lance. "Would you like to sign it tomorrow, Lance, after your baptism?"

"Hell, yeah," the boy gushed, and then clapped a hand over his mouth. "My bad, Father Mike. I been hoping you'd ask."

The priest smiled. "And you, Arthur?"

The king looked at Lance's eager face and suddenly realized a truth he'd always believed – even out of something so bad as this experience, God always provided something good. Had Lance not been arrested, this moment tomorrow would not be happening.

He smiled at Father Mike. "I shall be honored, Father." Then he turned his gaze upon Lance. "My son is the greatest warrior for right I have ever known, and he will be an outstanding warrior of light, as well."

Father Mike flashed that impish grin Lance loved and patted him on one shoulder.

"See you tomorrow, *mijo*." And off he went to talk with another family.

Arthur gazed across the table at Lance, causing him to laugh nervously. "What, Dad?"

Arthur must've realized he'd been staring because he lowered his eyes a moment and smiled, shaking his head. "Have I told you of late how proud I am of you, Lance?"

Lance looked embarrassed. "Thanks, Dad."

"What you are going through, son, would break the strongest of men, and yet you endure. No, more than that. You transcend. I love you more with each passing day, if such a thing were possible."

Lance fought back tears. "C'mon, Dad, you're gonna make me cry and that's a big bad in here."

Arthur laughed, and Lance joined in. They reached across the table and held hands. "We shall prevail, son, and you will be made stronger for this pain."

"I know. I just wish I wasn't embarrassing you so much with all this."

Arthur squeezed his hand and looked him dead in the eye. "You *never* embarrass me, Lance. Never."

Lance smiled gratefully, and had to swipe away the tears before he made a scene in front of the whole unit.

The rest of their visit passed with them talking over old times and making plans for the future.

Lance didn't sleep well that night because he was nervous about the morning. Most nights, it was hard to sleep anyway because overhead florescent lights were always on in their rooms so staff could look in and make sure they were okay. He was already up and pacing his room when door was opened for early morning head and water calls.

As soon as breakfast ended, Lance went back to his room as usual, and stood by his window waiting for his dad to arrive. At seven thirty, he spotted Father Mike walking with two people past Movement Control, but on the backside of the structure so he couldn't see who it was. When they came around the corner, his heart leapt. It was his dad, and Sergeant Ryan. Arthur was dressed in his more normal tunic, leather pants and boots. He even had his crown-like circlet on his head. Lance smiled at his dad dressing so formally for him, and here he'd be wearing the lousy county pants and gray t-shirt. Oh, well!

He kept his gaze pinned to them until they neared the Compound, and then Lance banged on the window. By now Arthur knew which one was his and looked that direction. He raised a hand in greeting and so did Ryan, and the three men moved on past the gigantic cage toward the chapel, where the regular, non-animal kids, went to church.

He sat on his bed and waited, picking up his Bible and reading the passages where John baptized Jesus in the River Jordan. By now, he'd read all four gospels and a good portion of Acts, and he understood the rite of baptism and its purpose.

When he looked back out his window, he saw the non-Compound kids—those who simply walked with their hands behind their backs and no shackles—as they made their way toward the chapel. He spotted Hector, now just a regular kid, and banged on the window. Hector looked up and grinned.

Arthur and Ryan were introduced to the other volunteers setting up the chapel for mass, and Father Mike explained that he would bring the king up as the service began to explain about Lance and talk about their proposition. Arthur thanked him and sat off to one side with Ryan as staff began leading in groups of kids, ranging in age from thirteen to seventeen, and seating them quietly in certain sections.

The dim, recessed lighting gave the small chapel a somber feeling, but the large cloth-covered altar, and the areas on either side of it, were brightly lit. There were banners and pictures of Jesus adorning the walls.

The kids and staff all noticed Arthur as they passed him and many an eye went wide with shock. As with Lance, there weren't many in the world that wouldn't have recognized the king. Once everyone was seated, there was an opening song. Then Father Mike, decked out in his white surplis and colorful stole, took hold of the microphone and stepped toward the assembled kids. Everyone blessed themselves, a gesture Arthur had never adopted, but did so now out of respect.

"We have a very special guest today," Father Mike began, and gestured for Arthur to approach.

The king joined him up in front, and smiled warmly at the assembled kids.

"I'm sure all of you recognize King Arthur and know of his accomplishments toward bettering your lives. I'm also sure you know that his son, Sir Lance, The Boy Who Came Back, is currently housed in the compound, charged with a very serious crime. Today, Lance is going to be baptized, and both he and his father will sign the Book of Life. King Arthur would like to say a few words of encouragement to all of you,"

Father Mike handed the microphone to Arthur. The king bowed respectfully and turned to the wide-eyed kids.

"I can see many of you are my son's age, and it saddens me to see you here. My son is innocent and we intend to prove that. But, the system wants him to have a trial. Given a choice, I would have any of you youngsters as jurors for my son before I would trust the job to most adults. I'm an adult and I know of what I speak."

The kids laughed and applauded.

"Our proposition will give you all real rights that are now only given to grown-ups, like the right to sit on a jury for someone like Lance. My son is an amazing boy, as my other son, Ricky, is so fond of saying, but any one of you can be just as amazing. New Camelot is open to you all, if it is your desire to join. There are no requirements other than to use your might for right. My son is the greatest warrior of right I know, and today, thanks to Father Mike, he shall become a warrior of light. I ask your prayers for him and for me and for our cause. Thank you for welcoming me this day."

He handed the microphone back to Father Mike as the kids broke into applause, and one boy up front threw his hand into the air. Father Mike pointed to him.

The boy looked at Arthur and asked, "How do we join up, King Arthur? I wanna be a knight too."

Arthur stepped forward and stood in front of the boy. "Your name?"

"Raul Ramos, sir," the boy answered, bowing his head respectfully.

Arthur reached into his pocket and slipped out a business card, handing it to the boy.

"Call me when you get out, Raul, and you shall be welcomed with open arms."

The boy beamed with amazement and grasped the business card reverently. More hands shot up and Arthur turned to Father Mike, eyebrows raised.

The priest said into the mic, "If you would like one of King Arthur's business cards, he'll be passing them out after mass."

That calmed the kids, and Arthur smiled at them before retaking his seat along the side. Ryan gave him a head nod as he sat. The rest of the service proceeded smoothly, and Arthur was impressed by Father Mike's deft way at handling these kids and relating the scriptures to their daily lives. He and Pastor Tom needed to meet one day, the king decided.

After mass, Arthur stood first at one door and then at the other, shaking hands with every kid and giving out his card to any who asked for it. Father Mike told him afterwards that, as a rule, staff take the kids out from both doors at the same time, but that today they wanted all the minors to meet Arthur. The king felt truly honored and said so, shaking hands with the staff, as well.

When they entered unit W-2, Lance stood right by his door, gazing out the little square window. Father Mike's smiling face appeared first, and then there was his dad, rock solid and strong and looking exultant. Lance felt warm inside and grinned like a fool.

Father Mike unlocked the door, and Lance rushed out to hug Arthur as though he hadn't seen him in weeks. Then he glanced shyly at Ryan and extended a hand. The detective shook it warmly.

Father Mike grinned. "You ready, *mijo?*"

Lance nodded eagerly and followed the three men through the control room and into the hallway where the service was always held. The usual volunteers were present, and everything looked set up and ready. Lance spotted the bowl of water on the altar and grinned. This time it was for him.

He sat up front, Arthur on his right and Ryan on his left, and chatted until the other kids entered and sat down. Most had seen Arthur at visiting, but none had really talked with him, other than to say hello and shake his hand. A few recognized Ryan as a cop and they eyed him warily. Once again, Father Mike asked Lance to read the gospel, and volunteers from among the kids did the other readings.

When it was time for the baptism, Lance took his place behind the bowl of water, with Arthur on one side and Ryan on the other. Father Mike instructed each man to place a hand on the boy's shoulder. Then he addressed Lance thus, "What is it you seek of God's church today?"

"Baptism," Lance said, taking a nervous breath.

Father Mike went through the litany of questions in which Lance professed his faith by answering, "I do" to each one. After this, the priest marked the top of Lance's head with chrism oil and asked him if he was ready.

"I am," Lance announced, feeling a strong sensation of peace well up within him. Father Mike nodded and indicated the bowl. Lance dipped his head over the water, his long brown hair spilling out and around his face, draping the outsides of the bowl and splaying out on the altar beneath.

Father Mike dipped the seashell and said, "Lance, I baptize you in the name of the Father," and poured the water over Lance's head before dipping in for more, "the Son," another pour and dip, "and the Holy Spirit." Another dip, the biggest one yet, and Lance's head and hair were doused.

Arthur and Ryan glanced at one another, and both men smiled.

Lance lifted his head, water dripping through his long hair, down his face, and onto the front of his gray shirt. He grinned, feeling a sudden overpowering sensation that everything was going to turn out well for him.

Arthur handed him the towel, and Lance dabbed at the water, not wanting to wipe it all off because it was holy water, and had made him holy by its spilling.

"*Fuerte applauso*," Father Mike told the kids, and they clapped loudly and with gusto. Lance was well liked, almost revered, just as he had been on the outs.

He hugged Arthur. Then he turned to Ryan and grinned shyly. "Can I get a hug from my *padrino?*"

Ryan pulled a questioning face, and Lance laughed. "That means godfather in Spanish."

Ryan nodded, but still looked uncertain, as though no one had ever asked him for a hug before.

"Well, *nino?*" Lance asked, his arms opened wide.

A big grin breached Ryan's face, and he hugged the boy who everyone knew had transformed his life in so many ways. "Congratulations, Godson," he said sincerely. When they separated, he winked. "Don't tell Gib we hugged or I'll never live it down."

Lance laughed. "No problem, *nino.*"

Ryan laughed too.

Father Mike continued the service until it was time for the Eucharist. At this point, Lance made his first holy communion and took the host into his mouth. It was dry and tasted like cardboard, but he knew the spirit of Christ was within and that filled him with joy.

After everyone else had received communion, it was time for Lance to be confirmed. Father Mike rubbed oil on his forehead and said, "Receive the Holy Spirit and be a powerful warrior of light."

Again, Lance felt an inner peace unlike any he'd ever known.

He was going to be fine. He knew that now.

The last part of the ceremony required Lance and Arthur to sign the Book of Life, which they both did. As godfather, Ryan was asked to sign too, and he did, happily. Father Mike held up the book, open to the page where they had signed, and nodded his head toward Lance.

"I give you Sir Lance, our newest warrior of light," and the kids burst into applause yet again.

One of the volunteers had taken photos with Father Mike's camera during the ceremony. When the mass concluded, several more were snapped of Arthur and Lance, and one of Arthur, Lance, Ryan and Father Mike. Then Arthur, Ryan and

Lance chatted with all the kids until the senior, Mr. Mansfield, said they had to return to the dayroom.

Lance was allowed to visit for a while with his dad and Ryan in the hallway. Father Mike bade them goodbye, shook their hands, grinned at Lance, and wandered out into the dayroom.

Lance looked at these two men, once adversaries, now best friends, now dads to him, and he couldn't help but smile.

"You look happy, son," Arthur told him.

"I am, Dad," Lance said. "When that water poured over my head, I felt deep inside that everything was gonna be okay, and I still do. Father Mike was right. God *will* take care of me."

"Glad to hear that, Godson," said Ryan, "because I don't know the first thing about being a godfather."

"Yes, you do, *nino*," Lance said quietly. "You already take care of me. You protect me. You're there when I need you. You've been my godfather all along. We just didn't know it."

Lance was shocked to see Ryan get choked up a moment, as if those words were the kindest he'd ever heard.

"Thanks, Lance," he finally said after a halting pause. "Appreciate that."

The three chatted, laughed, and joked around until Mr. Mansfield told the men it was time to leave because he had to get the kids ready for outside rec. Promising to be back for regular visiting, Arthur embraced Lance, long and lovingly.

When they separated and Lance turned to Ryan, the normally taciturn man didn't need an invite this time. He opened his arms and Lance hugged him tightly.

He accompanied the men into the dayroom because his room was near the exit. Just as a staff let them out, Lance said, "Dad."

Arthur turned, eyebrows raised questioningly.

Lance suddenly seemed shy and uncertain. "Tell Ricky I–" He paused, and expelled a nervous breath. "I love *him* more than anyone else. Okay?"

Arthur smiled. "Okay."

Then they were gone and Lance returned to his room to wait for lunch. He felt better than he had in the longest, and gazed out his window with peace in his heart. The future would be good. How, he didn't know. He just knew that it would. And that was enough for now.

When Arthur and Ryan returned to New Camelot late that afternoon, after Arthur's regular visit with Lance, everyone gathered around them to hear about the baptism and see the photos Father Mike had given him.

Jenny and Reyna almost cried upon seeing the shots of Lance having the water poured over him, especially the one of him standing just after, water droplets clinging to his hair and dripping onto his face. The look of extreme peace and joy on his features and in those bright green eyes touched them deeply.

"Wow," Reyna exclaimed. "He looks even more beautiful, doesn't he?"

Jenny nodded. "Yes, he does."

Ricky hovered around while everyone looked at the pictures, but made no effort to look for himself. He seemed distant and withdrawn. Arthur finally took the photos from Chris as everyone began dispersing, and approached him.

"Do you not wish to see these photos of Lance?" he asked cautiously.

Afraid to actually speak, Ricky nodded and accepted the photos. His breath caught in his throat upon seeing the one of Lance smiling at the camera, newly baptized, water droplets spilling around him. Reyna was right, Ricky thought – he *does* look more beautiful.

"I wish I could of been there, Dad."

Arthur wrapped an arm around his shoulders. "So do I, son."

Ricky didn't look up at his father. His emotions were too unsteady at the moment, too volatile.

"Can you keep these in Lance's room for me?" Arthur asked, indicating the photos. "We'll have copies made later."

Ricky nodded, still gazing down at Lance's angelic face. He felt Arthur's arm leave his shoulders and heard the man's steps walking away. Then they stopped.

"Ricky?"

Ricky lifted his head to look at his father uncertainly.

"Lance sent you a message," Arthur began, watching him carefully.

Ricky's eyebrows shot up questioningly.

"He said he loves *you* more than anyone else."

Ricky sucked in a breath.

His father smiled and retreated up the stairs, leaving an emotionally unsteady Ricky lowering his eyes once again to the face in the photo. His heart beat erratically and his breathing nearly stopped. The beautiful face of the most incredible boy Ricky had ever known smiled up at him with joy, and he felt some of that joy seep into his aching heart.

Throughout the week following his baptism, Lance found his mind drifting in odd directions. He kept going back to Father Mike's talks about forgiveness and how that might relate to him, and Richard, and Mr. D. Both men were evil, he knew, and his forgiving them wouldn't change that. But fixing the other person wasn't what forgiveness was about, according to Father Mike. Forgiveness was about fixing yourself.

He also found his mind returning again and again to Michael. He kept seeing Michael in that courtroom and wondering why he had suddenly reappeared in his life after so long. Could it be that maybe Michael had forgiven him for saying, "Drop dead" that last time they were together? Somehow, he didn't think Michael was the forgiving type and yet, he'd always had the sense of something deep within Michael that still made him human.

An intense desire to hear Michael's voice built up within Lance during that first week of September, and he couldn't shake it. One Thursday before dinner, he asked the staff if he could use the brown phone in the office to call a friend, because his friend couldn't take collect calls.

Since Lance was very popular with all the staff, the man, whose name was Lindsey, agreed immediately. He led Lance into the office and explained to the senior, Mr. Taylor, what Lance needed. The short, stocky man waved Lance over to his left, where the phone sat down low at the base of the console.

Lance thanked him and sat cross-legged on the floor by the phone, his face turned away from Taylor, who was busy doing paperwork. Lance nervously punched in Michael's cell number from memory. His heart pounded as the phone rang once. Twice. Three times.

His hopes sank until on the fourth ring he suddenly heard, "Yeah?"

"Hey, Michael," he whispered, unable to get much sound out for fear of choking on his words.

There was a long pause at the other end. "Lance. The hell do you want?"

Lance almost hung up. "Just wanted to say hi." He knew it sounded lame. What *did* he want anyway? What did he expect?

"Hi," came the curt reply. "We done now?"

Lance was afraid Michael would hang up so he said, "I saw you in court."

There was a pause. "Yeah. Got bored that day," came the dispassionate reply. "Thought it might be fun."

That hurt, but Lance forced himself not to let it show. "It wasn't fun, Michael. I gotta go to trial."

"Yeah. Bummer."

This was a mistake, Lance told himself. *Ricky was right all along.* But his heart wouldn't let him hang up. He tried another tack. "I got baptized on Sunday."

A derisive laugh. "As though you needed that."

Lance sighed heavily, and then said it. "I miss you, Michael."

That scornful laugh came again. "Last time I saw you, Lance, you told me to drop dead."

"I was mad, Michael. I didn't mean it."

There was silence on the other end.

"I really do miss you, Michael," he said again. "You know how I—"

"Don't go there again, Lance," Michael's voice said sharply, cutting him off.

Lance opened his mouth to argue, but closed it. As always, where Michael was concerned, his conflicted feelings refused to become clear.

"Any progress on your case? That D.A. has nothing."

"I know, but he's trying to turn everyone against me, make me into some kind of monster before the election."

Another pause. "You're not the monster, Lance."

Lance forced himself to breathe. "You aren't either, Michael."

There was a very long pause and Lance feared the other boy had hung up. Then he heard, "What happened after you left me that night?"

Lance stiffened. "Nothing, Michael, I went straight home. I didn't do this."

A chuckle. "Of course you didn't. Anybody who thinks so is an idiot."

Lance smiled, despite his nervousness.

"What I meant was, tell me everything that happened after you left me."

Lance frowned. "Nothing. I skated home."

"Did anybody see you?"

Lance considered. "No, nobody."

"Did you see any cars along the way?" Michael asked. "Did anybody wave at you or anything?"

"Some jerkbag ran a red and almost took me out," Lance said, recalling the guy on Hollywood Boulevard, "but I skated around him."

Lance was certain he heard a slight intake of breath from the other end. "Where?"

"Where, what?"

Impatience now. "Where were you when the guy ran the red?"

Lance thought back a moment. "I was crossing Hollywood around Schrader. No wait, it was Cherokee. Now I remember. I was in the middle of the street and he just shot through the red. I spun on my board and just missed him."

There was silence. Was Michael still there?

"Michael? Did you hear me?" He could almost see Michael's strong, handsome face with that indecipherable look on it.

"Yeah, I heard."

"Why does it matter?"

"Just conversating," came Michael's disinterested voice. The intensity of a moment before was gone. "So tell me, Lance, that dude in court who said you threatened him. What's his story?"

Lance recounted his and Jack's encounter with Mr. D. and how, according to Jack, the guy was a regular down on Santa Monica Boulevard. "Hopefully, my attorney's investigators can get something on him."

Michael snorted on the other end. "Scumbags like that who rape boys like Jack or you are too smart to leave tracks."

The tone of his voice had turned angry, and Lance suspected Michael was recalling his own rape, and his parents' indifference to it. He needed to change the subject before he ran out of time, because he desperately wanted to know something.

Expelling a deep breath, heart thudding even more loudly, Lance practically whispered into the phone, "Michael?"

"Yeah?"

"Do you miss me?"

He heard a breathy sound, but nothing more. He waited, but could only just detect Michael's breathing on the other end.

Then the line went dead.

Emotion twisting his insides into knots, Lance knew his face must be flushed. He slowly hung up the phone and sat a moment to compose himself.

He heard from behind him, "Everything okay, Lance?"

Without turning, he nodded. "Yeah, Mr. Taylor. Thanks for letting me use the phone."

He rose, his heart more heavy with sadness than it had been all week, and returned to the solitude of his room. Michael's rejection of him hurt more than he knew it should. Why did he allow it to?

He pondered his conflicted feelings for Michael until staff called him out for dinner. Then he put on his game face and pretended everything was good, because that's what you had to do.

With Lance's preliminary hearing the top news story all over the country, and especially with the media outlets running snippets of audio from that cell phone video, the boy's popularity with the always fickle public plummeted. According to Sir Techie, who kept tabs on the numbers, Lance's rating had dropped to forty percent favorable, fifty percent unfavorable, and ten percent undecided.

These numbers disturbed Ricky, and he wanted to go on TV and scream at the top of his lungs that Lance was innocent. But he knew that wouldn't work. Only he had ever seen Lance have those meltdowns whenever he flashed back to his childhood trauma, and no one who didn't already believe in Lance would believe him anyway.

The cable networks seemed to cover the story differently, everyone at New Camelot had noticed. CNN seemed more supportive of Lance. FOX and MSNBC, not so much. In fact, Lance was often the butt of jokes on MSNBC, and from comedians on TV, in nightclubs, and on YouTube. Ricky refused to even watch this stuff because it made his blood boil.

He still hardly slept at night, and nodded off daily during school lessons. Jenny understood, as did the other teachers, and no one gave him a hard time about it. The now-impending trial had everyone on edge, especially with the increase in negative media coverage. Their proposition seemed to be gaining more support amongst the populace, but not for the reasons Lance and the others intended.

It wasn't gaining in the polls because the people of California believed children had been abused for too long and needed more rights, but rather because there were too many 'latent monsters' like Lance out there and the public wanted them tried as adults and imprisoned. Another of those unintended consequences Michael had pointed out, Ricky realized, hating to agree with Michael on anything, but reluctantly accepting the truth of the older boy's words.

Lance got his weekly phone call on Friday night, and Reyna filled him in on some of the media drama, but no one shared how far he'd dropped in the public opinion polls. Once left alone with Ricky, Lance once again felt nervous, and guilty for thinking about Michael this week.

"You hanging in there?"

"Yeah, I guess," Ricky replied, his chest tight with uncertainty, his emotions all over the map. "I just can't believe how anybody could think you..."

He heard a deep sigh from the other end. "That's the way people are, Ricky." Lance tried to sound like it didn't matter, even though both boys knew it did.

"Have you talked to your lawyer this week?"

He heard a long pause with just breathing, and then a sigh. "No. Has Dad?"

"No."

There was silence between them.

Then Ricky said quietly, "Dad told me what you said."

A short exhalation came through the speaker. "Yeah."

Ricky hesitated, all tremulous lips and thudding heart. "I, uh... I love you, too, Lance, more than anyone else."

Ricky heard a sound, a reaction, from the other side, something like a gasp, but not that strong. More like what a smile would sound like if it made a noise. "You okay, Lance?" he asked, fearful he'd said too much.

He heard a deep sigh, as of relief. "Yeah, I'm good. I'm real good now."

Ricky didn't know what to say. His emotions cut off his tongue, conflicted his thoughts, even as they warmed his heart.

"I need you back here, Lance," Ricky blurted before he could stop himself. And then to cover his embarrassment added, "Este's too big for me and I need some ass to kick."

He heard a laugh from the other side. "You mean you need someone to kick *your* ass? Cause I'm your man."

Ricky grinned, and both boys chuckled, their emotionalism of a moment before swept away.

"I been working out like a madman, Lance," Ricky assured him, the old confidence back in his voice. "You won't even be able to beat me at arm wrestling anymore."

He heard delighted laughter. "Yeah, fool, well I been doin' plenty of arm wrestling in here, and I can still take you. Just wait till I get out. You're goin' down!"

Ricky laughed, and heard Lance's accompanying laughter from the speaker.

The call was about to end, so Ricky said, "Those pix of your baptism were dope, man. Wish I could of been there."

"Me too."

Ricky grinned devilishly, even though he knew Lance couldn't see him. "I'd have shoved your whole head into that bowl."

Laughter filled the lobby. "I bet you would have." A pause. "Hang in there, Ricky."

"You too, Lance."

And then the line went dead.

The weekend passed normally, with Arthur visiting both days and Lance attending church services on Sunday. This time the volunteers did the service because Father Mike was in Unit Z. But the priest dropped by during visiting to check on Lance and greet Arthur. Lance was happy that these two men, who were so important to him, liked one another and had so much in common, especially their views on social justice.

Arthur had not heard from Ryerson, so he did not know if the investigation had turned up anything as regards Mr. D. He promised to phone the attorney on Monday and ask.

It was now going into the second week of September, with Lance's jury selection looming in little more than a month, but neither of them wished to even speak of that right now.

Lance knew he was likely to be found guilty. Since his arrival, almost every kid in there who'd gone to trial had been washed up with sentences of fifty or sixty years in state prison. One boy got fifty years to life for being drunk and passed out in the back seat of a car while his homies shot somebody from the front.

Those who didn't lose in trial were forced by their public defenders to take deals of thirty-five years and two strikes, or twenty-five to life and one strike. One kid was even offered a deal of ninety years!

Do they think we're vampires or something? Lance kept wondering.

Nobody but Hector had gotten a second chance at fixing himself and having a real life. Nobody. Despite the momentary uplift of his baptism, these statistics dampened his spirits, and Lance held little hope that he would prevail, either.

But then, on Monday morning, everything changed.

CHAPTER NINE
AM I GOING TO PRISON ALREADY?

ONDAY STARTED OUT NORMALLY FOR Lance. Head and water calls. Breakfast. The wait in his room until school. The short march to the caged-in classrooms. But around ten a.m., a probation staff named Solano appeared in Lance's class and called him out of the room. Lance stiffened with dread, and Joey looked at him with concern, flipping him a head nod as he rose and crossed the room toward the waiting Solano. Even the burly kid who'd called him a faggot flipped him the head nod of support, and then Lance was out of the room and following Mr. Solano back toward the living units.

"What's wrong?" he asked, unable to mask the apprehension in his voice.

But Solano kept walking. "I was just told to come get you and bring you back to the unit, Lance. That's all."

Lance didn't respond and followed him through several locked gates and back down the sloped walkway to Unit W. Upon entering, the senior, Mr. Mansfield, ushered him forward, while Solano headed back up to the school.

Fearing the worst, Lance followed Mansfield into the office. The big man turned and looked down at him, who suddenly felt small and helpless and doomed.

"Looks like you'll be leaving us today, Lance."

Lance gasped. "Am I going to prison already?"

Mansfield looked startled a second. Then he smiled. "Looks like you'll be going home."

Lance's head swam with shock. "What?" Had he heard right?

Mansfield looked around as though fearing somebody might be eavesdropping. "I'm not supposed to be telling you this, but come here."

He led Lance over to where a real TV monitor was embedded within the workings of the console. All the other monitors displayed areas within the unit to keep tabs on the kids. The TV sound was down, but Lance could see District Attorney Dooley in front of some kind of formal looking podium, with Sergeant Gibson standing behind him.

What the hell…? Lance thought, and then Mansfield turned up the volume.

"Let me repeat," Dooley was saying in obvious answer to a question, "we do not yet know how this image came to be sent to Sergeant Ryan's computer. Someone hacked into the city mainframe and sent it, but left a very convoluted digital trail to cover his tracks. The photo, itself, as I said, is a red light camera photo taken on the night of July thirtieth at twelve thirty a.m."

He held up the blow-up of a picture, and the camera cut to a close up. Lance's breath stopped. The photo showed the front of a car, license plate partially covered by a kid on a skateboard.

A kid with long hair.

Dooley's voice continued behind the image. "As you can clearly see, the offending car very nearly ran over this boy on his skateboard." Image zoomed in even more. "And as you also can clearly make out, the boy is Lance Pendragon."

Lance's mouth dropped open in stunned shock.

The image vanished from screen as the unseen reporters murmured and threw out questions.

"Let me finish, please, and then I'll answer whatever questions I can," Dooley said, clearly irritated and very uncomfortable having to reveal to the world that he was dead wrong. "The time stamp on the photograph places Mr. Pendragon at the intersection of Hollywood and Cherokee at exactly twelve-thirty a.m., the time estimated by our medical examiner that the attack on Mr. Thornton occurred many blocks distant from that location."

He paused and gazed out at the crowd. Eating crow did not suit him, and he looked as though he'd prefer to be in front of a firing squad.

"In addition to this new evidence, there have been rampant rumors all morning that another attack has occurred, same M.O. as Mr. Thornton. I'm here to confirm the accuracy of those rumors. At approximately two thirty this morning, a man was attacked in West Hollywood and mutilated in the same manner as Mr. Thornton. Again, 911 was called, it appears, ahead of the actual attack to make certain the victim would survive." He sighed heavily, looking like he did not want to utter his next words. "In light of this new crime, and the red light camera photo, this office is in the formal process of dropping all charges against Mr. Pendragon. Once the paperwork goes through, he shall be released from Barney J. Nelson Juvenile Hall sometime today."

He paused another moment to collect himself. Gone was the smugness, gone was the arrogance.

Lance stood rooted to the spot, stunned with disbelief. Was this happening? Was he really going home?

Mansfield eyed him, as though fearful he might faint. "You okay, Lance?"

He nodded, but placed both hands firmly on the console to steady himself, just in case.

On the TV, Dooley cleared his throat. "It would seem this office was perhaps overzealous in its pursuit of justice, and we wish to extend our apologies to Mr. Pendragon and his family. While it is true that we could still charge the boy with making a terrorist threat to commit great bodily harm, based solely upon that video, we have decided he has learned his lesson on that score and have dropped those charges, as well. Now, your questions."

Mansfield switched off the TV. "Arrogant prick," he whispered before turning back to Lance. "Need to sit, Lance?"

Lance nodded, his emotions churning and twisting like a tornado. Mansfield rolled over his chair and eased Lance into it. Pale and still in shock, almost unable to process the reality of it, Lance looked up at him.

"I'm really going home?"

The big man grinned. "You're really going home."

Lance gripped the arms of the office chair hard, as though holding on to the reality of what he'd just heard before it could slip away. He began to cry. He cried for all the days he'd suffered. He cried for all the days his family had suffered with him. He cried tears of sorrow, and tears of joy. But mostly, he just cried because there were so many emotions fighting for control that crying was the only way to let them out.

Mansfield gave him tissue and let him cry, and then let him into the bathroom to wash his face and compose himself. When he re-entered the dayroom—eerily silent with everyone at school—Lance asked Mansfield what would happen now.

The man explained that the release paperwork would take hours, but that Lance should be out before nightfall.

Lance understandably didn't feel up to finishing school for the day, so Mansfield let him into his room and he lay on his concrete bunk for the last time.

And thought about Ricky.

Today, he'd see Ricky.

"Thank you, Lord," he whispered aloud. "I knew you'd take care of me. I'm sorry I doubted you the other day."

He was going home. He laughed, and then laughed some more.

Ryan had been in the Computer Lab at New Camelot checking his emails when the photo came through. At first he didn't understand what he was seeing or why anyone would send him a red light camera picture. But then the boy's hair caught his eye and he'd zoomed in. If ever his heart had skipped a beat, it was at that moment.

Everything happened rapidly after that. Ryan got on the phone with Gibson and quickly explained what he'd received and told his partner to "Get over here ASAP."

Then he found Arthur and showed him the picture. At first, the king didn't understand its significance, until Ryan laid out the timeline for him. Then Arthur hurried to Jenny's classroom to share the good news.

When Arthur explained what the photo meant for Lance, that their boy would be coming home, everyone in the classroom whooped for joy. Jenny grabbed him in a tight hug, and Darnell reached out to high-five Ricky.

But Ricky sat in shock-mode, unable to believe that his... that Lance would be coming home. He stared at Darnell a long moment, and then threw his fist into the air.

"Yes!" he shouted, and leapt to his feet. He high-fived Darnell and then ran to his parents, grabbing both in an intense hug of joyous relief.

It was decided that Jenny, Ricky and Reyna would prepare New Camelot for Lance's homecoming, while Arthur accompanied Ryan down to the district attorney's office for any needed paperwork the king might need to sign. From there, they would go to juvenile hall to retrieve Lance.

Ricky desperately wanted to go with the men, but Ryan nixed the idea on the grounds that they may have to physically enter the juvenile facility and minors were not allowed. Ricky understood, but felt crushed with disappointment.

By the time the other kids came back into W-2 for lunch, word had gotten around that Lance had been exonerated. Joey was so happy that Lance felt guilty, knowing his friend still faced murder charges and might never get out. The staff allowed the other minors to congratulate Lance even as they sat down to lunch, a clear violation of the "quiet during meals" rule. But this was an unprecedented moment – the most famous boy in the world was going home.

After lunch, Lance remained behind while the others returned to school. He gave Joey a man-hug, in case he was gone by the time the kids returned from school.

"You been an amazing friend, Joey," Lance gushed with complete sincerity. "I'm really gonna miss you, man."

Joey grinned, still confident he'd beat his case. It had clearly been self-defense, as he'd told Lance enough times, and he would walk. Eventually. "I'm joining up soon as I get out."

"You better, fool, or I'm comin' after you with my sword."

Joey laughed, and got into line to return to school.

Lance watched the boys queue up, and a lump caught in his throat. "Good luck, you guys," he told them, all watching him in silence. "I'll never forget you, and I'm not gonna let them out there forget you, either. I got your backs."

They grinned and the staff escorted them out of the unit.

Normally against the rules, Mansfield let Lance stay in the dayroom while he awaited word from Movement Control to bring Lance up front. Lance waited for an hour before anything happened, and even then it was only Father Mike who entered the unit. The presence of this deeply spiritual man calmed Lance's nerves, especially when the old priest flashed that impish grin.

"You were right, *mijo*," he said with that slight accent.

"No, Father Mike," Lance replied with a shake of his head. "You were. You told me God would take care of me and He did."

Father Mike nodded, and sat to await Lance's release. It finally came at just before two o'clock, when Mansfield got the call from up front to send Lance to Boys Admitting.

Lance turned to Mansfield and said, "Thanks, Mr. Mansfield, for taking good care of me." He reached out his hand, and the big man shook it gladly.

"I've never been so happy to see a kid go home, Sir Lance," he said, and clearly meant it.

Lance smiled. "Thank all the staff for me, 'kay?"

"You got it."

With Father Mike at his side, and no shackles or manacles binding his hands or feet, Lance left Unit W for the last time. One of the staff escorted him out of The Compound and down to Boys Admitting, back to where his incarceration begun.

As Lance looked around the facility, the red brick buildings surrounded by green sloping hills and interspersed with playing fields, he thought, not for the first time, how peaceful the place would be if it weren't a lock-up for kids.

Father Mike accompanied him into Boy's Admitting where Mr. Brown happily waited with Lance's original clothes. He handed the clothes to Lance.

Lance flushed with embarrassment. "I gotta change here, in front of Father Mike?"

The two men laughed.

"No," Brown told him. "This time you can use the bathroom." He pointed to a door across the hall.

Lance sighed with relief and hurried through the indicated door to change. Once back in his own clothes, Lance emerged carrying the county clothes and handed them to Brown, who tossed them into a laundry cart.

Brown grinned at him. "So, the boy who came back is now the boy who went home."

Lance and Father Mike laughed. They had to wait around with Brown for another hour before the paperwork was complete, but Lance and Father Mike chatted easily as though they'd known each other for years. Finally, another probation staff stepped into the office.

"Lance," she said, "Your father and godfather are outside. You ready?"

Lance looked at her like she was crazy. "I was ready six weeks ago."

He eagerly followed the staff and Father Mike down a long, fenced-in corridor leading to a glass door. There was a buzzing sound and the staff pulled open the door, ushering him through.

Lance stepped through the door. There was a glass-enclosed booth with a security guard stationed within, another closed glass door, a metal detector, and then the open door to freedom. Standing just outside were Arthur and Ryan.

Father Mike placed a hand on Lance's shoulder, and urged him forward. The security guard buzzed the door and Lance was through in a flash, bolting through the metal detector and right outside into his father's outstretched arms.

Father and son held each other a long moment, no words passing between them because none were needed. They were together again, and that said it all.

Father Mike shook Ryan's hand. "Reverend," the priest joked.

Ryan did something he seldom did – he grinned with joy as he shook Father Mike's hand.

Arthur finally released his son and turned to the chaplain. "Thank you, Father Mike, for all you have given my son. You, sir, are a gift from God."

The priest chuckled. "Sometimes the staff think I'm from the other guy."

Arthur extended a hand, and they shook. The old priest looked at Lance, and Lance at him. There was a moment of silence between them, and then Lance broke away from Arthur and hugged the priest, again without a word spoken.

Father Mike just held him and let the moment be.

When Lance pulled away, he had to brush a tear from his eye. "You'll come visit me, won't you?" he asked, desperate not to be seeing the last of this remarkable man.

Father Mike's eyes twinkled and that impish grin returned. "I never turn down free food, Lance."

All of them laughed. Then Father Mike watched Arthur and Ryan, with the boy between them, pass out of his view around the corner of the building and into the parking lot.

The ride back to New Camelot seemed to take forever in the late afternoon traffic and Lance was near to bursting with anticipation. He sat in back and watched everything pass by with newly formed eyes, as though he'd never seen any of it before.

Ryan told Arthur and Lance about the attack on Mr. D., which shocked Lance because Dooley hadn't identified him during the press conference.

"The attacker," Ryan said, "left a note attached to the victim explaining the man's penchant for picking up boys in West Hollywood for sex."

Lance was stunned. "Do they know who did it?"

Ryan shook his head. "Just from what you told me, Lance, it could've been any of the boys this guy preyed on. The only thing that made it different from—" He stopped suddenly and Lance could see him gazing back at him through the rearview. "You okay hearing about this, Lance?"

"Yeah. It's okay."

"What was different, Sergeant?" Arthur asked.

"This time the attacker wore a Halloween mask so he didn't have to blindfold the guy," Ryan answered.

Halloween.

That triggered something in Lance's memory. "Uh, what kind of mask, *nino?*"

"That Scream face," Ryan answered matter-of-factly.

Lance gasped, and Arthur turned quickly. "Is something wrong, son?"

Lance remembered something now, something that might be important. He paused, catching Ryan's intense gaze focused on him in the rearview. "No, nothing. Those movies just scared me when I's a kid."

He lowered his gaze to the floor and quickly looked out the window, so his father or godfather wouldn't see the lie plainly written across his face.

As Lance bolted excitedly through the front doors of New Camelot, Arthur and Ryan on his heels, he was sure someone would be there waiting. But the lobby was empty. He turned to Arthur in surprise. Grinning, the man pointed down the hall to the closed Throne Room doors, and Lance rushed to them, throwing them open to a thunderous, "Welcome home!"

The room was packed, Arthur's knights having come from all over the city to welcome Lance home. Jenny started forward, but Bridget beat her to it. She ran to Lance and threw her arms around him, almost knocking him backward. She didn't even give him a chance to react, she just planted her lips on his and kissed him.

Shocked and startled, Lance awkwardly kissed her back. His eyes caught something behind her.

Sensing something wrong, Bridget pulled back. "Sorry, Lance, but I missed you so much!".

"Missed you too, Bridg." But his gaze remained focused over her shoulder.

Frowning, she turned and looked.

Ricky stood there, Ariel at one side, Jenny at his other.

Bridget blushed. "Sorry, Lance. Just got carried away."

Lance nodded absently. "It's okay." But his eyes remained fixed on those of Ricky and he stepped around Bridget.

Everyone fell silent.

Lance stopped before Ricky, suddenly feeling little-boy shy and awkward.

Ricky lifted his chin a notch. "Hey," he said.

"Hey, yourself," Lance said right back, never breaking eye contact.

"You grew a little."

"You didn't."

"Still the same old dumb ass."

"Yep. Still the dumb ass who can whip your dumber ass any place, any time."

"You and what army?"

Lance broke into an enormous smile.

Ricky stepped forward, arms outstretched, and enveloped Lance in a genuine hug, which he greedily returned. They pressed together and Lance finally realized just how much of himself had been missing these past six weeks. At last, he was whole again, his soul mended, and he knew Ricky felt the same way.

At this point, Jenny rushed over to envelope him, and that perfect moment ended. Ricky had to take a step back as Lance was swamped. Chris grabbed him in a hug and it seemed he'd never let go. He handed Lance a drawing he'd been working on. It was a crude, childish rendering of The Ivory Tower atop of which Chris had written 'My Big Brother'. Lance gushed over his effort and grabbed him in another hug of joy.

Somewhere in the crowd and celebration, Lance lost Ricky, and felt empty once more, his eyes constantly roaming for a glimpse of his other half. Every time he did, Ricky's gaze instantly went to his, as though a sixth sense told him Lance was looking.

Of course, Reyna had to give Lance the once over, and after doing so proclaimed him thinner, but "Still younger and prettier than me," to which everyone laughed.

Bridget clung to Lance's hand the entire evening, as though afraid if she let go she'd lose him again. Lance was so happy to be home he couldn't even begin to express his feelings to her or anyone else.

He knew Ricky understood – he'd sensed that when they hugged. Ricky understood everything.

There was food and cake and talking and laughter and dancing. Of course, Reyna dragged Lance into "The Cha Cha Slide" and then a bunch of the kids melted into other crazy dances, which made Lance laugh at their outrageous movements and convulsive gestures.

Finally, Reyna hauled Lance up onto the platform in front of Arthur's throne and yelled, "Speech! Speech!" until the crowd quieted down.

Lance looked out at the sea of faces. His family. His huge, extended, wonderfully diverse family. God, how he'd missed them! Deep emotions clogged his throat and nearly suffocated him.

Fighting back that all-to-familiar burning in his eyes, Lance shifted in place. "I've never seen anything so amazing in my life."

Everyone burst into applause and cheers and hoots.

"Thank you for all your prayers and hopes for me, and for carrying on the campaign without me. One of the guys told me I got put in that place for a reason, so I could understand how important this fight really is. And I think he was right. We got six weeks until the election and we need to make it count. Those kids I was with in Sylmar are no different than me or you, except most of 'em will go to prison for a long time. We need to win this election, for me, for you, and for them. You have no idea how happy I am to be home, but first thing tomorrow, I'm gettin' to work and I hope you will too. We're gonna win this thing and we're gonna win big!"

The room erupted with cheers, applause, and foot stomping.

Lance smiled broadly out at them. He was home. He was in charge. He was loved. He caught Ricky's eye and grinned, because most important of all, he was back with Ricky.

Before leaving, Bridget expressed the hope that she and Lance could have some time together, maybe go out to dinner or something.

Lance saw the hope on her face, but he had to shrug weakly and say, "My goddad's not letting me out of his sight, Bridget, until after the election. He still thinks I'll be a target. 'Sides, I got so much work to do between now and election day."

He saw disappointment flit across her eyes, and placed both hands on her shoulders. He leaned in for a quick kiss, pulling away before she could make it deeper.

Lance didn't notice her frown of disappointment because his gaze was fixed on Ricky gently kissing Ariel goodnight. His face burned hot at the sight, though he knew it shouldn't. When Ricky pulled back from Ariel and saw Lance watching, his face reddened too.

Once everyone had returned home or picked a room to stay in for the night, it was finally Arthur, Jenny, Lance, Ricky and Chris seated in the Throne Room. They sat and looked at one another, as though the family members were afraid to let each other out of their sight.

"We are a family once more," Arthur finally said, and Jenny squeezed his hand, looking over at the three boys lovingly.

"You have no idea, Lance, how empty this house felt without you in it," she said with a sigh.

"Ricky's been reading me Neverending Story, Lance," Chris said.

Lance feigned surprise. "Funny. I didn't know Ricky could read."

Chris chortled with laugher and Ricky threw a cushion at Lance, who ducked and laughed.

A comfortable silence settled over them again.

Finally, Arthur spoke. "You know, Lance, you must speak to the media tomorrow about your exoneration and the pending election. Lady Helen told me the press conference will be at noon."

Lance knew he should be tired of all these press conferences by now, but after what he'd learned tonight from Techie, he relished this one like no other.

"I got it, Dad. No worries."

Chris piped up with, "Ricky did that stuff while you were gone, Lance."

Lance smiled at Chris, but smirked at Ricky. "Didn't know Ricky could string two sentences together, either."

This time Ricky charged him, and the two boys rolled around on the floor, each trying to gain an advantage, laughing like little kids. After a few moments, Chris leapt atop them and tried to pin them both. The three boys dissolved into laughter, panting and splaying outward on the floor side-by-side.

Jenny pronounced, "Bed time."

The boys groaned as Arthur stood and extended both hands. Lance grabbed one, Ricky grabbed on to the other, and Chris held on to Lance. Arthur heaved, and the three boys were laughingly pulled to their feet.

As Lance and Ricky undressed for bed, they shyly removed their shirts in front of each other. For Lance, being naked in front of strangers had been a daily occurrence. Now, in front of this boy with whom he was closest, he actually turned away as he tugged off the shirt and slipped under the covers. God, how amazing this bed felt after sleeping on a concrete slab for so long!

Ricky quickly snatched his own shirt up and over his head and slipped under the covers on the other side.

The two boys looked at one another across the enormous bed, each bathed in the light of his bedside table lamp.

"I haven't slept right since you left, Lance," Ricky admitted quietly.

"Me, either."

There was a long pause as they just looked at one another.

Finally, Ricky whispered, "I missed you."

Lance felt his heart pound. "I missed you too."

Suddenly feeling weak and exposed, both boys turned away from one another and doused their lights. There was so much unspoken between them that the room felt almost oppressively hot.

Lance's thoughts drifted back to the promise he'd made to Jack, and cursed himself for being so weak. Sometimes saying the things we've *not* been saying, Lance concluded once again, was the hardest thing in the world to do.

Despite their individual uncertainties, their joy at being together again won out, and both boys slept more soundly than they had for the past six weeks.

Lance awoke at six a.m. on the dot and his first thought was, "Why hasn't staff opened my door yet?" Then he remembered. He felt the soft bed beneath him, saw bits of early morning light peaking in through the heavy drapes, saw his beloved Ricky slumbering peacefully on the other side of the bed.

I'm home. I'm really home.

He took a moment to pray and give thanks for all his blessings, especially family and freedom. Then he simply lay there, unable to go back to sleep from all the thoughts and feelings coursing through him, but relishing the comfort and security of his own bed, his own room, his own home.

He thought of Joey, Hector, Angel and his other friends from juvy, and a darkness pulled itself over his heart. He had to help them. He had to! What they were going through was simply wrong. They had to win this election so those kids would have at least have a jury of their peers.

But then he recalled the men on the county bus, and in the holding tank. They wore shackles too. He wondered what happened to the man he'd prayed for. The whole system was screwed up, he realized, whether you were a kid or an adult.

And then a thought hit him, one he'd had before, but dismissed because he'd already gone so far in this campaign – might it be better if *no* kid could be part of that system, at least at the adult level? If all could be treated as kids, like Hector when he'd been released from The Compound, rather than like violent animals as Lance and Angel had been?

But that would mean a 'No' vote on their prop. Only then would kids remain kids until the age of eighteen. He'd been so certain all along that giving kids the right to vote and help make the laws was best for them. But was it? Or might a win for their prop give adults even more excuses not to parent, not to mentor, not to give second chances?

He didn't know the answer, but he knew what his father always did when undecided on an issue, and so he did the same. He asked God for insight. Then he rose quietly so as not to wake Ricky and went into his bathroom by himself, and took the longest shower of his entire life. It felt liberating.

When Lance stepped out of his bathroom to get some clothes, his hair was a frizzled mop from towel drying, and he sported a big, soft towel wrapped tightly around his waist.

Ricky sat up in bed gazing at him with a huge grin on his face.

Lance stopped and looked down at himself like maybe the towel had fallen. When he looked back up, Ricky was still grinning.

"What?"

Ricky just laughed. "You, fool. It's really you."

Lance understood, and smiled "Yeah, it's really me."

"And you look like the skinniest-ass drowned rat I ever seen."

Lance laughed, but then mockingly flexed his right bicep. "Watch your mouth, fool, or this skinny-ass rat'll take your flabby ass down for the count."

Ricky grinned, and then both simultaneously said, "You and what army?" and burst into laughter.

Ricky drifted into his own room to get cleaned up while Lance dressed and blow-dried his hair, his mind on the looming election.

What would happen afterwards? What should be the next goal for their crusade? He considered all he'd seen and experienced in juvenile hall and adult court. It was all about rights, or lack of rights, wasn't it? What if kids, *as* kids, simply had more rights? Then he smiled. He had the perfect follow up to this campaign, and it would help kids all over the country, not just in California. And it would work whether this prop passed or not. He and Ricky would work on it, he decided, and share it later on when they had something real to show. He grinned in the mirror, congratulating himself on his best idea yet.

For now, he had the press conference at noon, and he needed to spend some time with Techie in the lab beforehand. He went to the connecting door and pushed it open.

Ricky was shirtless, his lengthening hair a rattrap of waves and frizzes, pulling on a pair of jeans. He stopped in mid-motion, startled.

"What?" Lance asked. "Can't handle this much hotness so early?"

Ricky chuckled and slipped the rest of the way into his pants. "If this world depended on you for hotness, we'd all freeze to death."

Lance laughed, and Ricky eyed him, serious now.

"I just forgot what it was like having you come in my room every day," he said apologetically. "Sorry." He genuinely looked embarrassed.

Lance waved the apology away. "No worries. I had to get used to naked dudes in the showers or running around the unit just in towels."

Ricky eyed him, still serious. "Was that like, you know, embarrassing?"

Lance shivered slightly. "Yeah. But I had to deal. Listen, I'm grabbing a quick breakfast and meeting Techie in the computer lab. Gotta see how much crap was put out about me 'fore the press conference."

"I'll be right down."

"Oh, and fix up that hair 'fore birds nest in it."

"You're really fixin' for a serious beat down, aren't you?"

"Bring it on," Lance challenged with a grin.

"You got it. This afternoon, after you cuss out all them reporters who stabbed you in the back."

Lance frowned, their playful banter forgotten. "Were there a lot of those?"

Ricky nodded soberly.

Lance sighed and left for the dining room.

Ricky joined him in the dining room about ten minutes later, his hair dry and dangling more than halfway down his back. They ate a quick breakfast of cereal and milk and then headed to the Computer Lab at eight to meet Techie.

Sadly, Ricky had not been joking about the number of media outlets that had turned their backs on him. Having been fully in his corner prior to the arrest, they apparently saw better ratings and more readership by jumping on the 'Is Sir Lance Really A Sadistic Monster?' bandwagon. Needless to say, Lady Helen had stood by him, as had a number of other news outlets.

The boys went through and printed out some of the nastier headlines, and Lance also looked up some of the kids he'd been locked up with, to see press coverage of them, positive or negative. Sadly, it was all negative.

Lance asked Techie to compile a database of positive news outlets and commentators versus negative, so he'd know who not to talk with from this point forward. He and Ricky then went to find Arthur, to discuss the press conference and what each of them would say to the media and the public at large.

CHAPTER TEN
NOW YOU HAVE YOUR ANSWER

Once again, to accommodate the media circus, and the sheer number of people who wanted to see and hear Lance, the Mayor provided the front of City Hall, his outdoor stage, and sound equipment, while Police Chief Murphy arranged security. A lot of security, especially since the perpetrator of the bomb attack on Arthur and his knights had never been apprehended.

As Ryan and Gibson had told the family, the bomb had been made of fertilizer and commonly acquired items, thus its place of origin would be very tricky to pin down. The FBI was still investigating, but had turned up nothing of substance. This fueled suspicion that the culprit was no mere rabble angry about the proposition, but rather someone powerful enough to cover his or her tracks.

Per custom, Helen had a front row seat, courtesy of Arthur and Lance. Arthur, Jenny, Lance, Ricky, and Chris were driven downtown by Ryan, with Gibson meeting them there. The crowd was so vast, police had to completely close Temple Street in front of City Hall and reroute the traffic. Gibson met Ryan's car when it pulled into a reserved spot, and the two detectives escorted the family through the crowd and up onto the dais.

The crowd cheered them as they passed through, and so did the reporters and media. Lance noted their actions with incredulity as he made his way up to the chairs behind the podium.

Mayor Soto, who had remained convinced of Lance's innocence throughout, warmly embraced him and each member of the family. He stepped to the podium and expressed his sincere pleasure that Sir Lance had been exonerated, "As I knew he would be." Then he invited Arthur forward. The crowd cheered wildly until Arthur held up a hand to quell them.

"My son is going to do the talking today," he began, "however I did wish to express my thanks to anyone here who believed in his innocence as I did. Your thoughts and prayers were greatly appreciated."

There was loud applause, mostly from the regular citizens. Arthur smiled, and then held out his hand toward Lance and Ricky. He stepped back and joined in the applause as the boys stepped to the podium. Ricky held in his hand a manila folder stuffed full with papers.

Lance looked out at the crowd. He saw Helen below, beaming up at him with genuine happiness. He grinned and waved. Finally, the crowd settled down and Lance leaned in to the microphone.

"Thank you all for coming out today, especially those of you who didn't give up on me."

There was loud applause from the people, and Lance had to wait for it to quiet down.

"As you all know," Lance went on, "we have an election in six weeks and there's been a whole lot of drama with our Prop 51. The question I been getting for months is, 'why do kids need more rights like adults have?' I didn't know the answer before as well as I do now." He took a deep breath. "Because I just spent the past six weeks in Hell."

There were audible gasps from the crowd.

"I was handcuffed, had my head shoved into a police car by a cop who thought I should go back to Mexico, a country I never even been to. In juvy, I got stripped to check for drugs and had to be shackled like an animal just to go from place to place. I had to shower butt naked in front of anyone who happened to be in the dayroom 'cause there was no privacy. I had to sit on the toilet and wipe my butt in front of the whole dayroom for the same reason. I got taken to court in shackles and manacles, and got beat down and kicked in the ribs 'cause I stood up for my friend that the sheriff guys were punching around. I went to court and had to listen to some guy you all elected call me a sadistic monster that should be put away for life. I had no rights at all. I couldn't even get baptized without my dad's permission. The only right I had was the right to go to prison. Does all this clue you in why our prop is so important? Maybe a little?"

He stopped to catch his breath, forcing his anger back down. Ricky stepped up and placed a hand on his shoulder. Lance tossed a grateful smile.

"When I told my dad about the cops and sheriff guys beating on me, he wanted me to tell their names to Chief Murphy, or the mayor or somebody. But I won't. You wanna know why? Cause them and their homeboys'll get payback, maybe not against me, but against my family and friends, against other kids on the street. The cops and the sheriffs are a gang same as any other. They back each other up. They cover up their crimes. But you wanna know why they're *worse* than any street gang out there? Cause they got the power to kick the crap outta us and you all gave 'em that power, and not enough of you give a rip that they abuse it."

He paused to glare out over the crowd, allowing that accusation to sink in a moment. The faces gaping up at him in shock only strengthened his resolve.

"So no, I'm not naming names. Those guys know who they are and their homies know who they are. The only ones who can fix it are them. Are all cops like that? Hell, no. My *padrino* and his partner are two of the best guys I know. But there's enough bad ones, and enough others who cover up for 'em."

He stopped again, gazing at the looks of sheer horror on everyone's face. They must've either thought he'd lost his mind in juvy, or they knew he spoke the truth.

"Which brings me to you media people out there." He chuckled wryly and shook his head. "How you all loved me and wanted interviews and loved taking my picture, and filming whatever I was doing, 'cause I got you ratings and readership and made you money. A few of you out there, Lady Helen being the best, didn't turn your backs on me when I got arrested. You actually believed I was innocent until proven guilty. But the rest?"

He cast a baleful glare down at the now-squirming reporters, his fierce green eyes boring into them.

"Now I know what it's like to swim in a tank full of hungry sharks. Let's see a few of the better headlines, huh?"

He turned to Ricky, who opened the folder and pulled out a computer printout of a Los Angeles Times front page and handed it to Lance. He held it up for any cameras that wanted to zoom in.

"Los Angeles Times. Picture of me from that video, holding out a knife, scared out of my freaking mind, but making an angry face. Love the headline – 'The Monster Within the Hero'. Not even a question mark. No, I'm a monster, period."

Ricky handed him another.

Lance held it up. Same picture, or close to it.

"Check out this headline – 'Sir Lance Cuts Up!' Wow, that's funny, isn't it? I have more."

Ricky handed him several printouts and Lance leafed through them one after another, reading the headlines with great dramatic flair.

"'The Boy Who Came Back Is Now The Boy Who Turned Bad', 'Victim of Brutal Sir Lance Attack Recovering', 'Will Sir Lance Look As Cute in Prison Blues?' and this one, oh, yeah, this one's a riot. Check it out - 'Sir Lance: *Well* Hung Out To

Dry?' with the 'well' in italics. Damn, that's funny, isn't it, mocking a kid in trouble like that?" He put them down and sighed disgustedly. "There's way too many to read. Here, you can have 'em back."

He took the folder from Ricky and all the sheets from within and started flinging them out in every direction, over the heads of the journalists. The scattered stories and images caught in the warm September breeze and wafted lazily around to settle listlessly at the feet of the silent, abashed crowd like giant snowflakes.

"I was guilty because you wanted me to be, because it was good for business," Lance went on soberly. "And you do it every day. Those kids I met in juvy, you do the same thing to them. They're dangerous, violent, sadistic monsters, they need to be put away forever. Too bad we don't have the death penalty for kids, right?"

He stopped again and gazed sadly out at everyone.

"And you have the guts to ask me why kids in this state need more rights? You journalists out there, you're supposed to be uncovering the truth, not covering it up 'cause it's easy and makes you money. I was famous, so trashing me was good for business. But kids every day are getting falsely arrested, beat up by cops, sent to prison for crimes they didn't commit, and you all let it happen. All of you out here today. And I mean you, the people, too."

He fixed his intense gaze onto the crowd of citizens behind the media, sweeping his fiery eyes over them angrily.

"You vote for the laws, you give guys like that district attorney the right to get re-elected by putting kids like me in prison. And then that guy has the nerve to say he won't charge me with making a terrorist threat against the man who raped me and used me as a sex slave for three years, the man who was stalking me and tapping into my phone and following me because he still wanted to do that crap to me!"

Ricky stepped up to Lance, resting against him, shoulder to shoulder, to help calm him.

"I was scared," Lance went on, almost breathlessly, "and damn straight I pulled a knife on his ass and I'd do it again! And you know what? So would every one of you, even mister high and mighty district attorney. It's *your* job, you media people, to balance the scales for kids like me, to show *our* side of the story, to show where we came from and how we got to the point of that action or crime. But no. You just wanna throw us away, too. A bunch of your editorials say we don't need this prop, that voting either way on it will be bad for California. Well, it might be bad for you who like to abuse your power, but it can only help us kids, no matter how the people vote."

He stopped a second, visibly shaking, catching his breath. Ricky placed one hand on his arm. The crowd awaited his next words in breathless shock.

"Oh, and one last thing. I'm not taking any questions today. You wanna talk with me, call my mom or my sister at New Camelot and we'll work something out. I'll be campaigning my butt off these next few weeks and I'm happy to talk to anyone who supported me when I was in jail. I have no time for any of you who stabbed me in the back. And trust me, I know who you are, so don't even bother calling. You're on our do-not-call list as of now."

He stopped and caught his breath again, his face becoming visibly calmer, his rapidly beating heart beginning to slow.

"I got baptized in juvenile hall by an amazing man named Father Mike. He taught me a lot about forgiveness. So even though a bunch of you out there did your best to hurt me and I won't talk to you any more, I *do* forgive you."

The stunned silence of the crowd was staggering in its totality.

"I know I probably sound super pissed today, but I'm really not. I'm just sad, because everything I just told you? It all happens 'cause you grown-ups care a lot more about yourselves than you do about us kids." He smiled sadly. "You asked why this prop, and now you have your answer."

He turned to Ricky, threw his arm around his shoulders, and led him back to their chairs. The Mayor stared at Lance, mouth agape.

Lance shrugged. "Young Mr. Lincoln, remember? Those Douglas debates and stuff? My mom taught me about them."

The Mayor broke into a huge grin. Murphy did not look pleased, but Ryan and Gibson eyed Lance with approval.

Mayor stepped to the podium. "Well, that was quite a statement, Sir Lance," he said, trying to be as non-committal as he could. Then he looked gravely out at all the stunned faces. "And it was all true. Thank you for saying it."

Astonished ripples of conversation drifted through the crowd, especially within the media pool. Helen beamed with delight.

"It may cost me my own re-election bid, but dammit, I support this boy and what he's trying to do for this city. And I, for one, am proud to share a stage with him."

He turned and waved Lance over. Lance stood and walked to the Mayor's side. The man took his hand and thrust both into the air in a sign of solidarity. Lance grinned with delight as the citizens cheered them. Even some in the media applauded, but most of them looked angry and insulted. That made Lance grin all the more.

This campaign, he knew, had just kicked into high gear, and he was stoked.

It was something of a madhouse trying to get back to Ryan's car, but the family made it out unscathed. Many of the people cheered and clapped for Lance as he passed through the crowd, with Ryan and Gibson flanking him protectively.

When they'd finally broken free of the throng and gotten home to New Camelot, Lance was startled to find Ryerson in the lobby awaiting them.

Arthur frowned with concern. "Is all well, Mr. Ryerson?"

The man nodded curtly. "Oh, yes, quite well. I merely wished to see young Lance a moment."

"I thank you for helping my son." Arthur extended his hand and Ryerson shook it.

"That is my job, King Arthur," the man replied matter-of-factly.

Arthur and Jenny wandered down the hall into the Throne Room, where the low tones of television news could be heard from the flat-screen.

Chris followed them, but Ricky hung back with Lance. Ryerson eyed the other boy, but Ricky shook his head. "I'm not letting him out of my sight."

Ryerson frowned, and then made a sort-of resigned, grunting sound. The man seemed to be having trouble making eye contact.

"Mr. Ryerson?" Lance said, hoping to get at whatever the man wanted to say.

Ryerson coughed, and lifted his eyes to meet Lance's gaze.

"I have been in the Throne Room watching your, how shall we call it, your diatribe?"

Lance eyed him expectantly.

The man cleared his throat. "It was somewhat impressive. Even your grammar was for the most part exemplary. You might consider a career as an attorney."

Lance wasn't sure that had been intended as a compliment or not, so he just said, "Okay, thanks."

Ryerson suddenly looked uncomfortable, as though he had terrible indigestion. "I merely wished to tell you that, uh, I have never, before you, represented a juvenile in any judicial proceeding."

He stopped, and Lance waited, wide-eyed and expectant.

"It was an honor, Sir Lance," Ryerson blurted, then turned quickly and let himself out the front door without another word.

Lance stared after him, a flabbergasted look on his face.

Ricky eyed him uncertainly. "What?"

Lance shook his head, as though not certain he'd heard correctly. "The guy was a jerk to me the whole time."

Ricky shrugged. "Must be those pretty boy looks that won him over."

Lance narrowed his eyes. "You're just as much a pretty boy as me, you know."

"You're lookin' for a serious beat-down, aren't you?"

"Bring it on, boy."

Ricky grinned. "Let's go at it." He extended a hand to usher Lance forward to the stairs.

They started forward.

"Hey, Ricky."

"Hey, what?"

"What's 'diatribe' mean?"

"Beats me."

Lance laughed. "I will beat you!"

He bolted for the stairs. Ricky was caught slightly off-guard, but burst forward and pelted up the stairs two at a time, catching up to Lance as they neared the second floor landing. Their combined laughter could be heard wafting down the stairs as they ran into their rooms and slammed the doors.

Arthur and Jenny stepped out of the Throne Room and over to the foot of the stairs to check on the racket, and heard the boys' voices from the second floor.

"I will so kick your ass this time, Ricky!" Lance called, obviously from his room into the other.

"On what planet?" came the challenging reply, and then both boys could be heard cracking up.

Arthur and Jenny looked at one another, smiling with the simple joy of having the family whole once again.

Arthur gazed deeply into her eyes. "Have I told you yet today that I love you?"

Jenny smiled. "I think you just did."

They kissed, long and lovingly.

That afternoon, dressed in their workout clothes, Lance and Ricky, with Chris cheering them on, sparred with swords and shields for an hour, and mostly fought to a draw, according to Chris. Then they shot arrows for thirty minutes, and Lance was still the better archer. Afterward, sweating and panting, they stripped off their shirts and pulled out the wrestling mat. Now, as always, Ricky was on stronger ground, and easily took Lance down the first couple of falls. But Lance, despite his weeks in juvy, was still more muscular and taller, outweighed Ricky by a few pounds, and eventually managed to get a couple of pins.

Overall, Chris called the wrestling matches a tie, and then threw himself into the mix. The three of them rolled and pitched and tumbled and laughed, happy and content to be reunited, just regular boys for a change.

Later that night, Lance checked his phone, which he'd left in his room since returning home. There was a text from Michael: "You let 'em have it today, Lance, except for that forgiveness crap. That's for pussies."

Lance frowned, and texted Michael back. There was no response. Making certain Ricky didn't notice, Lance kept checking his phone until he turned it off to go to bed. Maybe this time, Michael really *had* given up on him.

The next few days were incredibly hectic for Lance, Ricky, and all of New Camelot. The prop promotion team asked Lance to record some new spots reflecting his time as an incarcerated minor, reiterating some of the points he'd made in his press conference.

Lance and Ricky worked most of Tuesday with the producer of those spots writing thirty-second sound bites for Lance to record. The fallout from his lengthy "diatribe," as Ryerson had called it, was mainly to reboot his image in the eyes of the public. Of course, comments, tweets, and Facebook postings flew fast and furious, some condemning his indictment of the police and justice system, but most in full support. Often, the supporters posted their own negative experiences with violent, abusive cops, overzealous district attorneys, or downright railroading by the justice system.

Lance received an enormous number of requests for interviews, which Reyna and Jenny filtered using Techie's compilation list. Any news outlet that had backstabbed Lance, or mocked his incarceration, was sent a polite response along the lines of: "Sir Lance has limited time available for interviews and is declining your invite for reasons you already know. Thank you."

Any interviews that he did do, with Helen, of course, as well as some other news outlets, were always filmed at New Camelot, in the Throne Room. Ryan and Gibson refused to allow him to travel. There were too many hateful postings and rather poisonous rhetoric directed at Lance, Arthur, and their prop, on broadcast media, talking heads shows, blogs and Internet sites.

Over the next week, Lance recorded several "Yes on 51" spots to air throughout the state, and he once again appeared on The Ellen Show. Of course, his false arrest and incarceration were the main topic of her questions, but he always tied it back to his belief that too many adults in the country were focused on themselves instead of on their children. The studio audience applauded his sentiments.

The days settled into a routine for everyone. Lance and Ricky, now in the eleventh grade, still had school in the mornings, did their workouts and wrestling after lunch, and spent the rest of their time chatting on Facebook or Twitter, blogging or making YouTube videos to "sell" their prop.

The polls showed the prop at almost 50/50, for and against. Clearly, the people of California were divided on the notion of giving kids more adult rights, despite Lance's experiences, and despite the opinions of their own children. Due to this extreme indecision, Lance and Ricky conceived a plan to at least make certain every parent in the state voted.

Once absentee ballots would be made available—probably in early to mid-October—kids who wanted their parents to vote on the prop would once again become silent until the parent proved he or she had voted. Those who wanted to do early voting would also have to prove to their kids that they had, in fact, voted, by showing them the "I Voted!" stub given out at polling places. For those who planned to vote on Election Day, the kids would institute their silence a few days in advance and would refuse to do any work in school that week in November until they were shown that all-important "I Voted!" stub.

Their plan received a lot of support on Facebook and Twitter, with kids all over California vowing to participate.

In addition to all these regular duties, Lance and Ricky spent hours alone in Lance's room on their post-election follow-up project, which Ricky had whole-heartedly endorsed, but they refused to tell anyone else what they were doing.

"It's a secret," each boy would respond when queried, always with a sly little smile. Only Jenny and Arthur knew their plan because the boys sought out their advice and knowledge.

Mr. D. and Richard recovered from their horrific mutilations, but both were now in trouble with the law. Ryan and Gibson uncovered other teen boys Mr. D. had used for sex, and those boys gave sworn statements under oath. Likewise, several boys surfaced to accuse Richard, one who knew him under his 'Thornton' name, the others under his alias 'Trimble'. A court order had to be procured to get DCFS to give up Richard's file. Once that was turned over, evidence arose that the agency had suspected Thornton of sexual abuse, but rather than charge him or turn over their info to the police, they'd simply fired him and sealed the file.

Now a huge scandal loomed, and Lance was asked by the media to comment on it. Since his experiences in the foster system were largely negative, he did not side with the agency, but rather expressed the hope that all their dirt would now be uncovered and other kids like him wouldn't have to go through what he had.

Lance also continued to text Michael, but never received a response, which saddened him a little when he had the time to think about it. Usually, the days were so hectic that by bedtime, he knocked out fast, barely able to say goodnight to Ricky. He longed for the election to be over.

On top of all this, Chris's birthday loomed on October twenty- fifth. Since Chris had not had a celebration last year, both Lance and Ricky were determined to do something special for his eighth. They felt guilty having to spend so much time on "business," as well as on their secret project, at the expense of their younger brother.

Lance conceived the perfect idea for Chris's birthday, besides the requisite New Camelot party planned by big sister, Reyna, of course.

Arthur thought Lance's idea delightful, and felt certain Mr. Mills would agree. Arthur had praised the man highly the previous year for helping him and Lance— though he never went into precise details as to the nature of that assistance—and Mr. Mills had been promoted to a high ranking position within the railroad company.

Sergeant Ryan would have to accompany them, Arthur told Lance and Ricky, or at least drop them off and pick them up at the end of the line.

Arthur called Mills, who was thrilled to hear from him and absolutely wanted "To do whatever I can fer you and that fine son a yours."

Arthur explained what Lance hoped to do for Chris, and Mills had one idea better. Rather than using an empty Metrolink train for the private birthday cruise, "Why not an authentic Union Pacific locomotive?" the man suggested in that slight drawl of his. "Give the lad a taste of real training, eh?"

Sunday mornings were fairly light, since commuters stayed home, Mills explained. He was certain he could get a section of track cleared, say from Pasadena into Union Station, and have the train on the track ready for a private ride.

"Wouldn't be that far, mind you, Arthur, cuz the comp'ny wouldn't let me hog that track for too long. Takes time to get the big engine on and off, don't ya know. But fer you, I'm sure I can swing it."

Arthur expressed his deep gratitude.

Lance got on the phone and thanked him too.

"Anything for you, Sir Lance," the man drawled. "'Specially after the hell you just been through."

Lance gushed, "Thanks, Mr. Mills."

Arthur took back the phone. "As a matter of security, Mr. Mills, it be of the utmost import that you tell your superiors not to speak of this to anyone. The police are still fearful that I or my sons may be attacked prior to the election."

"No problem, King Arthur," the man answered confidently. "I got yew covered."

Mills promised to get back to the king with the particulars and the conversation ended.

Arthur looked at his sons with pride.

Lance nearly turned red under the scrutiny. "What?"

"I'm happy that you take such a loving interest in your younger brother."

"Oh," Lance said, and then he and Ricky giggled nervously.

"Reyna'll handle the party stuff, right?" Ricky asked.

"She'll allow no one else to do so."

The boys laughed and went on with their day.

The days drifted by rapidly for everyone. Lance and Ricky texted their girls, and chatted when there was time. Bridget and Ariel occasionally came to New Camelot to hang out, but there really wasn't much time to socialize, so they would just get on a computer in the lab to tweet or message people about voting on the prop. They also responded with nasty retorts to anyone who dissed Lance or the crusade in general. They enjoyed being part of the operation.

October turned chilly, and the election loomed ever closer. The online rhetoric became more nasty and vitriolic, but Lance was happy to see a real debate going on. For the first time, adults throughout the state were looking at how children and teens had been treated. They were seriously scrutinizing the school and justice systems, and their own beliefs. Whatever the eventual outcome of the election, Lance felt good about "stirring the pot," as Helen had once described it.

The week before Chris's birthday, Ryan approached Lance as he and Ricky were exiting the Training Center, and asked for a word with him. In private.

Ricky was surprised, but got the message. "Okay, uh, I'll see you upstairs, Lance."

Lance nodded, shocked that Ryan would want to say anything Ricky couldn't hear.

"What's wrong, *nino*?"

Ryan looked cautious, but serious. "I wanted you to know we still don't have any leads on whoever attacked Thornton or Diosdado."

Lance eyed him questioningly.

"But I think you do," Ryan concluded soberly, his eyes pinned to Lance's face.

Lance sucked in a breath of surprise. He hadn't even thought of either of them since both had been put under the investigative microscope. He still got the shakes whenever he gave either man even a moment's consideration.

"I don't understand."

Ryan looked uncomfortable, shifting his feet nervously. "I kept telling myself I saw something that wasn't there, but my instincts about lying are like yours about people."

Lance's mouth dropped open. "When did I lie to you, *nino?*"

"When I told you the perp was wearing that Scream mask."

Lance gasped. He'd completely forgotten that, and he *had* lied. His face reddened, revealing his guilt for all to see.

"One of the best things Arthur's done for you, son, was to make you into a bad liar." Ryan said solemnly. "What do you know, Lance, that you're not telling me?"

Lance lowered his gaze to the floor. "Nothing."

"Lance, look into my eyes and say that."

Lance glanced up, and Ryan stood there, gazing at his face, patiently awaiting the truth.

"It's nothing, *nino,*" Lance said, squirming. "It's something I remembered..."

"What was it, Lance?"

Now Lance did look into his godfather's eyes. He shifted back and forth uncertainly. "*Nino*, I know what it's like to be accused of something I didn't do. I can't do that to someone else. Not 'less I know for sure. Let me see what I can find out first."

"No!" Ryan snapped, sounding like a gunshot, his eyes blazing with intensity. "Listen to me, Lance. Whoever did these crimes is dangerous. You could get hurt." He paused a moment. "I'm not supposed to tell you this, but homicide thinks these attacks might be related to some similar, unsolved mutilations three or four years ago."

That caught Lance by surprise. "The same thing?"

"Yeah. Five frat boys from UCLA."

Lance gagged, and the blood drained from his face in a second.

"What?" Ryan said quickly. He stared so intently into Lance's eyes that Lance had to look away. "Tell me, Lance. Tell me what you know, and let *me* handle it."

Lance kept his gaze lowered, and said nothing.

Ryan glared angrily. "Dammit, Lance! You think I can watch you die again? Well, I can't!"

Lance looked up at that, shocked to see fear on Ryan's stoic face. Fear mixed with love. Impulsively, Lance hugged him and said into his jacket, "I'll be okay, *nino.* I promise." He pulled back and looked into Ryan's doubtful, almost panicked eyes.

"If I ask you something, Godson, will you tell me the truth?"

Lance wore an uncertain look on his face. "Depends on what you ask."

"If you found out anything about this person you suspect, would you tell me?"

Lance hesitated, and considered the question. "If I think even for a second somebody could get hurt, I'll tell you. Okay?"

"That depends," Ryan answered gravely.

"On what?"

"On whether or not you're still *alive* to tell me," the man said sadly, and turned to walk away down the corridor.

Lance watched him go, considering whether or not to call him back and confess what he suspected. But no. He had to find the truth first. It was only fair. He'd seen way too much unfairness of late, and he needed to be sure.

When he got upstairs to change, he found Ricky waiting for him, pacing the room. Ricky hadn't even changed out of his sweaty shirt yet. The second Lance stepped into his room, Ricky pounced.

"What's wrong? Is everything okay?"

Lance nodded, feeling sick to his stomach for lying to Ricky. But he had no choice. "Yeah," he said evasively. "He just wanted to talk to me about the investigation, about how they still don't got any leads on the attacker."

Ricky frowned suspiciously. "Why couldn't he tell you that in front of me?"

Lance shrugged, and Ricky frowned some more.

Lance knew Ricky knew he was lying, and felt like scum.

Ricky entered his room without another word, closing the door behind him.

Once Ricky stripped off his soaked shirt and gazed at himself in the bathroom mirror, his tight breathing began to ease. He was angry at Lance for lying, but then, with a jolt, he realized that he'd been lying to Lance for months, so who was he to be high and mighty? His was a lie of omission, true, and it *had* been for Lance's good, he tried to convince himself.

Or is it so he won't reject me?

His stomach twisted into knots of despair as Ricky set about getting cleaned up.

CHAPTER ELEVEN

HE'S DANGEROUS, LANCE

LATER THAT NIGHT, WHILE HE and Ricky were playing scrabble with Chris, Lance purposely lost the current round and told them he was gonna make a quick food run to the kitchen. He snuck quietly downstairs to the lobby. He stuck his head into the Throne Room and found it empty. Then he checked the hallways leading to various parts of the hotel before scurrying back to the landline phone in the lobby.

Snatching up the receiver, he rapidly punched in Bridget's number. As he listened to the rings, Lance glanced around nervously. He'd never changed his own cell number, like he'd planned, and he couldn't use Ricky's phone. But out here, he was open to anyone walking in on him, and beads of sweat appeared on his forehead. Finally someone picked up.

"Hello?"

"Is Bridget home?"

Lance had never met Bridget's mom, but figured this must be her.

"I'll get her."

There was silence for a few moments while Lance fidgeted and cast his eyes nervously about.

Finally, Bridget's voice came on the line. "Lance? Why are you using the house phone?"

"I couldn't use my cell," he answered evasively. "I'll explain later. Listen, Bridget, I need a big favor."

"Anything for you, baby," she chirped into his ear.

"I need you to find out where Michael will be next Friday night."

There came an angry sigh over the line. "Michael. Again."

He heard the anger, the suspicion in her voice and tried his best to assuage it.

"It's nothing like that, Bridget. I just need to know where Michael's gonna be Friday night, like will he go to a party or what?"

There was a long pause, and Lance feared she'd say no. In addition, the longer he took, the more likely Ricky would come searching for him.

"I don't party with Michael anymore, Lance, you know that," he heard in his ear. "He scares me too much."

"I know, Bridg, but can't you find out from somebody who does hang with him, somebody at school?" There was a long pause. "I know how you feel about Michael, and I wouldn't ask, 'cept it's really important."

Another long pause. "Please tell me you're not gonna party with him, Lance."

"Hell, no. I just need the information."

He waited, his forehead beading with more sweat. He could see her in his mind's eye, cordless handset in one right hand, twirling her hair nervously with the fingers of her other, considering the ramifications of his request.

Finally, he heard, "Okay. I'll do it."

He let out a huge sigh of relief. "Thank you so much, Bridg."

"You want me to call when I find out?"

"No, just tell me sometime next week, when you're over here," Lance said, quickly adding, "And Bridg, you can't tell Ariel or Ricky. You can't tell anyone."

He heard a sharp breath on the other end. "Now you're scaring me, Lance. What are you gonna do?"

"Don't worry, I got it covered," he said, evading her question. "I gotta get off this phone. Remember, our secret."

Her next words struck straight to his heart, especially given the tremulous emotion he heard accompanying them. "I love you, Lance. I love you so much."

Lance became rigid, and even more sweat broke out on his forehead. She'd said those words before, but never with such passion, such intensity. She really *did* love him!

"Love you too, Bridg." He tried to sound convincing because he wanted to, but deep down was it really so?

He hung up the phone and stood there a moment. Then, cursing himself for his weakness, Lance hurried back upstairs to Ricky's room to rejoin the game.

The following week flew past in a blur. Lance, Ricky, and Chris did more online interviews and recorded last minute YouTube pitches. Reyna and Jenny set up news conferences for the day before the election and the day after, both at City Hall. The first, for a last minute push to get people to the polls, and the second, to discuss the results.

Everything was on track for Chris's birthday. Reyna pulled out all the stops for the party. Everyone felt badly that the little boy's birthday had been forgotten the year before. Lance, especially, knew the pain at that age of not having a birthday cake, or even a card. When he'd turned eight, Richard had come to his room and...

No! Don't go there!

He knew he had to put all that behind him, but it was *so* difficult. Even normal things like birthdays brought back traumatic memories.

Mr. Mills had also pulled off the impossible and gotten the head honchos at the rail company to allow him to use the requested track on Sunday morning at ten. The actual train ride would be short, probably no more than thirty minutes. But Mills planned to show Chris how the train operated and let him explore the controls before they got underway. The track would be cleared of all other trains for three hours, nine-thirty till twelve-thirty. Lance and Ricky were thrilled, for themselves, as well. Neither had ever been on a real train before, and it would be an adventure.

The plan was to leave New Camelot at eight-thirty, so Ryan could get the boys to the train in plenty of time. He would stay with them until they'd gotten settled in with Mills, and then drive down to Union Station to pick them up when the train arrived.

One time during that week, Chris came upon them in their room talking quietly and they clammed up the moment he entered.

"I know you guys are planning something," he said. "What is it?"

"It's a surprise, little man," Lance said with a grin.

"We're gonna make this the best birthday you ever had, Chris," Ricky added, and Chris beamed.

"Man, am I lucky you guys are my brothers," he gushed.

"Damn straight you are," said Lance with a grin.

Chris laughed and went back to his own room to do homework.

It was Wednesday before Bridget finally gave Lance the information he needed. When they were in the Computer Lab, she called him over to her computer on the pretense of showing him something. Ariel was at the computer to Bridget's right, but she was using headphones to listen to some of the YouTube postings. She smiled Lance's way, but then turned her attention back to the screen.

Lance leaned in to Bridget's left side and she slid a piece of folded paper into his hand. He opened it and saw an address.

"That's where he'll be Friday night," she whispered. "It's a big party, so he should be there late."

"Thanks, Bridg," he said, handing her back the paper. "I didn't need to know where, just that he wouldn't be home."

Her face dissolved into confusion. "Why?"

Lance looked away, and didn't answer. He felt her hand on his.

"What are you going to do?" Her voice was breathless with unease.

"Don't worry, I'll be okay," he whispered back.

She cupped his face with her hands, gently and lovingly, her eyes filled with trepidation. "He's dangerous, Lance. You know that. Please, don't do whatever you're planning."

Lance tried for a confident smile. "I'll be fine." He smiled reassuringly and headed back to his own station, leaving her gazing after him with fear painted across her soft features.

The next two days seemed endless to Lance, despite being busy with the campaign and getting ready for Chris's birthday celebration on Sunday, because uppermost in his mind was what he might unearth at Michael's house.

Finally, Friday arrived. Chris was especially hyper and couldn't even concentrate during his sparring sessions. Even though his birthday wasn't till Sunday, the little boy was already out of control with happiness. Lance and Ricky had told him they were taking him someplace special Sunday morning, just the three of them, and he was so excited Lance feared he wouldn't sleep the next two nights.

Lance knew he wouldn't get much sleep, either. Michael would likely be at the party until at least two a.m. Saturday, but Lance didn't want to take any chances. He planned on going to "sleep" early on the pretense that it would be a busy weekend. But as soon as he knew Ricky was asleep, he'd be up and out. By skateboard, it would take him forty-five minutes to an hour to get to Michael's house in the Hollywood Hills, like it had before. The return trip would be faster. Still, he wanted to be in and out of Michael's place by one, just to be safe.

The day dragged on, despite the usual routine. Bridget and Ariel did not appear because they were coming Sunday for Chris's party, and Lance insisted they not make the trip twice. He also didn't want Bridget around giving him "those looks" all afternoon, because she knew he was up to something questionable that night. He'd crack for sure, and then Ricky would know something was up.

Chris yammered on all through dinner about how Sunday would be the first real birthday party he ever had. "But the best part is spending all morning with my big brothers," the youngster chirped in his high-pitched voice. His round, milky white features danced with joy, and everyone speculated on what the older brothers were planning.

To keep the secret from Chris, only Arthur and Jenny and Ryan knew, so there were a lot of guesses thrown out over dinner, everything from swimming with sharks to bungee jumping off the Vincent Thomas Bridge in Long Beach. Of course, Chris knew they were all just kidding around, and he laughed harder with each outrageous suggestion. It was a delightful and relaxed family dinner. Only Lance felt tense, because only he knew what he was planning to do.

Finally, it was time for bed. Since they were almost finished reading Chris *The Neverending Story*, both Lance and Ricky sat with him and switched off as readers, making the finale as dramatic as possible. Chris listened in wide-eyed wonder as the story of Bastian and the magic book came to an end.

When they were finished, Lance asked, "Well, little man, did you like it?"

Chris nodded vigorously, but then tilted his head slightly as he regarded Lance.

"What?" Lance asked.

"They were right," Chris said after a long moment.

The older boys exchanged a look.

Ricky asked, "Who?"

"Those people on the Internet," Chris answered.

Lance looked at Chris questioningly. "About what?"

"You really *are* the Ivory Tower." Chris hugged him, throwing out one arm to pull in Ricky too, bringing the three of them together in mutual love and solidarity.

When Chris let them go, Lance eyed his little brother in wonder. "Thanks, Chris," was all he could say, feeling his face burn with embarrassment.

Ricky laughed and punched him. "Oh, look, Chris, you made him blush, for a change."

Lance laughed and shoved Ricky back. In seconds all three of them were hitting each other with pillows until Jenny came in and put a stop to the horseplay. Lance and Ricky bade Chris good night, kissed their mom, and returned to their own rooms.

Jenny leaned down to tuck in Chris and kiss him goodnight. "Mom," Chris said as she turned to leave. She looked back at him. "Lance and Ricky are awesome, aren't they?"

"That they are, Chris. Goodnight, sweetie." Then she left him and returned to her room.

Lance and Ricky changed for bed, no longer shy about taking off their shirts in front of each other. They'd still laugh a little and joke about whose pecs were too scrawny or whose abs were crooked, but it was all part of their good-natured rivalry.

Lance felt especially nervous tonight, however, hoping he wasn't trying so hard so play their usual game that Ricky would sense something was up. Because of their uncanny ability to know the thoughts or emotions of the other, Lance kept his distance as much as possible.

Finally, both boys slipped beneath the covers on either side of the bed. Usually they'd talk for a while about well, just everything, but tonight Lance was too high-strung. He knew he'd trip up and give himself away. So, he said he was wiped out and bade Ricky a quick goodnight before rolling over to face the curtains.

"Oh, okay, 'night, Lance," he heard from behind him, the hurt evident in Ricky's voice.

"'Night, Ricky."

It seemed to take hours as Lance stared endlessly at the red numbers changing ever so slowly on his night-table clock. By the time he heard Ricky slumbering away, it was eleven-fifteen. Slipping quickly out of bed, Lance cautiously slunk past Ricky's side and into his bathroom, where he'd hidden his clothes and skateboard behind the shower curtain. Making not a sound, he dressed and slipped into his skate shoes, gently lifting his board to avoid the slightest sound, and stepped from the bathroom.

Ricky was facing his direction. Lance froze and watched. But the even breathing told him Ricky was still asleep. Lance darted to the door, eased it open without so much as a creak and slipped out into the hall, closing the door just as silently.

As on the night John died, the journey to Michael's house was an uphill battle along the steeply sloping streets. Most of the time he carried his board in hand and jogged up the shadowy, dimly lit streets into the Hollywood Hills. Even in the dark, the mansion that Michael's parents owned loomed large near the end of its shady, tree-lined cul-de-sac. His board wheels scrapping against the pavement made so much noise in the stillness of the night that he jumped off and carried it up to the massive entry gates. Sliding the board through the slats of the gate, Lance deftly clambered up and over, alighting quietly on the balls of his feet like a cat. Grabbing his board, he started up the expansive driveway.

Skirting the main house, which seemed deathly quiet and dark, Lance used his key to open the side gate and slipped into the back yard. He stopped and listened for any sounds. There was nothing except his own ragged breathing. Up ahead, on the other side of the pool, through the jungle, lay Michael's back house, dormant and quiescent. Lance slipped out his phone and checked the time: twelve-thirty. Damn! He had to move fast.

Jogging lightly on the balls of his feet, Lance skirted the pool, ran over the stone blocks through the jungle, and stopped before Michael's front door. He glanced back at the main house. There was no movement, no sound. Lance cautiously inserted the key into the heavy deadbolt and turned. With one more backward glance, he slipped into the house and eased the door closed.

The interior was pitch black, and Lance had to let his eyes adjust. He knew if Michael had kept any evidence, which Lance suspected he would because of his supreme ego, it'd be on his computer or somewhere else in his bedroom. So, that's where Lance went without hesitation. As he passed by the kitchen, his eye caught sight of the wet bar, now closed and apparently locked, and felt not the slightest urge to drink.

He paused at the door. He recalled the video he'd seen of himself and Ricky that first night they'd been here. Might those cameras be recording him again as soon as he stepped into Michael's private world? He suspected they probably would, but also knew he had no choice. He had to know the truth. As long as he didn't get caught in the room, he'd have Ryan and the others for protection.

He used the key to unlock Michael's bedroom door and, upon entering the shadowy room, understood that he couldn't turn on any lights. If anyone was in the main house, that would alert them. He took out his phone and activated the flashlight app, keeping the beam aimed at the floor. He first went to the computer desk and sat. The screen was in sleep mode, but it woke up when he touched the mouse. Remembering Michael's old password, Lance typed it in.

'Incorrect Password' popped up on screen.

"Damn," he cursed quietly. Michael must've changed it. Sighing heavily, Lance turned and scanned the room. Knowing Michael as a paranoid individual who beat people up just for taking his photograph, where would the boy hide evidence he wished to hold as keepsakes, but didn't want anyone else to find?

Rising from the chair, Lance made his way to the closet. He remembered it as an enormous walk-in number. Maybe there was a secret room in back somewhere. He opened the door. Racks of very expensive clothes hung on either side, with rows of shoes, mostly basketball, lining the floors. All the basketball shoes were Nike, and there must have been a hundred pair, he noted with awe, which explained why Michael had never worn the same pair twice.

Shaking off his amazement, Lance crept slowly into the closet. It extended back at least ten feet, and then angled off to the left. This closet was almost as big as his bedroom, he thought, as his light bounced off plush beige carpeting, and up at even more clothes, mostly suits and slacks, hanging primly, awaiting use. Nothing. The closet ended just ahead, and there didn't seem to be any hidden offshoots.

Feeling a desperate sense of defeat, Lance decided to tap along the walls of the closet, the way people always did in movies to find hollow spaces. He began right where the closet turned left, using his knuckle to gently rap a few times against the wall. Solid. A foot further along. Solid. Another couple of feet. Solid. Damn! Nothing! He got to the end, and tapped the wall behind some designer suits. A dull echo answered his knock, and his heart leapt into his throat.

Bingo!

Feeling along the area with his fingers, Lance found a small catch near the bottom, hidden behind some black dress shoes. He flipped the catch up and over, and the door swung outward an inch. Taking a deep breath, Lance raised his phone light and pulled the door out cautiously. Once it was wide enough, he stepped through into Michael's secret domain. He raised the flashlight, and gasped.

Eyes wide with horror, Lance took in his surroundings. Papered to all four walls were news stories about the five frat boys who'd been attacked and mutilated. The dates read from four years ago. He also saw more recent articles, from this year, detailing the mutilations of Richard and Mr. D. Lance also saw hundreds of articles about him and the crusade papering the walls, some dating as far back as his first interview with Helen in Eucalyptus Park. Propped up in the corner, as though on some kind of clothes dummy, was a child's Halloween costume, all black, with the Scream mask resting on top.

But these weren't what set his gorge rising into his throat.

It was the color photos lining the walls, bloody, nauseating images of the maimed victims that Michael must've taken with his cell phone. Some were extreme close-ups, others full body shots. But all made him feel sick, despite the fact that one of these mutilated men had raped him.

"Oh, Michael," he whispered, his legs shaking with terror. "What have you done?"

Not knowing what else to do, feeling certain Michael would know he'd been in here, Lance opened the camera on his phone, quickly pulled on the overhead light after closing the door, and snapped pictures of the photos, and the costume.

As near as he could tell, these seven were the only victims, and Lance knew that each of them had brought it upon himself. What goes around comes around, as he'd always heard growing up. An eye for an eye, Michael had told him before.

But Michael *was* a monster, after all.

What if he got mad at the wrong guy and did something like this to an innocent person? And what if I could've stopped it by turning him in? Like I could've stopped Richard so long ago!

Lance didn't know what to do, but he did know he needed to get out of there before Michael came home and found him. He trembled at the very thought of the unhinged boy's reaction to his snooping.

Careful not to disturb anything, he flicked off the light, backed slowly out of the hidden room and closed the door, making sure the catch clicked and the shoes were back covering it. Then he slipped quietly out of the room and out of the house.

Carrying his board to avoid waking any of the neighbors, Lance jogged as fast as he could quietly manage down the street and away from the neighborhood. When he was far enough away, he leapt onto his board and frantically skated the downhill slopes back toward home.

Michael sat on a couch at someone's house he barely knew, but the party was big and loud and he was Michael so, of course, they'd let him in.

He sat between a brunette with tattoos on her naked arms and piercings through her lips, and a skinny, floppy haired boy wearing a muscle shirt that did nothing but display how scrawny his arms were.

Michael was making out with each of them in turn, nearly suffocating them with his rough affections.

The phone in his pocket vibrated, and Michael pulled his tongue from the gasping boy's mouth to slip it out and check the screen.

There was a flashing alert.

Michael leapt to his feet, practically tossing his playthings aside in the process. He opened the alert and read it:

'Security breach bedroom; Security breach closet'.

His eyes narrowed to slits and everyone looking his way stepped back instantly.

He cursed, his features turning violently animalistic. And then he was running, out the front door and down the driveway to his car.

FOR EVERY CHILD THERE
COMES A TIME

CHAPTER TWELVE
MICHAEL CAME BY WHILE YOU WERE OUT

B Y THE TIME LANCE GOT home, it was after one-thirty. He managed to slip back into bed without waking Ricky, but couldn't even begin to sleep. He lay in the dark, staring at the ornate ceiling, images of those maimed and bleeding men filling his mind and tightening his stomach.

Oh, Michael... what am I gonna do?

He wrestled with that question, going back and forth in his mind. Yes, Michael had done monstrous things, horrible atrocities, worse even than those committed by the creature in *Frankenstein*. Ricky had been right about Michael, after all.

But then Lance would consider the victims. His mind replayed Michael's torturous gang rape, his own violation at Richard's hands, Jack's handsome face twisted into patterns of deep humiliation in the presence of Mr. D.

What goes around comes around... an eye for an eye... forgiveness is for pussies... These were Michael's philosophies, and Lance couldn't blame him for having adopted them. What had been done to Michael had turned a boy into a monster. But hadn't Lance always seen something in Michael's eyes that eluded everyone else, something deep down, something that was still good? Had he been wrong about that? Had he seen what he'd wanted to see, like Ricky said?

He tossed and turned for hours, fighting to block out the images assaulting him, struggling to reconcile what he'd been taught by Arthur and Father Mike, versus what Michael believed, and had done. He felt certain Michael would know about his snooping. Michael was too paranoid not to have fail-safes set up. Should he confront Michael? Everyone would say no, that Michael wouldn't hesitate to hurt or even kill him.

But Michael wouldn't do that to him. To others, maybe. But not him.

"Would you, Michael?" he whispered into the silent dark. But the dark didn't answer. Finally, exhaustion from stress overcame him, and he drifted into a fitful slumber.

He awoke to Ricky shaking him. Popping open his eyes, Lance quickly jerked upright in fear. "What? What's wrong?" He'd been dreaming. A nightmare, actually, of Michael stalking him with a sharp, gleaming knife.

Ricky scrunched up his face in confusion. "Nothing." He eyed Lance peculiarly. "It's just, like, ten o'clock already. Thought I should get your lazy ass up."

He grinned, but Lance's fearful gaze drifted to the curtains, his mind somewhere else.

"You okay, Lance?"

"Uh, yeah," Lance mumbled. "Just didn't sleep good. Weird dreams."

"About how I'm stronger and better looking and how everyone likes watching me kick your ass? Those kinds of dreams?"

That drew a tight smile to Lance's lips. "In *your* dreams."

Ricky grinned. "C'mon, fool, get your ass up and lets go shopping. We gotta get something cool for Chris, remember? Reyna's coming to take us in her Escalade." He wiggled his eyebrows to indicate they'd be traveling in high style.

"My godfather coming with us?"

"Of course. Protection, remember?"

Lance nodded.

"What's wrong, Lance?"

Lance raised his gaze from the bed cover he'd been staring at, and turned red with embarrassment. "Nothing, man. Let me jump in the shower and we're good to go."

Ricky scrutinized him carefully, but Lance refused to meet his gaze. "Okay. But don't crack the mirror when you look at it."

Lance looked up and saw Ricky's grin. He smiled and climbed out of bed.

With all the donations coming into the crusade—many from anonymous donors—Arthur and Jenny had no shortage of money with which to take care of any kid who needed to stay at New Camelot, as well as to fund the needs of their campaign.

Lance, Ricky, and Chris, as well as any other kids who stayed over, like Justin and his current group of knightly security guards, were paid for handling all their duties. Thus, Lance and Ricky had money to spend on Chris, and they wanted to get their little brother some nice gifts, besides the secret train ride.

When Reyna picked them up, she'd already swung through Boyle Heights and gotten Esteban, who rode shotgun as he always did, jokingly commenting on her erratic driving skills. Chris wanted to come along, naturally, but they told him he couldn't because it was a secret for his birthday and he'd have to wait until the next day. He was both disappointed and supremely excited. Jenny held his hand as the others drove off.

Lance sat in between Ricky and Ryan, and would not look over at his godfather. He still hadn't decided what to do about Michael. He had all the evidence he needed right on his phone, but did he want to share it? Since Ryan knew him so well, and could always tell when he was lying, Lance made it a point never to look into the man's eyes all the time they were shopping, not even when they stopped for lunch.

Thanks to Jack's influence, Chris loved football, so the boys bought him a brand new football, a very cool, authentic jersey, and *Madden NFL* for iPad. The iPad, itself, was Reyna's gift to Chris. They also found an ultra-cool watch that was mathematical, because Chris was probably the only football-loving, sword-wielding, arrow-shooting math geek in the world and this watch seemed to scream "techno math geek."

Esteban bought Chris a high quality bow and some arrows. Reyna thought Chris might not be strong enough yet to pull back on the bowstring, as the tension level was high, but Esteban laughed and said, "That's 'cause you think like a girl."

She punched him. "I do not. I just think it's too hard for him," she said as she eyed the bow appraisingly.

All the boys stood looking at her until she threw out her hands. "What?"

The guys exchanged a look, and then in unison said, "You're such a girl, Reyna."

They knew she hated being thought of as "just" a girl, and when her face became a thundercloud, they all laughed. Getting the joke, she relaxed and laughed with them.

Esteban leaned in, right there in the sporting goods store, and kissed her. Lance and Ricky exchanged a look between them, embarrassment overcoming them both.

"Okay, kids, break it up," Ryan cautioned, and everyone cracked up. They finished their shopping, and returned to New Camelot without incident.

When they returned home, Arthur and Jenny greeted them in the lobby.

"Go wrap your presents quickly," Jenny advised them. "I've got Chris playing a math game in the lab."

Even Ryan had purchased Chris a book that Lance picked out, and he followed Reyna and Esteban toward the back of the hotel, where the wrapping paper and sundry items were located in a large pantry.

Ricky and Lance started to follow, but Arthur said, "Lance, a word alone, if you please."

Lance frowned, and Ricky's eyebrows shot up questioningly, but then Jenny threw her arm around Ricky's shoulders and led him after the others. He turned his head to look back at his dad and Lance, his face scrunched with worry. But Jenny gave him a tug and they disappeared into the vastness of New Camelot.

Standing awkwardly within the cavernous lobby, Lance eyed Arthur curiously. His dad looked worried. "Everything okay, Dad?"

"You tell me, son. Michael came by while you were out."

Lance could almost feel himself going ashen with fear. "Uh, what did he want?" He tried to keep the tremor out of his voice.

Arthur eyed him intently. "He did not say, but he appeared more angry than usual, somehow harder than the last time I spoke with him. It disturbed me greatly. Do you know the reason?"

Lance shuffled his feet uneasily. "Why did, uh, he say he came?"

"He wanted you." Arthur's penetrating look sought his eyes, but Lance could not meet it.

"I haven't seen him since I got arrested, Dad," he offered, knowing it sounded feeble. "Why would he want to see me all of a sudden?"

"I asked him the same question," Arthur replied evenly, with a note of suspicion. "He said you would know."

Lance flicked his gaze back up into his dad's, and then just as quickly back down. He didn't want to lie to Arthur anymore, so he said nothing.

Arthur paused, and then placed both hands on his shoulders, forcing Lance to raise his head once more. "Tell me, son."

Lance hesitated. The truth was right there on his lips, the proof in his pocket. He very nearly blurted it all out. But instead, he just sighed. "It's no biggie, Dad. Just something him and me gotta work out."

Lance could tell his dad wasn't buying it, could tell the man knew he was not telling the full truth, but Lance just couldn't say anything about Michael. Not yet.

At least not until he'd confronted him.

I owe him that much, don't I? He wrote our prop, after all..

That was his excuse, anyway. He knew, deep down, that it was feeble, but it was all he had right now.

Arthur released his shoulders. "You know you can tell me anything, do you not, Lance?" His deep brown eyes practically begged for the truth.

"I know that, Dad."

Arthur gazed at him a moment longer. "He said he'd be back."

Lance gulped, too afraid how his voice might come out if he answered. Michael was coming back? When?

"May I be excused now?" Lance asked, and Arthur nodded. Lance scurried off down the hall after the others. He felt his dad's intense gaze on his back, and knew Arthur was afraid.

So am I.

Lance spent much of the afternoon with Ricky and Chris, training and wrestling, so the others could start decorating the Throne Room for the party. But try as he might to focus on Chris, all Lance could think about was Michael. Of course, Ricky wanted to know what Arthur needed to see him about, and Lance had said it had to do with a message from the Mayor about Monday's press conference. Nothing important. Ricky looked suspicious, and Lance knew Ricky saw through the lie, but pressed no further.

Of course Michael knew he'd been in the house, Lance told himself.

He had cameras everywhere. He was paranoid. And they recorded me, just like I thought.

So Michael knew that *he* knew.

The question haunting Lance throughout the day and into an uncertain night was: what would Michael do about it?

Getting Chris to sleep was even harder than the night before because he was even more excited, and they'd already finished *The Neverending Story*. Jenny had lots of other children's books in the library downstairs, so Ricky went down to find one while Lance talked and joked with Chris about his birthday, teasing him without telling him anything. Chris laughed with delight. Lance had never seen him so happy, so at peace with the world.

This is what being eight-years old should be, he thought wistfully.

By the time Ricky returned with *Peter Pan*, Chris was getting sleepy.

"You want us to lie here with you, Chris, till you fall asleep?" Lance asked, thinking back to the old days when Chris would sleep next to no one but him.

Chris shook his head and gave Lance that knowing, all-too-adult look. "I'm too big for that, Lance," he said, as if it was the most obvious thing in the world.

Lance was caught off-guard a second. "Never too old to hug your big bro, though."

Lance hugged him, and Chris grasped him tightly around the neck, like he knew everything was changing, that this kind of moment between he and Lance might soon be a thing of the past. They held each other a moment longer, and then Chris kissed him on the cheek.

"Love you, Lance."

"Love you more."

Chris lay down and smiled up at Ricky. "Love you too, Ricky," he gushed. "You're the best thing to happen to Lance, ever." He paused when Lance reddened. "And me too."

Ricky also looked embarrassed, but leaned in to kiss Chris on one cheek. "Love you too, little man. Now get some sleep. Big day tomorrow."

Chris snuggled down under the covers. The older boys turned out his light and returned to their room, Lance wondering what Chris had meant when he'd said that about him and Ricky.

He again avoided conversing with Ricky while they lay in bed that night, once more feeling certain he would give himself away and spill his guts about Michael. He hated keeping anything from Ricky, but he knew Ricky had no perspective on Michael. He would go to Ryan even if Lance told him not to. So he steered the small talk toward the train ride tomorrow and the party, keeping it all focused on Chris and how fast he was growing up. Finally, both grew tired enough to sleep.

For Lance, his dreams were haunted by blood and knives and Michael's leeringly handsome face.

Chris was beyond excited the next morning. Pastor Tom did a shorter-than-normal service at eight, using the library this time so Chris wouldn't see the decorations in the Throne Room, and blessed the boy for his birthday. Lance once again thought how he'd like to get Father Mike over to do a service, too, but it couldn't be on Sunday because the priest was too busy at Sylmar.

Because they were going on a train ride, and in case of any sudden stops, the boys could not bring their swords or knives with them. As a rule, they seldom did when out in public, except for appearances where the swords were rather expected as part of the package. Besides, they knew Ryan would be nearby to protect them, and the sergeant was always armed.

Unknown to Chris, but known to the boys, Arthur had arranged for Reyna to drive he and Llamrei, in her trailer, down to Union Station where he planned to surprise Chris when the boys arrived. Arthur would put Chris into the saddle and let him steer the horse back to New Camelot. Chris had never gotten much time on horseback and had often complained about it to his dad. Of course, with so much of Arthur's life now relegated to cars, he longed for more time with his beloved mare, as well. The horseback ride would also delay Chris's return home, so all of the knights could assemble and surprise him when he arrived.

Despite his worries over Michael, Lance felt great excitement. He hadn't seen Mr. Mills since the previous year and he liked the kindly, older man. He'd also never been on a real train before and it sounded awesome.

Ryan drove them to Pasadena where Mills told them to meet at the Sierra Villa Station. Normally, this was a Gold Line Light Rail stop, but those trains ran less frequently on Sunday mornings and this particular track had been cleared for Mills to use. His plan was to switch over to a more commercially used track after exiting Pasadena, thus freeing up the Gold Line track as quickly as possible.

The boys had dressed casually in long-sleeve flannels and jeans and skate shoes, and all three sported beanies, including Chris who'd adopted the style to emulate his big brothers. Lance made their arrival even more mysterious and dramatic by blindfolding Chris as they neared the station, so he couldn't see the train until it was upon them. But Lance saw it and was slack-jawed with awe. It was just the locomotive, but it was freakin' huge! Much bigger than any Metrolink car he'd ever been on.

The locomotive was painted yellow, with "Union Pacific" in bold red letters along the side. There was a kind of American flag shield on the front, just above a huge metal extrusion protruding out in front to dislodge potential debris from the path of the moving train. There was a railing flanking both sides and a thin platform for walking along the outside.

He doubted Mr. Mills would let him, but Lance really wanted to walk outside the train while it was moving. It looked like it had four sets of wheels, but he wasn't certain he was counting correctly from this angle, and the entire engine looked to be a hundred feet long. It sat idling on the track, spewing out black smoke like a whale with lung cancer.

Wow!

Ryan pulled his sedan into the station. There were several LAPD officers standing guard, making certain the area was cleared of everyone but Ryan's group. Being a Sunday morning, there was no one around anyway. A couple of the uniforms glowered at Lance, but he purposely ignored them as he stepped from the car. He and Ricky led the giggling, still-blindfolded Chris from the car and walked him over to where he'd face the train at an angle. Ryan trailed behind, scanning the area protectively as he did so.

"Ready, Chris?" Lance asked.

The boy nodded vigorously.

Lance exchanged a grin with Ricky and then whipped off the blindfold.

Chris's jaw dropped open in amazement. "Oh, wow!" His eyes widened as he took in the monstrosity that was this massive locomotive.

Mr. Mills stood just to its front, grinning at Chris's reaction, and waving to Lance. He wore what looked like a typical train conductor's uniform, no doubt, Lance decided, to better impress Chris.

It had only been a year, but Mills looked older, grayer and thinner. Still, the man grinned broadly as the boys hurried up to him. Lance was shocked to see he was now taller than the older man. Mills noticed too, based on his surprised reaction.

"Well, well, well," the man enthused, looking Lance up and down. "If it ain't my pal, the great Sir Lance. And tallern' me to boot!"

He stuck out his hand and Lance happily clasped it. "Good to see you, Mr. Mills," he gushed, "and I grew three inches since last year."

Mills grinned. "That you have, my boy." His eyes drifted to Ricky, standing just to Lance's right. "And this must be the equally famous Sir Ricky."

Ricky smiled, a trifle embarrassed. "Oh, uh, thanks." He shook the man's calloused hand.

Mills looked over at Chris and smiled broadly. "And this must be the birthday boy, Sir Christopher. Howdy do, young one?" He stuck out his hand again, and Chris shook it, his face one big, happy grin.

Mills pulled his hand back and surveyed the three boys. "I owe yer dad a lot, that's fer sure, boys. It was his good word to my superiors that got me my promotion, don't ya know."

Ricky looked slightly uncomfortable. "So, uh, how do know our dad?" he asked, quickly adding, "You know, besides that he's famous and all?"

Mills nodded toward Lance. "You never told him the story?"

Lance shrugged. "It just never came up." He turned to Ricky with a chuckle. "When dad and me were running from the cops on Llamrei, Mr. Mills here hid us in an empty train car so we could get away."

Ricky laughed. "That's mad cool. Wish I could of been there."

Lance smiled shyly. "Me too."

"Those were the good ole' days," Mills said wistfully and clapped Lance on the shoulder. He looked down at Chris, who was bouncing up and down, bursting with energy. "Well, little man, you ready for a train ride?"

Chris nodded vigorously. "You think maybe I could drive some?"

Mills smiled conspiratorially. "Well, we'll just have to see about that, won't we?" He winked.

Chris laughed and the man ushered them forward to the five steps leading up into the engine. Chris ascended first, followed by Lance, then Ricky, and finally Mills.

Ryan sat in his car, watching until they all entered the cab of the engine. Just as he was starting the car, his cell rang. He saw the caller: 'Gibson'. Curious, he snatched it up and pressed talk. "Yeah, Gib, what's up?"

"You with the kids?" he heard over the line.

"Yeah. They just boarded the train."

"Listen, Ry, we got a lead on that red light camera pic. Our IT guy finally figured out how it was rerouted through practically every country on earth."

"Yeah, so?" Ryan kept his eyes pinned to the train.

Gibson's voice sounded excited. "We know where it originated."

Ryan sat up now, his heart rate quickening. Finally, a real lead. "Where?"

"Some hotshot entertainment lawyer in the Hollywood Hills," came Gibson's tired voice. "Been up for hours getting a search warrant. On our way there now."

"I'll be at Union Station waiting for the kids," Ryan said. "Keep me posted."

"Will do," he heard, and then the call ended.

Ryan sat and watched the train. The station was empty except for his officers, and there was no reason to wait until the locomotive actually departed. If they got up any speed along the way, the train might beat him to the station. True, Arthur was there, but he wanted to be on site anyway, just in case. So he started his car, backed carefully from the parking space, and drove out of the lot toward Los Angeles.

Inside the locomotive, Mills showed the boys the engine and pointed out the various controls. "This is an old diesel model, boys," he said, "Not much in use no more, which is why I could get hold of it today. Most new trains are electric, you see."

"How fast can this go?" Chris asked, dazzled by all the switches and levers and control buttons around them.

To Lance, it looked like being in some kind of old-school space ship or something.

"This old girl got six axles and four-thousand horse power, Chris, my boy. Since we're not pulling any cars, she could make eighty miles per hour, maybe more."

Chris's mouth dropped open in amazement.

"Course, we're not gonna be goin' that fast, just so ya know."

The little boy looked disappointed until Mills reached into a small cupboard tucked in beside a big white control panel loaded with black switches. Pausing dramatically, Mills pulled out a well-worn, child-size conductor's cap.

Lance whistled in surprise, because it really looked like an antique.

"Now this here," Mills said, holding the faded, bent and soiled cap out to Chris, "was my hat when I's your age, Chris."

"You were driving trains when youse eight?" Chris asked in amazement, his eyes as big as boiled eggs.

Lance and Ricky exchanged an amused look and did a quick low-five.

Mills shook his head. "No, but me pappy was, and he started teachin' me when I's your age, Chris. Now, I don't got no kids 'a my own, son, so I'd be honored if you'd take me old hat as a little gift, for your birthday and all."

Lance didn't think Chris's eyes could get any wider as he reached out and took the hat, staring at it like it was a pot of gold.

Lance chuckled. "Well, put it on, little man, or else you can't drive the train. Right Mr. Mills?" He winked, and the man grinned.

"Right you are, Lance."

Chris pulled off his beanie and handed it to Lance, who shoved it into his back pocket. The little boy slipped on the cap, and it fit perfectly, his long blond hair splaying out from beneath it. "Wow, this is so cool. Can I really drive the train? Can I, please?"

Mills appeared to consider a moment, as Chris bounced up and down excitedly. "Well, once we get out of the station, I'll turn her over to you for a couple a miles. Will that do ya?"

Chris's mouth dropped open so far that Lance and Ricky burst out laughing. Chris turned to them, mouth still drooping. "Did you hear that?"

They nodded, giving each other a high-five this time. Lance felt good about himself for coming up with this idea. Chris was stoked, and the shadow of Michael and his monstrous actions became shorter by the moment.

Mills sat Chris in the conductor's chair, up high where he could see over the protruding front end and out at the track ahead. Then Mills flipped a bunch of switches on the white panel and stepped forward to where Chris was seated. In front of the boy was a console of sorts. It looked like something Lance thought he might see in an old-fashioned airplane. There were buttons of differing colors, dials, gauges and indicator lights in green and red and white.

Mills pointed to a black handle that looked like the stick shift in a car and said, "That there is the throttle. It's how we speed up or slow down." Then he pointed to a big red handle to the right of the throttle. "This here is the brake. You ready, birthday boy?"

Chris nodded excitedly.

"Okay. Gimme yer hand." Chris extended his hand and Mills placed it atop the blacktopped throttle, and placed his own hand atop Chris's. "Okey dokey, Chris, let's get this baby moving."

Pressing forward with Chris's hand beneath his, the throttle clicked forward one notch, and the train began to move.

Gibson and several squad cars pulled into the enormous circular driveway of the mansion and stopped. When he'd pressed the buzzer at the large front gates, he expected to have to identify himself. But a buzzer sounded and the gates swung open. Gibson and his fellow officers exited their vehicles, guns drawn. Gibson nodded the men forward. He approached the front door, officers ducking to both sides of the entrance as back up. He rang the doorbell.

After a few moments, the door opened and a woman answered. She looked surprised to see them, as though she'd been expecting somebody else. She was an attractive woman, Gibson noted, the kind who'd clearly had "some work done," as the saying went in Hollywood, tall and regal.

"Mrs. Maitland?" Gibson asked, all business.

"Yes?" the woman replied, obviously annoyed by the interruption. "I'm expecting company. If you're Mormon or Jehovah, we're not interested."

Gibson flipped open his badge. "Sergeant Gibson, LAPD, ma'am. Is your husband home?"

She looked surprised by his badge, but barely gave it a glance as he slipped it back into his pocket.

Cool, this one, he thought.

"He's out playing golf," she announced, but offered nothing more, her lips drawn into a tight expression as the officers flanking Gibson moved into her line of sight.

"Does anyone else live on the premises?"

"My son," she answered curtly, obviously feeling put out by such a contemptible interruption.

Gibson slipped a paper from his pocket, holding it out for her to scrutinize. "We have a warrant to search the house and grounds, ma'am," he announced, just as curtly. Two could play this game.

"This is outrageous, Sergeant," she protested, with an arrogant tilt of her head.

"That may be so, ma'am, but as you can see, this warrant is duly sworn out and signed by a judge. Now, are there other buildings on the estate?"

For a moment, it looked like she wouldn't answer, but then she sighed. "There's a back house, behind the pool."

"Would the back house be open or do my men need a key?"

The woman glared daggers. "I'll send a servant around with the spare key."

Gibson nodded to the two officers and they took off toward the pool. Then he looked at the woman, who still blocked the entryway. "Ma'am?"

She eyed him again, and the team of officers behind him, and then stepped to one side. Gibson ushered the men into the house.

She called out, "If you damage anything, I'll sue."

Gibson turned to her soberly. "We'll be careful, ma'am."

As he started to cross the enormous entry hall, she called after him, "I'm calling my husband."

Gibson turned back. "Please do. We'd like to ask him some questions." Then he disappeared into the cavernous house.

When Ryan arrived at Union Station, he found Arthur standing beside Reyna, holding the reins of Llamrei. He hadn't seen the magnificent white mare in some time, and had to admit the horse looked impressive beneath the bright morning sun.

It hadn't taken him but fifteen minutes to get there – Sunday morning was the only light traffic day of the week.

Arthur and Reyna greeted him warmly, and Ryan said he wanted to scout around inside the terminal, just to make sure his men were on duty and everything looked secure. He retreated into the historic landmark.

The massive locomotive eased its way slowly out of the station and into downtown Pasadena. Normally, the Gold Line would make multiple stops on its way into Union

Station, but for now, local citizens up and about on a Sunday morning were treated to the rare sight of a real locomotive cruising slowly through their city.

Chris sat wide-eyed, his hand still on the throttle, with Mills' hand atop his. The train chugged noisily along, making its lazy way along the tracks.

Lance and Ricky gazed out the front windshield, and then darted over to look out the side windows, as well. Though neither wanted to say it aloud, both of them felt giddy with little boy excitement, something not usually cool for a teenager to display. Despite their attempts at nonchalance, each caught the other grinning foolishly at the experience of riding in a real train.

Gibson watched as his men carted computers from the house, laptops as well as desktop models. His radio beeped. Unclipping it from his belt, he clicked the talk button. "Gibson here."

A crackling voice came over the radio. "Officer Williams, sir, in the back house. You need to get back here, sir. You won't believe what we found."

Gibson clicked 'talk'. "On my way." He slipped the radio back to his belt and hurried toward the back door leading into the yard.

CHAPTER THIRTEEN
IS THIS WHERE YOU FINALLY KILL ME?

A S THE BOYS GAZED IN wonderment out the windows of the moving train, watching people and cars and the city of Pasadena slip evenly and casually past, Lance's phone vibrated. He saw it was Ryan, signaling for him to do a video chat. Lance touched the appropriate button and Ryan's face appeared on his phone.

"Hey, *nino*, what's up?"

"Just checking on you boys," Ryan said in reply. "Everything's set over here."

Lance knew what he meant and nodded silently. To say more might tip off Chris.

"Can you put your phone on the dashboard, or whatever those engineers call it, so I can see you guys at all times?" Ryan asked. When Lance frowned, Ryan added quickly, "Okay, call me overly cautious. I just got that feeling in my gut. Humor your old G-dad, okay?"

Lance smiled. "Sure, old man, no problem."

Ryan cracked a grin.

As Lance turned toward the console, his phone signaled an incoming text.

The name read: 'Michael'.

Lance's breath caught in his throat, and he quickly turned away from the others to hide his reaction. He fumblingly opened the text message.

'I'm at the back of this train. DO NOT alert Ricky boy unless you want him seriously hurt. This is between you and me'.

Lance's heart began thundering in his chest. Oh, God... He glanced cautiously back toward Ricky, and then he remembered Ryan, quickly closing the text. His face must've indicated something wrong because Ryan asked immediately, "You all right over there, Lance?"

Lance forced control into his voice. "Yeah, *nino*. No prob. Here, I'm gonna put the phone up front."

Hopeful the vibrations of the train beneath his feet would mask his trembling hands, he placed the phone in front of everyone, away from the controls, but in a position where they could see Ryan, and he them.

"Hey, birthday boy, how's it going?" Ryan called out from the phone, working the best smile he had onto his wrinkled face.

"I'm driving the train, Sergeant Ryan!" Chris gushed, and Ricky gave a little wave.

"Uh, Mr. Mills," Lance asked, fighting to sound calm and casual. "Is there a bathroom in back? I forgot to go."

Chris grinned at him. "Should a gone peepee when you made me go, Lance."

Lance looked embarrassed. "I know."

Mills kept his eyes glued to the moving track ahead and threw a thumb toward the back. "You can't miss it."

Ricky eyed him peculiarly. "I thought you went at home."

Lance fought to meet his gaze, his palms sweating, his heart beating louder than the rolling of the train. "Drank too much water, I guess. Be right back."

He turned and hurried through the door into the main cabin of the locomotive. He closed the door and looked around. There was no one there. Had Michael just been screwing with him? There were some bench seats, upholstered with a kind of smooth-looking mustard yellow material, and small windows at either side for viewing the passing scenery as you sat on those benches. But nothing else.

He hesitantly made his way down the length of the train car, glancing furtively to his right and left in case Michael might be hidden behind one of the benches, and then stopped at the very rear. He spotted the bathroom easily enough, tucked into a corner.

But no Michael.

He glanced out of a window first to his left, and then to his right, before standing upright in the center aisle, bewildered, and gazing back toward the front of the train.

A click sound made him whirl, and he gasped.

Michael stood just outside the bathroom door. He wore his usual tight black shirt, designer pants, and Nike's, but his face blazed with a demonic fury Lance had only glimpsed a couple of times before.

Only now that fury was directed at him.

And he'd left his phone up front.

Michael's nostrils flared like an infected animal, his breathing sounded almost guttural, and his eyes drilled holes right through Lance.

"You and me, Lance, we have a *big* problem."

Lance stood there, rooted to the spot, gazing back at the boy, and seeing only the monster. Was this the day he'd die? For good this time?

When Gibson had skirted the pool and entered the lavish back house—noting that it made his own place look like a hovel by comparison—a young officer in uniform quickly approached.

"Back here, Sergeant," he said and indicated the door to the bedroom. Gibson followed. "We were checking the closets for anything suspicious," the young man said as he led Gibson into the bedroom with its king size bed and luxurious appointments. Other officers were unhooking two desktop monitors in preparation for removal.

Officer Williams led Gibson into a long, massive walk-in closet that actually turned to the left into another huge space.

Enough Nike's here to outfit the whole NBA, Gibson thought as he passed the shoe racks.

Officer Williams pointed to the corner. "Back there, sir. We found a secret room."

Gibson eyed the young man peculiarly, then stepped forward with a deliberate pace. The suits had all been pulled off the racks and laid on the floor to provide easier access to the hidden room.

Gibson stepped beneath the overhead clothes bar and into the room itself. He stopped up short and gazed in horror at what he saw papering the walls around him. "Holy crap!"

Michael held out one arm. It was taut with tension, every vein bulging. "Gimme your phone."

"I don't have it."

But I wish I did.

The brown eyes narrowed dangerously. "Do I have to take it from you?"

Lance shrugged. He was more afraid than he'd ever been in Michael's presence, but he couldn't show it. He held up his arms. "Search me. I left it up front."

The eyes narrowed even further. "Why?"

"Cause my *nino* wanted to be on video chat with us the whole time, to make sure everything was all right."

Michael glowered again, and then stepped forward aggressively. Lance flinched, but stood his ground. Michael's huge hands swept over his body, hard, probing, with not even a pretense of the gentleness as he'd shown in the past. When the hand got to Lance's crotch, he tensed, waiting for Michael to grip it painfully or otherwise torment him. The palm of Michael's hand lingered, sending a jolt of fear racing up Lance's back, but he fought it down and gazed at Michael as calmly as he could.

The bigger boy stood back, satisfied Lance had not been lying. Those brown eyes fell on him again like bullets piercing his head.

Lance refused to be intimidated. "Why, Michael? Why'd you do those things?"

Michael's angry look turned to shock. "You of all people have to ask me that? After you saw what they did to me? It's called justice, Lance! An eye for an eye. They'll never rape another kid again. I made sure of that. I even took care of your two problems 'cause you didn't have the balls to do it. *That's* justice!"

The words ripped into him, appalling him with their animalistic brutality, and making him feel like a failure at the same time. "I was just a boy, Michael," he protested weakly. "What could I have done?"

Michael sneered. "I was a boy too, Lance! Those rapists made me a man real quick. And I took care of business." His entire body looked like a spring ready to snap.

Lance gazed at Michael as though seeing him for the first time. "They really did turn you into a monster, didn't they?"

Michael laughed, and the sound chilled Lance's very soul. "Just like in Frankenstein." Then those eyes bored into him once more. "Now you look me in the eye, Lance, and tell me you feel sorry for Mr. D. or that son-of-a-bitch Richard. You tell me that!"

Lance tried to hold the gaze, tried to open his mouth to tell Michael he did feel sorry, that what Michael had done was too much. Too over the top.

But he couldn't.

Because he didn't feel sorry.

What goes around comes around.

He lowered his gaze to the floor of the train in shame.

Michael cackled. "I knew it. You and your lofty speeches about forgiveness."

Lance gulped, hating his own weakness more than his fear of Michael. "I get the guys who raped you, Michael, but why the others? They never touched you."

Michael's face darkened. "Mr. D. tried to rape you, and he *did* rape Jack."

That caught Lance by surprise. "Why would you care about Jack?"

Michael laughed again, derisively and mockingly. "For a guy who can look in someone's eyes and see their whole frickin' soul, you still don't know?"

Lance tilted his head uncertainly.

Michael met his gaze and pointed to his own eyes. "Look, Lance, really look into my eyes and tell me you don't see."

So Lance looked, more deeply than he ever had. Something about those eyes had always confused and enticed him. All he saw now was coldness and fury and emptiness. But then, for a split second, he saw it – gentleness.

"Oh, my God..."

Michael laughed hollowly. "I stand before you a living stand-up comic's favorite joke, Lance – separated at birth. Pretty funny, huh?"

Lance felt numb, suddenly understanding why he'd felt close to Michael from the beginning, why he'd trusted the boy when no one else did. "Twins?"

"Fraternal. Me blond, him brunette, but we both got the same eyes."

Lance expelled a breath, suddenly realizing this was the information Reyna had uncovered and tried to tell him about. "Did, uh, did Jack know?"

Michael shrugged disinterestedly. "I doubt it. I only realized it when I saw a close-up of Jacky boy on TV and lo and behold, there were my eyes looking out at me."

Lance's whole body trembled from this new revelation. "How'd you find out?"

Michael just tapped his temple with one thick finger. "The Pentagon, remember?"

Lance nodded. But something still didn't add up. Was that all that existed between him and Michael? The ghost of Jack? He felt certain there was more. Much more. "Okay, I get Mr. D. But why Richard?"

Michael flinched slightly, and something brief and uncertain flickered across those brown eyes. Then the hardness returned. "You were six years old, Lance! How many other little kids you think he raped over the years?"

"That's the only reason?" Lance asked in a taunting fashion, knowing he could be treading dangerous waters with Michael as unhinged as he was right then. "You just wanted to save innocent kids from a rapist?"

Michael didn't answer, but that flicker washed over his eyes again. He actually seemed hesitant. There was a moment of silence between them, with only the vibrations of the train and the rolling of its wheels against metal track between them.

"You're Jesus and Harry Potter and The Ivory Tower all rolled into one," Michael finally said, but his voice had dropped to a whisper.

Lance saw the facial expression shift momentarily from monster to boy, and had a sudden insight. "You posted that up, didn't you? *You* started calling me that."

Michael refused to answer. The hardness was back. The brown eyes glared, squinting once more with malice and fury.

Lance sighed, and met those cold, dead eyes straight on with his own. "So, is this where you finally kill me, Michael?"

Michael flinched slightly, but otherwise maintained the same taut posture, and demented facial expression.

Lance gazed at him with resignation. "The poisoned vodka, the runaway roller coaster – those were just warm-ups?"

Still Michael stared, silent and unmoving as a wax statue.

"So how you gonna do it, Michael? Throw me off the train and make it look like I fell? Or do you not even care enough to hide it anymore? You gonna just choke me out and watch my life slip away? Tell me, Michael. I wanna know before I die."

His voice remained calm and cool, and he felt unexpectedly composed. For whatever reason, he no longer felt afraid. Maybe it was the revelation about Jack, or maybe it was the uncertain look that still remained hidden behind Michael's outward glare. Whatever it was, he calmly awaited Michael's response.

Michael didn't move a muscle and looked like one of those Greek gods carved into marble, cold and hard and toweringly beautiful. Like Jack, but not like Jack.

"I didn't do those things," Michael whispered, his eyes never wavering. "I tried to find out who did, but I couldn't. And I didn't think they'd arrest you for Thornton." He paused. "I never would've let you go on trial."

Lance gazed soberly at him. Did he believe him? Did it matter anymore?

"You don't believe me, do you?" Michael asked, his voice still without inflection.

Lance continued staring, but did not respond.

Michael met his gaze with such intensity that Lance was tempted to break eye contact. But he didn't.

"You could be the first thing I've ever been wrong about, Lance," Michael continued dispassionately. There was a pause. "But I don't think so."

He reached into his pants pocket, slipped out a flash drive and held it out.

Lance took it and turned the drive over in his fingers, his expression quizzical. "What's this?"

Michael never broke eye contact. "Everything. My rape video, my V-log describing how I got justice, the photos I took, everything."

Lance's mouth dropped open in shock. "Why would you give me this?"

"Because you'll know the right thing to do," Michael said, his voice but a whisper, barely audible over the rolling of the train. "Like always."

Lance's breath stopped a moment, and his hand closed over the flash drive, his arm dropping to his side. Without breaking eye contact, he slipped the drive into his pocket and stared long and hard at Michael. Into those eyes so like Jack's, and yet so different.

"Why, Michael?" he asked, his own voice more breathy than he'd have liked.

Michael just stared at him. What was in those eyes of his?

His heart pounding, Lance said, "You give me enough evidence to put you in prison forever and you're just gonna let me walk away? I wanna know why."

No response.

"Tell me the truth, Michael!"

If Michael ever planned to answer, Lance would never know, for at that moment an enormous explosion rocked the train, jolting the entire locomotive upwards slightly, sending both startled boys tumbling hard to the floor of the moving car.

CHAPTER FOURTEEN

I ALREADY HAD MINE

G IBSON'S MEN AWAITED THE FORENSICS team to dust the hidden room for prints and catalogue the evidence, while the sergeant stood by the pool, sending Ryan a text message with an attached photo. Then he dialed Ryan's number.

Ryan hovered within Union Station, watching his phone and enjoying the looks on the faces of the kids.

Wait a minute!

Lance hadn't come back yet. That was odd. Just when he was about to ask Ricky, a text from Gibson caught his eye. He put the call on hold and opened the text.

'This is the perp, Ry. Did the mutilations. And he had pix of that coaster at Manic Mountain. This is one of Arthur's kids, right, the new one?'

Ryan opened the attachment. As it slowly revealed itself, Ryan found himself gazing at a cold, hard, chiseled young face topped with scruffy blond hair. Michael. The phone beeped. It was Gibson. Leaving the train call on hold, he put the phone to his ear.

"Yeah, Gib, I got it, and yeah, he's the arrogant one."

"Name's Michael Maitland."

"You got him?"

"No. Not here."

"Hellfire!" Ryan cursed.

"Where's Lance?" Gibson asked, anxiously.

"On board the train. Hold on, let me click back." Ryan placed Gibson on hold and re-opened the video chat to the train. "What the hell?"

The image he saw was a corner, very indistinct, but what wasn't indistinct was the thick, black smoke swirling around it. And then the image cut off.

"Crap!" He switched back to Gibson. "Get over here now, Gib, something's gone wrong on that train!"

"On my way!" The call ended.

Ryan knew he had to find an engineer, somebody who could make contact with that train, but first he dialed Arthur. He controlled his voice as best he could. "Get in here, Arthur. There's a problem."

He hung up and searched for someone in charge.

Outside the station, Arthur hung up with Ryan, a chill enveloping his soul such as he hadn't felt since that night so long ago when Jack had returned alone, without Lance. That had been the beginning of the end.

"What's wrong, Arthur?" Reyna asked, easily picking up his change of expression and body language.

He tried to affect a calmness he didn't feel. "Sergeant Ryan needs me inside. Would you watch Llamrei for me, please?"

She eyed him carefully, and he knew she could see his fear. "Sure."

He handed her the reins and trotted off into the station as quickly as he could without alarming Reyna or anyone else milling about.

Lance's head struck one of the seats when he fell, momentarily stunning him. He felt strong hands pull him to his feet and shake him hard. The train was still moving beneath them, he noted, as he looked into Michael's stony face.

"Did you do something, Michael?" he asked, pushing the hair out of his face, ignoring the pain in his head.

Michael released him and started toward the front of the train.

Fear for Ricky and Chris engulfed Lance and he staggered forward, pushing himself past the bigger boy and blocking the aisle leading into the engine room. Heart pounding, he stood his ground. "I'm not gonna let you hurt them, Michael."

Michael stood, body coiled, anger flaring in those eyes again, and then he held out his arm. "You first."

Backing up cautiously, keeping his eyes on Michael, Lance neared the door before turning around and flinging it inward toward him.

Black, oily-smelling smoke belched out of the cab into the car, choking him and forcing him backward. Michael leapt forward, flinging open windows on either side of the train to suck out the smoke before both of them could be overcome by it. Then he muscled his way past the gagging Lance and into the cab of the train. Lance coughed and spluttered against the noxious fumes, and staggered after him.

Smoke spiraled up from the front of the engine, and more spewed from the main console. Ricky lay crouched in one corner cradling a crying, smoke-blackened Chris.

Ricky gasped fearfully when he saw Michael. "What's he doing here?"

Lance squatted down. "Is Chris okay? Are you okay?"

Ricky nodded, still clutching Chris to him. Both faces had been blackened, and Chris's blond hair was quickly going dark from the swirling, oily black smoke.

Squinting against the invading fumes, Lance stood and glanced around, assessing the situation.

The glass windshield was cracked, and smoke billowed up from the front engine. The control panel looked fried, with all the circuits and dials and light switches dark, and sending up tendrils of ominous-looking smoke.

There was no sign of Mills.

"Where's Mr. Mills?" Lance asked frantically, his eyes burning from the acrid smoke.

"He heard the engine making some strange noise," Ricky said, his voice sounding raw and fighting for calm. "He went out to check if we ran over something, and then the thing blew. He fell off, Lance!"

"Oh, no!" Lance whispered.

Ricky pointed at Michael. "He sneaks on board and the engine blows up? Don't tell me that just happened!"

Michael's eyes bored furiously into Ricky. "You still wanna piece of me, bodyguard? Let's go at it! But *after* we fix this problem!" He didn't even squint, seemingly unaffected by the roiling smoke.

Lance put out both hands. "Enough!"

Ricky clambered to his feet, setting Chris down and taking the terrified boy's small hand in his.

Lance's eyes teared up fiercely from the smoke, and he had to fight to keep from coughing. He spotted his phone, tossed into a corner. He snatched it up. The screen was cracked, but miraculously, it still worked when he pressed the power button. The train continued moving forward as smoke curled skyward and wafted back into the cab through the two side windows. He frantically unlocked his phone screen. From the corner of his eye, he saw Michael examining the lifeless control panel.

"We're speeding up," Michael announced calmly, tossing a quick look back over his shoulder.

Lance nodded.

The smoke continued to swirl around them, but most of it quickly whooshed out the side windows as the train picked up speed and rattled relentlessly down the track. They'd left Pasadena behind and were clattering along through an industrial area of warehouses, with more railroad tracks on either side.

The video chat re-opened and Ryan's frantic face reappeared. "Oh, thank God!" Ryan exclaimed when he saw Lance. "Is everyone all right?"

"Mr. Mills fell off the train," Lance answered as evenly as he could, coughing a couple of times and squinting at the image of his desperate godfather. "Ricky and Chris are okay, but the train's still going, *nino*. How do we stop it?"

"I'm talking to an engineer now, Lance," Ryan said, "but there doesn't seem to be much he can do. That's an old diesel and he can't control it from here, not with everything blown at your end." His face paled. "Get him away from those controls!"

Lance whirled. Michael was tinkering with the dials and switches.

"Hold the phone up so Michael can see me, Lance," he heard Ryan say with more intensity than usual.

Michael stood upright and turned, chest puffed out, face without discernable expression, his back to the console. Lance held the phone up so Ryan could see him. Ricky clutched the shaking Chris tightly as both pressed in next to Lance.

"Listen to me, Michael," Ryan said, keeping his voice steady and calm. "We know everything."

Michael flinched, and Ricky cast a questioning look Lance's way.

"We have your computer, and we've been in your secret room."

Lance sucked in a shocked breath, his eyes whipping from the phone to Michael's stony face, fearfully awaiting the explosion to come.

But Michael only nodded, and then the old familiar smirk returned. "How'd you make me?"

"We have a good IT guy," Ryan replied with forced calmness. "Figured out your pattern when you sent that red light photo."

Michael nodded again, with no trace of anger on his features—only a sense of inevitability. "So Lance got me busted after all." He shrugged, as though that was exactly how it was supposed to happen.

Lance gazed at him in stunned realization of what Michael had done. Michael had saved him from prison. True, he hadn't confessed to the crime, but he had gotten him set free.

"He didn't tell us anything, Michael!" Ryan said quickly, his voice sounding muffled and far away beneath the rattling and rolling of the train wheels. "Don't hurt him. Or the others. Please."

Michael looked soberly into the phone. "I wouldn't hurt him."

Ryan paused, keeping as much of a poker face as he could. "You're the chief suspect in the roller coaster tampering."

Lance watched Michael's facial expressions, and Ricky watched Lance.

"You sent in that red light photo?" Lance finally said, focusing as hard as he could on Michael's face, which wasn't easy with the smoke burning his eyes.

Michael stared back, strong, like a rock, still unaffected by the smoke except for a dusting of black in his blond hair, making him look more like Jack than ever before. He merely shrugged as if to say 'Who else could have done it?'

"Don't trust him, Lance," Ricky implored, his own blackened face contorted with fear. "He's a monster, like I been telling you all along."

Lance looked a long moment at Ricky, and then back at Michael. The bigger boy hadn't budged, but those eyes fixed on Lance with a look he'd seen maybe once before, that night he'd been so drunk and Michael had taken him to his bedroom. The kind of look Jack used to give him.

Lance looked at Ryan's terrified face, floating within the cracked phone screen like a phantom.

"*Nino*, Michael's the only one smart enough to stop this train," he said, eyeing Michael expectantly. "I have to let him try."

"No!" both Ryan and Ricky screamed at the same time.

Then Ryan said, "Please, Lance, the boy is unstable. He *is* a monster, like Ricky said. Don't let him touch the controls!"

Just then, Arthur's face appeared beside Ryan's.

"Dad!" both boys called out, and Chris looked up at the phone with tearful hope.

Arthur's face was chiseled with worry and fear, and Lance could tell he was struggling to remain calm. "Lance. My son. I agree with Sergeant Ryan. Michael cannot be trusted. Please."

Lance looked straight into the phone, so Arthur could clearly see his face. The train rattled ceaselessly forward. Smoke continued unabated from the damaged engine. He was afraid, but he was also sure of himself.

"Dad, do you trust me?" Lance held his breath.

Arthur looked caught off-guard for a split second, and then replied, "I love you, Lance."

"I know you do, Dad," Lance said quietly, and lovingly. "But do you trust me?"

Now Arthur hesitated, glancing over at the unseen Ryan before turning back to face Lance. "Yes, son, I trust you."

Lance let out that breathy little laugh, and warmth suffused him, despite their danger. "I love you, Dad, more than you may ever know." Then he turned to Michael. "Go, Michael!"

Ricky cursed under his breath, but the bigger boy didn't hesitate. He leapt for the console and examined every dial and switch. Lance exchanged a look with Ricky, whose brown eyes flashed fear and distrust. Lance tried for a little smile, placing a comforting hand on Chris's smoke blackened hair. Michael dropped to his knees and opened a rectangle beneath the control panel.

The wiring and all the working parts inside were blackened and smoking. Michael stood and took another look at the throttle. It jiggled back and forth uselessly. So did the red brake switch.

He turned to face the boys, and shook his head.

Chris started to cry again, and Ricky pulled him closer.

Lance met Michael's eyes and nodded his thanks. Then he turned back to the phone. Ryan's face was there, but not Arthur. "Where's my Dad?"

Ryan looked hopeless. "He's coming for you."

"There isn't time," Michael said quickly, his voice calm as steel. "We've gotta get off this train before it goes any faster."

Ryan reluctantly addressed Michael. "How fast is it going now, Michael? We've got nothing at this end with everything off at yours."

Michael glanced out the window. Lance followed his gaze. The world sped past at a much faster rate than last he checked. Faster by the moment. The rattling of wheels against track had intensified.

"Thirty, maybe thirty-five," Michael answered, and then turned back to Lance and Ricky. "We've gotta get little man off this train now." He indicated Chris.

The two older boys just stared at Michael, and Lance didn't know what he meant. Get off how?

Michael ignored them and bent toward Chris. The little boy cowered between Ricky and Lance. Michael sighed with obvious frustration. "Listen, little man, you know how to fight, right?" Chris eyed him fearfully. "You remember how to tuck and roll when you fall? I know you do, 'cause I've seen you do it."

Chris still stared, blue eyes petrified with fear. Michael's intensity was clearly scaring him.

Exasperated, Michael stood and looked at Lance. "Tell him to listen to me, Lance."

Lance looked down into Chris's frightened eyes. "It's okay, Chris. He's Jack's brother."

Chris gasped, and Ricky's mouth dropped open.

"What the...?" Ricky spluttered.

Lance nodded.

"When did you find that out?" Ricky blurted.

"Just now," Lance replied.

Ricky turned his open-mouthed expression of shock on Michael.

"Now you finally understand what you were fighting, don't you, Ricky boy?"

Ricky flinched, but said nothing.

Lance's eyes burned from the smoke. "Understand what?"

But Ricky refused to answer, and Michael just shrugged.

With a frustrated sigh, Lance said to Chris, "Listen to him, Chris. He knows what he's doing."

Chris nodded, squinting against the oily smoke in the air.

Michael squatted down to look him in the eye. "Now when I tell you to jump, Chris, the second you hit the ground, you tuck and roll. Cover your face and ride it out. Ricky boy'll be right behind you."

"Hell, no!" Ricky exclaimed. "I'm not leaving you alone with him, Lance."

Michael stood and expelled an annoyed breath. "We'll be right behind you."

Ricky shook his head. "No. You go with Chris and I'll go with Lance."

Michael looked down at Chris. "That work for you, Chris?"

The small boy shook his head. "I wanna go with Ricky or Lance."

"See. Now get ready to jump, bodyguard."

Ricky gazed imploringly at Lance. "I don't trust him, Lance. *Please* don't make me do this!"

"I do trust him. Please, Ricky. Protect Chris. He's more important." He met Ricky's gaze straight on. "So are you."

Ricky's eyes widened, despite being irritated from the swirling smoke, and Lance saw something in that look that confused him. "Lance, I..."

"*Please*, Ricky."

Michael sighed heavily. "Sometime today, ladies, before this train gets too fast for any of us?"

With obvious fear, and extreme reluctance, Ricky nodded.

"Good," Michael said, and led Chris to the door and slid it open, squatting down with the small boy. Onrushing wind whipped everyone's hair in all directions, and the ground sped past with alarming speed. Chris cowered back into Michael's arms, gripping the bigger boy in panic. Startled, Michael froze.

Chris studied his face. "You have the same eyes."

Michael nervously nodded. Then he gently placed his hands on Chris's shoulders. "Remember what I said, little man – tuck, roll, and cover."

Chris nodded, his light blue eyes wide pools of terror.

Michael turned Chris's head to look outward and lowered his hands to his upper back. "Don't be afraid. You're as badass as they come, Chris. Get ready."

The ground started to get grassier and less rocky.

"On three. One. Two. Three." Michael pushed and Chris jumped at the same time, quickly disappearing into the grasslands behind the train. Michael leapt to his feet. "Now you, Ricky boy!"

Ricky stepped to the door, cast one last heartbroken look at Lance, then jumped. He too, vanished from sight.

Michael turned to Lance, his face set, his voice rock solid steady. "Our turn."

Lance suddenly blanched white as a thought occurred to him. He held up the phone. Ryan's face was still there, but turned away. Lance could barely hear muffled voices speaking with him from off-camera somewhere. "*Nino!*"

Ryan looked back quickly. "What is it?"

"We got Chris and Ricky off but, *nino*, where will this train crash if we can't stop it?"

Ryan looked grave. "Right here in Union Station."

Lance sucked in a breath. "Where *you* are?"

"No. It'll hit the platform, where people board."

"What?"

"Lance, we don't have much time!" Michael hissed, his eyes glancing over at the spinning world outside the open door.

"Quiet, Michael," Lance hissed right back before looking again at Ryan. "How many people are down there, *nino*?"

Ryan shrugged. "We don't know. We're trying to evacuate, but... do you have any idea how fast you're going now?"

Lance glanced at Michael, who cursed under his breath and looked out the door again. The rattling of the wheels against the metal track had gotten louder, more frantic. He turned back.

"Maybe forty."

Lance saw Ryan glance to his left, pause, and then turn back. "Not enough time.

Your ETA at that speed is approximately seven minutes. Get off the train *now*, Lance. Save yourselves."

Michael looked relieved. "Finally, somebody with sense. C'mon, Lance, you heard the man."

Lance lowered the phone, arms at his side, body tense with dread. "Michael, all those people…"

"Are not our problem, Lance," Michael insisted, his body taut with tension. "Getting off this train is!"

"But they'll be killed!" Lance insisted, his throat raw from smoke inhalation. His mind filled with horror at the thought of so many innocents dying because of him.

"So?" Michael's face flared with anger. "How many of those men down there raped kids like us, huh, Lance? How many women down there stood by and let 'em do it? We owe them nothing! Let 'em all die!"

Lance looked at Michael, horrified, his face settling into a soft, compassionate expression. He placed a gentle hand on Michael's hard, powerful shoulder. "That's not true, Michael. Most people are good. You know that now."

"I know nothing!" Michael shot back, shrugging his shoulder away.

"Please, Michael," Lance insisted, his voice tremulous, but insistent. "There's gotta be some kind of emergency brake, like the hand brake in a car."

Michael shook his head emphatically. "Won't do any good at this speed, Lance. Not when we're this close."

Lance gave Michael the imploring look that had melted hearts and minds ever since he'd taken center spotlight on the world stage. "*Please*, Michael. There must be a way."

Michael cursed loudly, turning his attention back to the console. He crouched down and spotted the emergency hand brake – a blue pull handle – set back and below the main controls. He bent to examine it, pulled slightly and felt pressure. Then he turned and snatched the phone from Lance. "Ryan. There any curve in the track 'tween here and the station?"

Ryan looked to his left again, paused, and then turned back. "Yeah. Less than a mile out."

Michael put the phone down on the console and stared at Lance.

"What?"

"You want a solution, Lance, here it is," Michael intoned dispassionately. "When this train hits the curve, yank that emergency brake as hard as possible and she'll jump the track."

Lance scrunched up his face. "Jump the track?"

"Crash, Lance."

Lance broke into a grin. "Well, that's great! We yank the brake and then jump."

Michael shook his head soberly. "No can do. That brake has to be pulled and held tight at exactly the moment the train hits that curve."

The blood drained from Lance's face. "You mean…"

Michael nodded. "Titanic time, Lance. Whoever pulls that brake goes down with the ship."

Lance stood a moment, frozen in place, his whole life swirling around him like the wind whipping his hair in every direction. He trembled, feeling sad and lost and hopeful and alone and a hundred other emotions all at once. He knew what had to be done. There was no other way. He looked at Michael compassionately. "You go, Michael. I'll stay."

"What?" Michael exclaimed, his furious face dissolving into shock.

From the phone on the console, Ryan shouted, "No, Lance, you can't!"

Michael stared at Lance as though he were crazy.

"Please, Michael," Lance implored, knowing he sounded weak. "I want you to live."

Michael's face darkened into such monstrous fury that Lance thought he might kill him on the spot. But Michael just slammed one fist sideways into the metal control panel so hard he made a dent. "The hell, Lance! You wanna die for a bunch of strangers?"

Lance shrugged, his eyes filled with hope. "They deserve a second chance, Michael. So do you. I already had mine and I screwed it up."

Michael clenched and unclenched his fists, suddenly seeming so like Jack. He raised his eyes and drilled them into Lance's very soul.

Lance's gaze didn't waver. He refused to cower. He could do this. He was tired. He'd messed things up too many times. Now he had to make something right. "Go, Michael," he whispered softly.

The rattling of the train beneath his feet grew louder, the vibrations stronger.

They were accelerating.

Death was finally coming back to claim him.

Michael glared a moment longer. "Screw it!" erupted from his mouth like volcanic lava and he shoved Lance out of the way, taking his place in front of the emergency brake.

"No, Michael," Lance said, struggling to move the bigger boy, gripping solid muscles that felt like steel. "I said I'd do it."

Michael didn't budge, and Lance felt like he was trying to move the Rock of

Gibraltar. Sweat broke out on his forehead as he tried to force his way back to the emergency brake.

"You're not strong enough, Lance!" Michael hissed, his eyes fiery.

"Am too!" Lance retorted, his pride stung. Then he released his futile grip on the boy and stepped back, panting from the exertion. "How do you know that?"

Michael just gave him a look that said, 'How do I know any of the stuff I know?'

Lance sighed, his body tight with emotion. "Okay, but I'm staying to help."

Michael nodded and looked out the cracked windshield a second before turning back. "I'll pull the brake handle. Stay behind me and be ready to pull my arm when I say so. Got it?"

Lance agreed, sweat dripping from his hair into his smoke-stung eyes, causing him to blink furiously.

"Lance," he heard Ryan's frantic, muffled voice seemingly coming from the air itself, barely audible anymore over the howling wind and rattling wheels. "Don't do this! Please!"

Pain shot through his heart at the anguish he heard in Ryan's voice. But he ignored his godfather and just looked at Michael. Michael looked at him. Their eyes met and held.

"Do something for me, Lance, before we..."

Lance raised his eyebrows questioningly.

Michael indicated the open door with a nod of his head. "Stand there and look out a second."

Confused, Lance obeyed. He turned and stood at the top step watching the world whiz past at a dizzying speed.

"What do you see?" he heard Michael ask from behind him, the boy's voice nearly drowned out by the pounding of the train.

"The world, going by really fast." He turned to look at Michael, but Michael used his huge hands to gently turn Lance's head back toward the open door.

"Exactly. The world. See, this is how it is, Lance. You're the boy who came back. *I'm* the boy who got screwed. And it's gotta stay that way."

A chill raced up Lance's spine, and he was just starting to turn around when Michael yelled, "Jump!" and shoved him outward with both powerful arms.

Suddenly Lance was airborne, out the door and flying downward at an alarming rate of free-fall.

"Noooooo!" he screamed, and then his feet slammed hard into solid ground. Pain lanced up his right ankle like a thousand scorching knives, and his skating instincts took over. He tucked and bent forward. His shoulder pounded into the ground, knocking the air from his lungs in an instant, and then he was rolling and pitching out of control down a hard, gravelly slope.

Inside the cab, Michael stood a moment at the open door, though Lance was long gone.

"It's gotta stay that way, Lance," he whispered, his face dissolving into a look of resignation. He turned back to the console. He saw Ryan's stunned face watching him from the damaged surface of the phone. They looked a moment at each other.

"Lance was right about you, Michael," the detective said, his voice tinged with admiration.

Michael smiled wryly. "No. I was right about him."

He reached for the hand brake, his eyes fixed on the track. The sharp curve loomed just ahead. He held his breath. The train rattled forward with pounding intensity, and swung sharply into the curve. Every muscle in his arms and back taut with tension, Michael gripped the emergency brake and pulled.

Arthur galloped Llamrei at a frenetic pace across the gravelly train yard toward the fast-moving locomotive in the distance. He could hear sirens approaching from behind, and knew the emergency personnel were close.

But not close enough.

The train whipped into a high-pitched, screeching turn, and Arthur watched in open-mouthed horror as, with a terrific rending and shrieking of metal, the locomotive jumped the track, sailing upward like a breaching whale and landing at an angle on its wheels, flipping over onto its side and grinding its way forward along the rocky ground.

"Lance!" he screamed from the depths of his very soul, his heart almost frozen, and dug in his heels, spurring Llamrei into a frothing gallop.

Lance tumbled and rolled and pitched over and over again, covering his face as his arms and elbows crashed hard into this rock or that ridge. Bits of gravel flew everywhere, stinging his face and gouging his back. The fall seemed endless, and instantaneous at the same time, until he finally slammed into some bushes that entangled him like a prickly fishnet, and his forward motion suddenly ceased.

Dazed and fighting for breath, he heard an unearthly rending and tearing and screeching, then the crashing of metal and wood. He sat up quickly, tearing his sleeves on the branches, his head swimming, his ankle throbbing, his beanie gone and his hair a tangled mass of brambles and dirt.

"Michael!" he shrieked before staggering to his feet and stumbling forward. He felt dizzy and unsteady, his eyes swimming in and out of focus as he pressed on.

He spotted the wreckage in the distance, the crumpled locomotive lying on its side like a downed buffalo, smoke rising from the engine, and he lurched and staggered and stumbled toward it. Pain ripped through his ankle, but he didn't care. He saw from the corner of his eye his dad galloping furiously toward the wrecked train. But his heart and mind were fixed on one thing only – the boy who'd saved him.

As he tripped and rose, tripped again and fought to clear his head, Lance haltingly forced his way closer, calling out shrilly, "Michael!" He could scarcely breathe from fear and shock and had to keep swatting dirty, sweaty hair off his scratched face.

He scuttled over the gravel like a wounded crab, saw the spinning wheels, the oily black diesel fumes spewing forth and further burning his eyes. He lurched his way around the front of the engine, arms outstretched to maintain balance.

"Michael!"

He heard a groan. He stumbled onward over the hard ground until he spotted a body lying in the grit about ten feet from the damaged train.

"Michael!" he called out, and pelted forward. He halted abruptly when he saw the boy sprawled on his back, burned and bloody and broken, one leg twisted grotesquely back at the knee, the joint clearly shattered.

"Michael," he wheezed, his breathing raspy and ragged, as he dropped down beside him. Lance gently placed his hands on Michael's cut and bleeding cheeks, cupping the boy's face and turning the head carefully toward him.

Michael's eyelids fluttered open and he blinked a few times with confusion. Then he clearly recognized Lance. His handsome face was bloody and bruised, but he tried for a grin. "Jumped, like you said, Lance," he coughed out hoarsely. "Missed."

He lifted his right arm slowly, grimacing in agony as he did, and Lance gasped in horror. A piece of metal protruded from Michael's chest, the shirt torn, the muscle and flesh ragged and bloody, and the boy was bleeding out quickly.

"Oh, God," Lance said, frantically patting his pockets. "My phone! I don't have my phone!"

Then he staggered to his feet and saw Arthur in the distance, closing the gap.

Behind his dad, further back, were the flashing lights and wailing sirens of emergency vehicles.

"Hurry!" he screamed desperately.

"It's okay, Lance," Michael croaked and Lance dropped back to his knees, his eyes brimming with tears.

"Why, Michael? Why did you do it?"

Then Michael did something Lance had never seen. He blushed and looked away in embarrassment.

And suddenly Lance knew.

"Oh, Michael..." he whispered, barely an exhalation of breath. "Why didn't you tell me?"

Michael turned his head back. The brown eyes weren't hard anymore. They were soft and gentle. Jack's eyes. "What for?"

Lance's tears dropped onto Michael's bloody, shattered chest. "Because I love you, too, Michael."

Michael flashed that hard look again, but then his eyes softened once more. "Knowing you, Lance, you probably do," he said, his voice becoming raspier. "But not like that." He paused, his eyes wide and tender. "We both know who you're *in* love with."

Lance sucked in a breath, gazed into those eyes, and saw the truth.

Oh, God, no!

Michael must've seen something in Lance's face, because he smiled. No smirking or sneering. A human smile.

Fearfully pushing those other thoughts away, Lance leaned down and kissed Michael gently on his soot-blackened forehead, raising his head to see a look of surprise mixed with thanks on his face. "Please don't die, Michael."

"The monster always dies at the end, Lance," he coughed out, blood dribbling from between his lips. "Didn't you know that?"

Lance's vision blurred with more tears. "You're not a monster, Michael."

Galloping hooves caught his ears and then he heard, "Lance!"

Turning, he saw Arthur leap from the still moving white horse and run toward him. Lance pushed himself to his feet and lurched forward, his head still swimming. "Dad, I need Excalibur!"

Without hesitation, Arthur unsheathed the blade and handed it to him, gazing downward in horror at Michael's bloody, broken body.

Lance staggered back to Michael and stood over him, panting and fighting for control.

Michael's eyes went wide with wonder. "Gonna put me outta my misery, Lance?"

Lance shook his head, tears streaming down his face. He stood as straight as he could, hair a mass of tangled dirt and branches, face blackened and scraped, and pointed the tip of the sword at Michael, who looked wide-eyed and expectant. He gently touched the tip to Michael's left shoulder, and then to his right, his voice trembling with love. "I hereby dub thee Sir Michael the Good..." His voice caught in his throat a second before he could continue. "Knight eternal... of the Table Round."

Then he pulled the sword back and stuck it into the ground, using its stability to lower himself to one knee beside Michael, and saw the boy's face light up with a childlike wonder he would've said was impossible.

Then Michael laughed that breathy little laugh he'd gotten from him. "Hell, Lance," he gushed, his voice growing weaker. "I feel like a kid again."

"You are a kid, Michael. A good kid."

Michael's eyes glistened. "You were the only one, Lance," he started to say. Then he coughed up blood. "The only one I ever..."

He choked a moment, and more blood dribbled from his mouth.

Lance wiped it away tenderly with his fingers. "The only one what?"

Michael tried for a smile. "Who I..." And then he hesitated. "Who could... save... me..."

His head lolled to one side.

"Michael!" Lance called out, releasing Excalibur's hilt and cupping Michael's face with his hands.

But Michael was already dead.

Tears cascaded down Lance's face as he held the head of his friend tenderly in his hands. He felt a hand lightly fall upon his shoulder. He looked up into Arthur's saddened face. He gently lay Michael down and stood, looking at his dad with immeasurable pain.

"Oh, Dad," he said through his tears, and grabbed the king tightly around the waist. Arthur hugged him back. "He *was* good. He wasn't a monster like everybody said."

Arthur stroked his hair. "No, son, he wasn't. You were right, Lance, and I was wrong."

Lance pulled back, his eyes widening as he saw Ricky stagger toward them, Chris wrapped tightly around his neck, Ricky's arms cradling the smaller boy.

Ricky stopped, and Lance met his gaze. He saw so many things in those briefest of moments, and he knew Ricky saw a myriad of emotions in him, as well. They held each other's gaze for a few seconds before emergency personnel leapt from their vehicles and surrounded all of them, taking Chris from Ricky's arms, guiding Ricky to an ambulance, surrounding Lance, and rushing to Michael's lifeless body.

Within seconds, Ricky was lost to Lance's view, but the look of betrayal in the Ricky's eyes would haunt him forever.

CHAPTER FIFTEEN
YOU WOULD SEE A TRUE HERO

BY THE TIME LANCE, RICKY and Chris had been treated, the coroner had arrived to remove Michael's body. Lance had severely sprained his ankle, and a paramedic had iced and wrapped it. Both he and Ricky had gotten cuts and bruises, but neither was seriously hurt. Chris fared best of all. His small size and flexibility turned him into a little ball that rolled along the ground until he was able to stop himself. Ricky had found him a few minutes after and carried the terrified child to the crash site.

Mr. Mills, as it turned out, had broken an arm and a leg, and likely suffered a concussion. He'd been rushed to emergency, but the paramedics assured the family that the older man would recover.

Arthur stood with the boys as Michael's broken body was lifted onto a stretcher and covered with a sheet. Then it was slid into the back of a coroner's van as Lance shed more tears.

Chris held Lance's hand lovingly, while Ricky looked desolate and lost.

Of course, the news helicopter hovered overhead filming the cleanup, and reporters hurried to the scene to interview the survivors. Naturally, Helen was there, but Lance was too distraught to even talk with her. Arthur answered most of the questions, with Ricky and Chris describing the situation on board the train.

Ryan also fielded questions about the cause of the crash, and he said they had a lead on the mutilations case that also tied into this one and further information would be forthcoming. Then he directed the boys to his car while Arthur returned Llamrei to her trailer for the return trip to New Camelot. He asked Reyna, who'd been frantic when she'd arrived on the scene, to drive the horse back so he could go with the boys. After practically crushing all three boys with suffocating hugs many times over, Reyna got into the Escalade and left the scene towing the horse trailer.

At New Camelot, everyone had been gathered for hours and saw everything on TV, mostly from the news copter point of view, but also from the many news cameras on the ground, as well.

Despite his sorrow, Lance had told Ricky on the drive home that they had to celebrate Chris's birthday as planned, and Ricky agreed. Those were the only words spoken between them. Michael wasn't mentioned.

Lance knew that somewhere deep inside, Ricky thought he'd chosen Michael over him, had made Michael more important. Was that true, he'd asked himself on that sad, silent ride home? Had he done that? And what about what Michael had told him just before he died? And that look in his eyes? Just the remembrance made Lance squirm all the more, and kept his eyes fixed out the back window so he wouldn't have to look at Ricky.

After everyone greeted them lovingly and excitedly, the three boys went upstairs to shower and clean up.

Lance and Ricky said not a word to each other as they readied themselves for the party. Lance walked with a painful limp, and had to keep his ankle wrapped. After showering, and drying their hair, both boys went into Chris's room to help him get ready.

While he was blow drying Chris's hair, and Ricky rummaged in the dresser drawers for some clean clothes, Chris looked at Lance in the mirror.

"Michael was a hero, wasn't he, Lance?" Chris asked with wide eyes. "Just like Jack."

Lance glanced through the open door into the bedroom, where he saw Ricky freeze, awaiting his answer. Lance turned back to Chris, waving the blow dryer around the little boy's mop of blond hair. "Not the same as Jack, but still a hero."

He heard a drawer slam loudly before Ricky strode into the bathroom with a fresh tunic and clean pants in hand. He practically shoved them at Lance, who took them without meeting his gaze.

"Did you love him like you loved Jack?" Chris asked innocently. Lance was so caught off guard he nearly dropped the blow dryer and clothes. His eyes instantly flicked to Ricky's face, and the scowl he saw cut straight to the heart.

"No, Chris," he answered truthfully. "Jack was amazing, and I loved him like an awesome big brother."

Chris squinted his eyes in the mirror, regarding Lance quizzically, as though saying, 'That's not how it looked to me.' But the little boy said nothing more, and Lance wondered just what Chris had thought about him and Jack.

Lance and Ricky barely looked at each other as they helped Chris dress for his big event.

Despite the trauma of the afternoon, Chris was so overwhelmed by the party that he almost forgot about the crash. His body was sore and he winced with pain whenever someone hugged him, but the adrenalin rush of having a real birthday party superseded his discomfort.

Ricky and Lance put on happy faces for their little brother's benefit, but deep within, Lance felt broken and bereft over Michael's death, and Ricky appeared unwilling to even talk about any of it.

Bridget and Ariel obviously sensed something between the two boys and gave them space, not hanging all over them as usual. Instead, they helped Reyna with presents and cake and fawned over Chris.

Reyna had recovered almost instantly upon returning to New Camelot, and quickly became the mistress of ceremonies, handling the distribution of cake and presents with a stoic professionalism that amazed Lance.

Of course, no one but him had liked Michael anyway, and thus the boy's death had little impact on any but himself. That bothered Lance more than he cared to admit. Michael had saved his life, and that of both Ricky and Chris, but no one seemed to care that he was dead as a result.

Then there was Ricky. Lance watched him play pin the tail on the donkey with Chris. Ricky was clearly angry with him, and hurting inside. He felt rejected, but he was so wrong about that, and Michael's death made Lance realize just *how* wrong. But what could he do about it? He couldn't give in to the truth because then his greatest fear might come true.

As he gazed intently across the room at Ricky laughing and playing with Chris, Lance felt another set of eyes on him. He turned.

Bridget was staring at him, watching him watch Ricky. There was something in her eyes that Lance could not read. Was it anger, or maybe resentment? He couldn't tell, but the moment he looked into her eyes she quickly turned back to Ariel and Reyna.

What was that about?

The next few days, all the news was about the train crash, the election, and Michael. Postings came from kids all over the state on the New Camelot website and Facebook pages that their parents had absentee voted, and thus the kids were once more speaking to them. It had not been part of the deal for parents to say which way they voted – merely to prove to their kids that they had, in fact, voted.

The train crash had induced some media outlets to hype 'The Curse of Camelot' and what that might signify for Arthur and his crusade.

But the main story was Michael, no doubt because its prurient nature brought out the voyeur instincts in the media and the populace like no reality show ever could. The atrocities he'd committed were front and center of every broadcast, radio talk show, and Internet site.

Lance scanned these stories daily, appalled at the vilification Michael was getting. He was a monster, a fiend, and a demon.

All the labels that had been applied to Victor Frankenstein's creation.

The preliminary police investigation had pinned the Manic Mountain event at Michael's unhinged feet, and the media ran with it. Michael had been obsessed with Sir Lance, and in his dementia couldn't handle seeing the boy with anyone but himself. They'd even speculated that the train crash was designed to kill them all, himself included, because Michael had finally decided if he couldn't have Lance, no one else could, either.

Bridget believed that version, as did Ariel. So, Lance concluded, did almost everyone at New Camelot, which sickened him. He had done one interview with Helen, which had been picked up by the wire services, in which he'd defended Michael. He'd told how it was Michael who'd saved him and Chris and Ricky, had saved everyone at Union Station that day.

Alas, most of the people seemed to believe he was just sticking up for his mentally disturbed friend, and they preferred to focus on the crimes Michael was known to have committed. Some outlets even expressed sympathy for Richard and Mr. D., interviewing them as victims.

But nowhere did Lance see what he kept searching for – mention of the video he'd watched, the one of Michael's rape, the event that had unhinged him in the first place. The more he searched, the angrier he became.

The cops had Michael's computer and the video had been on it! Why were they covering that up? To make their case stronger? He couldn't believe Ryan and Gibson would be part of something like that!

Because they felt any imminent danger to Lance had ended with Michael's death, Ryan no longer stayed over at New Camelot, and thus Lance hadn't seen him since the crash.

And then there was Ricky. The Monday after the crash, Lance had awakened to find that Ricky had moved back into his own room. His entire body ached and his ankle throbbed, but these physical ills couldn't begin to touch the pain in his heart at not seeing Ricky on the other side of the bed when he awoke.

Later, when he asked Ricky why he'd moved back into his own room, Ricky's reply was short and laced with sadness.

"You don' need me no more, Lance, now that Michael's dead."

Not even meeting Lance's eyes, Ricky stepped into his own bathroom and closed the door, shutting Lance out of his life and opening a hole in his heart that could never be filled. He wanted to say something, but what could he say? If he said what he really wanted to say, Ricky might never talk to him again. That was a risk Lance wasn't willing to take. So he took Mark's old advice to heart and decided to let it be.

He worked perfunctorily in the Computer Lab, tweeting and posting messages to get out the vote the following Tuesday, but his heart wasn't in it. Arthur and Jenny could see something had shifted between him and Ricky, but neither boy wanted to talk about it, so the adults didn't push.

On Wednesday of that week, with still no stories about Michael's gang rape in the media, Lance called Ryan on his cell.

"Hey, Lance, how you feeling, godson?" Ryan asked, sounding happy to hear from him.

"I'm okay," Lance grumbled. "Ankle's getting better."

"Good," he heard Ryan reply, and the man sounded relieved.

Lance took a deep breath. "*Nino*, why are you and the cops trying to pin everything on Michael?"

There was a pause, and then Ryan said quietly, "Because the evidence points to him, Lance. He'd been stalking you before you two even met."

"What do you mean?"

"In his secret room he had pictures of you from the Internet, from your cleanup campaigns last year, and a lot from the night you..." he hesitated, "well, died. We also recovered his phone. He'd been tapping into your line for months before you *accidentally* met him that day on the street."

Lance was stunned, but it still didn't fit. "Yeah, but—"

"And," Ryan continued, "despite what you said about Thornton stalking you, there's nothing in his background to indicate he could rig a roller coaster to fail or even get himself near a party you were at to poison you. A party, I might add, at Michael's house."

Lance's head spun. They were connecting all the dots, like police did, and the image they got was Michael. And listening to Ryan, Lance could almost see the logic. "Yeah, but what about his computer?"

"What about it?"

Lance nearly cried out in exasperation. "Didn't you guys look at everything on it? All his videos?"

"There was nothing on it, Lance," Ryan replied, and Lance's heart skipped a beat. "Hard drive was empty except for a homemade screensaver."

"What!" Lance couldn't believe it.

All the evidence, the rape video, all gone? Why would Michael do that? Had he suspected the cops were about to raid his place? Knowing Michael, that was a possibility. But did he really want everyone to think he was just a monster?

And suddenly Lance knew.

That's exactly what Michael wanted.

The monster always dies at the end.

"Uh, Lance?"

Lance pulled himself back into the conversation. "Yeah, *nino*, I'm here."

"The screensaver was a message," Ryan was saying, though Lance was only half listening. "About you."

That caught his attention. "About me?"

He could almost see Ryan's wrinkled face nodding as he heard, "It was just one of those messages that float around the computer screen."

Lance swallowed hard. "What did it say?" he whispered, his heart thumping, wondering what Michael may have told the world about him at the end.

"It said," Ryan's voice continued, "let me check my notes." There was a brief pause. "It said, 'The Boy Who Came Back will do the right thing.' Any idea what that means, Lance?"

Lance's heart beat so loudly he was certain everyone in the house could hear it. Those words, so similar to what Michael had said on the train.

When he'd handed Lance the flash drive.

The evidence.

All of it.

Both sides of the monster.

He'd left it up to Lance to decide what to do.

Oh, Michael...

"Lance?" he heard from the other end of the phone. "You still there?"

"Yeah, *nino*. Look, I gotta go, okay. Talk to you later."

He pressed 'end' and sat back in his chair, glancing around at the other kids in the lab. They were all eyeing him questioningly, but looked away when he caught them staring.

Lance needed to talk to somebody about this. Ricky was out because Ricky couldn't talk objectively about Michael, even though he knew the truth. Dad or mom? Maybe.

Then it hit him. Merlin.

He hadn't talked with the old wizard for ages, and suddenly felt need of the man's wisdom.

As usual, Lance found Merlin in the library. Over the past months, the wizard seemed to hide out in this room, reading about all that had happened since he'd sojourned in Avalon. Lance also suspected he didn't want to influence events by revealing something he may have seen with his unique "sight."

Merlin lounged comfortably in a high-back, heavily stuffed armchair, wearing a Guns N' Roses shirt, and looked up from a book when Lance entered. He pulled one bud from his right ear.

Lance heard heavy metal blasting from the now dangling ear bud.

"Ah, my dear Sir Lance," he greeted the boy warmly, closing the book without marking his place.

Lance wondered how he'd find it again.

"How are you healing?"

"Still sore everywhere."

The older man smiled, a twinkle in his eye. "Rather like you had been thrown from a moving train?"

"Yeah, kind of like that."

"Tell me about this dilemma you face over Michael."

Lance's eyebrows shot up. "How'd you know?"

"My gift. Or perhaps it's a curse. I've never fully decided." He smiled ruefully.

Lance hesitated, not sure how to begin. "It's like, well, I know something about Michael that nobody else knows and I think he wanted me to decide whether to tell it to everyone or not."

"He trusted you, obviously, to make the right choice, Lance. So why do you doubt yourself?"

"Something happened to him when he was a kid that was, like, really humiliating," Lance explained, somehow sensing the wizard knew this already. "I'm not sure if he wants the whole world to know or if he'd rather they all think he was badass and a monster."

Merlin's face looked thoughtful. "You have a gift yourself, young Lance. You saw something in that boy even I could not read, something good. He is gone now. How would *you* like him to be remembered?"

Lance answered at once. "As a kid who was turned into a monster, but then turned himself into a hero."

"Because of you, no doubt."

Lance reddened.

"Michael sounds much like the epic hero I've read so much about in these marvelous books of yours. The innocent who turns evil, but ultimately regains his goodness in the end."

Lance's eyes went wide. "That's exactly right. That's what I want people to think about him."

"Then you have already made your decision."

Lance nodded. He *had* made his decision.

"Consider this, however," Merlin continued in a cautionary tone, his light gray eyes fixed intently on Lance. "Michael as monster seems to have pushed much of the populace in favor of your proposition, if the Internet stories are to be believed. His crimes were so horrific, people cannot see him being treated as anything but an adult, despite his age at the time he committed them. If you show them Michael the tragic hero, could that perhaps undermine your cause?"

Lance frowned. He hadn't thought of that angle. He *could* wait until after the election, he knew. But should he? More and more lately, he'd questioned his own beliefs about kids being adults at age fourteen. He was almost sixteen, and after everything he'd been through this past year, he felt more like a kid than ever. He wasn't sure what to do now.

"Thanks, Merlin. You gave me a lot to think about."

He turned to exit the library, but Merlin called him back.

When Lance turned back around, Merlin said, "Ricky weighs upon you, as well. Do you wish to speak of that?"

Lance turned red again, looked down and shook his head.

"If I may say something, Lance."

Lance looked up, his emotions conflicted, his heart heavy.

"In this era there seems to be an obsession with the perfect male and the perfect female and if you cannot live up to those ideals, you are somehow a failure. Would you agree?"

Lance nodded slowly, again feeling a dread well up within him that Merlin knew exactly what was in his heart.

"In your father's day, there was no such demand to perfection. You, Sir Lance, are far from perfect. So is your father. So is Sir Ricky. These idealized notions of perfection are like your Hollywood movies, Lance – pure fantasy. You are quite extraordinary, even more so than your father at your age. Do not destroy yourself because you cannot measure up to the fantasy image of the perfect boy. Would that you could see yourself through my eyes, or through Ricky's, you would see a true hero, an amazing young man who is more real than most."

Lance stood slack-jawed, stunned by the man's words. Merlin had never said so much to him at one time, and Lance never knew the wizard thought so highly of him. Did Ricky really think of him that way too? Did Merlin know his deepest fears? Is that why he mentioned the "real" part? He broke into a hesitant grin of gratitude. "Thanks, Merlin. Now I know how my dad got so smart."

"And now I shall return to the decline and fall of the Roman Empire. Quite fascinating, really. Much like this country today."

"Thanks again, Merlin."

As he left the library, from the corner of his eye Lance saw the wizard open the book seemingly at random and resume reading.

He trudged painfully up the stairs, his ankle throbbing dully, and decided that he would reveal the other side of Michael to the world – on Monday, the day after Michael's funeral. There was an afternoon press conference scheduled, a last minute get-out-the- vote rally in front of City Hall. But what he planned would require Helen's cooperation, and he silently prayed she'd be willing to help him pull it off.

He also considered the realities of Michael's funeral. The boy's parents had been in hiding, refusing to speak to reporters, and only answering basic questions from the police. In the media, they were likened to the parents of the Columbine killers, a reference Lance had to Google to understand.

Their plan had been to cremate Michael's body as soon as the coroner was done with it, but Arthur contacted them at Lance's behest and urged them to allow a funeral, and that he would take care of the arrangements. Michael's parents were curt, but agreed, so long as they had nothing to do with it.

Pastor Tom agreed to have the funeral at his church in West Hollywood, and Lance called Father Mike to see if he would join Pastor Tom in performing the service. Father Mike agreed without hesitation, which made Lance feel very grateful. He knew hardly anyone would show up, but he wanted to honor Michael properly. Bridget and Ariel planned to attend, and wanted to come over every day after school, but the boys kept putting them off.

Bridget sensed something wrong when they Skyped that night. "Did you and Ricky have a fight or something?"

Lance shook his head. The opposite, really. They'd barely talked since the train crash on Sunday, and Lance felt that emptiness in his soul growing larger and larger.

"No. We're good. Just need to recover. I still feel like crap."

Bridget nodded, but her expression showed she didn't believe him. "Lance, um, my parents will be gone this weekend."

He looked at her uncertainly.

"Since you can go out now," she went on, "you know, without a bodyguard, you could come over on Sunday, after the funeral."

Lance stared at her, and his heart began to pound.

Bridget bit her lower lip nervously. "And you could stay over."

Lance sucked in a sharp breath. Was she suggesting...? He gazed into her eyes, as best he could on his iPad.

She smiled uncertainly, and added, "If you want. If you're ready, I mean."

He let out the breath he'd been holding, his heart thumping wildly now. "Bridget, I..."

"I love you, Lance, more than I've ever loved any boy." She sounded so sincere and her declaration of love made Lance feel warm inside.

Nervously, he stammered, "I, uh, I don't know," and looked away in embarrassment.

She obviously sensed his hesitation. "It's okay if you don't want to."

"No!" he blurted. "No, I do want to."

She smiled back shyly. "Can you make some excuse to your parents for staying out late?"

"I'll figure it out."

Her smile got bigger, filled her entire face, and she signed off.

Lance sat on his bed, stunned, his heart pounding and head swirling with expectations. She wanted him. Like *that*. He would be a real boy. He could do this. It would save his relationship with Ricky. He could love Bridget. He *did* love Bridget, right? And it would wash away all his fears and doubts and guilt, even the fear he'd never shared with anyone.

He set down his iPad and turned his head toward the adjoining door. Ricky stood there, looking at him with an unreadable expression.

"Hey, Ricky, guess what?" Lance said, hoping his news might jumpstart their relationship again and close the door Michael had forced him to open.

"I heard," Ricky said quietly.

Lance looked down, feeling shame when he wasn't sure he should. Looking back up, he saw Ricky's expression hadn't changed. Or had it? Did he see sadness in those incredible brown eyes?

"Congrats, man," Ricky said tonelessly. "You'll be a real boy now." Then he turned and entered his room, closing the door and leaving Lance alone.

Lance sat there stunned. Ricky should be happy for him, just as he'd be if Ricky and Ariel were going to.... He found himself flushed with uncertainty at the thought. *Would* he be happy for Ricky? Or jealous?

He shoved such thoughts to the back of his mind. This was what couples did, right? He'd finally know what it felt to be normal. But was it right? Did he really want this? Esteban's words came back to him, about proving something to himself. Was that what he was doing? Using Bridget to prove something? Hell, it was her idea, he told himself, so how could he be trying to prove anything to anyone, except to show Bridget that he cared about her?

He considered all the times Bridget had touched him, or tried to get more passionate when they kissed. He'd nearly freaked out every time, memories of his childhood violation overwhelming his senses. Could he seriously go all the way without melting down?

Frustrated and not wanting to think any more, Lance headed downstairs to the Training Center and shot arrows at targets, over and over again, until his arms grew tired and sweat burned his eyes. The workout exhausted him, but did not quell his thoughts and fears. And Ricky wasn't there to help him sort through them.

That hurt most of all.

Dinner that night was rather quiet. Lance and Ricky did not horseplay or even converse, and their somber mood settled on Chris, who also remained silent. Merlin eyed him and Lance met his gaze a moment before looking back down at his food.

Arthur and Jenny exchanged worried looks. Arthur had asked Esteban and Reyna to dinner, as well, hoping their presence might enliven the others. In addition, he wanted them all to bear witness to something he hoped would remove the pall that had settled on New Camelot.

After dinner concluded, Arthur eyed Merlin across the table, and the wizard winked. Then the king rose and addressed everyone.

"I have created a special dessert for Lady Jenny," he announced, and everyone looked at him with questioning expressions. "It has been a difficult week – no, a difficult year – for us all, and it is my wish that my gift will bring joy to you, as well to her."

He exited into the kitchen, leaving everyone to exchange quizzical looks. Reyna eyed Jenny, but she shrugged, obviously having no idea what the king was up to. Arthur re-entered carrying something on a small plate with a napkin covering it. More looks were exchanged as he smiled and handed the plate to Jenny.

Mystified, she took the plate and eyed him as he grinned down at her. She removed the napkin, and gasped, her hand flying to her mouth. Sitting on the plate was a cupcake, but that wasn't what made her gasp. Adorning the top of the cupcake, embedded within the white frosting, was a sparkling diamond ring.

The others watched with stunned expressions as Arthur knelt before Jenny and said, "Lady Jenny, it would be the greatest honor of my life if you would consent to become my wife."

Reyna almost screamed aloud in excitement.

Tears streamed down Jenny's face, and she nodded. "Yes. A thousand times yes."

Arthur grinned even more broadly. He took the plate from her and removed the ring. Setting the plate on the table, he used the napkin to wipe the ring clean of frosting, and then slipped it over her trembling finger. She looked speechless, and merely stared at the ring with elation. Then she kissed him.

"All right!" Chris yelled, and Reyna grabbed Esteban's hand joyfully. Even he had a big grin on his face.

Lance and Ricky stared at their parents, speechless and gaping. Then they looked shyly at one another.

"Pretty cool, huh?" Lance said.

"Yeah. Pretty cool."

They held each other's gaze a moment longer, and then the boys averted their eyes as Reyna leapt from her chair to envelope Jenny in a huge hug of joy. She turned to Arthur with a reproachful look. "It's about time, Arthur!" and then laughed at his comical expression, hugging him, as well.

Arthur looked at the boys. Chris gave him a big thumbs up, but Lance and Ricky just sat there uncertainly. "Lance? Ricky? I had thought my announcement would make you both happy."

The boys did their best to smile.

"We are happy, Dad," Lance assured him. "At least I am."

Ricky cast him a hard look before saying, "Me too, Dad."

Lance and Ricky gazed at one another a moment more, both with a sense of longing and something painfully unspoken. Then all three boys rose to hug Jenny and Arthur, and offer their heartfelt congratulations.

From across the table, Merlin watched them all with an unreadable expression, focusing, in particular, on Lance. But at the moment, the boy's heart and mind were closed to him.

CHAPTER SIXTEEN
YOU CAME FOR ME

The next few days were spent preparing for Michael's funeral and for the final campaign rally on Monday. Of course, Reyna was ecstatic about the upcoming wedding, and so was everyone at New Camelot. Even little Chris gushed over it, desperately wanting to carry up the rings like he'd seen little kids do on TV.

Ricky kept to himself, leaving Lance to mope around and lament the fact that no one seemed to care that Michael was dead. No one but him. If Lance was reading everyone right, they all seemed relieved. Would they feel bad once they knew the truth? He didn't know, and it didn't matter anyway. He owed Michael the truth, and he hoped it might better help voters decide on Tuesday which way to cast their ballots.

Helen came over on Saturday morning, per Lance's invitation, and spent some time alone with Lance in the Computer Lab. When she finally left the house, she looked nauseated and ashen.

Lance bade her goodbye. "See you on Monday, Lady Helen."

She waved, but didn't smile. He understood. He felt sick again too. Closing the door, he turned and found Ricky looking at him from the stairs. Their eyes met and held.

"You, uh, you wanna spar with me?" Lance asked hesitantly, shyly.

Ricky nodded.

There was none of their old spark, the old banter, the one-up- man-ship comments flung back and forth. It was like they were two boys who'd just met and were going to play a game against one another.

But when they began thrusting and swinging at each other with swords and shields in the familiar confines of the Training Centre, it felt good to Lance, like old times. As each scored against the other, laughter ensued. Finally, after Lance knocked the shield from Ricky's grasp, he chuckled. "Got you that time, dumb ass."

Ricky grinned. "Oh, yeah?"

Lance laughed, and Ricky charged, slamming into Lance and knocking them both to the ground. Ricky leapt up and pointed his sword to Lance's throat, effectively ending the match.

"Who's the dumb ass now?"

Lance grinned, and Ricky pulled the sword back, extending his hand to Lance. Almost shyly, Lance took the hand and they locked eyes a moment. Then Ricky pulled Lance to his feet and the moment was gone. The boys pushed and shoved their way back to the armory and stowed their swords, bragging about who had scored more hits.

When they closed the door to the weapons room, Ricky turned to Lance. "You still gonna," he said awkwardly, "you know, go with Bridget tomorrow night?"

Lance reddened. "I *got* to."

Ricky frowned, his brown eyes glossy with sadness. "No, you don't."

Lance eyed him uncertainly, trying to understand his expression. "I need to, Ricky. All I know is being Richard's sex toy." His face clouded with anger and he trembled at just uttering the man's name.

"That's all I know too." Ricky paused, and fixed those soulful eyes on Lance. "But isn't sex supposed to be about love, not just something to do?"

Lance lowered his eyes shamefully. "I do love Bridget." He looked up and saw Ricky gazing levelly at him, silent and sad and almost accusatory.

"What about Ariel?" Lance asked nervously, to change the subject. "Do you think she...?"

Ricky burned red. "I think she would, if I asked. I'm just not sure. I don't wanna be like those guys on the street, you know, a user?"

Lance again had the feeling that Ricky knew exactly why he was doing this. Given their intense bond, he felt *certain* Ricky knew. But it didn't matter. He couldn't end up a monster like... He shivered, even though he was hot and sweaty.

"Can you, you know, cover for me tomorrow night, with Mom and Dad? In case I stay out too late? I'm not sure what time I..."

Ricky nodded, but refused to meet his eyes.

He studied Ricky's taut posture a moment and then slapped him on the back. "Let's get cleaned up."

They left the Training Centre to go back to their rooms.

Michael's funeral was scheduled for Sunday afternoon, to give Father Mike a chance to get there from juvenile hall. Out of respect for Lance, many of the knights attended. Even though none had liked Michael, they wanted to show Lance they supported him. Even Jaime came with Sonia and the baby. He'd met Michael once or twice at a gathering, but, like the others, attended for Lance.

Arthur had convinced Michael's parents to allow a burial, after explaining about Jack, because Lance wanted them buried side-by-side -- the two brothers who never got to meet in life. The parents agreed, but didn't want to foot the bill. Arthur agreed to all burial expenses.

When Reyna drove up to the church in her Escalade, with Arthur, Jenny, Lance, Ricky, Chris and Esteban with her, there were picketers outside, waving signs and shouting things like 'Monsters go to hell, not heaven' and 'No church funerals for demons!' The signs were peppered with epithets like 'Murderers Burn in Hell!' and 'Evil Boys Should be Buried in Unhallowed Ground'.

Lance didn't even know what unhallowed meant, but he was so sickened by the signs and the chants that he didn't even care to ask anyone.

Once they were inside the church, Lance saw the casket. It sat up front by the altar. He turned to Ricky, who'd been silent the entire drive from New Camelot. When Lance asked what was up, he'd shrugged disinterestedly, and Lance knew something was wrong, something other than the funeral.

Ricky refused to make eye contact, so Lance walked forward up the center aisle, Ricky and Chris following silently behind him. The head portion of the casket was propped open, and Lance stepped up on to the altar to look in.

Michael lay within, suddenly not so big and powerful and scary. His face looked soft, his features handsome, despite the pallor of death, blond hair combed with gel, his hands crossed peacefully over his chest.

A tear worked its way down Lance's cheek. Reaching out his hand to Ricky, he felt a surge of relief when Ricky clasped it. He reached out his other to Chris, and the little boy took it.

Lance gazed down at Michael, a heaviness clamping around his heart and soul.

I love you, Michael, he silently said. *But you were right – not that way.*

"Thank you, Michael, for saving me, for saving my brothers. You may have been a monster for a while, but you didn't die one."

He was startled to hear Ricky whisper, "Thank you, Michael."

Chris echoed the sentiment.

At that moment, Pastor Tom and Father Mike entered from behind the altar.

Lance hadn't seen Father Mike since Sylmar, and warmly embraced him, suddenly realizing just how much he'd missed this gentle man.

Bridget arrived, wearing a dark blouse and skirt and fancy shoes, but without Ariel. Lance glanced over at Ricky, who immediately looked away, and then went up to her with a questioning look on his face.

"She said she didn't feel well," Bridget explained, and Lance didn't ask questions. He was too afraid of what he was expected to do later.

As though reading his mind, she whispered, "You ready for tonight?"

Lance nodded, his mouth too dry to speak. She sat and he returned to his family.

Other than them, and the knights who'd chosen to show up, the church was empty.

Lance sat next to Chris and Ricky in the first pew with Arthur and Jenny. Reyna and Esteban and Bridget sat in the second one with Jaime and Sonia, and the other knights were scattered about the church. Ryan and Gibson showed up just before the service began, but chose to sit in back.

Pastor Tom introduced Father Mike and the two men proceeded to do a mix match of a service, part non-denominational and part Catholic. When it came time for the eulogy, the men called Lance to the podium.

His heart and soul heavy with regret, Lance stood, tugged at his tie because he suddenly felt suffocated beneath it, and made his way to the podium, glancing once more into Michael's casket. He looked out at the assembled, his eyes taking a moment to drift over everyone gathered there, lingering longest on Ricky, who hesitantly met his gaze without looking away.

"I know you're all here 'cause of me, not 'cause of Michael," he began, pausing to take a deep breath. "That's okay. None of you knew Michael like I did. You only knew the monster, the face he wanted you to see. But he wasn't just a monster, and you'll all know what I mean tomorrow afternoon. For now I just wanna say that Michael taught me a lot this past year, and it wasn't all good, and it wasn't all stuff I wanted to learn, especially about myself."

He glanced at Ryan and Gibson before continuing.

"I don't believe he ever tried to kill me, because I knew Michael, and if he wanted me dead, I'd have been dead. Even on the train, he could've killed me, or even escaped and let me die, but he didn't. He saved me. He saved Ricky and Chris, too. He died a hero, no matter what else he did before that. And it's the hero I honor today, a fallen knight of the Round Table, Sir Michael the Good."

He unsheathed his sword and held it aloft to the heavens. Arthur stood at once, unsheathed Excalibur, and also held it high. Filtered light from the stained glass windows danced off its blade like a glittering rainbow. Then Ricky stood and raised his sword. After that, Chris, Reyna, Esteban all rose and followed suit. The other knights, who'd come from home, stood and raised a fist into the air in lieu of a sword.

Lance lowered his sword, and everyone sat.

At this point, the back door to the church cracked open and a head stuck its way inside. Lance scowled, and thinking it was the protestors trying to ruin the service, leapt from the altar and pelted down the aisle, his sword out and ready. All heads turned to follow him. He stopped at the door, his sword pointed threateningly, his face flushed with anger.

The newcomer held up a hand of peace. "Please, we're not here to disrupt anything."

He sounded frightened, and Lance realized how scary he must look waving his sword around. He sheathed it. "We?"

The man pulled open the door, and Lance gasped, stepping forward to look out at seventy-five to a hundred people—men, women and children, various ages and races—waiting patiently to enter the church.

Lance turned to the man quizzically.

The man indicated the people behind him. "We're them."

"Who?"

The man looked almost apologetic. "From Union Station, last Sunday."

Lance still didn't quite grasp what the man was saying.

"We're here to pay our respects to the boy who saved our lives."

Lance's eyes traveled to the sea of faces before him, solemn and respectful. And he understood. These were *them*, the people who wouldn't be alive but for Michael's sacrifice. Chest constricted with emotion, he stepped back and allowed the man to open the door fully.

"Please, come in," Lance croaked, his heart thudding, and ushered them forward.

He returned to his pew and watched in silent amazement as one by one they filed past Michael's casket. Some made the sign of the cross, some knelt for a moment, others bowed. Lance looked at Arthur and his dad smiled warmly. Lance turned to Ricky beside him. Ricky's eyes were wide with stunned surprise, but as their gazes met, he grinned, and Lance grinned back.

"Oh, Michael," he whispered to the heavens, "I hope you're watching this."

The procession continued until all had paid their respects. Then Father Mike and Pastor Tom stood to conclude the service.

The graveside service was brief. The boys had left their swords in Reyna's car and stood solemnly as the priest and the minister blessed the gravesite. Lance held Ricky's hand in his right and Chris's in his left to watch the casket lowered into the ground beside those of Jack and Mark. Once all was concluded and Pastor Tom had departed, Father Mike chatted a bit with Arthur and Jenny. Arthur asked him if he would perform their wedding alongside Pastor Tom, and the priest said he'd be delighted. He warmly embraced Lance, Ricky and Chris before returning to his car. Bridget hovered nearby, and Lance nervously walked up to his parents.

"Dad, mom, Bridget invited me to her house for dinner and to hang out a while," he said, trying to keep his voice steady, knowing what a bad liar he was. "Is it okay? I mean, I'm not in danger anymore, right?"

Arthur and Jenny exchanged a wary look.

"There is still the election on Tuesday." Arthur had a touch of worry in his voice.

"We're just gonna be at Bridget's, not out in public anywhere."

Jenny eyed Bridget appraisingly. "Your parents are home, Bridget?"

Bridget smiled sweetly, and without batting an eyelash, said, "Of course, Lady Jenny. They don't let me have company when they're gone."

Lance glanced down so he wouldn't give anything away, marveling at how easily she could lie to someone's face.

Arthur and Jenny exchanged another look. Arthur studied Lance a moment, and then nodded.

"All right, Lance," Jenny said, "but don't stay out late. Tomorrow's a big day."

Lance nodded, nervous as hell, but trying not to show it. "Thanks, Mom."

Bridget smiled gratefully. "Thanks, Lady Jenny, King Arthur." Then to Lance she said, "I'll bring my car around." She walked across the grass, back to where all the cars were parked.

"Drive carefully, Bridget!" Jenny called out.

Bridget turned, walking backwards for a few steps. "I will. No worries." Then she continued on her way.

Arthur observed him so keenly that Lance felt certain he suspected something. "You acquitted yourself well today, Lance. I'm forever proud of you."

Lance flushed with embarrassment, and guilt flooded his heart and soul.

Arthur turned to Ricky. "Shall we go, son?"

"Be right there, Dad. I'll wait with Lance till Bridget comes back. You know, my old bodyguard thing." He grinned, but it came out nervously lopsided.

Arthur didn't seem to notice. "And I am forever proud of you, as well, Ricky."

"Me too," Jenny echoed. "Both of you."

Arthur took her hand and they slowly made their way back to the Escalade, where Reyna and the others awaited them.

Lance and Ricky stood awkwardly, side by side, both shuffling their feet, uncertain what to say. Then they raised their eyes and looked at one another more intently than they ever had.

"Uh, I'll cover for you, don't worry," Ricky said, a bit breathlessly, as though it was hard for him to speak.

"Thanks." Lance couldn't look away, wanting to say more, but not trusting his tongue to get it right.

Ricky tried for a little smile, but didn't quite make it. "I really hope tonight is everything you want it to be, Lance."

Lance nodded, his heart racing, his breathing unsteady.

Ricky broke eye contact. "There's Bridget's car. I'll be going now." He turned quickly and started to walk away.

Lance watched him go, wanting to stop him.

Then Ricky turned around, and Lance was startled to see tears glistening in his eyes.

"I broke up with Ariel today," he announced, his voice hitching with emotion.

"Why?"

"I lied to you, Lance, and I lied to her," he said quietly, his voice filled with remorse.

Lance took a few steps closer. "Whadda you mean?"

Ricky bowed his head in shame. "Remember I told you how my father thought I was crushing on a boy and that's why he called me queer?"

"Yeah, so?"

Ricky looked up, his face filled with shame, tears trickling down his cheek. "I *was* crushing on that boy, Lance, and still am. In fact, now it's worse 'cause I'm like, completely in love with him." He must've seen something of shock or maybe revulsion in Lance's face because he went on quickly. "I'm sorry, Lance, I'm *so* sorry! I tried to be a real boy and love Ariel like you love Bridget, but I just can't. All I could think about was him, even when I was kissing her. God, I'm so sorry for letting you down."

He turned to hurry toward the waiting Escalade.

From the corner of his eye, Lance spotted Bridget striding his way. He called out desperately, "Ricky!"

Ricky turned, head bowed in shame.

Lance cleared his throat hesitantly. "This other boy... do I know him?"

Ricky looked up and met Lance's eyes.

Lance saw it then, that "look" he'd seen so many times before, but had misinterpreted—the same look he'd seen in Michael's eyes right before he died—and gasped with comprehension because now he knew *exactly* what that look meant.

"So now you know, Lance, what a pathetic loser I really am. God, I hate myself!" Ricky turned again, looking like he was about to run.

Rooted to the spot, Lance could barely croak out, "Ricky, wait!"

Ricky turned back, eyes tearful and filled with shame.

"I—" Lance began.

But then Bridget was at his side, touching his arm. "You ready, Lance?"

His eyes wide with confusion, Lance glanced over at her, and then back at Ricky standing helplessly a few feet away. Ricky raised his damp, poignant brown eyes, his expression one of abject despair.

Bridget eyed the two boys uncertainly, first Lance, and then Ricky.

"Ricky?" she asked hesitantly. "Is everything okay?"

Ricky and Lance kept their gazes locked on one another, as though Bridget wasn't even present.

Ricky said sadly, "Yeah, Bridg. It's all good." He sprinted toward the Escalade, not once looking back.

Bridget lightly squeezed Lance's arm, but his gaze never left Ricky until he had been swallowed up within the black SUV and it pulled away into the dusk.

"You ready, Lance?" Bridget repeated, her voice sounding scared and uncertain.

Lance finally turned to her, looking bereft.

"Are you okay?"

He nodded slowly and, with halting steps, allowed her to lead the way to her car.

Ricky sat silently in the Escalade all the way back to New Camelot, waves of shame and guilt and self-loathing washing over him the whole way. Everyone could tell something was wrong, but attributed his mood to the funeral, and Lance's somberness. Chris took Ricky's hand and held it. Ricky squeezed his little brother's hand, and didn't let go until they arrived home. No one spoke as everyone went their separate ways to change out of their funeral clothes and clean up for dinner.

Dinner was a gloomy affair. Very little was spoken by anyone. Arthur and Jenny realized it had been a difficult day for the kids, especially seeing all those strangers file in to bid farewell to Michael, strangers who wouldn't be alive if it weren't for the boy they had all so disliked and distrusted. Arthur knew a certain amount of guilt ran through everyone, so he let silence rule the night as they gave thanks and ate their food.

Lance had never been to Bridget's house except that one time for the Manic Mountain trip, and he hadn't gone inside. It was large, two story and expansive, but not palatial like Michael's. Still, her family had money. Lots of money. Lance took off his nice jacket and hung it on a large wooden coat rack in the entry hall. At Bridget's suggestion, he also removed his tie and hung that with his coat.

After giving him a quick tour of the downstairs, she suggested they grab something to eat in the kitchen before going upstairs. She said "upstairs" with a shy smile, and Lance blushed nervously as she took his hand and led him into the spacious kitchen that sported a refrigerator larger than most of the bathrooms in his foster homes.

After dinner, Ricky played Madden football with Chris on his new iPad. Ricky had wrestled, but never played football and didn't even know all the rules, so Chris kicked his butt every time.

Ricky's mind kept going to Lance and Bridget, and he'd continuously check his phone to see the time. Had Lance become a real boy yet? Hell, a man! That's what he'd be after tonight. At least, that's what everybody said makes a boy into a man. Somehow, Ricky didn't think it was that simple, but what did he know?

Chris noted him checking his phone, and finally asked if he was thinking about Lance.

That surprised Ricky. "What makes you think that?"

Chris shrugged as he simultaneously executed a play in the game. "You always have that look on your face when you're thinking of Lance."

Ricky squinted uncertainly. "What look?"

Chris shrugged again, his eyes still on the game. "I don't know what it's called. It's just a look."

Ricky attempted to digest the boy's observation while losing his fourth game in a row.

Bridget had heated up a chicken casserole her mom had left for her and made some salad to go with it, while Lance wandered around downstairs taking in more of the place where she lived. She was an only child, and there were pictures of her at various stages of growth along the wall adjoining the stairs. He ascended slowly, taking in each one. Her hair had been long until what looked like her junior high school pictures, then it was short from that point on.

When he'd ambled back into the kitchen to help her get dinner ready, he asked why she'd cut her hair, commenting that she'd looked pretty with it long.

She tilted her head back with a slight mad dogging look. "What, I don't look pretty now?"

He flushed with embarrassment. "No, I didn't mean it that way. You just have amazing hair, that's all."

She punched him on the shoulder. "Just messing with you, Lance." He visibly relaxed. "It was a rebellion thing. My mom wanted me to keep it long, so I cut it."

He nodded, but didn't say anything more. God, he was so nervous. And guilty. He shouldn't even be here, especially after Ricky's confession. So why was he? To prove something to himself that he knew wasn't true?

As they ate, she watched him appraisingly, almost making him squirm with discomfort.

"What?"

"Sorry. You're just so beautiful."

That made him look down at his food. "I'm a boy, Bridget. You're not s'posed to call boys beautiful."

"Sorry, but in your case it's true."

They ate in silence for a few more moments, and then Bridget asked, "You still don't think it was Michael who tried to kill us on that roller coaster, do you?"

Lance's face darkened like thunderheads. "No. But no one wants to believe me."

"It *is* possible, Lance."

He glared at her across the table.

"You remember the first time I met you, at that party Michael brought you to?"

"How can I forget?"

"Do you remember him leaning in to me and whispering something before he took off?"

Lance thought back. "Yeah, now that you remind me. What did he say?"

"He told me I could play with you, but that you were his and his alone. Those were his exact words."

"What did that mean?"

"I think that was Michael's way of saying he was in love with you, Lance." She paused at his startled reaction. "You didn't know that?"

"Not till the end, when he died."

She eyed him in amazement. "You don't think you're worth being loved, do you?"

He averted his eyes, and shook his head sadly.

She reached out and lifted his chin, so their eyes met. "If someone loves you, Lance, do you know what that means?"

He knew. Jack told him.

"It means you're *worth* being loved," she continued quietly.

Lance glanced away, not because of what she said, but because it brought to mind Ricky's confession at the cemetery.

Ricky loves me.

And I...

"Lance, can I ask you something?"

He looked up, his thoughts interrupted.

Her eyes were expectant, and uncertain.

He nodded, not trusting himself to speak.

"Do you love me?"

"Of course, I do."

She eyed him a long moment. "The same way I love you?"

He hesitated, and she must've seen the answer on his face because her hopeful expression dissolved into one of sadness.

"I knew it." She sounded resigned, and not nearly as hurt as Lance expected.

"I really wanted to, Bridg," he stammered, hating that he made her sad. "I tried my best, but I just..." He trailed off and stared down at the empty plate before him.

"I understand, Lance. I've known for a long time. I guess I just ignored the signs because I wanted to." She paused and took his hand. "Have you told him yet?"

Lance looked up sharply. He trembled and began to shake, feeling the beginnings of a freak out coming on.

Bridget leaped up. "Be right back." She hurried from the kitchen, leaving Lance hunched over and hyperventilating.

It was true. He knew who he loved, who he was *in* love with. Did that mean his worst fear would come true? He couldn't face that. He'd rather die first, permanently this time.

Bridget hurried to his side and slid an open bottle of vodka in front of him. Lance snatched it up and guzzled as much as he could swallow in one gulp. The alcohol burned his throat, but also relaxed him and slowed the impact of his freak out.

"Whoa, slow down, Lance. I just wanted to calm you." She reached for the bottle, but he snatched it back, taking another long, desperate swig.

He noted her concerned expression, yet he clutched that bottle like a lifeline and took another drink.

Once Ricky had gotten Chris into bed and read some of *Peter Pan* to him, Chris dropped off to sleep immediately, as only young children seemed able to do.

Then Ricky went to Arthur's room to say goodnight, something he normally did not do. But tonight would be his last night, and he wanted the man to know how much he loved him. Arthur sat up in bed reading a book of his own. He looked surprised when Ricky entered.

"Is Chris asleep?" he asked.

Ricky nodded. "I'll wait up for Lance, Dad," he said as casually as he could. "He said he'd be home by midnight."

Arthur frowned at that. "Do not tell your mother. She expects him before eleven."

Ricky made a zipping motion across his lips, and Arthur gave him a confused look.

"It means my lips are sealed."

Arthur smiled his understanding.

Impulsively, Ricky reached over and hugged his dad. Surprised, Arthur hugged him back. When Ricky pulled away, Arthur eyed him quizzically. "What was that for?"

Ricky just shrugged. "Just 'cause I love you, Dad," he said quietly, almost breathlessly due to the pounding of his heart. "Thanks for everything you done for me."

Arthur eyed him soberly. "Is everything well with you, son?"

Ricky looked down at the carpet around his feet. "Yeah, fine, Dad."

"And with you and Lance?"

Ricky looked up and knew his face must look bright red. "Yeah, Dad," he replied quickly. "Everything's good." Arthur looked dubious, and Ricky said again, "Really, Dad. We're good. 'Night."

He tried for a little smile, but it felt more like a grimace of pain on his face. Then he hurried from the room before Arthur realized that something was terribly wrong.

Ricky wanted to say goodbye to Jenny too, who'd been a better mom to him than his own ever had. But he knew how sensitive she was and felt certain she'd pick up right away what was going on inside him.

So he returned to his room. The house was quiet. Reyna and Esteban had gone out for a drive and there wasn't much happening until the rally tomorrow. Ricky slipped into Lance's room via the connecting door and proceeded to stuff extra pillows under the covers on Lance's side of the bed, so if Arthur or Jenny stuck their head in the door during the night, it would appear Lance had returned.

Then he went back to his room and sat on the bed. His eyes roamed the expansive bedroom, his home for nearly a year. His birthday was on Wednesday, but he wouldn't be around to celebrate it. His eye caught sight of that photo wedged into the corner of his vanity mirror, and he crossed the room to pull it out.

He gazed at the image: him and Lance, one arm each over the other's shoulder and the other scrunched into a fist punching each other in the gut. They were laughing with pure delight. Ricky nearly cried recalling that moment, and the hundreds of other moments he'd shared with Lance this past year. He considered taking the picture, but decided he wanted Lance to have something good to remember him by.

He looked around the room. Was it worth even taking anything with him? Most of the clothes belonged to Arthur, and he wasn't a thief. But he could take some of the things he'd been given for his birthday last year, and Christmas. That seemed fair.

He hated how miserable Arthur and Jenny would be when they discovered he was gone, but there wasn't anything he could do about that.

And Chris... The little boy would be devastated, he knew. But there was just no possible way he could have Lance continue looking at him with horror like he'd done tonight. Despair threatened to drown him. He had to go.

There was no other way.

But he had to leave a note. He had to apologize to Lance for his weakness and failure, and apologize to his parents for taking off like this. So he found a piece of paper and sat down at the roll top desk and fished a pen out of the drawer.

He considered what to say, and as he considered, he realized a great irony had occurred. He and Michael, who had hated each other from the start, both had hopes that Lance would save them – Michael from himself, and him from being the *maricón* of his father's name-calling. Michael had succeeded, but he had failed. Despite his best efforts to be like Lance, he'd failed. Seeing that as perhaps the best place to start, Ricky put pen to paper and began to write.

When he finished, he entered Lance's room and looked around. Two books lay on Lance's night table – *Frankenstein* and *The Neverending Story*. Since Ricky had given him *The Neverending Story* for his birthday, it seemed the perfect place for him to leave the note.

He folded it over once and slipped it into the book where there was a picture of The Ivory Tower, making sure the paper stuck up high enough to be obvious. Then he left the book atop the pillow he'd used for so many months.

Ricky returned to his own room and shoved himself beneath the covers, his phone with him to check on the time. He knew he'd have to wait until the middle of the night to slip away or risk getting caught. The patrols were still active, per Ryan's request, until after the election on Tuesday.

Ricky lay in bed with his shirt off, in case his mom came in to check on him, as she sometimes did. He lay and stared up at the dark ceiling, thinking back to the moment he'd first seen Lance on the Internet, to the first time he'd heard the boy speak when Helen interviewed him and Arthur at that park.

God, that seemed so long ago.

And meeting Lance on the street that night? That's the moment Ricky knew he'd found the other half of his soul, but of course he couldn't have told Lance that. No way in hell!

So, he'd tried. He'd tried for a year to be what Lance wanted him to be, to make the choice not to love another boy. He'd tried with every ounce of willpower he had. Ariel was an amazing girl, a great girl. But she wasn't Lance, and Lance was the only one he loved.

She'd reacted badly when he told her that morning, but as they talked about it, she grudgingly admitted that she knew something was wrong. He insisted it wasn't her, that she was perfect. *He* was the problem. *He* was the screw up. She was hurt, he knew, but at least he'd convinced her that he never tried to use her, that he honestly loved her. He just wasn't *in* love with her.

It was eleven-thirty when Jenny stuck her head into his room and noticed he was awake. She entered quietly and padded over to his bed, wearing a nightgown and slippers.

"Is Lance home?" she whispered.

Ricky nodded in the darkened room. "He was still really bummed about Michael and just wanted to go to sleep, so I didn't bother him."

She studied his face in the shadowy darkness. Her scrutiny made him squirm with nervousness.

"Are you all right, sweetie?" she asked, her voice as caressing as a sprinkling of water. "You were unusually quiet at dinner."

"Yeah, Mom, I'm fine."

She hesitated, still eyeing him carefully. "You know you can talk to me, Ricky. Did you and Lance have a fight or something?"

Ricky blushed, grateful for the dark shadows to hide it. "No, Mom. We're good."

She nodded, but even in the darkness Ricky could see she didn't entirely believe him. She leaned down and kissed him on the cheek before turning back toward the door to the hallway.

"Mom?" Ricky called out quietly.

She turned back expectantly.

"I love you." That was all he could get out before he'd choke on his words.

She smiled. "I love you too, Ricky." Then she was gone.

Ricky's eyes welled with tears at the thought of never seeing her again, and he turned to weep quietly into his pillow.

His phone woke him, vibrating in his hand. Ricky lurched awake, startled by the thrumming in his hand. He saw the time on the phone – one a.m. – and the name of the caller – Lance.

Ricky bolted upright in bed and pressed the 'talk' button. "Lance?" he whispered into the phone.

"Ricky..." he heard in a desperate, slightly slurred tone.

"Lance, what's wrong?" Ricky was wide-awake now, shards of fear piercing his soul. He heard crying over the phone. "Lance, what's wrong? Tell me!"

"Ricky, can you come get me?"

The words were thick with tears and alcohol. Lance was drunk again.

The hell, Bridget! What did you give him?

"Where are you?" Ricky was out of bed now and scrambling for his shoes in the dark, phone to his ear. He found the first shoe as he listened to Lance cry. "Lance, where *are* you?"

There came sniffling and choking noises over the phone, and Ricky was about out of his mind.

What the hell could have happened?

"I'm up the street, Ricky," Lance sobbed, "where we met Michael." There was a pause and Ricky feared Lance had passed out. "I can't walk any more. Too much to drink. I'm sorry, Ricky. I'm so sorry. For everything."

"Hang on, Lance," Ricky whispered into the phone as he slipped on his other shoe. "I'm on my way."

He ended the call and snatched up his shirt from under the covers where he'd hidden it. Then he slunk from the room as quickly and quietly as he could, down the back stairs and out past the patrolling guard into the back yard, out the gate and down the street at a run.

As Ricky approached the large shade tree under which he and Lance had first met Michael, he spotted someone slumped against it, visible beneath the glowing street light. He broke into a run.

He stopped up short as he got closer, heart in his throat, gasping for breath. Lance leaned against the tree, hair splayed wildly about his shoulders. His dress shirt was rumpled and untucked, and his jacket was open. Clutched in one hand was what looked like an empty bottle. He looked asleep, or dead.

Ricky dropped to his knees, gently felt Lance's face, and breathed a sigh of relief. Warm. Thank God! But Lance was passed out cold. Ricky slipped the clear glass Smirnoff bottle from Lance's grasp and held it up to the light. Empty.

"Oh, Lance," he murmured as he tossed the bottle into some bushes behind the tree.

He studied Lance's tear-streaked face for a few moments, his heart lurching. "What happened?" he whispered to the night, knowing full well the darkness had no answer. Lance still held his phone in hand, and Ricky slipped it into his own pocket.

Lance was dead weight at this point. There was no way he could move under his own power, which meant Ricky had to carry him. He'd carried Lance up the stairs that one night when Michael had brought him back, but that was months ago. Lance had been shorter and lighter, and the distance wasn't great.

Ricky considered a moment. Then he remembered some of those firefighter movies he'd seen as a kid. The firemen always threw somebody over their shoulders to carry them.

He leaned down and took Lance's hands in his. They were clammy, and slippery, as though Lance was sweating out the alcohol. He struggled to pull Lance to his feet, while at the same time ducking his already sore shoulder beneath Lance's midsection.

He reached back and grabbed one of Lance's dangling hands, pulling his upper body around his neck so Lance's weight was better distributed over both his shoulders. Powering upward with his legs, Ricky rose to his full height, Lance slung awkwardly over his shoulders. Ricky held onto Lance's feet and arms with each of his hands.

He groaned under the weight. His body still ached everywhere from the train jump, and Lance was all muscle, in addition to having gotten taller. Ricky stumbled forward, feeling like a little kid learning how to walk for the first time. No doubt looking drunk himself, Ricky staggered and stumbled his way back to New Camelot.

He fumblingly made it through the back gate, and zigzagged slowly and painfully through the stillness of the gardens, his heart pounding from the exertion, his legs turning to jelly. As he neared the back door, he awkwardly slipped out his phone to check the time: two-forty-five. The patrol would be passing right now. He'd have to wait a few minutes.

Lance's dead weight bore him downward, and his legs were already trembling beneath the strain. Ricky finally understood that old saying about muscle weighing more than fat. He kept eyeing his phone, forcing himself not to groan. His shoulders and neck felt numb beneath his brother's limp body. Two-fifty. Finally!

Ricky yanked open the door, and stumbled into the house, closing and locking the door. He was already dead on his feet and wanted more than ever to take the elevator, but the old gears made too much noise. With no other choice, he forced his way down the hall to the back stairs. Then, one lurching step at a time, he trudged up the now-seemingly endless flight to the second floor, Lance's body weight nearly driving him to his knees on several occasions.

Feeling as though he was scaling the slopes of Mount Doom itself, Ricky fought and groped and dragged himself upward one stair at a time, pausing at the top step to recapture his fleeing breath. Knowing their mother to be a light sleeper, he listened a few moments for any sounds from down the hall.

Silence ruled the night.

Ricky gripped the wooden bannister and pulled, awkwardly rising from one knee and then from the other. He shifted Lance slightly to ease the pain in his injured shoulder, then staggered as quietly as possible down the hall to Lance's door. Reaching out, he turned the knob and pushed the door inward carefully so it wouldn't bang against the wall. Then he hurried across the room, depositing Lance on his side of the bed with an exhausted sigh of relief before dropping agonizingly to his knees on the floor.

Ricky panted and heaved, swiping sweat away from his eyes as he gazed sadly upon the slumbering Lance. After a few moments to catch his breath and quell his shaking limbs, he rose and shut the door. Then he returned to the bed and undressed Lance. As he pulled off the jacket and shirt, and Lance's naked torso came into shadowy view, Ricky flashed back to the anger he'd felt when Michael had undressed Lance that one night last summer. No, not anger, he now admitted, jealousy.

Forcing his eyes away from Lance's exposed skin, Ricky slipped the shoes off his feet, and then removed his socks. Feeling almost like the pervert he knew most people in the world would call him, Ricky tugged gently, but firmly, at Lance's pant legs, one at a time, until the pants slipped down over his buttocks and slid completely off. Ricky tossed them onto the bed with the other clothes and gazed down at Lance, clad only in his boxers. His blood pounded with equal parts love, shame, and self-loathing.

He rapidly removed the pillows he'd stuffed under the bed cover and pulled back the cover and sheets. He had to lift Lance slightly to get the covers out from under him, and the feel of Lance's sweaty skin against his hands unnerved him. He gently rolled Lance over onto his back and covered him with the sheet and bed cover.

Sadly, Ricky stepped back and gazed down at this boy who meant more to him than anyone on earth. His mind raced with memories of the good times they'd shared. But front and center was that look he'd seen on Lance's face at the cemetery — that look of supreme disappointment.

"I'm sorry, Lance," he whispered, and then turned to leave.

Lance groaned, and shifted, causing Ricky to stop in his tracks. He looked down, and Lance's eyes fluttered open. The room was dark and Ricky was grateful he could not discern Lance's expression. He couldn't bear it if this boy above all others gazed upon him with revulsion.

"Ricky?" Lance gasped, his voice tight and hoarse.

Ricky swallowed hard. "Yeah, it's me."

There was a moment while Lance processed that information, maybe even processed where he now was. Ricky heard him groan some more and shift around on the bed.

"You came for me, Ricky."

Tears burned Ricky's eyes so suddenly he didn't have time to fight them off. "Course I did," he said quietly, aiming for a bantering tone. But his tongue felt thick and heavy in his mouth. "Somebody's gotta watch over your dumb ass." Tears trickled down his cheeks, and he was grateful Lance couldn't see them.

"You came for me," Lance repeated, his words mumbled and slurred. "Like always." He paused. "I have to tell you something…" Then he fell silent.

Ricky was going to crack. He had to leave and he had to leave now. "Go to sleep, Lance," he whispered in as soothing a tone as he could muster. "Everything'll be better in the morning. You won't even remember this."

Hopefully you won't remember me, either. That'd be best.

Lance grunted and then seemed to settle back into his pillow, drifting off into a drunken slumber.

Ricky sighed, wiping tears from his eyes. He felt an extreme temptation to kiss Lance on the forehead, but knew that would be wrong.

"Goodbye, Lance," he whispered into the dark. "I love you."

Then he hurried around the bed and slipped into his own room. Within minutes he was gone, down the back stairs, out of the house, and out of Lance's life forever.

He wandered the dark, forbidding streets of Hollywood, eyeing warily the night dwellers he hadn't been around for over a year. He was dressed in jeans, a band t-shirt and leather jacket with a beanie covering his head. He honestly didn't know what to do, or where to go. He just roamed the streets without hope.

He had to disappear somehow. But how could someone as famous as him do that? Where could he go? People all over the world knew his face. Plus, he'd brought no money.

He suddenly knew where to go first. At least he might find some closure, and she could lend him the money he needed to leave California.

He had the address on his phone, and the GPS map app directed his every move. It took him two hours to walk the distance.

In the dark, her house seemed larger than the first time he'd seen it, but then he'd never had a lot growing up, so this kind of lifestyle was still a mystery to him. It was four in the morning when he finally got to the front door. He was cold and hungry and tired. The house was quiet, of course, but one light burned in a room upstairs. He rang the bell.

He shivered in the autumn night air as he waited for the door to open. He heard footsteps running down the stairs and then the peephole opened. An eye appeared, and widened in surprise. The door swung open, and Bridget looked stunned to see him.

"Ricky!" She looked over his shoulder, as though expecting someone else. "What are you doing here?"

"Sorry, Bridget," he mumbled. "Been wandering the streets. Didn't have anywhere else to go."

She grabbed his arm and dragged him inside. "It's freezing out here."

Once inside, she closed the door and locked it, turning to face him, a look of fear on her face. "What happened? Is Lance all right?"

Ricky nodded, but said nothing. He noticed she was wearing a t-shirt and the same skirt she'd worn to the funeral. He couldn't look her in the eye, knowing who she was to Lance, knowing what they'd done just hours before.

She seemed to sense his feelings because she gently took his arm. "C'mon up to my room and we can talk there."

He nodded, and followed her up the flight of stairs to the second floor. Glancing around her room, he saw the rumpled bedcovers and blushed with embarrassment. He turned instead to the laptop computer on her desk with a YouTube video open, but paused.

Doubting his decision to come here, Ricky distracted her by pointing to the computer. "Uh, what're you watching, Bridg?"

She wandered over in front of him, glancing back and making eye contact. Her expression looked sad and thoughtful, which surprised him.

"Did you see that movie *Les Miserables*?" she asked, and he shook his head. "I loved it." Her voice was tinged with regret. "Especially this song."

She turned to the computer and pressed the play button, and the video unspooled.

Ricky watched as a beautiful young woman with dark hair and incredible eyes walked through rain in some dark street singing about some guy she was in love with. But the guy didn't love her back – he loved someone else. The song was melancholy and wistful, and as it played out Ricky grew more and more uncomfortable, squirming and fidgeting with dread.

Gradually, his anger rose, and he began to think Bridget was mocking him. How could she be so cruel? How did she even *know*? Had Lance told her? By the time the girl on screen sang her final words about how she loved him, but only on her own, Ricky trembled with rage. With a torturous cry, he slammed the flat of his fist into the wall by her door, causing Bridget to jump slightly with fear.

He turned to her, his face anguished and incensed. "I don't know how you found out, Bridget, but *that*—" and he pointed to the frozen image of the girl "—is not me, okay! I am not a girl, dammit! I'm a boy! A real boy, all right? I'm just a boy who happens to—" He paused to choke back a breath. "—to love another boy, a boy who doesn't love me back. And I wish more than anything I wasn't like this." His torment turned tearful, and that made him even more angry. He pounded the wall a second time with a sharp exhalation of breath. "I gotta go!"

As he moved to the door, the shocked Bridget finally found her voice and said, "Ricky, wait."

He stopped and turned, his body tight with rage, his face twisted into a mask of pain. "What?"

She gave him a look of genuine remorse. "I'm sorry. I didn't mean to upset you." She glanced at the girl on the computer screen. "That wasn't supposed to be you, Ricky. It's me. It's how *I* feel about Lance."

That caught Ricky off-guard, blindsiding him, in fact, and his ire dissipated into confusion.

"What are you talking about, Bridget? You won! He chose you... over Michael. He chose you over... everyone." He paused, barely able to utter these final words, "He loves... *you.*"

He lowered his eyes in painful wretchedness, and didn't even notice her approach until he felt a hand on his arm. He looked up into her soft blue eyes.

"We need to talk, bodyguard. Let's go make some hot chocolate. It'll warm you up."

Her expression was unreadable, but her tone soft and caring. Reluctantly, he got his breathing under control and slowly followed her out of the room and down to the kitchen.

Lance awoke. Darkness surrounded him. He had dreamed Ricky was there, but as his eyes adjusted to the dark and he looked around, Ricky was gone. He sat up suddenly as an unexplained fear pierced his heart. Dizziness assailed him. His head swam and he had to hold it steady to keep from puking. The sensation gradually subsided, and he was able to get his bearings.

Where was he?

He eyed his surroundings in the darkness, felt the soft downiness beneath him, and realized that he was in his own room. He'd been outside, drinking. That's what he remembered. He'd asked Bridget to drop him off a couple of blocks from home so he could walk and think. He'd already drank some at Bridget's, even though she tried to stop him. He took the bottle – he remembered that much. Then what? The tree. That's right! He'd sat by Michael's tree to think and, oh, God! He'd drunk the entire bottle!

And now he remembered why.

"Ricky?"

There was no answer.

Slowly, head swimming, his stomach queasy, Lance slipped his bare feet out from beneath the covers and planted them on the floor. He paused to steady himself, and rose shakily to a standing position. What time was it anyway? He glanced over at the clock. It's red numbers proclaimed four-thirty.

Using his hands for support, Lance made his way around the outside of the bed to Ricky's side, and felt around.

Empty.

Then Lance remembered. Ricky was sleeping in his own room now. As Lance's hand felt around the pillow, it struck something. A book.

Knowing it would hurt, Lance closed his eyes and groped for the switch on the table lamp. Muted light struck his pupils even beneath the closed lids, and made him wince. He forced his lids to rise, letting in such stabbing pain it felt like his brain was being used as a pincushion. It took several moments for his eyes to adjust to this vicious invasion before he was able to focus on the book.

The Neverending Story.

A folded piece of paper protruded from it.

With trembling hands, he reached for the book. He opened to the marked page, to the artist's rendering of The Ivory Tower.

And to the folded paper.

A sudden dread nearly overwhelmed him as he set the book down and clutched the paper in his left hand. With his right hand pressed to the night table, he supported his unsteady legs. He flipped the paper open and scanned the first line.

And almost cried aloud with despair.

"No!" he hissed, his brain suddenly wide-awake and very sober. He lurched for the knob and yanked opened the connecting door to Ricky's room. Not even caring how much pain it would cause, Lance flicked on the overhead lights. Like the sun itself frying his eyeballs during an eclipse, he felt searing pain stab into his brain. But the pain in his heart was worse.

The room was empty.

His eyes began to tear up as he looked around. All that was left of Ricky was that picture stuck in the vanity mirror. With unsteady gait, Lance moved toward it, hand outstretched. His fingers gripped the corner of the picture and slid it out, holding it up to gaze desolately at his face, and that of Ricky.

"Oh, my God..." he murmured before lowering his eyes back to the note in his hand.

'Hey Lance,

'By the time you read this I'll be gone. You already know why, so I don't gotta say it again. I saw your face when I told you and that was enough. Just wanna say I'm sorry I couldn't be what you wanted me to be, but I hope you believe I really tried hard. I don't know why I only love you, but I do. It's like half of me is missing without you, but that's my problem, not yours. I hope everything went great with Bridget and you'll be happy together. I mean that. You're so amazing, Lance, and you deserve to be happy. I hope you remember the good

times we had, like me kicking your ass over and over again. LOL Let mom and dad know I love 'em more than anything, and Chris too. They were the best family a guy could ask for. Goodbye, Lance.

The Other Half of the Toy,

Ricky

You are por siempre, Lance, la guardián de mi corazón'.

Lance's tears stained the paper like blood by the time he finished reading, and he collapsed to his knees in anguish.

"What have I done?" he asked the darkness as he lowered the paper to his side. Tears streaming down his cheeks, he looked angrily up toward heaven. "Oh, God, why did you bring me back?"

He collapsed onto the floor, curled into a fetal position, and sobbed.

CHAPTER SEVENTEEN
WELL, ARE WE ADULTS OR KIDS?

CHRIS ENTERED LANCE'S ROOM THE following morning at eight o'clock to see if Lance wanted to have breakfast with him. Frowning at the sight of Lance's empty, rumpled bed and clothes tossed haphazardly about, Chris saw the open door to Ricky's room and entered.

Then he saw Lance, wearing only his boxers, curled up and unmoving, and yelled, "Dad, come quick! Something's wrong with Lance!" He ran to his brother's side and knelt beside him, shaking him gently. "Lance, wake up," he implored, his face scrunched with fear. "It's Chris."

The door from the hall flew open and Arthur and Jenny were there, already dressed, a look of dread on their faces.

Jenny gasped when she saw Lance on the floor. Arthur dropped down beside Chris and rolled Lance over gently onto his back, checking his eyes and feeling for a heartbeat. He sighed with relief and turned back to Jenny.

"He's alive." Then he bent closer and sniffed the air around Lance, and understood. "Jenny, would you mind taking Chris down to breakfast while I tend to Lance?"

Reading his expression, she understood.

Chris eyed his father fearfully. "Is Lance gonna be okay, Dad?"

"Yes, son." He sighed. "He just drank too much again."

Chris allowed Jenny to lead him from the room.

Arthur pulled the photo from Lance's hand and smiled at the memory it evoked. Then he spotted the paper in the other, and tugged it free. Lance's dried tears had smudged Ricky's writing, but the note was still readable. Arthur's breath caught in his throat as he read, and his heart beat frantically with loss and anguish.

Lance stirred beneath him, and his eyes opened. Seeing Arthur kneeling above him, he realized it was morning. When he saw the note in his father's hand, everything came flooding back, and he began to cry.

Arthur scooped him up and enfolded him in his arms and allowed Lance a few moments to release his grief and remorse.

"Tell me, Lance," he said quietly.

With Arthur cradling him, Lance haltingly, between gulps and sobs, told how he and Ricky so desperately wanted girlfriends so they could feel like real boys. That was why they went out with Michael in the first place. But everything had gone terribly wrong because they'd both been trying so hard to be something they weren't. And he told of Ricky's confession at the cemetery.

"He thinks I hate him, Dad," Lance said, his face tortured with regret. "Ricky thinks I *hate* him."

Arthur attempted to soothe him. "He knows you do not."

"*No*, Dad, you saw the letter," Lance insisted, swiping at the snot running from his nose as he leaned up against Ricky's bed. "The look I gave him when he told me. It didn't... that's not what it meant..." He trailed off, and gazed longingly at the photo on the floor beside them. "Oh, Dad, what if we never see him again?"

"Ricky just needs time to think, son. I'll alert Sergeant Ryan to search for him, but I feel in my heart he will return to us."

"How do you know?"

Arthur smiled, though it was tinged with sadness. "He's my son."

Lance didn't understand that answer. "I really screwed everything up, Dad, like I been doing this whole year."

Arthur shook his head. "No, Lance, you have simply made mistakes."

Lance shook his head, the tears continuing unabated. "No, Dad, you don't understand."

Arthur gazed at him with compassion. "Then help me to."

Lance sniffled, more snot dripping from his nose. "It's because of *him*!" he hissed. "Richard!"

Arthur scooted over and held him, handing Lance a handkerchief from his pocket.

Lance used it to wipe his nose, but the tears would not cease. He took a moment, not sure he could actually say it aloud.

His deepest and greatest fear.

"Richard liked boys, you know, and he did those horrible things to me," he said, his words coming out like hiccups between sobs, "and so I always thought if I, you know, liked boys too, that I'd be..."

He couldn't finish, but saw with relief that Arthur understood.

"Like *him*?"

Lance nodded.

Arthur sighed heavily, his look one of sadness and deep empathy. "Oh, my son, there truly is no word for a child's fear."

Lance looked confused.

"Lance, Richard did not do those things because he favored boys over girls."

Lance's eyes went wide, and his breathing nearly stopped.

"He did them," Arthur continued, "because he enjoyed the power it gave him over you. He relished the fear and pain he created in you because it made him feel dominant and strong. You could *never* be like him, son. Not if you lived a thousand years."

Lance's mouth hung open. "How do you know I couldn't?"

Arthur gazed into his eyes lovingly. "Because you are my son, and I know your heart."

Lance stared at him a moment, stunned and frozen. Then he threw his arms more tightly around him, resting his head against his father's chest, and wept quietly, despairingly. "Oh, Dad, my whole life I thought..."

"That there was no one to understand your fear even if they heard," Arthur whispered into his ear. "But I understand, Lance."

Lance cried some more, and Arthur cradled him gently.

Lance finally pulled away and took the handkerchief and blew his nose. His blotchy red eyes gazed at Arthur, and he felt in his heart more gratitude than ever before. His greatest fear, a child's fear, was finally gone, because this man had taken it from him. "Thank you, Dad," he whispered, almost shyly. "God, I love you so much!"

Arthur smiled. "And I love you more."

"Dad, today at the rally, I'm gonna talk about Michael. And me. Is that okay?" Arthur nodded.

"Don't you wanna know what I'm gonna say?"

Arthur shook his head.

"Why not?" Lance asked. "If I say the wrong thing again, I could blow the whole election."

"I trust you, son, remember?"

Lance looked deep into his father's eyes and saw the truth of those words. Despite his guilt and his shame, he felt an overwhelming love for this man and his unconditional love. "I so don't deserve a dad like you."

They remained together on the floor, leaning up against the bed, clutching each other, and then Arthur pulled away. "Now, Lance, why not put on some clothes and tell me about last night with Bridget."

Lance expelled a sharp breath of surprise. "You knew I was planning to…?" His face burned with shame. "How?"

Arthur gazed at him without expression. "You are my son."

Lance stared a moment, his eyes filled with amazement. "Why didn't you say anything last night?"

Arthur took on that wise look Lance usually associated with Merlin. "That's where the trust part comes in."

Lance's mouth dropped open in shock. Then Arthur nodded toward the other room and Lance climbed stiffly to his feet. In moments he was back, wearing gym shorts and a plain t-shirt.

Father and son sat on the floor of Ricky's room, facing each other with legs crossed, as Lance told his dad everything that happened the previous night, and what was in his heart. And Arthur listened.

Lance called Helen later that morning to ask if everything was set for the rally at four, and she assured him it would be broadcast live on local, national and cable networks. He thanked her and hung up. He spent the rest of the day in Ricky's room just sitting and staring at the photo, the note, and the dog-eared copy of *The Neverending Story*.

Ricky's favorite book.

Except the story had ended, after all.

At least, for him and Ricky.

Arthur and Jenny had told the others as they began trickling in throughout the day that Ricky was gone, but did not elaborate.

Reyna entered the room to check on Lance, but he wouldn't talk to her. He just handed her the letter and she read it in shocked silence.

"Oh, baby boy, I'm so sorry." She leaned down to hug him, but he didn't even respond to that. Her face etched with sadness, she handed him back the letter and quietly left the room.

Lance sat there all day, refusing to see anyone, refusing to eat, refusing to speak until the rally. Finally, Reyna knocked on the door at two-thirty and told him it was time to leave.

With a heavy sigh, Lance stood, folded the paper back into the book, laid the book reverently on Ricky's pillow, and followed Reyna down to the car.

They arrived at the rally sight almost forty-five minutes before it was to begin. Crowds had been gathering for some time, the family was told by Ryan and Gibson, as they made their way to the raised dais. Both detectives had been alerted that morning to Ricky having run away, and Chief Murphy had put out an all-points bulletin for him. Ryan tried talking with Lance when he'd arrived to pick them up, but Lance would not leave his cocoon.

Behind the podium, chairs had been set up for Arthur and his family, as well as the Mayor, police chief and city council members. All were expected to attend, whether they agreed or disagreed on the prop, because everyone knew that no matter which way the voters went the following day, monumental changes were coming to California and Los Angeles.

Lance glanced sadly at the number of chairs, knowing one of them would remain empty. His head pounded from the hangover, but he had chosen not to take any aspirin or other pain reliever because he believed he deserved to suffer. Each thrust of the knife through his brain only accentuated the ones through his heart.

Ricky had run away, and it was his fault.

Lance sat in a plastic chair, barely acknowledging fans in the crowd calling his name. He'd turn and smile and give a perfunctory wave, but that was it. The rest of the family mingled with the crowd, chatting, thanking them for their support, urging adults to vote tomorrow and kids to make sure their parents voted. Gradually, the Mayor and other dignitaries trickled in and greeted Arthur and the family. The Mayor noted Lance seated alone, without Ricky, and queried Arthur, but the king merely commented that Lance would explain himself shortly.

As Lance looked out over the crowd, he was surprised to see Father Mike beside Pastor Tom. They caught his eye and waved.

There was a festive atmosphere that trapped everyone in its snare – everyone but Lance. His odd behavior and sullen demeanor were not lost on the crowd, and there was much speculative murmuring drifting through their ranks.

Lance spotted Helen, and she nodded in his direction. Big screen TVs had been erected at her instigation so the crowd could see and hear everything being broadcast, especially for those far back from the dais. Cameras were everywhere, Lance could see, from all the major news outlets, and he was as ready as he could be.

Finally, it was four o'clock and Mayor stepped to the microphone to speak. He gradually quelled the crowd and thanked everyone for their attendance. He urged all who hadn't voted by mail to "Get out there tomorrow and help shape the future for your children and grandchildren."

Cheers followed his remarks.

Council President Sanders rose and spoke on behalf of the city council, also urging everyone to vote on this, "The most significant ballot measure Californians have ever been asked to consider." He did not state which way he, himself, planned to vote.

Finally, Vice President Gale rose to introduce Arthur. The crowd went wild with thunderous cheers and applause as Arthur stepped to the podium. He grinned and waved, looking resplendent in his finest kingly attire. The crowd settled down and Arthur spoke.

"On behalf of my family and extended family of New Camelot, I welcome you all and thank you for your attendance." He paused as they clapped anew. "As you well know, children, to me, are and should remain our highest priority as adults in this society." More applause. "To that end, I urge every one of you who is eligible to vote to take a stand tomorrow for the children of this state, and vote your conscience. We have made our case, and now it is up to you."

More applause. Arthur turned and extended a hand toward Jenny.

She rose, taking Chris's hand and nodding to Lance, who also rose. Chris took Lance's hand and they stepped up beside Arthur. He took Jenny's other hand before turning back to the microphone.

"As you all know, this year I adopted three boys."

There was more applause, but some obvious uncertainty wafted over the crowd. They had obviously noted the absence of one of those boys.

"It is always in the best interests of children, whenever possible, to have two parents who love them. I cherish this woman like no other, and so do my sons, who already call her 'mom'. I have asked the Lady Jenny to be my wife and she has happily accepted. Soon after we marry, she will adopt my boys and a unified family we shall truly be in every sense."

The crowd went wild with cheers and applause. Arthur turned to Jenny and they kissed briefly, still holding on to their children.

They heard someone in the crowd call out, "Where's Sir Ricky?"

Lance flinched at that, and Chris squeezed his hand more tightly.

Arthur gazed out at the crowd, his face settling into something resembling sadness.

"Alas, my other son could not be with us today."

"Where is he?" came another voice.

Arthur turned back to the microphone. "I give you my son, Sir Lance."

The confused crowd applauded, but restlessly, as though sensing something was terribly wrong.

Arthur and the others returned to their chairs and a somber Lance stepped up behind the podium and scanned the crowd. Father Mike grinned and gave him a thumbs up sign. Lance nodded his thanks, fighting to control the earth-shattering hammer that pounded inside his head.

"I wanna thank everyone for coming out today and supporting us."

There was applause and some cheers, especially from the hundreds of children present.

"I thank the media for being here, especially the ones who weren't always so voyeuristic and focusing on my mistakes, but on the things I actually got right."

More applause, this time from the media pool, as well.

"Before you all vote tomorrow, I need to tell you some things," Lance went on, fighting to keep his voice steady. "About me, and about Michael."

Uneasy murmuring wafted through the crowd, and Lance waited until it subsided.

"Before I tell you these things I'm gonna be like my mom the teacher for a minute. Raise your hand if you ever read the book, not seen the movie, but read the book, 'Frankenstein'."

There were some laughs and a few hands rose in the crowd.

"For you guys who didn't, that's your homework assignment." The crowd laughed, but Lance didn't smile. "That book was written by a teenager, like, two hundred years ago," he went on soberly, "an eighteen-year-old girl who sure seemed to understand us today better than we do. In the story, Victor is this young guy, super smart and all, who wants to find a way to cheat death. While he's studying, he discovers how to bring life to the dead. So he figures he doesn't need God and puts together this, like, giant man from different body parts. You all know this stuff from the movies. He thinks what he's making is beautiful until he brings it to life. Then he sees how horribly ugly and deformed it is and, like my own father when I was born, Victor splits. He abandons his 'baby' and leaves it to face the world alone. And the world hates it because it's ugly and different, and everyone treats the creature like crap. It doesn't even have a name. The creature just wants what all us kids want – love and acceptance, you know? But all it gets is hate. And that's why it becomes a monster."

He paused to gauge the crowd reaction. They were rapt with attention.

"Michael gave me that book to help me understand. Yes, Michael was a monster. He did monstrous things. And I know a lot of you will be thinking about him when you vote tomorrow, thinking how what he did made him not a kid anymore and he shouldn't be treated like one. But you don't know the whole story. You don't know *why* he became a monster, and you need to know that before you vote." He turned to Helen, who stood patiently down in front. "Lady Helen."

She stepped forward and he extended a hand, helping her up the steps to the dais. Then he moved back, amongst much agitated murmuring from the crowd, as she assumed his spot at the podium.

"Good afternoon, ladies and gentlemen," she began. "You all know me, Helen Schaeffer of Channel 7 News."

There was some applause and a few catcalls.

Helen frowned. "There are many children here today and many more watching at home. I strongly advise parents at home to remove your preteens to another room, and parents here may wish to cover their children's ears."

She glanced back at Lance and he nodded.

"This video was given to Sir Lance by Michael, himself," she went on, "though Lance had stumbled upon it by accident some months ago. The crime was filmed by friends of the perpetrators, who apparently thought what happened amusing enough to film it for posterity." Her voice hardened, and her face crumpled into one of disgust. "It is quite simply the most horrific thing I've ever witnessed."

There were gasps of surprise from the crowd.

"The thirteen-year-old boy you will get a glimpse of is Michael. He was raped by the five men he later mutilated in an act of revenge. Per obvious FCC regulations, the video may not be broadcast. After you get that glimpse of his face, the image will go black and you will only hear his cries for help. The video was an hour long. This is only fifteen seconds of his torment."

She motioned to one of her crew, who pressed the play button on a computer. Michael's terrified face appeared for a moment before the image went dark. Then Michael's cries of pain and anguish poured forth from the speakers.

Lance cringed at hearing even the audio again.

For Arthur and the others on stage, it was revelatory. Reyna gripped Esteban's hand, her face dissolving into revulsion and guilt.

The crowd stood in stunned silence, unable to move or make a sound until that seemingly endless fifteen seconds finally ended.

When it did, Lance turned back to the crowd. Some were crying, others staring up at the stage in shock.

Helen turned back to Lance. He stepped forward and helped her down the stairs to resume her place as a member of the media pool.

Lance returned to the microphone and surveyed the crowd.

"Michael was an arrogant kid, yeah. He got that from his parents. Did he deserve what those guys did to him? Hell, no. Was there ever any justice for what was done to him? No. His father didn't want the embarrassing publicity, so he ignored the whole thing. And Michael became a monster. He took his own justice against those guys. And he took justice for me with the other two. Yes, Michael was a monster, and what he did monstrous. But now you know why. And you know why I pulled a knife on Richard that night that got me arrested. But you don't know about all the other kids you want to put in prison because, like this video, it's too hard to see the truth and easier just to pretend us kids wake up one day and decide to be evil."

He paused to catch his breath. "Michael was a boy who became a monster, and then chose to be a hero in the end. He saved my life. He saved my brothers and he saved everyone at Union Station. He could've jumped off that train and saved himself, but *he* chose not to. Remember that when you vote tomorrow. We're kids, and kids need more than one chance to get it right."

He stopped again and sighed, gazing outward over the sea of spellbound faces.

"Which brings me to me," Lance went on, taking a deep breath before continuing. "I've had a tough year."

There were a few chuckles and a lot of head nods.

"I'll be sixteen-years-old on Wednesday, and I've learned a lot this year. You guys have seen me at my best and my worst, and some of you liked seeing me at my worst. I didn't, but I learned from what I did, like all us kids do. I learned I can't handle alcohol."

There were a few laughs. Lance didn't smile.

"I learned that alcohol won't hide my pain, and that partying won't, either. The pain is still there in the morning, just like it is today." He paused, glanced down, and then back up, knowing the cameras had him in close up. "I broke my promise again. I'm hung over today, because last night I got drunk."

There were agitated murmurings from among the assembled.

"As many of you know, for most of this past year I had a girlfriend, though I never told you her name. You saw all the pix, me making out with her. That's how I am when I get drunk. This girl is amazing and special and perfect, and I love her to death. Problem is, I'm not *in* love with her, and had to tell her that last night."

He paused, scanning the crowd for Bridget, but not wanting to draw attention to her.

"For the longest time I been struggling to be what all of you out there wanted me to be — a real boy, a real man, 'cause to be less is wrong. That's the message I heard my whole life. A real boy gots to be tough and fall in love with a girl and make lots of babies. No exceptions. And I tried my best. God knows I tried to be in love with that amazing girl. I tried to make a choice, like you all said I could. If a boy loves a boy, you say it's wrong and it's a choice. So I tried, for you, and for me, so I wouldn't hate myself. But I failed." He lowered his eyes a moment, caught his breath, and then looked out again at the enthralled, expectant faces. "I'm hopelessly, painfully, definitely in love with... another boy."

The crowd erupted with animated chatter, and cameras flashed unceasingly.

Lance waited again, his heart thumping wildly, his legs weak with fear, until they quieted.

"It was mostly what I heard my whole life that made me hate myself so much. If I loved another boy, I was dirty and weak and girly and... a pervert." He shuddered. "I even thought I could end up like Richard and... do horrible things to children like he done to me. That's what you grownups taught me."

He paused and met Father Mike's eye. Even from this distance, Lance could make out his impish grin.

"But I met a man in juvenile hall, a great man who told me I was exactly what God had in mind when He made me, and that God doesn't make mistakes. It took me a long time, but I believe that now. The mistake was what *you* taught me, how you made a kid hate on himself and feel worthless for something he couldn't control. But I learned those lessons too late. The boy I love more than I love myself is gone, because I pushed him away, and I'll have to live with that for the rest of my life, with half of my soul missing."

He paused again, a tear dribbling slowly from one eye down his cheek.

"I guess what I'm saying is, and I could be in a crapload of trouble from my fellow knights for this, but I'm okay with you voting 'no' tomorrow."

There were major gasps and animated exchanges drifting through the crowd. Faces frowned, some became angry, others grinned, but Lance ignored them. He exhaled another deep breath.

"It's because of all that's happened to me this year, the way I almost ruined my life because I listened to you, because of all the mistakes I made." He blew out a nervous little breath. "I'm not ready to be a grownup yet. I wanna be better than the adults who made me hate on myself, and I need more time to get my act together. And I don't wanna see even more kids my age chained up like animals 'cause some D.A. wants to get promoted or something. So yeah, I'm okay with a no vote. All I ask is that you think of me when you vote tomorrow. And Michael."

His piercing eyes scanned the crowd below.

"If a monster like Michael can change, can't we all? He told me I saved him, but all I did was not give up on him like everyone else did. Is that too much to ask?"

Lance was so engrossed in his speech that he failed to notice the crowd grow even more silent, staring up at the big screen uncertainly.

As he concluded his statement, Lance caught the angle of their eyes and turned to the screen. His heart leapt into his throat.

Ricky stood on the dais, right behind him.

Lance whirled round in stunned surprise.

Ricky stood there, hair streaming from beneath his beanie, wearing a band shirt and jeans, gazing uncertainly at him. "Hey."

"Ricky!" Lance gasped quietly. It wasn't a name. Or even a word. It was an emotion. "Are you okay?"

Ricky nodded.

The crowd waited in cautious silence. Arthur gripped Jenny's hand. Jenny gripped Chris's, while Esteban had his arm around Reyna.

"How long you been here?" Lance asked uncertainly, his body trembling with expectation.

Ricky shrugged. "Pretty much the whole time." He grinned. "You talk too much."

Lance let out his breathy little laugh. "Where'd you go?"

"Bridget let me kick it with her."

Lance flushed with embarrassment, and lowered his gaze to the dais, hands dangling at his sides listlessly. "So now you know. I couldn't even go through with it."

"Because you weren't in love with her," Ricky said, causing Lance to raise his eyes. "She loves you even more for that."

Lance sighed. "Yeah. She's incredible."

"So, Lance," Ricky went on quietly, a slight tremor in his voice, "this boy you're madly in love with. Do I know him?"

A tiny grin graced Lance's face. "I think so. He kind of looks like me, but not near as hot and buff. He's kind of a dumbass..."

Ricky raised his eyebrows.

"...but not as big a dumbass as me." God, was he scared! Even more scared than he'd been last night with Bridget. "I think maybe he's been running through that dark place, too."

"He has."

Lance expelled a deep breath, and extended his hand.

Hesitantly, Ricky reached out to take it.

A jolt, like warm electricity, flew up his arm and straight into his heart. Lance pulled him closer, heart thundering in his chest, relishing that basic human contact. Ricky's hand felt perfect in his, like it belonged there. Like it had always belonged there. "You think maybe two dumb-asses can help each other out of that place and into the light?"

"Yeah, I do."

"I'm scared to death, Ricky." He lowered his eyes again, fearing his admission would make him seem weak.

"Me too."

Lance raised his eyes and found Ricky's soft brown ones fixed on his. He saw that look, the one he'd seen so often before, the one whose meaning he now understood. "Can you ever forgive me?"

Ricky paused, tilting his head as though considering the idea.

Lance's breath stuck in his throat, fearing maybe Ricky could not.

"On one condition."

"Name it."

Ricky's eyes locked on his and nearly melted his heart. "Can I kiss you, Lance?"

Lance shook his head to make sure he'd heard right. "What?" He saw the longing in Ricky's wide eyes and trembled. "Here? Now?" The thought terrified him, the old fears flooding in on him.

"Lance, I been wondering what it'd feel like to kiss you for, like, two years almost. I don't care if the whole world is watching."

Lance swung his free arm weakly toward the crowd. "Ricky, the whole world *is* watching."

Ricky didn't even glance in the indicated direction. "Still scared?"

Lance looked deeply into those soft brown eyes. "Hell, yeah." He paused a second, riveted to that perfect face, with Ricky's lips so close to his. "But screw 'em."

He leaned in and pressed his lips gently to those of this boy whom he loved above all others, whom he had loved from the beginning. He didn't want the kiss to be rough like those he'd shared with Michael, or desperate like those with Bridget. No, he wanted it to be perfect, like that first kiss with Jack.

So their lips stayed pressed together, thrilling excitement tingling every nerve in his body. Ricky's soft lips against his felt perfect, like pieces of a puzzle that were meant to be together. He kept his eyes open, and the love and devotion reflected back at him from within Ricky's thrilled him more deeply.

His arms slipped up and enveloped Ricky's shoulders and Ricky's slipped around his waist. They were two halves of the same boy, together and complete. The kiss seemed to last forever, and no time at all. Lance actually felt weak in the knees as they separated, and thought he might melt right down into his boots.

Breathlessly, they gazed at one another, faces flushed, eyes wide with wonder, leaning in to rest their foreheads gently against each other's.

"Wow," Lance whispered, his breath wavering on his lips, his whole body shaky and helpless.

Ricky smiled, all poignant eyes and ragged breaths. "Double wow."

"Jack was right. That was like a hundred Fourth of July's."

They pulled apart, Ricky's arm sliding awkwardly down to clasp Lance's sweaty hand as they turned to gaze out at the stunned and gawking crowd.

At this point, someone in the throng shouted in a dumbfounded voice, "Sir Lance, you're in love with your own brother?"

Lance stepped shakily to the microphone, his hand still within Ricky's. He was terrified, but refused to show it anymore. He'd never again allow these people to frighten him with their false expectations.

"Ricky is the other half of my soul," he told them with conviction. "He's my brother, yes, but we're not related by blood. Only by love. And we've been in love the whole time. We were just too scared to say it."

There was uncertain babbling and murmuring from the people as they digested this new image of The Boy Who Came Back. Lance turned to Ricky with a shrug of indifference. He didn't care what these people thought. Not anymore. They finally had each other, and each other was everything.

"Can we take a picture of you and your boyfriend, Sir Lance?"

Lance looked out over the crowd for the source of the voice, and sucked in a shocked breath. It was Yellow Hair, the tabloid journalist who always heckled him.

"*You're* asking my permission?"

Yellow Hair grinned. "We wouldn't wanna be *too* voyeuristic, now would we?" He held up his camera, but didn't try to take a photo.

Lance chuckled, and turned to Ricky.

The boy he loved tossed off a little smirk. "Is that what I am? Your boyfriend?"

Lance looked at him in wonder. "Hell, no!" He turned back to the microphone. Yellow Hair, and everyone else, awaited his response. "You can take our picture, but don't call Ricky my boyfriend." He glanced shyly Ricky's way. "This boy is *ahora y por siempre, la guardián de mi corazón.*"

Some in the crowd sighed with delight, while Yellow Hair looked up quizzically. "For those of us who don't speak Spanish, Sir Lance?"

Lance blew out a little breath and cast his eyes toward Ricky's radiant face. "He is for now and always, the keeper of my heart."

Their eyes locked for a moment. Both grinned, shyly raised their clasped hands above their heads, and stepped away from the podium.

The crowd went wild, clapping and cheering and whistling. Cameras clicked like crazy. Lance glanced up at the screen and saw the two of them looking larger than life. He giggled and nudged Ricky, who eyed the screen and grinned foolishly at the sight of him and the boy he loved together at long last.

Behind the boys, Arthur held a tearful Jenny in his arms. Chris leapt from his chair and ran toward his brothers. Happily, they scooped the little boy up and onto their shoulders, hefting him between them with Chris sitting half on Lance's right shoulder and half on Ricky's left.

The cameras went wild again. The boys grinned happily, and Lance finally felt at peace with himself. It had been a long and painful journey, but he'd survived. He locked eyes again with Ricky, and saw the same peace within that amazing boy who'd snuck in, stolen his heart, and made his life worth living.

Reyna and Esteban applauded with the crowd, but then she turned to punch him hard in the chest.

"Ow!" he called out. "What was that for?"

She looked sternly at him. "How come you never talk to me like that?"

Esteban's face fell into embarrassment. "Oh, baby, c'mon, you know Lance is the smooth one."

She glowered at him and threw both hands to her hips.

Sighing, he took her hands in his and dropped to one knee. "Reyna, *ahora y por siempre, eras la guardián de mi corazón.*"

She grinned broadly.

"Happy now?" Esteban said, rising to his feet.

Her smile broadened. "It's a start." Then she kissed him.

The rally ended shortly after the photo ops concluded. It seemed everyone wanted pictures with Lance and Ricky, and insisted the boys hold hands for each one. They were still shy with each other and giggled slightly when their hands touched. But they never disliked that basic human contact. And their entwined fingers never felt anything less than perfect.

Lance thanked Helen for what she'd done, and she hugged him. Then she hugged Ricky, expressing her sincerest hope that the boys would be happy together, though she did say it might take the public some time to accept their newfound relationship.

"Brothers to boyfriends is a big jump," she added before handing the flash drive back to Lance.

"It's a big jump for us too, Lady Helen," Lance replied with a shy glance at Ricky.

Ryan stepped forward and Lance looked at him sheepishly, handing over the flash drive.

The older man pocketed the drive and peered at his godson with an unreadable expression that worried Lance.

"Are you okay, *nino*?" he asked breathlessly, suddenly trembling with the fear of rejection by someone he loved and admired. "You know, with me and Ricky and all?"

The man's face broke into a grin. "Damn straight."

Lance laughed and hugged him.

Dinner that night was a festive affair compared to lunch because the rally had been a success and Ricky was home. The air felt different for everyone now that the boys' feelings for one another were out in the open, but nothing else really seemed different. Lance and Ricky bagged on each other like always and tried to one-up each other, causing everyone to laugh with delight, Chris most of all.

When it came time for bed, however, Arthur and Jenny arrived together in Lance's room, where the two boys sat, still fully clothed, talking quietly atop Lance's bed. As soon as Lance saw their anxious and worried expressions, he knew what they wanted.

Both adults pulled up chairs and sat before the bed, looking woefully uncomfortable and nervous.

Jenny eyed Arthur as though to say, 'You're the dad, this is your job.'

Arthur grimaced and turned to the boys, stroking his beard thoughtfully. "Boys," he began haltingly, "your mother and I are... well, happy that you have found each other as you have. It had been rather obvious for some time and—"

Startled, Ricky cut him off. "You knew how we felt?"

Jenny smiled warmly. "You're our sons and we love you," she said. "Of course, we suspected."

Lance blanched with embarrassment. He suddenly remembered Esteban's comment about Ricky so many months ago. "Did everybody know?"

Arthur smiled and shrugged. "I do not believe the mail carrier was aware..." He let the rest of the thought trail off.

Lance was aghast. Everybody knew how they felt before they did? How freakin' embarrassing!

"How come you never said nothing?" Ricky asked, his heart pounding.

"It's 'anything', honey," Jenny correctly softly, "And it wasn't up to us to tell you how you felt."

The boys exchanged another shy look.

Lance's lips curled into a wry smile. "We're pretty dumbass, aren't we?"

Ricky grinned, and agreed.

Arthur cleared his throat nervously. "As to the sleeping arrangements..."

Lance felt his face burn. "*Dad...*"

"We want you to sleep in your own rooms from now on, alone," Jenny said, slight annoyance in her voice over Arthur's obvious inability to step up and handle this.

Both boys flushed with mortification.

"You guys, this is *so* embarrassing," Lance whispered, unable to look at either of them.

"It is uncomfortable for us, as well, Lance," Arthur replied, his voice thick and edgy.

Lance looked at Ricky and Ricky at Lance. Both nodded in unison.

Lance turned to their parents. "Dad, Mom." He paused, took in a long breath, and let it out. "Ricky and me aren't gonna be having sex."

Arthur's eyebrows shot up and Jenny looked at him in surprise.

Arthur looked confused. "But we understood you today to—"

"To say we're in love with each other?" Lance finished for him.

Arthur nodded.

"We are, but that doesn't mean we wanna jump into sex or anything like that." He shivered. "I get the shakes every time I even think about it. All that making out I did at the parties I had to get drunk to do, and I'm done with drinking."

Ricky eyed them soberly. "My experiences weren't as horrible as Lance's, but they were painful and, like, really humiliating to be used that way."

Lance squeezed Ricky's hand in a gesture of support. Then he eyed his parents again. "I guess what we're saying is, yes, we're in love with each other. It's what John said – we're like two parts of the same toy and neither of us can work right without the other. But we're not ready for the physical stuff. That's way down the line somewhere. I mean, I think we've been, you know, in love the whole time, way before we became brothers. But now we are brothers and that's all, well, kind of weird too, you know?"

The adults nodded.

Lance sighed, glancing again at Ricky for moral support. "We wanna go slow. We're still kids, and kids screw up. We don't wanna screw up anymore."

Arthur and Jenny exchanged a long, uncertain look.

"Do you trust me, Dad?" Lance asked quietly.

Arthur smiled. "Yes, son, I trust you."

"Mom?" Lance repeated to Jenny.

She met his gaze with her soft blue eyes, and nodded.

"What about me?" Ricky asked uncertainly. "Do you guys trust *me?*"

The adults looked at one another, and laughed.

"Of course we trust you, Ricky. Both of you," Arthur said. "And it sounds like you've made a very adult decision. You are both, to use Lance's favorite word, quite amazing."

The boys grinned and climbed off the bed, each trading off hugs with both parents.

Then Arthur and Jenny quietly left the room.

Lance's face clouded over.

"What's wrong?" Ricky asked, suddenly worried, one hand snaking out to grasp Lance's.

Lance looked into those soulful, anxious eyes. "What if I, you know, never can—"

Ricky put a finger to Lance's lips to quiet him. "Don't go there. I'll love you no matter what." Then he grinned. "And I'll still kick your ass in wrestling."

Lance laughed and Ricky entered his own room to get ready for bed. The boys decided to keep the connecting door open so they could hear each other's breathing throughout the night. Just knowing each had the other half of his heart a few feet away made everything perfect.

The next day, Election Day, was nerve-wracking. Since Arthur wasn't yet a citizen, he was barred from voting. However, Jenny went with Reyna and Esteban to their polling place and cast their ballots, later reporting that there were long lines of people waiting to vote.

For Lance and Ricky, it was a day holed up in the Computer Lab finishing the project they'd secretly been working on – the next phase of the crusade. They knew that tomorrow would be yet another press conference at noon to respond to the election results, and they wanted to be ready with their announcement.

Lance got tweets from many supporters congratulating him and Ricky, and wishing them best of luck in the election.

Jenny, Arthur, Reyna and Esteban began watching election returns as they trickled in after the polls closed at eight that night, but Lance and Ricky chose to play Scrabble with Chris. In their minds, however the voters decided in California, their secret plan would hopefully jumpstart the whole country down a better path when it came to the needs of children. By the time they went to bed, the polls showed a virtual tie on Prop 51, with most precincts yet to report in, and absentee ballots still to be counted.

Later, before going to sleep, the boys stood together, arms wrapped around each other, hearts beating against each other's chest. They were nervous over the eventual outcome and needed the closeness of the other. How long they stood together neither could later recall, but they finally separated into their own rooms feeling anxious and uncertain about the morning to come.

"'Night, Ricky," Lance called out through the darkness. His voice felt as weightless as a snowflake.

"'Night, Lance," Ricky called back, sounding almost breathless.

There was a long pause as both boys lay in their respective beds, gazing up into the dark, and contemplating the future, until exhaustion began to take them.

Eyelids heavy with drowsiness, Lance said quietly to the dark, "I love you, fool."

He heard drift in from the other room, as though carried on a mere wisp of air, the three most important words he knew he'd ever hear: "Love you more."

Content and at peace, both boys dropped into the best sleep of their lives.

When Lance awoke the next morning, his first thought was of Ricky, and whether the other boy slept as well as he had.

Then he remembered.

The election.

The results.

Leaping out of bed, Lance slipped a t-shirt over his bare torso and crept into Ricky's room. The most amazing of boys still slept, looking peaceful and content. Gently, he shook Ricky awake, and with pure delight watched him open those marvelously soft brown eyes and look around a moment in confusion. Then realization enlightened his face and he grinned, activating those dimples Lance so loved.

"Morning, dumbass," he murmured.

Lance grinned. "Morning to you, dumber-ass." Then he punched Ricky on the chest. "C'mon, fool, we gotta get downstairs and see what happened."

Ricky punched him back. "Okay, fool!"

Laughing, he leapt from the bed and both hurried into their bathrooms to get cleaned up.

A short while later, as Lance and Ricky uneasily descended the stairs, they saw Reyna and Esteban entering the lobby from the direction of the Throne Room. The older kids looked up at the younger ones in silence. Lance and Ricky slowly closed the gap between them, alighting to the lobby floor feeling almost weightless with anticipation. Still, the older teens said nothing.

Lance sighed, his insides churning anxiously. "Well, are we adults, or kids?"

Reyna and Esteban exchanged a look between them, and then Reyna smiled at him.

"Well, we're adults no matter how you cut it, baby boy. But thanks to what you said yesterday—" She paused for dramatic effect, almost making Lance leap out of his skin, "—you and Ricky are still kids. They voted no. By more than two thirds."

Lance nearly sagged with relief. "Has the hate email started coming in yet?" he asked, certain that his followers statewide who had worked so hard to pass the initiative would be furious.

"Not that much, according to Techie. Most seem relieved, actually, especially the kids. I think seeing what happened to you, all those pictures and videos of you chained up like some dangerous animal, I think that woke people up. According to the exit polls, anyway."

Lance eyed her cautiously. "You're not mad at me?"

"I could never be mad at you, baby boy."

"Besides," Esteban put in, his deep voice sounding more grown up every day, "now the adults, and that means us, too, gotta do something real for kids. Can't just throw 'em away anymore, can't just dump 'em in prison. Now we gotta get together and really help kids from neighborhoods like mine to make sure they stay out of trouble or get a second chance if they don't. You did a good thing, *carnal*. I'm proud of you."

Lance looked at Esteban shyly, suddenly uncertain. "You're okay, Este, with, you know, me and Ricky?"

Esteban squinted with amusement. "Hell, Lance, I was the one who told you to pick him in the first place." He held up a meaty fist.

Ricky looked startled at that, but Lance grinned, punching Esteban's fist with his own.

"Oh, and the best news," Esteban went on, grinning, "is that scumbag D.A. lost. You took him down, Lance. Now that's some mad politicking skills."

Reyna threw both hands to her hips. "Now, I know you two have been plotting something for weeks. What is it?"

"C'mon," Lance said, and led them to the Computer Lab.

He logged into his account and called up the document he and Ricky had spent so many hours drafting.

Reyna's eyebrows shot upward, and Esteban whistled in surprise. With Lance and Ricky standing off to the side feeling rather proud of themselves, Reyna and Esteban leaned in and read every word.

Reyna turned to face them. "It's brilliant."

"Man, Lance, you and Ricky boy make some kick-ass team," Esteban said with a shake of his head.

The two boys eyed each other with a grin and simultaneously said, "Damn straight," before busting up with laughter.

Reyna looked at the boys appraisingly. "You realize, of course, that you have to travel the whole country and sell this, right? It'll be a long process and I'm in."

"Me, too," Esteban echoed, grabbing Reyna's hand and squeezing it lovingly.

"You guys have college," Lance reminded them.

"College?" Reyna retorted with a laugh and a wave of her well-manicured hand. "We'll take classes online. You think I'm gonna let you have all the fun? Hell, no, baby boy. You might still be younger and prettier and a better shot than me, but you're sure as hell not a better party planner. And this is gonna be the biggest party ever!"

Lance laughed and Reyna leaned in to engulf him in a tight hug, making him squirm.

"Reyna, you're embarrassing me," he mumbled, glancing shyly at Ricky once she released him.

She gazed at Lance in wonder. He was now taller than her. His long hair draped his shoulders perfectly and spilled all the way down his lean back. He'd gotten more muscular and his face slimmer. "Happy birthday, baby boy." She kissed him on the cheek.

Lance blanched with surprise. "Oh, my God, I forgot."

Ricky looked equally embarrassed. "Me too."

Reyna laughed. "And happy birthday to you, baby boy number two."

She enveloped Ricky in a hug, nearly squeezing the air out of him. Then she eyed them both with an appraising air. "You two are so amazing. I'm, like, *so* proud to be your sister."

Both boys reddened, and then punched each other out of embarrassment.

Leaving Lance and Ricky to finish tinkering with their document, Reyna and Esteban returned to the Throne Room to discuss their big get-together after the press conference. The plan was for all the knights to be present at City Hall and then everyone could head to New Camelot for a victory party.

Later, as the boys dressed in their rooms to go downtown, Lance remembered the shirt he'd gotten Ricky. It was still in a bag because he hadn't had time to wrap it yet. As he stepped to the connecting door and pulled it open, he nearly collided with Ricky on the other side, heading into his room.

They both laughed, and Lance noted that Ricky, too, had a package in hand, also in a plastic bag. The boys eyed one another, eyed their packages, and then burst out laughing.

"Happy birthday, dumbass," Lance said, shoving the bag at Ricky so hard he staggered back a step.

Ricky grinned and shoved his bag at Lance just as hard. "Happy birthday, dumber-ass."

Grinning, they tore open their bags and held up two t-shirts. Lance's was green and Ricky's red. They simultaneously dropped open the shirts to see what was on the front, and cracked up.

"We gotta wear these today," Ricky gushed.

"You know it, fool," Lance agreed, and they high-fived in delight.

Once again, as on Monday, the area around City Hall was packed with media and dignitaries and regular citizens, though not as many kids because of school. Lance did note a few large groups of children, apparently on field trips with their teachers.

Lance wore the 'Team Ricky' shirt Ricky had given him that morning and Ricky sported his 'Team Lance' birthday gift, as well. The shirts generated a lot of laughs and a few cheers from the crowd when the boys walked on stage. Lance noted people scowling, too, haters who apparently thought the boys less than human because they loved each other instead of girls. He couldn't be bothered with those people anymore. Way too much to do.

Arthur made a brief statement about how the voters had spoken and that everyone must abide by their decision.

"Since the adults of this state have given childhood back to their children, it remains my sincerest hope that they will all work diligently to preserve and protect that childhood. I have learned much about being a parent over this past year." He sighed heavily and glanced a moment at his three boys, seated behind him with Jenny. "And I have the gray hair to prove it."

He smiled warmly, and the crowd laughed. The boys bowed their heads in embarrassment.

"I've learned that my sons do not think as I do because they are not yet grown," Arthur went on, a touch of wistfulness in his normally commanding voice. "I've learned that it is ever and always my job to set a right and proper example for them. I've learned to trust them, and to never, ever give up on them. I pray all of you can do the same, with your own children and those of your neighbors."

There was tremendous applause and Arthur waited for it to subside. "Some may consider yesterday's vote a loss for our crusade, but it is not, for we have a plan to move forward, to secure a better future for all youth in this country. To tell you about the next phase of our crusade, I give you Sirs Lance and Ricky."

More applause arose from the throng as the boys almost shyly approached the microphone. The people began clapping all the louder as the two stopped at the podium. There were whistles and whoops from the crowd. A few catcalls, as well. The boys exchanged a look and shrugged.

When the crowd finally settled down, Lance thanked everyone for voting, and for their support.

"Like I told you guys Monday, at first I wanted this to pass, to give more rights to kids. But after everything that happened to me, I thought maybe a yes vote would just give adults more reasons to turn against us. Now, like my big brother Este told me today, you grownups have to do some real work to make things better for kids like me, since you can't just throw us away any more."

There was some applause and some cheers, but mostly a lot of uncertainty in their eyes.

Lance's face clouded slightly, and he fought to quell his emotions. "I don't know if my incarcerated brothers in the Compound at Sylmar are watching this, but come January first, no more shackles for you guys. Or for any other kids in this state. You won't be animals anymore. Just kids. You got your second chance, Joey and Angel and even you, the kid who called me a faggot."

There were some gasps from the crowd.

Lance sighed. "I kept asking myself why God brought me back, and maybe now I know the answer. For this. To help make kids kids again. I know how us teenagers are. We wanna be all badass and grown up and that makes us do stupid things. So I say this to all the teens out there - enjoy your time as a kid. Don't try to be adults before you are, because then you're just giving real adults excuses to *pretend* you are, like it was before. Use the time you got back to get it right, 'cause that eighteenth birthday'll come real fast. I know I need more time. *Man,* do I ever."

There were chuckles, and scattered applause from the assembled citizens.

Lance offered that radiant smile he knew the public cherished. "Find good adults to copy, like I got. I know how blessed I am to have my dad and mom. Hopefully, you kids out there got somebody good, too, but if you don't, find someone. You good adults out there, be those role models to *every* kid, not just your own. But we kids also gotta watch the bad people, too, you know, so we can learn how *not* to act. Please don't be mad at me because you don't get to vote yet. You'll be there soon enough. For right now, we got a plan that'll make sure every kid in this country has their rights protected, for now and always."

That generated a lot of buzz through the crowd, and Lance grinned at Ricky.

"Ever since I got out of jail, Ricky and me have been working on something that won't go live on the Internet till Monday, so you'll all have to wait till then to see the details." Groans floated up to them, but Lance waved them away. "Here's the deal, like we see it. The U.S. Constitution has the Bill of Rights, ten of 'em, right?"

Heads nodded in the crowd.

"Problem is," Ricky took over, "those rights don't apply to us kids. Only to people eighteen and over."

There were mystified murmurings from the crowd below.

"So," Lance went on excitedly, "on Monday next, on our website, we will roll out ten new amendments to the Constitution that will guarantee rights to everyone under the age of eighteen." He held up a piece of paper. "We call this 'The Children's Bill of Rights'."

The crowd went wild. There were protests. There was cussing. There was applause. There were cheers. And there was stony-faced, open-mouthed silence from many.

Lance and Ricky grinned with glee at the uproarious reaction, exactly what they had hoped for.

Helen, momentarily stunned like everyone else, threw up her hand. "Sir Lance! Sir Ricky!"

Still grinning, Lance pointed to her. "Lady Helen has a question, everybody. Let's calm down."

The crowd gradually quelled its shock and awe.

"Sir Lance," Helen began, the disbelief obvious in her voice, "are we to understand that you want to sell this idea to the whole country, to actually amend the Constitution of the United States?"

"That's the plan, Lady Helen."

Ricky nodded vigorously beside him.

"But the Constitution hasn't been amended since, maybe, 1992? And before that it was around 1971."

"Sounds to me like we're due for an update," Lance said, grinning at the shocked expressions on everyone's face. "Monday, twelve noon, our website and Facebook page. The Children's Bill of Rights goes live. And the campaign begins. Thanks, everyone!"

With a wave, Lance and Ricky turned from the podium and returned to where Arthur and Jenny sat with the mayor.

The mayor gawked. "What's next, Mr. Lincoln, you going to lower the age requirement so you can run for president?"

Lance pretended to consider the idea. "Hmm. Good idea." He laughed and Ricky joined in.

The mayor shook his head in amazement.

The party downstairs was still going on, but Lance needed some air, and a moment to think back over this tumultuous year. So he slunk away and crept up to his favorite place to think – the roof. He sat on the parapet, legs dangling over the edge, gazing down at the twinkling, almost magical, lights of his city.

He thought of Jack, whom he had loved. At least it was the beginnings of love. He knew that now. Had Jack lived, who knew where it might have gone? But just like Lance's horrific time in jail having assisted the greater good, perhaps Jack's sacrifice had done the same. Because of him, kids had their childhood back. And, like Esteban, Jack had mentioned Ricky in his letter, as though foreseeing the future. It was like he and Ricky had been destined to be together, except everyone knew it before they did. Irony. He remembered that word from his lessons. That's what it all was.

So engrossed was he in his thoughts, he didn't even hear the roof door open. Before he knew it, Ricky had slipped over the parapet and sat beside him.

"You okay?" Ricky asked quietly.

"Yeah. Just thinking. About you and Jack and Michael and Bridget and, well, the whole year, really."

The cool night breeze caught Ricky's hair and tossed it haphazardly into his face. He brushed it away and looked thoughtfully at Lance. "Michael really loved you, you know," he said, almost a whisper. "That's why I hated him so much. I was afraid you were falling for him."

"I thought I might be," Lance said quietly. "But he knew the truth. He's the one who made me realize it was you I loved."

Ricky's eyes widened with surprise. "How?"

Lance gazed out over the cityscape. "Right before he died, he told me we both knew who I really loved. And he had this look in his eyes." He turned back to Ricky, gazed deeply into those haunting brown eyes, and saw it.

"What look?"

"The one you have right now. The one you always have when you look at me. The one I didn't wanna see 'cause it made me feel things I was too scared to feel."

Ricky smiled, and they fell silent a moment, looking out at the bright city lights and listening to the humming of freeway traffic eight stories below.

"What are you thinking?"

Lance turned his head. "That I don't deserve you."

"That's true, but you're stuck with me."

Lance laughed, brushing strands of loose hair from his face. Then he shyly reached down and took Ricky's hand, never breaking eye contact. "We're gonna be all right now, aren't we, Ricky? You and me?"

Ricky grinned slyly. "Like the *guardián de mi corazón* always says, damn straight."

Lance blew out his breathy little laugh and lowered his gaze a moment. "He does say that, doesn't he?" Then hesitantly, little-boy shy and cautious, he raised his eyes, gently took Ricky's other hand and placed it against his fearfully beating heart. "He *is* the keeper of your heart, and you're the keeper of his. And he's never gonna let you go, for now and always." He paused, suddenly timid and small and insecure. "Is that okay?" It was barely a wisp of breath above the breeze.

Ricky cocked his head to one side, as though considering his options. Then he tossed off that haphazard grin Lance so loved and leaned in conspiratorially. "Tell him—" he whispered, as though it were the biggest secret in the world, "—that'll work."

Lance expelled the breath he was holding and gave a husky laugh. "Okay. I'll tell him."

Shy and uncertain, they gently and ever so softly rested their foreheads against one another, green eyes locked on brown, two hearts beating as one. Then they raised their heads, and Lance released the hand he held to his heart. But their other hands remained clasped together, as though joined for eternity. They grinned bashfully at one another, and then turned to gaze once more out over the city.

And so, letting everything be, secure in their oneness, two boys sat in peace and solitude, legs dangling, hands linked in solidarity, each for now and always the keeper of the other's heart.

Once upon a time in the City of Angels, hope endured, and childhood survived.

EPILOGUE

HE SAT ON THE ROOF, enjoying the cool breeze on his face as his eye focused through the scope. The two boys sat side-by-side on the parapet of New Camelot, oblivious to everything but each other. Easy take down. Not as inventive as the previous attempts, but still the job would be done. For good.

Lowering the high-powered sniper rifle to his side, he flipped out his phone and speed-dialed the boss.

"Yeah?" he heard from the other end.

"Thought you'd like to know your two favorite fag boys are up on the roof of their place," he said into the phone. "I got 'em both in my sights. You want me to take 'em out now and be done with it?"

There was a long, weighty pause from the other end. Then he heard, "Do it. But leave your phone on. I want to hear the shots."

He grinned and lowered the phone to the grainy roof beside his crossed legs. Scanning the area below for any sign of police presence, he chuckled and raised the rifle to his shoulder. He placed his right eye on the scope and closed his left. The one they called The Boy Who Came Back suddenly filled his field of vision, gazing out into the night almost straight at him.

"Let's see you come back from a head shot," he whispered to the night, his finger closing on the trigger with rock-solid steadiness. "Like shooting fish in a barrel." He chuckled, and began squeezing the trigger.

The Lance Chronicles Continue in Book IV:

AND THE CHILDREN SHALL LEAD

THE LANCE CHRONICLES

Book I:

CHILDREN OF THE KNIGHT

Book II:

RUNNING THROUGH A DARK PLACE

Book III:

THERE IS NO FEAR

Book IV:

AND THE CHILDREN SHALL LEAD

Book V:

ONCE UPON A TIME IN AMERICA

Michael J. Bowler is an award-winning author of nine novels—*A Boy and His Dragon*, *A Matter of Time*, *Children of the Knight*, *Running Through A Dark Place*, *There Is No Fear*, *And The Children Shall Lead*, *Once Upon A Time In America*, *Spinner*, and *Warrior Kids: A Tale of New Camelot*.

His screenplay, "THE GOD MACHINE," won First Place in the 2017 Scriptapalooza competition.

He grew up in San Rafael, California, and majored in English and Theatre at Santa Clara University. He went on to earn a master's in film production from Loyola Marymount University, a teaching credential in English from LMU, and another master's in Special Education from Cal State University Dominguez Hills.

He worked producer, writer, and/or director on several ultra-low-budget horror films, including "Hell Spa," "Fatal Images," "Club Dead," and "Things II."

He taught high school in Hawthorne, California—both in general education and to students with learning disabilities—in subjects ranging from English and Strength Training to Algebra, Biology, and Yearbook.

He has been a volunteer Big Brother to eight different boys with the Catholic Big Brothers Big Sisters program, and a decades-long volunteer within the juvenile justice system in Los Angeles.

He has been honored as Probation Volunteer of the Year, YMCA Volunteer of the Year, California Big Brother of the Year, and 2000 National Big Brother of the Year. The "National" honor allowed him and three of his Little Brothers to visit the White House and meet the president in the Oval Office.

He has completed three new novels aimed at the teen market, and one for middle grade.

His goal as an author is for teens and middle schoolers to experience empowerment and hope; to see themselves in his diverse characters; to read about kids who face real-life challenges; and to see how kids like them can remain decent people in an indecent world. The most prevalent theme in his writing is this: as a society, and as individuals, we're better off when we do what's right, not what's easy.

Website: www.michaeljbowler.com

FB: michaeljbowlerauthor

Twitter: https://twitter.com/MichaelJBowler

tumblr: http://michaeljbowler.tumblr.com/

Pinterest: http://www.pinterest.com/michaelbowler/pins/

Amazon: http://www.amazon.com/Michael-J.-Bowler/e/B0075ML4M4

YouTube: https://www.youtube.com/channel/UC2NXCPry4DDgJZOVDUxVtMw

Google+: https://plus.google.com/u/0/+MichaelJBowler

Instagram: michaeljbowler

www.ingramcontent.com/pod-product-compliance
Lightning Source LLC
Chambersburg PA
CBHW070438120726
47910CB00003B/837